Also by Bella Pollen

All About Men

Hunting Unicorns

Daydream Girl

bella pollen

midnight cactus

BLACK CAT
New York

First published in Great Britain in 2006
by Pan Macmillan Ltd, London

Printed in the United States of America

FIRST AMERICAN EDITION

Library of Congress Cataloging-in-Publication Data
Pollen, Bella.
Midnight cactus / Bella Pollen.
p. cm.
ISBN-10: 0-8021-7031-5
ISBN-13: 978-0-8021-7031-6
1. British—Arizona—Fiction. 2. Mexican–American
Border Region—Fiction. I. Title.
PR6116.O55M53 2007
823'.92—dc22   2006048712

Black Cat
a paperback original imprint of Grove/Atlantic, Inc.
841 Broadway
New York, NY 10003

Distributed by Publishers Group West

www.groveatlantic.com

07 08 09 10 11   10 9 8 7 6 5 4 3 2 1

For my husband,

David,

and my children,

Mabel, Finn, Sam and Jesse

Why is it that society exalts imitation rebels but is so intolerant of the real ones?

Dale Maharidge,
The Last Great American Hobo

Prologue

Once there was a way to get back homewards
Once there was a way to get back home
Sleep, pretty darling, do not cry
And I will sing a lullabyee

The Beatles, 'Golden Slumbers'

The Border, 1983

It starts raining on the mountain first. Clouds which have been hovering since early afternoon finally crack open and spew their contents in a freak summer storm that lasts no longer than twenty minutes. It's June and there's been not a hint of rain since spring. In truth there's precious little of the stuff now, an inch – an inch and a quarter tops, but this is more than enough. The creosote bush, school bully of desert plants, whose twisted yellow petals are currently in bloom, is the first to suck up the spoils of the storm. Next, a Gila monster, stomping belligerently from its shelter, absorbs the water through the pores of its blotched skin. Surfacing from deep under the sand where it has burrowed to escape the sun, the stink beetle fractionally tilts its shell to allow the raindrops to trickle down its legs and into its waiting mouth. Soaring ten feet above, a saguaro cactus collects its own drops and transports them to its roots via a thousand needles, affording this hoary old veteran of the desert its survival for another year.

Less than a mile away, Estella, a young Mexican girl, will not be so lucky.

Estella has no ingenious method of survival at her fingertips. Right now her best chance is brute will. She is desperate and desperation leads to blind faith and whatever religion sustains it, so as she picks her way carefully through the cholla, carrying her two-year-old son, feeling for holes in the ground with the toe of one sandalled foot and keeping a fearful eye out for snakes, she prays. She casts her devout net wide, sending out entreaties to Our Lady of Sorrows, to Mary the Blessed Mother, to the Virgin Sagrada; and, just in case, she directs an extra missive to Santa Elena, Discoverer of the Cross, perhaps reflecting that she too had the temerity to fall in love with a man outside her social status – and no one could say things hadn't turned out well for her.

From the day Estella was born, some twenty years earlier, in the small southern town of Chocan, many things were preordained. That she would be poor, that she would have straight black hair. That she would press perfect tortillas by the age of six and that when it came to crossing into the US in search of whatever brand of American dream she might be chasing, the Sonoran

Desert, hottest and most desolate of the four deserts of south-western America, would be her entry point. To be fair, this was less a question of fate, and more one of geography. The Sonoran Desert was simply the closest. That she chose to cross it in summer with the ground temperature peaking at 115 degrees was naivety. The rest was just plain bad luck.

Half a mile from the base of the mountain, not far from where Estella is winding her way north, the rainfall is now much less intense. Already the inch is down to a lousy centimetre which soon dwindles to a pathetic millimetre until the downpour is represented by nothing more than a smell, the wistful aftermath of moisture in the air. The rain had fallen so close – just not close enough. In the way that a speeding bullet has the velocity to tear through the heart of one man, but will drop harmlessly at the foot of the next, so too does the rain peter out just before it can be any use to Estella or the three men she is travelling with.

Originally, there had been twenty others in the truck. Twenty sweating bodies piled together like the heaving ribs of a panting animal. Estella knew none of them, but they were men from small towns like hers, all following different strands of America's labour trails. From snatches of overheard conversation, she knew some were heading to Florida to pick oranges, others to construction jobs in Colorado and still more making for states further to the north, ones she hadn't even heard of. None had been thrilled about her joining the party at the eleventh hour, least of all the smallish campesino with tightly curled hair and insubstantial moustache who had

3

been ordered to make room for her. By the time a large rock broke the axle of the truck's back wheel, the group had reached northern Arizona, their arrival on American soil justifying half the $500 they had each paid their coyote for the privilege, but they were still eight miles away from the safe house – and a good coyote might have got them there. A good guide might have led them single file, a shepherd guiding his sheep across the soft sand of the drags, perhaps using a broken-off branch to sweep clean the patterns of their shoes and boots. A good guide might have done everything in his power to keep them clear of the ever watchful eyes of the Border Patrol. But then this coyote was no good guide and hey, eight miles was nothing for a bunch of such young, fit men, he reassured them before scuttling sideways into the shimmering scrub of the desert. The safe house was indeed north-east and, true, it was only eight miles, but these were crow miles. The Mexicans could not fly and swoop over the dips and rises of steep canyons. Instead they were forced to pick their way round their perimeters in ill-fitting shoes that soon blistered their feet, hauling backpacks and suitcases that rubbed the skin off their shoulders and hands. Degree by degree they lost their sense of direction and before long the eight miles turned to ten, and those ten soon to fifteen.

As the heat of the day grew stronger the group grew weaker. Nobody was carrying enough water for a journey on foot. Nobody could have carried the amount required. Dissent broke out amongst the leaders – which direction to go, from which direction they'd come, which way really was north. At 30 per cent dehydration, simple decision-making becomes a murky business at best; 50 per cent dehydration is more like the final stage of drunkenness, the one where you have to concentrate really hard to decide whether jumping out of a tenth-storey window is a good idea or not.

When the group finally split, Estella chose to stay close to her co-sardine from the truck. Though he now regretted telling her, he was heading for California and so was she, to Santa Monica. She had no idea where Santa Monica was but I imagine she liked the name. Two men, for reasons no one would ever be quite sure of, elected to go with them. The campesino watched them vigilantly for signs of bad behaviour but they were soon far too busy retching and gasping to think of behaving in an ungentlemanly fashion towards the woman and child who were now nominally in their charge.

Estella is weak and dizzy. She can feel her tongue, a great swollen thing all but blocking her throat. She hasn't felt this sick since the first few months of her pregnancy when she'd become quite adept at chucking up in the flowerbeds of her neighbours' gardens back in Chocan. She'd had bad luck in pregnancy too. The birth had been breech and she could remember the agony as the old witchdoctor turned the baby inside her with her bare hands. At the time she thought it worth the pain to bear a white child. Well white-ish, anyway. At least the lottery of skin colour had favoured her. Of her four sisters and two brothers she was by far the lightest. But when the baby had finally been hauled out, she'd still been shocked by how *alien* he'd looked. Even the campesino, once or twice looking into the baby's blue eyes to make sure he was still alive, sussed something a little untoward with his parentage. Now he no longer wastes precious energy turning round to check the baby. For the last few hours he has felt his own life leaking out through the pores of his body and he has nothing left to sweat. When the two other men, the pair who had got drunk on King beer the night before, suddenly sit down within a hundred yards of each other and fail to get up again, the campesino knows he must find water or they will all die.

By the time the truck rumbles towards them along the dirt road, the campesino has given up on his crossing. He no longer cares whether the truck is full of swim-suited Miss Mexico contestants dispensing maps and free Fantas or fully armed agents of the USA Border Patrol. It was 1983 then and the divide between America and Mexico was not the great monstrous thing it is now. In 1983 the border was still an ideal, just a concept really, and it was supposed to be easy to cross. If you didn't make it the first time, you cracked it the second or the third or the fourth. So when the dust from the approaching truck is almost upon him, he steps out from behind the scrub and waves the wave of a resigned man.

It's at this point that bad luck strikes Estella for the third and final time. The vehicle is neither full of Fanta-dispensing goddesses, nor border guards. It's a shabby black camper van with a turquoise strip down the sides and it's being driven by another coyote and two of his men, who, on finding four of their fellow citizens in dire need of emergency assistance, quickly identify the situation as an opportunity for a windfall.

The coyote's name is El Turrón. He's a young Mexican, no more than twenty-five, with a receding hairline, unusually small hands and a juvenile paunch. His manner is entirely pleasant as he orders his men to round up the inert Mexicans' remaining money and valuables. While he issues these instructions he chews, littering the ground with sweet papers. His round squirrel cheeks masticate the lump of nougat, his mouth open to reveal a wide gap between his front teeth. After helping the three men lighten their load for whatever journey they might have remaining to them, El Turrón rewards himself by raping Estella.

The campesino has three sisters, all younger. Nevertheless they had married before him in quick numerical succession and it had thus fallen to him to chaperone them on dates. Innumerable times he'd sat at a table in the square while Florencio led Elena off to dance. He'd tramped a discreet ten paces behind as Ramiro walked Ysabel to and from the corner shop and by the time poor little Rosa was up for dating, he was heartily sick of the whole business.

'It's your duty,' his mother had rebuked him when he finally found the nerve to complain. 'It's every good brother's duty.'

Estella was neither the campesino's sister nor even a distant cousin but he knew the burden of her protection fell to him anyway. That's just the way it is in Mexico.

'¡Oye! ¡Parada!' he shouts. Stop! In his head, the word sounds like a yell, but the noise that escapes his throat is barely louder than a croak. '¡La se baja de!' He stumbles across the road to where the buckled legs of the

girl are pinned under the men. Before he can get anywhere close to pulling El Turrón off, one of the coyote's
men steps forward and, turning the gun in his hand until
he holds the muzzle, strikes the campesino hard across
the side of his face.

Estella feels the crushing weight on her chest. The
second of Turrón's companions has helpfully knelt on
her while Turrón spreads her legs with his boots and
folds his mirrored sunglasses into his pocket. She has
been kissed by only one man before. Not that you could
call this mashing of mouths a kiss. The cowboy had
kissed her hungrily, but Turrón kisses her greedily, like
she is a forbidden helping of fruit he knows he'd better
take while it's still on the table. Considering the searing
heat, Turrón's lips are surprisingly wet, his breath sweet
and sickly. The cowboy's lips had been so dry. His
fingers always cracked with dirt. Estella had tried to keep
the pregnancy from her parents, believing he'd return for
her long before they noticed the swelling under her dress.
'I could take you back home with me,' the cowboy had
said in a moment that meant little to him and everything
to her and at the time she had no reason to disbelieve
him.

The first time El Turrón hits Estella she tastes the
desert. The second time, her front teeth smash against a
rock and her mouth fills with blood. Most people don't
really believe they're going to die. It's a state just too
far removed from anything they are familiar with. So
while Turrón grinds her into the ground, Estella hangs
on to life and she hangs on to hope. She tries to think of
everything she is walking towards but all she can conjure

up is her past, those things she has left behind: the dirty faces of the Indian kids under the bridge, the smoke from roasting chickens drifting across the road. The smell of fresh corn. The naked light bulb which dances shadows across the doorway of her mother's house.

After they're through with her the Mexicans sift through Estella's possessions. They take her pendant of the Virgin of Guadalupe, and of course the money – those bills of pesos that are the fuel of border economics, already slashed from the trouser pockets of the men and now ripped from the hem of her dress – but the cowboy's letter, in which the money is wrapped, the men let fall to the ground. Words and sentences are of no use to them, but to Estella this letter is by far the most valuable thing she owns. It is the key to her future.

Of course this is not really Estella's story because she has no future, and I have only pieced this much together as best as I can, but in some strange way my story starts where hers ends. Our lives have parallels and opposites. Both are governed by roots and destinations, by running away, by the possibility and impossibility of escape, and so I think of Estella in this moment as I have thought of her so many times, as I have imagined every hard-fought step of her journey – I think of her trapped, unable to move as her life melted away in the awful heat of that desert. The summer of 1983. Estella's flight from south to north ended through lack of water. In 1983, over in my world, a wind was rising across the Orkneys, Scotland, the wettest place imaginable. An island so drowning in water it seems that the earth must be tipped unfairly on its axis. In the summer of 1983 my journey from north to south was only just beginning.

The campesino lies on the scrub, bleeding from his mouth and cheek. Across the track Estella lies dying. Three of her ribs are broken, she has difficulty breathing and her vision has begun to fade. By the time the campesino makes it to her side, she has felt for the letter on the ground and is agitatedly smoothing it against her dress as she calls out the name of her son. For a moment the campesino cannot register what she's saying. He has forgotten about the existence of the child, but when he screws up his eyes he can replay the last fifteen minutes like a cheap video from the market. El Turrón grabbing her by the hair; Estella calmly placing the child on the ground. The boy's reproachful cry. Benjamín looks into the glare of the sun, but he can see nothing and when Estella begs him to deliver the child to the address at the top of the letter, he can promise nothing – his broken jaw hangs uselessly. Instead he reaches over and takes her hand and when she stops breathing he lays it over her heart, then he stands up stiffly and looks around. Despite the searing pain in his jaw he feels a knot of something far worse in his stomach. There is no child on the edge of the road – there is no child to be heard a few yards off, howling with indignation, the spike of some cactus sticking out of his finger – there is no child anywhere to be seen. The boy has gone.

part one

1

January 2002

Thousands of feet up, somewhere between space and earth, night seems to go on forever. For hours, a never-ending sunset has been doggedly following the plane, trailing its woolly strands of orange and purple like an exotic jellyfish. Only now as I press my nose against the perspex window do I see that we've finally left it behind. There is nothing out there any more – just a world so black and vast it makes me want to topple into it and disappear.

I check my watch: two a.m. English time. New Year's Eve. Looking around at my fellow travellers, slack-jawed and mute with exhaustion, I wonder what will happen to us all in this year to come. Who on this plane will die? Who will become a grandparent, embezzle funds or burst into tears at their first grey hair? And the idea makes me unaccountably sad. What is it about flying that makes people so hopelessly sentimental? Something to do with the lack of air, I suppose, too much breathing in other people's anxieties and emotions. The DNA of strangers.

bella pollen

The man across the aisle, corpulent by even the most liberal of standards, loosens the leather belt from around his trousers, no doubt feeling the acid burn of dinner's coq au vin. The rest of the passengers shift uncomfortably under blankets or scratch drowsily at itches they can't quite locate. The atmosphere of somnolence in the cabin is so overpowering that were the pilot to streak naked through the aisles, just for a lark, I doubt very much anyone would notice – much less care. Even Jack and Emmy have passed out, mouths open, as though sprinkled mid-bicker with sleep dust by a kindly British Airways fairy.

God knows, I wish I could sleep on aeroplanes. Disconnected and temporarily excluded from life on earth below, it seems the only sensible thing to do, but as soon as the plane reaches cruising altitude, the moment the signs are switched off and the clink of the drinks trolley soothes the nerves of even the most neurotic of flyers, I fall prey to philosophical musings. While down on earth babies are being born, wars are being fought and couples argue over burnt steak dinners, I sit buckled into my seat and make endless pacts with God. I can spend long hours in this way, plotting personal revolutions, planning get-outs, but always with the safety net of knowing that as soon as the wing begins its downward tilt and the reality of hard ground rises up to meet us, this brave new me, this ghost of my future, will fade back into the ether where it belongs.

But not tonight. As the blinking lights of Phoenix airport appear below like a defiant grid of life on an inhospitable planet, I feel a surge of adrenalin. Tonight will be different. Tonight there is no turning back. In about an hour's time we will be at the head of the immigration queue. Poised for entry. The customs official will give me and the children no more than a cursory once-over before stamping our visa forms.

'What is the purpose of your visit?' he will ask.

The pickup truck has a side-swinging motion that the Mexican corrects every few seconds, bringing it back into line on the right side of the road. Every time my eyes begin to close with the rhythm, the wrench of the wheel forces them apart again. Right now I'd give anything to slip between clean sheets, sleep until it's time to let tomorrow begin, but the silence in the truck feels reproachful. No doubt the Mexican is pissed off at having to pick us up – well, too bad. Quite apart from the fact that I would have killed the three of us falling asleep at the wheel, the town is so remote I would never have found my way there in the first place.

I study his profile surreptitiously. He is more Spanish-looking than I remember – though it wasn't until we cleared customs that I experienced a moment of panic: what on earth *did* he look like? What if I didn't recognize him? What if he didn't remember me? What if he didn't show up at all? I'd held a vague picture in my head over the last few months of a shortish middle-aged man with tightly curled hair greying at the edges and a brushstroke of a moustache, but the truth is, all I could be really sure of was that he looked, well . . . Mexican, and at Phoenix airport, as it turned out, that wouldn't exactly have made him stand out from the crowd.

It's cold in the truck: 10 degrees above zero, if the crackle on the radio is to be believed. My hands are numb. I burrow them between my legs and check the heating dial on the dashboard. The thin white line is swivelled to maximum and I can feel pockets of warmth coming from somewhere, but they're no match for the freezing air leaking through the distressed seals of the cab's windows. The cold takes me by surprise. The last time I'd driven down this road it had been over a hundred degrees, hot enough to bubble the tarmac and melt the soles of my trainers, hot enough to sting the back of my throat and lodge there like some solid mischievous thing. It had been late September then and, on both sides of the road, grassland had rolled towards the hills like a golden sheet billowing in the wind. On the other side of the windscreen now, there is nothing to be seen. The road ahead is completely deserted and whatever might lie on either side of it hidden by the density of night.

Jack sighs from the back seat and I turn round to check him. His fringed suede water bottle, bought at the airport, is slung around his neck in a potentially lethal knot. His face is filthy. A still-life of the journey's bribes and snacks. The corner of his mouth droops slackly and a trail of dribble has leaked down his chin onto his neck where it has dried into a chalky mark. He sleeps in his customary upright position, a pose I'd always assumed was the result of all those years imprisoned in unforgiving baby car seats, but recently have come to understand is simply a mark of his independence, his two fingers up to the adult world. Jack has always had a certain irritation and impatience at being small, as if his babyhood and now youth were no more than inconveniences unfairly foisted on him, and consequently he's always treated them as something of an affliction, an accident of birth that he'd have to overcome, like a club foot or a squint.

'When are we there?' Emmy slumps self-pityingly against the opposite window. 'I'm sooo tired.' Her voice cracks with exhaustion and tears. As I prop her up again, she opens a cyclopian eye in order to fix me, the mother of all her woes, with a baleful accusing scowl.

How can my children possibly understand what's going on? Why they've been dragged on this endless painful journey, away from their home, from their friends, their father – and for what? To spend a year in some jerry-built cabin in the middle of God only knows where because of a whim, some barely explicable desire for escape that I had no longer been able to ignore.

'I still don't understand why you insist on going on ahead,' Robert had said for the umpteenth time as he'd kissed the children at the departure gate. 'It could be months before I can get away.'

I hadn't answered him because what was there to say? Once you lose the power of communication with some-one, nothing makes sense between you any more and months were exactly what I was counting on.

Unhappiness is a dangerous thing, like carbon mon-oxide. You don't smell it, you don't taste it, it's formless and colourless, but it poisons slowly. It seeps into every pore of your skin until one day your heart just stops beating. And I've been wondering. How did my mother put it? The summer she took off? A wind was rising over the Orkneys the day she upped and blew out of my world forever. But before there's any debate about repeat behavioural patterns and the hereditary nature of bolters, I have to point out one significant difference. In the summer of 1983 my mother didn't take her children with her. She didn't pack their favourite chewed teddies and leaking finger paints and Emmy's clock with the cat's eyes, whose tail wags along in time with the seconds. No. My mother left me behind, sitting on the beach, the underside of my trousers packed down with cold wet sand as I dug for lug worms, happy, oblivious, dreaming of beans on toast while my father knelt behind me and cried fat salty tears into a pile of nearby seaweed.

Sleep must have somehow come then, because when I open my eyes, the truck has stopped. I unclip the seat-belt and feel stiffly for the door handle. The Mexican is hauling suitcases out of the back and tossing them to the ground, small puffs of smoke gusting out of his mouth at the exertion. Even unconscious, Jack is not an amenable child, his limbs remaining obstinately rigor-mortified. I shake him awake and push him out into the cold night air, then scoop Emmy into a fireman's lift and the three of us stumble towards the cabin's deck where the Mexican stands silently, holding the fly screen open. Once we're safely inside he nods his head curtly and climbs back into the truck, leaving all the luggage in a sloppy pile outside the cabin door. I bite my lip in irritation as the ignition fires into life.

I push the children up the narrow wooden staircase, tossing Emmy onto my bed before going back to rescue Jack, who has somehow got left behind and is hunched, wide-eyed, on the top step as though shot by a sniper in the first wave of a surprise attack. At least the cabin has been made habitable. There are sheets on the bed and a shrunken striped woollen blanket on top. The sink in the corner still has rust stains down one side but hot water trickles from the taps, and the loo, whose incessant gurgling drove Robert crazy last time we were here, appears to have been fixed. Most luxurious of all, a reading light has been rigged up via the central overhead beam and connected to a yellowing switch on the wall. The children quickly lock themselves into their familiar sleep positions. Emmy, stretched out horizontally across the pillows, her long black hair splayed around her head in tangled Medusa locks, while Jack lies in repose in a T-junction with her shoulder. There is a bout of feral growling when I attempt to wash their faces and I give up. What does it matter if they spend the next year encrusted with dirt? What do I care if they run naked through the brush and their feet grow over with soft fur like baby wolverines? In this 'big adventure' of ours, there must surely be perks for them too. Jack's hair smells of cauliflower and urine. The H&M label on his T-shirt is sticking up against his neck. Height 125 cms, 7/8 years old, it reads and for a second I sit down on the bed, overcome by a wave of emotions I am simply too tired to identify.

After a few minutes of dozing upright I have the brilliant notion of peeling off my own clothes and getting into the bed, but as I move around the room I feel a nubble of something on the floor which, though solid initially, yields under the pressure of my foot. I kneel down and flip back the rug. It's a dead mouse. Or the putrid, rotting remains of one. Squashed flat, its legs and paws are spreadeagled across the floorboards like a miniature hunting trophy. For an optimistic moment I wonder whether I can get away with leaving it till morning, but the revulsion factor is too high. There's no obvious mouse-scraping utensil to hand and a quick rummage through the overnight cases produces nothing helpful. In desperation I yank open the drawer of the bedside table and finally luck out with a box whose hinged lid lends itself nicely to the task. Balancing the corpse gingerly on the lid with one hand and fumbling with the rusted catch on the window with the other, I shake the whole disgusting mess out. Then as soon as it's safe to, I laugh, thinking of the fuss Robert would have made. 'I mean surely it's not unreasonable to be angry!' I can hear him shouting. 'Haven't we been paying him to caretake the place? I mean, haven't we, Alice?'

Up in the sky, the stars are out in force. Cold air blows around the room. It smells earthy and unfamiliar. Except for Emmy's snoring, a faint puckering of air in and out, there is absolute quiet. What a miracle this silence is. No car parking outside, no slamming of doors, no heavy tread on the staircase to the bedroom, no reek of cigars or hand laid expectantly on my shoulder. Ha! We're here, we are finally here and to hell with poor little dearly departed Mickey Mouse, to hell with Robert's bombastic rants, because this is it, we've made it, and as I climb into bed, curl around my children and wait for sleep to come, I feel as smug as a cat who has taught herself to swim.

2

I'm woken by the phone ringing. 'You sound sleepy.'

Next to me the children barely stir, their eyes half closed, like a pair of alligators lying in wait for some unsuspecting prey to disturb the surface of their watering hole.

Outside the window, night is still inky black. I fumble for the watch under my pillow. 'Robert, it's five in the morning!'

'Sorry,' he says a little sulkily. 'I'm in Geneva, I got the time difference confused.' There's an awkward pause, then, 'Look, I just wanted to know you'd arrived okay.'

'We're okay,' I tell him and promise to call later.

'Love you,' he says, then waits a couple of barren seconds before hanging up the phone.

Relieved, I close my eyes once more but it's no good. It's there again. A subconscious prick of puzzlement which takes a few minutes to work through the fog in my head.

The wooden box is on the floor where I'd left it, its lid still smudged with a veneer of mouse goo, its contents strewn on the wooden boards – a small hollow silver cross and a roll of paper secured with a faded strip of cloth. I ease off the tie and carefully unravel the paper, half hoping for missing deeds or a treasure map, but it's just a letter. Strange. Unable to face a single night on the pitiful excuse of the cabin's resident mattress, I'd had our spare bed and bedside tables, along with some crates of books, shipped over from London. But neither this crudely made box nor its contents belong to me and whilst it's a romantic notion that one of the full-bellied removals men should have stolen away to a dark corner of the van for a chocolate Hobnob and a perusal of his morning mail, it's an unlikely one; the letter is written in Spanish and headed the University of California.

The Mexican then – had he slept here last night? Had he put on his pyjamas, waxed his moustache and thrown back the covers of the bed before turning his attention to the contents of the box, pausing only occasionally to glance out at the moon as it waxed and waned over the town? Perhaps. The paper is old and brittle, the ink so faded it's hard to make out the words. Curiouser and curiouser. I trace my hand down the lines as though their secrets might rise up like Braille beneath my fingertips and inexplicably I'm overcome by a sense of foreboding. A deep chill, like the proverbial phantom, passes through my body, and I quickly roll the letter up again and stow it back in its box.

The kitchen, too, is chilly in the stillness of the morning. I pull on jeans and a jumper while the water gathers bubbles in the saucepan. Tiny mouse turds cling to my feet. I brush them off and hurriedly add shoes. There is nothing so useful as a dustpan and brush in the kitchen, but I find two more saucepans, one with a stunted handle, a scratched frying pan, still with a layer of congealed grease from God only knows what, and a few loose pieces of mismatched cutlery the size of gardening tools. Except for the pack of coffee, the fridge is empty and I curse myself for forgetting to ask the Mexican to buy supplies, then reverse this and curse the Mexican instead, adding lack of breakfast-buying initiative to the man's growing list of crimes, which so far includes indefensible ill temper, poor house-cleaning and, of course, lousy pest control. There's nothing to feed the children except some fruit bars still in the zip pockets of their aeroplane backpacks which have already been passed over in disgust. So much of my energy in the past few months has been concentrated on pressing the pause button on our lives, that I'd given precious little thought as to what lay ahead, feeling in some superstitious way that to do so might jinx our exit route.

Outside the air is clear and still. I sit cross-legged on the wooden boards of the deck, feeling steam from the coffee condensating against my face. After a while tiny sounds become discernible – the rustle of a leaf, a bird cry, a noise, amplified by silence, of a door banging against its frame. It's the near light of dawn and all around the whispers of night time are fading as creatures disappear down warrens, drop bottom first into holes, crawl backwards into fissures in the ground. My head starts whirring with all the things I need to do, and I begin making a list – a lifelong solution for keeping panic at bay. For starters, the cabin needs a lot of work if we're to survive living in it for a whole year. A repaint, a better kitchen, curtains at the very least – abruptly, I put down the pen. A weak orange sun is creeping over the furthest peaks of the mountains to the east. It lights up every successive range, finally sweeping across the immediate landscape, glinting sharply as it touches on the tin roofs of the other cabins, just visible a few hundred yards down the hill.

Temerosa is a ghost town, one of hundreds of abandoned mining communities which sprang up out of the silver rush of the nineteenth century and consequently died in the glut of the twentieth. The town is built into the cleft of a hill on a small rocky plateau from where the landscape extends back as far as the eye can see, which is, in fact, forever. To the south lies Mexico. To the north are the flat plains and snow-tipped peaks of the Patagonia Mountains beyond which lies the great American West, a strange and wild country representing an escape and freedom so great that, for a long moment, I find it hard to breathe.

'Where are we going?' Jack asks.

'To see the town.'

'I'm cold.' This from Emmy.

'Come on, don't be silly, it's not that bad.' But she's right; despite the sun, it *is* cold and the air is dry. I can feel it greedily siphoning the moisture out of my skin, pore by pore. I touch a finger to my lips, already chapped and rough.

'I want to go home,' Emmy says.

'Let's walk quickly then.' I take her hand.

She snatches it back. 'No, home, London.'

'Why do we have to see the town?' Jack says, trudging two steps behind us.

'Because it's so pretty here! It's so different! We're going to have such fun!'

'How?' This last one from Jack, of course.

It's a perfectly reasonable question. How are we going to have fun? Right this second, with the children grouchy, listless and hungry, with no food in the fridge, no truck to get us to a shop, I haven't the faintest idea. How are we going to have fun in the long term? How will this adventure pan out? What will it be like to be alone with Jack and Emmy for the foreseeable future? I don't know either, but the hanging of curtains aside, I've been making plans. They may not be practical enough to ensure eggs in fridges but they're plans all the same: we're going to read a hundred books and complete 3,000-piece jigsaw puzzles, we will jog up mountains, learn to speak Spanish and make chipotle sauce. We are going to buy a pickup truck and head off west of the sun and east of the moon – stop in one-horse towns with names like Rattlesnake and Fort Defiance. But before we do any of these things, we will search out the most shamelessly greasy bacon 'n' cheese burger in the whole of America and kiss the bow-legged short-order cook who has grilled it.

'Will there be a shop?' Emmy asks.

'Don't be stupid,' Jack snaps.

'Mummy said it was a town.' Emmy's mouth turns down; close to tears, she's clutching the top of her arm.

'Jack! Did you pinch her?'

'Certainly did not!' Jack says furiously.

'Did Jack pinch you, Emmy?'

'Yes.' Emmy starts crying. 'I just wanted to know if there's a shop. That's not unreasonable, is it? Surely that's not unreasonable?' I turn my head away to hide a smile. What is unreasonable is how endearing it is in a five-year-old, when it's so annoying in Robert.

'Look, it's a ghost town,' Jack says wearily. 'There are no shops in ghost towns.'

'Why?'

'Ghosts don't have any pocket money.'

'Why not?'

'Because they don't have chores.'

'But I'm hungry. I want breakfast.'

'I know, me too,' I pacify her. 'I'm sorry. We'll get some breakfast soon.'

I smooth-talk the children on. Temerosa consists of seven cabins apart from ours, each separated by windy stretches of path covered in twisted desiccated leaves which crackle noisily under our feet. The cabins are different sizes, but all variations on a common vernacular of porch, deck and gabled windows. The first two we explore have stone foundations and outside walls covered in reddish cedar-wood shingles, most of which have warped and flipped up at the bottom revealing longer horizontal wooden planks beneath. Although at some point there appears to have been a cursory attempt at decoration, no one paint colour has been used to finish any one cabin. Some walls are whitewashed, some raw wood, others have remnants of a faded turquoise around the door frames. To the back of the second cabin, we climb down a dry wash and short-cut our way to the third. An enormous cottonwood tree is growing at the bottom of the wash, its branches drooping tiredly towards the ground like an overworked giant. I touch my hand to the trunk, which is carved with graffiti: initials, nicknames; 'Li'l Foozy' and 'Pearl' linked forever by arrows piercing a roughly scratched wooden heart.

'Mummy, I'm so hungry,' Emmy says again.

'I don't understand why we can't have breakfast now,' Jack says. 'Why do we have to wait till later?'

'Because we don't have any food right now.'

'But without food we'll starve,' Emmy whimpers.

'Eat Jack then,' I suggest and she giggles. Jack is less easily diverted. He has smelt blood and prepares to close in for the kill.

'And why,' he eyes me meditatively, 'do we not have any food?'

'Because I forgot to buy any.'

'So how are we going to have breakfast, *for God's sake*?'

'Don't say "for God's sake",' I say automatically. 'In a bit, we'll borrow a truck and go to town.'

'Why can't we borrow the truck now?'

I take a deep breath. Currently, I am the fly whose wings Jack likes to pull off.

'Cos it's a little early and I don't want to wake up the man who drove us here.'

'But I'm hungry *now*,' says Emmy.

'So eat the fruit bars,' I say, playing my trump card. I fumble for them in the backpack and wave them in front of her face.

'Nooooo,' she wails.

I nip at the wrapper with my teeth. 'Come on, it's good, what's wrong with it?' I tear off the end strip and chew determinedly. 'Yum, yum, see how delicious?'

'It's disgusting.'

She's quite right, of course. It's filthy. Nevertheless I hold it irresistibly close to her nose, hoping that some olfactory instinct will snap into action and send a signal to her mouth to open. Instead she knocks it to the ground and stamps on it. 'I'll die before I eat that. Die, do you hear?'

'Die then, brat,' says Jack, nudging at a stone with his trainers.

Emmy drops to the base of the cottonwood and adopts a squat position. Her favoured form of protest is 1960s university student and she does it really well, refusing to be bulldozed by threats or moved by entreaty. Only total capitulation to her petition of human rights will normally shift her. Still I go through the motions.

'Emmy, if you don't get up, I'll have to leave you here.'

'Leave me then.' Her voice begins to rise and screech like a string quartet warming up. 'Just leave me here to die – to die, d'you hear, because I'm starving to death. STARVING TO DEATH.'

I look at her helplessly. My job as a landscape designer has allowed me to spend most of my children's lives studiously avoiding the drudgery of childcare, calling on impossible work deadlines, meetings of vital importance, phone calls that simply couldn't be delayed, all in order to back up my case for not having to give in to the tedium of pushing-swings-in-park duties. I know there are some parents who can make space stations from toenail clippings and igloos out of potato peelings and I wish I were one of them, truly I do, but the patience and imagination required for that kind of activity simply never made it through to my gene pool. Now, as realization slaps me in the face that I have committed myself to an extended period of au pair/babysitter/nanny-free single parenting, I am tempted to fall into a heap of quivering motherhood.

'Look, Emmy.' I squat down. 'This is my fault, so I'll make you a deal. You stop making a fuss right now and you can eat whatever you want for a whole week.'

The snivelling stops and a look of true cunning passes over her face. 'Anything?'

'Well, okay, obviously not *anything*—'

'You said anything,' Jack reminds me coolly.

'Well obviously you can't just eat chocolate all day long, but you can choose any meal you want for a whole week and I promise I will give in without a fight.'

'Me too?' Jack asks.

'Both of you, okay?'

Emmy pretends to weigh up the offer but, God knows, she can recognize a good deal when it's on the table. 'Okay.' She stretches out her arms to be picked up and I pull her onto my lap.

'It's just that I'm tired,' she whispers.

'I know.' This is Emmy's standard apology and I

accept it with good grace. I try to set her on the ground, but she clings, rubbery-legged, around my hips.

'Mummy Mummy wait there's something else. I just have to ask you a question.'

'Okay.'

'Because it makes me scared in my body and I don't know if it's true and I don't want you to just say it's okay I want to know the truth because it really makes me sad.'

When she's upset or tired, Emmy talks like this; very long sentences without punctuation, all delivered with great seriousness and sense of urgency in a desperate pleading voice that flips my heart over. I steel myself for something apocalyptic. Has Emmy, with her child's extra-sensory perception, picked up that something is a little out of kilter with her parents' marriage? Has she decided after careful deliberation that living 7,000 miles apart is not exactly a normal state of affairs for your average nuclear family? And if so – then how to answer? Questions about God, sex and lesbians, I can field without difficulty, but justifying the big D, for any parent, remains the final frontier.

'Look, she's gone,' was how my own father chose to put it that first evening as he placed a plate of beans on toast in front of me. 'And she's not coming back.'

'Never?' Only later did it occur to me that this was an event way out of the ordinary.

'I'm sorry, Alice,' he said. 'But I'm going to look after you now and I'm going to do everything just as well as your mother.'

'Okay,' I said. And suggested he start by heating up my beans.

I look into Emmy's trusting face, knowing that whatever she asks, I will inevitably fail her. She glances nervously at her brother, then yanks my ear towards her mouth.

'Is it true that Jack is really a vampire?' she whispers. 'Because he says he is and he swears he is and if he IS a vampire AND he sucks my blood then I will have to be a vampire as well and I don't want to be a vampire because I don't want to live on blood.'

I hold her close to me while she cries, rolling my eyes at Jack over her shoulder, then I hoist her onto my back and walk on.

The rest of the cabins are in a grim state of repair, their doors and facades peppered with gunshots like constellations of black stars. Inside, the floors are littered with great mountainous piles of poop, rusting metal cans and little shiny pieces of broken crockery.

'Treasure,' Emmy says hopefully, dropping to the ground.

'Rubbish,' Jack says dismissively. He kicks a can against the wall.

The seventh and final cabin is bigger than the others, a long rectangular building with nine windows down each length and a wide porch wrapping around three sides. This was once the main boarding quarters of the town, housing both the kitchen and dormitories. We circle the outside, sizing it up. A hefty chunk of the side porch is covered by a bush with a trunk the colour of ox blood, its texture so smooth it feels as if it's been planed and sanded by a sculptor. A length of mosquito netting has been nailed over the front porch and the rusted spring base of an old mattress leant up against the hand rail. A workman's boot sits on top of a lubricant barrel as if admiring the view, which, to be fair, is spectacular. I shade my eyes against the sun. I can feel its strength now, almost as though someone has placed a warm iron on my back. The snow on the mountains looks like a wash of silver. There's nothing that far out, not a telegraph pole, or pylon, not a house, or a road or a living soul to be seen.

'What's that?' Emmy whispers. The fly screen is banging rhythmically against a mouldering door frame.

'Wowaaaaaaa.' Jack waves his arms around his head in the universally accepted impersonation of a person wearing a white sheet with snipped-out eyes.

'Ghosts?' Emmy, the uncynical, queries, wide-eyed.

We stare at the fly screen as it opens and shuts but if it's not from ghosts, it must be from boredom because there's not a whisper of wind. Not a shrivelled leaf moves on the oak trees. The air is absolutely still.

'Come on,' I tell the children, 'there are no ghosts here.' But of course this isn't true.

Over a hundred husky old miners have at one point lived and died in Temerosa and there are nights to come when it feels like a haunted wind blows through this town. Sometimes I lie in bed and think of them; sleeping cheek to jowl, hungry, frostbitten, wiring candles to their hats, boiling leather shoes and sucking on spaghetti laces as those interminable winters went by, as their bodies froze inside out and their minds slowly rotted with obsession for that one giant nugget they dreamed of holding – and they'd not been the only prospectors who dreamed of riches out here. Up until last fall, Temerosa had been owned by a conglomerate of developers from Toronto, one of whom, an old friend of Robert's, had come to him for a loan pending a more formalized investment in the business. As a property developer, nothing appeals to Robert quite so much as the 'big idea' but unfortunately his feverish optimism is never tempered by much sound commercial rationale. His Toronto friend's big idea was buying up deserted towns all over the American West then renovating them for resale. Before he got very far the stock market crashed and their funds withered. For once, Robert lucked out. He would never get any of his dollars back but instead we found ourselves in possession of a mystery 500-acre property in Arizona.

I yank back the screen and put my foot to the wooden door. Inside the big front room, wooden planks have been torn up and the floor is covered with stacks of pebbles and yet more animal droppings. A blackened burnt-out fridge stands in one corner and a sofa in another, stuffing oozing from a succession of gaping tears, as though it had gone mad from loneliness and indulged in a frenzy of self-mutilation. To the back of the room, a door opens onto a long corridor which runs the length of the building, cutting through a maze of smaller interconnecting rooms. The whole place smells rotten and musty. But there's another smell as well, one harder to identify, which creeps up my sinuses like ammonia, some lethal mining gas about to render us unconscious. I'm about to grab the children and pull them out when, just behind me, Emmy starts to wail – a high keening noise that rises and increases in volume with each intake of breath. I'm on the verge of panic myself until I see what has spooked her. On the walls of the adjoining room, animal skins – bats, skunks, deer and even a lion – have been stretched and pinned into menacing vampiric shapes.

I clamp my hand over Emmy's mouth and we beat a retreat. Outside, in the safety of bright sunlight, I suck fresh air into my lungs and glance back at the boarding house. The glassless windows stare back at us like the eyes of a blind man and for a moment, overwhelmed by the enormity of the job in hand, I feel a knot of unease deep in my stomach.

'Mum!' Jack whispers, tugging on my sleeve. 'Someone's coming.'

The Mexican, with his averted eyes and sad moustache, is slowly making his way up the track towards us, the dour expression on his face a dead giveaway. What a cushy job he's been used to. Self-appointed sheriff of a town with no citizens, being paid for taking care of a bunch of cabins so dilapidated there is nothing he could possibly maintain. No wonder he is surly and unhelpful. Up until now all he'd had to contend with were a couple of self-satisfied developers waltzing in once or twice a year to throw their weight around. And now here I am, with my snivelly whiter-than-white urban brats, crashing in on his own peace and refuge. I take the children's hands and we slowly head down the hill to meet him. I wonder whether to ask him about the letter but it's hard to know how to phrase the question 'Have you been sleeping in my bed?' without sounding like a peevish Goldilocks – besides, there is the small but not irrelevant fact that he has been caretaking this place for the last five years.

When we'd first come, Robert had attempted to cross-question him. What exactly had this so-called 'caretaking' entailed? But he'd got nothing more enlightening than a shrug and a 'No ispeek Ingless.' Irritated by what he'd perceived as deliberate lack of respect, Robert had been in favour of firing him on the spot, but I thought I'd noticed something else in the man's eyes, an expression I couldn't quite put my finger on.

'Yeah, a willingness to rip us off,' Robert said sourly once he'd realized that we were now solely responsible for the Mexican's wages. 'Besides,' he'd added petulantly, 'I hate Mexican food.'

Still, if he's been here five years, then he and he alone would have been around to oversee the building works to our cabin. He would know where to get the propane for the stove, how to pump the water from the well, how to unblock the sewage and restart the generator. If anyone has an idea how to access the local contacts or find inexpensive labour, it's going to be him. Besides, dammit, at this point in time, he is the one and only person I know in the entire state of Arizona.

'¡Buenos días, señora!' he mumbles gruffly, eyes sliding away from mine.

'¡Buenos días!' I nod back at him. It would really help if I could remember his name, but I can't and I don't know enough Spanish to ask it.

He bends down to Emmy. '*¡Buenos días!*' he says softly. Emmy turns and presses her face into my jeans. He straightens up again and holds out a paper bag.

'*Desayuno.*'

I'm confident that my scanty three words of Spanish will soon be augmented by a course of language tapes I bought from Waterstone's a good month before leaving. The only reason I picked them out from the legions of Biarritz-style offerings on the shelf was because I read on the blurb that the teacher had taught Doris Day to sing '*Que será será*' in flawless tones, but despite this inspiring recommendation, I have so far failed to start the course. The Mexican, however, is undeterred.

'Breakfast,' he translates.

'*Gracias*,' I say, surprised. '*Gracias.*'

He thrusts his hand into the bag and draws out a packet of Fruit Loops, a carton of milk, and three slim paper sachets of cherry Kool-Aid. '*Por los niños*,' he adds. 'The children.'

Jack and Emmy stretch out their hands and make cawing noises like starving baby crows and in response to this he suddenly grins. With a shock I wonder whether I have misjudged him. It's possible that his perpetual look of sullenness is less of a mean-spirited thing and more of a physical unkindness. When he smiles, the right-hand side of his mouth shoots up in the traditional manner, but the left side seems loath to follow, instead remaining stubbornly horizontal, which in turn gives his face the frozen look of a mild Bell's palsy sufferer.

'*Gracias*,' I say again.

'No problem.' He smiles again and this time I notice the gaps where two of his back teeth are missing.

I smile as well and stick out my hand. 'Alice.'

'Benjamín,' he says. His J is soft. *Benjhamin.*

I have absolutely no intention of firing him.

3

'The truck is good,' Benjamín says. I step up onto the metal footplate and hop into the cab. He slams the door after me, giving it a couple of slaps with the palm of his hand before walking round to the front. 'See?' He holds up the towline and hook still attached to the front fender. 'Big engine, very strong.' Then he presses his fingers to the hinge of his jaw, as though necessary to relocate it back into its proper place before committing himself to a final declaration. 'The truck is safe.'

The truck is a 1986 extended Dodge pickup and to those who believe the glamour of their ride correlates directly to the state of its disintegration – and I happen to be one of them – then this surely represents a very grand set of wheels indeed. First and foremost, it's a wonderful colour. I've never before seen a car or truck that was butterscotch coloured. I've certainly never heard any car dealer say, 'Why, yes, Mrs Coleman, you can have it in forest green, black, or could I perchance interest you in the butterscotch?' Anywhere else in the world a toffee-apple truck might look a little out of place, but here, under the orange sun, against the ochre and red of the rock face, well, it just looks tastefully camouflaged.

Size-wise, the front cab seats five people and the flatbed at the back is long and wide enough to transport a small Boeing 747. This back section also comes with an optional shell, like a lid on a giant re-usable can of sardines, so if you wanted to, you could even sleep in it. Above the Arizona plates Benjamín has fixed a spare tyre and wired an extra brake light through its centre.

Sitting up in the cab, yanking down on the clunky gears, brings on every Thelma and Louise fantasy I've ever indulged in, and I soon begin to visualize myself and the children, glowing and bronzed from regular outdoor activity, lying in the back, smoking roll-ups, covered in a great shaggy skin of a bear – possibly a bear that I have myself wrestled and overcome in an altogether separate fantasy – and staring dreamily at the heavens while meteorites flame across the night sky from Jupiter to Mars.

I clip Emmy and Jack behind stiff webbing seatbelts and after some unintelligible directions from Benjamín, we set off along the Temerosa road, a meandering dirt track of roiling dust and treacherous switchbacks. The truck is unwieldy to drive with a loss of control and marked rear-end sway every time it negotiates a corner, like a big-bottomed woman encountering a revolving door for the first time, but then Benjamín paid only $600 for it so anything over and above moving forwards and backwards has to be considered a bonus.

'So is this our car?' Jack says.

'Yup. What do you think? Do you like it?'

Jack sniffs the worn upholstery disdainfully. 'It smells.'

'It smells like poo,' Emmy says and giggles wildly at her nerve.

'Why can't we have our old car?' Jack demands.

This would be the point when, under normal circumstances, a watertight defence re the matter of the car would have to be prepared, but the road is so terrifyingly narrow in places, it's hard to work out how to keep all four wheels within its confines without either busting a tyre on the sharp rocky hillside or, worse, sliding across the pebbles that are scattered on the cliff edge like marbles and toppling into the abyss.

'We can't have our car, because Daddy's got it.'

'Why can't Daddy bring it here?'

'Because Daddy's using it.'

'Why can't Daddy get another car and send our car here?'

An effortless and exhausting litigator, no statement is too trifling for Jack to take issue with. He argues every point to its ultimate conclusion with the dogged tenacity of a prosecution lawyer, which has the knock-on effect of making me feel culpable of some oblique crime I was unaware had been committed.

'Come on, Jack, I like this truck. It's fun to have a truck. Maybe one night we'll sleep in it.'

'Tonight, Mummy,' Emmy immediately says, 'can we sleep in it tonight?'

'Well no, probably not tonight.'

'You said tonight.' Jack waits, glare intact.

What are my rights here? What constitutes the Miranda Escobar of parenting? There's no question I can remain silent, but I'm equally aware that anything I say can and most definitely will be taken down and used against me. Jack is a startlingly beautiful child with pouting junior heart-throb looks. Unlike most eldest children who emerge from their mother's womb, usually after a long and arduous labour, as hesitant, neurotic creatures, painfully reflecting their parents' total capitulation to terror at their arrival, Jack, a controlling child even during pregnancy, announced his readiness to be born by breaking my waters on the dot of four a.m. (the shock of which sent Robert rolling from bed to floor amidst weary apologies, 'Sorry, so sorry, was I snoring?') and two hours later shot into the world as a supremely confident, fully functioning dictator.

And still he waits, his streaky brown hair flopping over one self-righteous eye.

'No, I didn't say *tonight*, Jack – I said *one night*. One night soon,' I add for Emmy's benefit.

'Okay, soon,' Emmy agrees placidly. Emmy has a tenderer heart, it's true, but before we get all judgemental here, one of her greatest joys in life is to beat her teddies to a pulp so that she can have the pleasure of comforting them afterwards. Jack grunts with disgust at the malleability of his sister and within seconds I hear the Klingon signature tune of his Game Boy pinging into life. I watch in the rear-view mirror as his fingers and thumbs fly across the key pad as if he were typing up a deposition for the impending trial of Jack Coleman versus his mother. Down goes his head and down it stays for the remainder of the journey, impervious to any and all feeble exhortations to admire the view.

After about five miles of sandy track, I steer the truck over cattle grids marked with orange and black diagonal tin strips, which, like the facade of the cabins, have been shot through with bullet holes. The track becomes rockier as it cuts through the mountain. The verge on the hill side is sculpted into long crumbly sand stalagmites and above these, dotted between bushes and scrubby trees, cacti of every kind are growing. I don't yet know any of their names but some look like giant porcupines, others like green afros which would make ferocious gangland weapons if used for headbutting purposes. The south side of the slope is degraded and bare, blistered by sun. 'Quick, look!' I tell the children. A roadrunner, comically identical to the cartoon version of itself is running below us, parallel to the car. The truck veers around another corner and it disappears out of sight.

'Did you see that, Emmy? Jack?'

'See what?' Jack says.

Our nearest town, Ague, turns out to be a pretty strange place. Population 1,000, it's thankfully far too small to have had any of the McDonald's, Wendy's or Burger King franchises stuffed down the throat of its main drag, but the juxtaposition of old Victorian buildings – hotel, post office and saloon in its centre – and the more modern adobe slabs of a petrol station, Uzed car business and hardware store on its outskirts (Ague's centre and outskirts, by the way, being no more than a couple of blocks from each other) leaves the town looking like a set for some post-modernist spaghetti western which ran out of money just before shooting started.

Even after we turn into the main road, there's little traffic. Now and again we overtake a pickup with a spindly looking cowboy behind the wheel, flatbed weighed down with long planks of wood, and a beady cross-bred dog balancing precariously on top. Behind us, an ancient maroon Buick creaks to a stop at the lights, and drawing into the parking space in front of us is a Cadillac whose bodywork is so beat up that the butter-scotch truck looks right at home as I edge it in alongside.

Historically speaking, Ague's pièce de résistance is Prestcott's Hotel, built in 1882, and named after the prospector and founder of the town, Adam Prestcott. Originally, the place consisted of twenty-five cabins and seventy people and its very first property lot sold for the princely sum of $3.50. Ague sprang up on the luck of a group of miners to whom every wash in the area had brought new riches. Right now the town was struggling to claim its lawful place as a site of historical interest, which was tough considering it boasted only one famous gun battle – and that a dubious one – between two warring prospectors who had discovered a bonanza strike at more or less the same time but were both so geographically inept they failed ever to find it again. All this learned from the two girls behind Prestcott's big oak bar reception, Candy and Sharleen, who wear white lace aprons over neat black skirts and who virtually weep with gratitude when I ask whether Emmy and Jack can use the loo – or restroom, as they politely inform us it's called. The interior of the hotel is shabby Victoriana with a faded plum carpet, and the whole place has the faintest whiff of school cabbage dinners to it. Brass keys to the bedrooms hang on hooks in an old mail-sorting box but every single one of them appears to be present and accounted for.

'Quietest little place you ever saw this time of year,' the girls sigh, bringing out a plate of shortbread for the children to gnaw on. But according to Sharleen, in the spring when the desert bursts into bloom, and again in late fall after the sun has ceased pounding the earth with quite such ferocious intensity, people arrive from all over the United States, pop their parents into one of the innumerable retirement homes in Phoenix then celebrate their new-found freedom by touring the old mining towns or visiting Ague and taking part in one of the mock-up Doc Holliday/ Tombstone-style gun battles staged there daily.

'Oh yeah, it's sure rip roarin' those times,' she says wistfully.

We eat lunch in the Stage Stop Saloon, where a waitress with impossibly frizzy hair brings us glasses of mineral-tasting iced water and marvels at our accents. The place is decorated with a stuffed buffalo head, old guns and pictures of anaemic-looking miners nailed skew to the walls, and on first glance it might be taken for one of those themed Cowboy 'n' Injun restaurants in Leicester Square, were it not for the two actual real-life Indians slouched in a corner booth, dipping tortilla chips into a bowl of salsa. In between staring and pointing behind her hand at the Indians, Emmy orders a plate of ketchup and a chocolate milkshake. Jack gets a hamburger which is so overcooked it arrives as black and hard as a hockey puck and the mystery dish I settle for, Navajo bread, turns out to be the sort of thing the God of Impending Obesity might send down to earth as a light starter. It sits on the plate, an airy pillow of golden fried bread covered in chilli beans, chopped tomatoes, grated cheese, shards of iceberg lettuce and diced green chillies. I wimpishly order a child's portion, which is nevertheless the size of a trampoline, and though it remains in my stomach for many weeks to come there's no question it's quite the best thing I've ever eaten. While I'm gasping for breath, the waitress comes over and says, 'Are you still working on that, honey?' as though it's a set of accounts that I must diligently sign off on before our bill can be settled.

By this time, we've all had more than enough. It's late afternoon and the flu-like symptoms from a combination of sleep deprivation, constipation and an eight-hour time difference have crept up on all of us and we trundle back towards Temerosa, shopping bags flapping in the pickup, the children huddled together, eating Reese's Pieces, dull-eyed and silent.

I entirely fail to notice the police car on my tail until it snaps on headlights and flashes me. It's a big white Ford Explorer with a green strip down one side and the whirring red lights of looming trouble. I pull the truck over. I have no idea what the speed limit is round here. The road has been deserted for the last ten miles except for a single rabbit breaking cover and some hairy little things, which I took to be chipmunks, zigzagging under the wheels as though engaging me in a highly amusing game of Russian Roulette.

The Explorer pulls over behind us. A man in uniform climbs out and adjusts first his hat, then his sunglasses and finally the leather gun holster slung around the hips of his dark beige trousers. Only when he ambles up to the window do I see he's not the redneck sheriff I assumed, but an Indian boy, a young one, early twenties maybe, with a round, almost Asian-looking face, black hair and skin the colour of a coffee latte.

'Afternoon, ma'am,' he says politely, tipping the wide brim of his hat.

'Hello,' I say, examining him tentatively. He's heavy-boned and muscular, but it's the kind of muscle that with enough BBQ chips and beer might easily turn to fat.

He peers through the passenger window at the children who stare back at him with reciprocal curiosity.

'May I see your driving licence, please?'

I confess to not having it on me.

'It's an offence not to carry your driving licence, ma'am.' His English is strongly accented and he speaks in a hesitant, truncated way as though the words are being jerked out of his mouth one by one by a fishing rod and line.

'An offence? Really?' I fix him with a winsome Joyce Grenfell smile. 'I didn't know that.'

'Yes, ma'am, it's a requirement of the law.'

I look suitably grave but explain that in England you're supposed to keep important documents like birth certificates and driving licences all safely locked up in a drawer at home, then nod vigorously as though endorsement of such common sense will confirm me as the very acme of responsibility.

'Uh-uh,' he says non-committally. 'May I see some ID, please?'

I try to remember what's in my wallet. A switch card, a library card, some dollars . . .

'You know, I'm actually not carrying any ID either. See, the thing is, we don't really have ID in England. In fact even our driving licences are just scrappy old bits of paper without actual photographs on them!'

The cop's trousers strain across his thighs as he shifts weight from one leg to the other. 'Name please, ma'am.' He hauls a pad out of his back pocket.

'Of course, it's Coleman. That's C-o-l-e-m-a-n.'

'Is this your vehicle, Mrs Coleman?'

'Yes, yes it is.'

'May I see the registration documents, please?'

Any ground gained from my naive-foreigner routine recedes. So overexcited to drive the truck, I never thought to check the whereabouts of any documents, let alone make enquiries as to their existence. For all I know, the truck could have fallen off the back of a lorry – so to speak.

'I'm sorry, I don't have the registration documents.'

'Are you an Indian?' Emmy squawks from the back.

'Emmy!' I turn and glower at her.

'Ma'am, is this your truck or isn't it?'

'Yes, it is my truck, it's just that it's new – well new to me, anyway, and somebody else bought it on my behalf and . . .'

'Ma'am, it's a requirement of Arizonan law that

registration and insurance documents be kept in the vehicle.'

'Oh,' I say vaguely, keeping a nervous ear tuned to the whispering coming from the back seat. 'Well . . . maybe they are in the vehicle! I mean, where might they be?'

The cop leans through the window and flips open the glove compartment. Inside is a plastic bag of official-looking papers and I send up a silent prayer of thanks to Benjamín.

'Are you going to scalpel us?' Emmy now bellows.

'Emmy! Be quiet!' I turn round. 'Jack, will you stop it!'

'Stop what?' he queries.

The boy unsheathes the papers from their bag and painstakingly begins writing on his pad.

'Did you know you were speeding, Mrs Coleman?'

Heigh-ho.

'The speed limit on this road is fifty mph. You were making sixty.'

'Gosh,' I say weakly, 'who would have thought this old thing could go that fast.'

'Do you have a gun?' Jack says.

The boy/cop stops writing. 'Uh-huh.'

'What about a knife?'

'Yuh.' He slides a penknife out of a hard-leather pouch attached to his belt. 'You want to see it?'

'Does it have leftover brains on it?'

'Nuh-uh.' He puts it away again. 'I just cleaned it.'

In the mirror I see Jack's mouth form a silent Oh.

'Mrs Coleman.' The cop tears off the ticket. 'The fine for speeding is a hundred dollars.'

'A hundred!'

'Yes, a hundred dollars. You can pay me now.'

'Or?'

'Excuse me, ma'am?'

'Well what if I can't pay you now?'

'Mrs Coleman, if you don't pay me you have to follow me back to town and we have to go see the judge.'

'At this time of day?' I say craftily. 'Won't the judge have gone home?'

He shrugs. 'Then you can stay in town till morning.'

'In prison?' Jack says. 'That would be so cool.'

'Come on, Mummy, in jail! Can we?' Emmy is drunk with excitement.

Throwing myself on the cop's mercy, I swear I will never speed again and explain that today is literally my first day in America.

'Certainly is not,' Jack says. 'Liar.'

'Liar, liar, pants on fire,' Emmy croons.

'I'm sorry, ma'am.'

Defeated, I reach for my bag. The boy relieves me of five twenties and hands back the registration documents.

'Well, don't be in too big a hurry, Mrs Coleman.' He slaps the side of the window cheerfully. 'I spend a lot of time pulling freeway drivers like yourself off that Temerosa road.'

'I'm sure you do.' I eye him sourly, quite sure he's going to pocket the money for himself.

'Are you a cop?' Jack says.

'What's your name?' Emmy asks.

'Because you don't look like a cop,' Jack adds.

The Indian peers again at the children through the window. Unexpectedly, a dimple opens up in his cheek. 'Winfred,' he says. 'Winfred Tennyson. I'm with the Border Patrol.' He touches his finger to the brim of his hat. 'Glad to have been of service, ma'am.'

'A delight all round,' I mutter at his departing backside. God knows, there used to be a time when you could charm your way out of a simple speeding fine. 'Hey, wait!'

I stick my head out of the window. How on earth did he know we were heading to the Temerosa road? 'Wait!' I shout. But it's too late. Winfred Tennyson adjusts his hat and under the darkening edge of afternoon eases his bulk behind the wheel of his patrol truck and pulls out quickly into the road.

4

'Have you ever been to England, Benjamín?' I ask casually.

'Noh, Alice.' He puts down the *London Museum Guide* and hastily straightens up.

'I mean that's not one of them, but there are some good books here.' I wipe the spine of the *Roget's Thesaurus* with a damp cloth, 'Borrow anything you want, okay?'

Benjamín's eyes flick towards me by way of polite acknowledgement. He takes the knife from his back pocket and slices through the masking tape on the next crate.

'What about this, have you ever seen this?' I hand him a Folger's *Guide to Mexico*.

'Noh, Alice, no.' He scrunches up the used masking tape and yanks open the flaps.

I like the way Benjamín drops my name into every sentence as if it were a dot of punctuation. You'd feel compelled to shoot an American who did the same, but the cadence of Benjamín's English is sing-song. When he says 'no', for instance, he lands on the 'n' as if falling

51

from a great height, but as the 'o' is approached his voice swoops up again before coming to rest quaveringly on top, turning what would serve for anyone else as a curt negative into a multi-syllable word capable of expressing a whole range of other nuances – in this particular case, surprise.

Now whether this is surprise at a silly question, 'Of course I haven't seen this, what do you take me for – a goddamn tourist?' or surprise that such a thing exists, 'No! Wow, I've never seen such a fascinating and informed guide to my own country. Fancy!' it's hard to say. On balance I think it unlikely that Benjamín wants to borrow my Folger's guide book to Mexico just as it's a long shot he's going to want to sign out my copy of Anne Tyler's *A Patchwork Planet*, also fresh from the crate, but you know – I want him to know he can. Benjamín purses his lips and glances towards the window. Outside the children are pottering around beyond the deck. This afternoon they're on clean-up duty. Unaware, as yet, that they're being screwed on the exchange rate, they're picking tin cans and bits of plastic off the ground and putting them into rubbish bags for the agreed sum of one dollar a bag. The sky above them is deep blue. The sun strong. Idly, I wonder whether I should top up Emmy's Total Block.

We're beginning to get the hang of our new way of life now. For a few days after we arrived I found myself looking over my shoulder, fearful that at any moment someone, namely Robert, would barge into the town and drag us kicking and screaming back to reality, but once it dawned on me that Temerosa was our new reality, I was overcome with a delicious feeling of decadence, the kind you get on holiday, when the luxury of sleep is temporarily returned to you, when you can loaf around all day and think about nothing more pressing than what flavour jam to spread on your toast.

I wake early in the mornings. As the dark blue of night fades to milky indigo, as the outlines of trees slowly develop through the cabin window, I stretch a lazy toe across the cool unused sheets on the other side of the bed, knowing that right around this time, in London, I'd be woken by the whine of the garbage truck, the whirr of the milk float, followed by the clanking of scaffolding as one or other of our neighbours embarked on their seemingly endless quest for home improvements. Then would come the mind-numbing morning rush hour with its child waking, shaking, washing, dressing, breakfasting, teeth brushing, and homework finding, all played out against the clock, against the surly traffic, against the black and white television set that is London in winter.

Here, though, the iron bars of routine and habit we'd been so imprisoned by in the city have begun to soften and bend. In our brave new world, early mornings are spent wallowing in the old copper bath. The generator boils the water up hot. After we get out, Emmy and I stand on the deck in our towels, looking down at our cooked lobster feet steaming on the wooden planks. As the heat seeps from our bodies into the cool morning air, we watch the sun climbing round the edges of the mountains. This morning I noticed a smudge of nail varnish on my big toe, like a souvenir from another, different life.

'I can clean that off for you, Mummy,' Emmy offered, 'when I have time.'

And time is what we now have. Time is everywhere, ours to spend how we please and we're making good use of it. We explore the hills around town and play on the carcasses of mining equipment. We collect grasses to press (Emmy) or set up rusted cans on rustier barrels and throw rocks at them (Jack). We moon around like lovesick teenagers, waxing lyrical about the view or going on and on and on about the beauty of the mountains and the glorious sounds of silence (me) until the children's eyes roll back in their heads and they start choking on their tongues.

These days it's goodbye to those hellish evening meals where the children stare in mute fury at their enemy in its cold green uniform of vegetable, whilst Anneka, our duo-syllabic au pair, squats at the table like a prison wardress, denying probation, removing pudding privileges. These days, thanks to the ratification of the Treaty of Nursery Food, we are allowed to live on tinned chicken noodle soup and macaroni cheese for a further two weeks and moreover we get to eat it whilst playing the Memory game or Boggle or painting our bedrooms in lurid colours. (Emmy and Jack – green and pink, me – mustard.) These days it's goodbye to the hurrying, begging, shouting, pleading, cajoling of children into bed because there's an evening plan, a dinner to be cooked for Robert's business cronies, or just something better to do; these days, of course, there is nothing better to do. Here in Temerosa we all go to bed at the same time, at around nine o'clock. Sometimes even eight-thirty! Good

Lord – will the debauchery never end? And if it's all a little strange and new for them, then stranger and newer for me is that, for the first time in my life, I'm finding sole motherhood addictive.

'Night night, John-boy,' I call from my room. 'Night night, Mary Ellen.'

'Night night, Maw,' Jack and Emmy chirrup back even though the joke sails way over their heads, even though they have never seen *The Waltons*, a television show, hailing as it does from those days of yore when I was young and dinosaurs still roamed the earth.

'Lights out, Granny Walton,' they chorus, and I am grateful that despite Jack's swinging moods, despite Emmy's geographical confusion (Can we walk to London today?) they are trying their best, they really are, to like their new little house on the prairie.

Benjamín tears his eyes away from the window and dutifully takes the book from my hand.

'Really, Benjamín, take anything you want,' I press. 'I mean I don't even have bookshelves yet.'

'Thank you, Alice.'

Why am I pushing this? I don't want to embarrass him. I have no desire to make him in any way uncomfortable because, quite apart from the way he speaks, there are a host of other things I like about Benjamín: the tightly fitted shirts he wears tucked into his jeans; the stiff leather belt with the steer engraved on its oval buckle. I'm fascinated by the length of his legs (very short), and the fact that he takes a smaller shoe size than me (5 English). I like that his eyes turn down at the corners and the way his nose, disproportionately large compared to his other features, cuts through the topography of his face until it hovers over his lopsided mouth, another feature which I find charming, though one I have not yet dared ask how he came by – but then I haven't yet dared ask much in the way of personal questions because those I tentatively lob into the conversation, 'Which part of Mexico do you come from?', 'How long have you been living in America?', are met with evasive answers, ones which imply, ever so cordially, that I am downright nosy and should mind my own business.

But see, that's the problem. Benjamín's business is becoming my business and vice versa. He is lonely, that much is obvious, and thus, I suspect, glad to have us around the place. Benjamín gives the impression of someone who knows he should be mean to us, but simply can't overcome his inherent kind nature to be so, and the thing I like absolutely best about him is that he seems to have taken over nannying by default and this strikes me as an excellent turn of events. I'm only too aware that my children have spoilt city ways and the sooner they're taught to swear fluently in Spanish and kill things the better. To that end, they have taken to hanging out in his cabin. There are no books in Benjamín's cabin, nor pens nor writing paper for that matter. In fact there's precious little in the way of material possessions and it's a great deal cleaner and tidier than ours. On the walls hang a Madonna and child clock and a tin effigy of the infant Jesus in St Joseph's arms, the baby tugging playfully on his father's beard, which is nailed (the effigy, not beard) inside a makeshift altar underneath which, rather audaciously, sits a television powered by the generator.

midnight cactus

When Emmy is not watching Mexican soap operas she likes to help cook Benjamín's lunch. This takes the form of her balancing precariously on a bar stool and spooning cold shredded mystery meat into quesadillas, folding them in half, pinching down the edges with her filthy little nails before dropping them from a great height into lethally hot spitting fat while Benjamín offers silent encouragement, strokes his chin and mixes a third jug of Kool-Aid. Jack, meanwhile, addicted to *Baywatch* reruns, sits in Benjamín's tweedy upholstered chair, in a 36D-cup-induced stupor, picking fitfully at a selection of Ring Ding doughnuts, pop tarts, Twinkies and strange fluffy pink marshmallow things covered in coconut, all of which Benjamín believes constitutes a wholesome child's meal. As a nanny, Benjamín is unusually good at taking criticism. For instance, when I tentatively broached the subject of the children contracting scurvy, he merely said, 'Okay, Alice . . . no problem,' and announced he would make them chicken soup instead. Sure enough, the next time the children went round there was a huge pan of water heating on the stove and on the counter next to it, a freshly strangled chicken. When the water boiled and the lid began to jump, Benjamín flipped it off with a wooden spoon and popped in the chicken: legs, beak, feathers – and an onion as an afterthought.

So, given all of the above, I don't know why I'm pushing this except that there remains a smidgeon of curiosity, a lingering doubt about the letter-and-cross-in-a-box mystery that I would like to lay to rest once and for all and, however obscurely, this seems like a good way of working my way round to mentioning it. 'What about this one?' I hand him a pedantic-looking tome on desert life. 'It's got a lot of information on this area.'

Benjamín stands up stiffly and brushes dust from the knees of his jeans. He reclaims his knife from the bottom of a crate and slides it through his belt.

'I can't read, Alice.'

'Oh.' I sit back on my haunches. Now I've done exactly what I hadn't wanted to do and offended him. 'But you speak such good English?'

'Nooooo, Alice.' This particular roller coaster of Os implies rank amazement that I could possibly think such a thing.

'Well what about Spanish? Can you read in Spanish?' Good God, what's wrong with me? Every instinct I have tells me to drop this before it goes any further.

'No,' he says, refusing to meet my eyes.

Okay, so fine, I've got the whole thing wrong. Benjamín can't read. Benjamín does not wax his moustache by the light of the moon and he has never slept in my bed. The letter belongs not to him but to one of the dead miners, proof of a forbidden love, kept in a secret box, hidden under a squeaking floorboard. Then suddenly it dawns on me why I find this so difficult to believe.

'But, Benjamín, you must be able to read. I mean you *can* write!'

'Noo,' he says, then, too late, remembers.

'Benjamín, I know you can write!'

He looks at the floor angrily.

He was lying, I was sure of it. The first time we came to Temerosa, Benjamín gave Robert a file of notes and guarantees on the cabin which minutely catalogued everything that had been installed and how it worked. In the last few weeks I've spent long hours poring over manufacturers' manuals, boning up on pipe flows and instructions for fixing the pump, all of which are hand-written. I don't exactly remember how Benjamín put it, but certainly he'd left me with the impression that it had been his work. But one thing's for sure – if you can't read, you can't write.

'Benjamín, you were here when the cabin was reno-vated, right?'

He takes his hat off the chair and puts it on.

'Benjamín?'

'¿Sí?' Out comes the jaw.

'Who wrote all the notes in that maintenance file?'

He scratches the stiff hairs by the side of his ears.

'Was it somebody from the building company?'

'Building company?' he parrots.

'The guys who put in the well,' I say patiently, 'and the generator. Who were the men who did the improve-ments on this cabin?'

'They're gone,' he says, unwilling even to give up this seemingly innocuous bit of information.

'Yes, but where did they come from in the first place, who hired them? Was it the previous owners?' God knows, I don't mean to heckle him but I have a bona fide reason for asking these questions. Before going belly-up, the Toronto owners had sunk a substantial amount of money into Temerosa, putting in the basic amenities of electricity, telephone and, thank God, water – in the form of a 250-foot well – and my game plan is to take up where they've left off. Renovate the rest of the town and sell it on as a spa, or a retreat. Considering I have only the most basic idea how to go about this, it's fair to say I'm going to need all the help I can get.

Benjamín just shrugs.

'Was the job run by some kind of a foreman?'

'Four men?' he queries artlessly.

'Foreman – uh, you know, somebody who tells the builders what to do.'

'Okay, *sí*, yes, a man.'

'Okay, good. So was it someone local to here? Was it an outside person the developers brought in?'

'No,' he repeats stubbornly.

'Come on, Benjamín, if it wasn't you, who wrote up the maintenance file? Who organized the work? Who paid the workers, drew up the plans, kept the records? *¿Quién lo hizo?* Who did it and what was his name?'

Benjamín runs his hand over his jaw then pulls down on his moustache.

'Duval,' he says croakily. 'His name is Duval.'

5

Jack is the first to hear it. The children are lolling around on the kitchen floor, apathetic and fractious from tiredness or possibly my refusal to make them jam sandwiches for the fifteenth night running, when Jack sits bolt upright, clamps a hand over his mouth and looks to the door, eyes widening.

'Vinny!' he whispers through his fingers.

Vinny is our dog from London, a handsome if very stupid lurcher currently boarding with my father in Scotland. 'Oh, Mummy, it's Vinny, can you hear?' He jumps up and starts a headlong rush towards the door but I whirl round and catch him by the arm. It's stormy outside and the wind is rattling the glass in the window frames but, even so, I can hear it, a whining and scratching against the wood. I hold Jack tight and listen.

Earlier this afternoon, out of a blue sky, grey clouds began to collect and a wind rose over the mountains. The children and I stood out on the deck, wrapped in blankets, listening to the oak trees squeaking in arthritic protest as their branches were bent this way and that, then, just as suddenly, the wind dropped, there was absolute quiet and snow began falling silently and relentlessly, coating the landscape in the thinnest layer of white.

'Look.' Emmy lifted her finger and pointed. There it was, in the gathering darkness, padding across our eye line, pausing only briefly to stop and stare at us.

'What is it?' she whispered.

'I don't know.' I squinted out into the gloom. 'A coyote, maybe?'

Certainly, it was our first real wild animal. Road-runners yes, chipmunks yes, deer, any number of them, soundlessly crossing the mountain road in their ones and twos, hindquarters bobbing as they leaped from track to bush, and even funny little prairie dogs with velvety newborn-looking skin, but I'd yet to see a coyote in the flesh and imagined them brownish, hunchback, of the same mangy, insolent mould as the hyena. This creature, however, was huge with grey, almost silver-streaked fur.

'A wolf!' Jack breathed.

'Wolves walk in every dream,' or so said Rudyard Kipling, but when I rubbed my eyes it had vanished.

Now the whining outside the door turns to a yip and then to an urgent-sounding bark.

'Mummy!' Jack digs his elbow into my ribs, but no way am I opening this door. There are mountain lions out here and only last week I'd read a story in the Ague newsletter about a grizzly bear up in Idaho who had lumbered onto the deck of some local's house. This homeowner, presumably out of relief that the grizzly was outside while he was safely in, did a little na na ne na na victory jig right in front of it, whereupon the grizzly smashed his way through the glass door and ate him right up, an Act Three I found hilarious at the time, but less funny now that the scratching and barking persists.

'Vinny, Vinny!' Emmy takes up the call. 'Mummy, let him in. Don't be so mean.'

'Open the door,' Jack shouts. He renews his efforts to claw free.

Emmy's eyes well up with tears, and her bottom lip quivers pitifully. 'Let him in, Mummy, I beg you to death, he'll catch cold . . . he'll catch cold and then he'll die, DIE . . . do you hear?'

I look at my children, so shaky and miserable. Now that the novelty of the first few weeks has worn off, things have not been going well just recently. There's no question that both children are missing home and who's to say my dream of freedom and romantic isolation won't turn into their nightmare of lonely imprisonment?

Emmy has started waking in the night. Quite unprompted by me she has taken to dressing like a whore from the Last Chance Saloon. She sleeps with her long hair twisted up into a bun, her frilly nightie nicely setting off the suede thong, purchased for 20 cents from the Ague thrift shop, which she keeps tied high around her throat. I kneel by the small wooden bed and smooth a hand over her forehead. Her flat bosom heaves with sobs.

'I want Vinny! I want Barbie! I want Anneka! I want Daddy!' she howls. With a pang I realize that the repulsive plastic Barbie is the only one of these I can produce and I think back to Robert's call earlier that morning.

'Our friends think we're having a trial separation,'

he'd said. Down the line, that fragile wire of communication that still binds us, I could hear him gulping air.

'Are we?'

'Are we what?'

'Having a trial separation? Is this what this is?'

'Robert—' I began, but stopped. The truth is there are six non-retractable words which mean the end to a marriage, but when it came to it, they'd stuck in my throat like fishbones. We'd gone to a restaurant and I remembered looking at the other couples sitting in awkward familiarity at their tables for two and wondering how many people were lucky enough to feel a real passion for someone, one that endured. When the grand scheme of marriage becomes mundane with disappointment, wrecked by the sheer ordinariness of life, how many end up settling for less? Settling for so very little. The world was full of couples like me and Robert, moving through life together, the principal dancers in a ballet choreographed by the Joker.

Blindly, I reach under the bed for the doll. A fresh outpouring of grief threatens but Jack comes to the rescue.

'Barbie's a lesbian,' he mutters sleepily and Emmy chuckles.

'Shut up,' she says amiably and, mollified, sinks back against the pillows.

Last week Benjamín took Jack down to the puddle of the river where the Temerosa miners used to pan for gold. I watched as he bent down and scooped gravel and silt off the bottom before handing the sieve to Jack. After a tentative bout of shaking, Jack was left staring at nothing more exciting than obsidian, volcanic-looking sand.

'If I ever find gold,' Jack said bitterly, 'I'm going to buy a rocket and fly away from here.'

There are nights, too, when even I feel strange and displaced, when I fall prey to sudden bouts of cabin fever and find myself standing at the window, staring out at the nothingness beyond as if my missing social life might suddenly drive into the town in the form of friends scrunched together in the back of the butterscotch truck, bearing videos of movies, theatre reviews, and prints of photographic exhibitions I'd missed. But there is nothing out there, just stars and darkness and silence. I open the window and breathe it all in, go on breathing until I think my insides might freeze. Then I go upstairs and sit on the children's beds and watch them sleeping, put my hand on their chests, because there are times when you need absolutes, things you can count on, like their inno-cence and sweetness. As for loneliness – well, for all the exoticness of sleeping by myself, there are nights when I miss a man in my bed.

So as the barking continues outside and I look at the longing on their faces I'm overcome with a crippling sense of guilt and, against all better judgement, open the door to the stormy night. The creature stalks in and sniffs the air, clearly offended at the amount of time it's been kept waiting. It turns and stares right at Emmy as though sizing up how much of her face to take off with the first lunge.

Emmy presses herself against my legs. 'Mummy,' she breathes, 'it *is* a wolf!' and she's not far off the mark. A strange-looking animal, half cattle dog, half Hound of the Baskervilles with a meaty stub of a docked tail and different colour eyes.

'Here, boy, here.' Jack holds out his hand. The dog growls and bares a set of thin frighteningly sharp teeth.

'Don't touch it,' I snap. Herding the children behind me, I swing the door back open.

'Here, boy, come on, out you go. Go on now. Out!'

'No,' the children shriek in unison.

The dog pays absolutely no attention to any one of us. It sniffs its way round the kitchen, eats two of Emmy's cheese doodles with their accompanying bugs and dust off the floorboards, then, folding its shaggy legs beneath its body, flops down under the table, throwing a quick challenging look in our direction.

And there it stays.

6

The children are starting at Devil's Slide, a small local school just outside Ague. We leave the house on the dot of eight a.m. Jack and Emmy trudging down the hill behind me towards the butterscotch truck. The ground is still covered by snow, the surface crisp and frozen into a layer of ice as delicate as the sugar crust on top of a crème brûlée. The morning is quiet and still. Lumps of snow balance precariously on the ends of boughs like dumb-bells in the hands of a man on a tightrope. Occasionally one falls and hits the ground with a soft plop. The sun is only halfway up the mountain and the town is in shadow. It's cold and the children complain. I daresay Jack is dreaming of his overheated-car run to Wormley House, maybe Emmy is suddenly feeling nostalgic for her happy clappy morning assembly at the local nursery – or maybe they just want to dispense with the notion of school attendance altogether.

I get the door of the truck open before noticing that Emmy has turned tail and deserted. Her tartan skirt flaps up to show pink pants as she legs it back to the cabin, kicking up puffs of snow in her wake. When I catch up with her she shrieks and drops limply to the ground.

'Oh, please come on Emmy.'

I try to hook my hands under her armpits but she cunningly changes tack from 1960s college student to paraplegic.

'I can't walk,' she announces.

'Why not?'

'My neck hurts.'

'What's wrong with it?'

'Broken,' she mutters.

'Oh, that's not good. How did that happen?'

'Don't know.'

'Was it broken when you woke up this morning?'

Five years spent with Jack have made her understandably wary of the fourth degree and she quickly spots the potential ambush in this one. 'No,' she says carefully, 'it broke just now.'

'Do you think it will be broke for long?'

'Yes, forever,' she says, voice cracking bleakly. She turns her head away and I take her shaking body in my arms.

'Mummy, Mummy.' Tears leak down her face, 'I can't go to school today because my neck is broken and you can't go to school with a broken neck and that's not just it I've got nits in my stomach and nits are catching and so I can't go to school with nits in my stomach and a broken neck.'

'Oh, Emmy.' I look at her blotchy face. Her eyes are wet, her thick lashes clumped together like black spikes of a garden rake. Oh, God.

'Children have to go school and that's that,' I lecture as I clip her into her seat.

'Why?' says Jack.

'Because they have to.'

'But why?'

'Because it's the law. Everyone has to go to school.'

'What would happen if we don't? What would actually happen if we broke the law? It's not like we'd *die* or anything, is it?'

'No, you probably wouldn't *die*, Jack, but you'd certainly have to go to prison.'

'They can't put us in prison.' Emmy looks outraged. 'We're very very small children.'

'Of course we wouldn't have to go to prison, Emmy. Mum's just saying that.'

'Okay, well maybe you wouldn't have to, but I would.'

'You should go to prison,' Emmy scowls, 'for making us go to school.'

'Anyway you wouldn't even have to go to prison, you'd probably just have to pay them money or something,' Jack points out.

Indeed. Under clause 1 of US educational law 7668, as my son, the District Attorney, correctly identifies, they would probably just fine me.

'Okay, Jack, I'm sure you're right, because, you know, why wouldn't you be right? After all, you're all of eight and I'm, like, thirty-four, so clearly you've been around the block a few more times than I have, but you'll see, I won't send you to school and then, one day, we'll all be having a nice time, eating cottage pie and minding our own business, when the sheriff will burst through the front door and haul me away and I'll have to spend the rest of my life doing hard labour, wearing an unflattering orange boiler suit and all because you wouldn't take my word for it, you know, just *for once.*'

'You don't have to be mean,' he says, sulkily.

'Jesus, Jack,' I say just as sulkily.

I manoeuvre the truck roughly down the road, nearly slamming into an elk on the first bend. At this hour of the morning you can smell the sulphur rising from the deserted mine shafts in the hills. The court of Jack is in temporary recess. He sits silently on the front bench and sneaks tropical-flavoured Skittles into his mouth one by one.

'So do they know I'm coming?' he says eventually. 'Will they like me?'

'Yes, they do know you're coming and yes, they will like you.'

'How do you know?'

'Because I like you,' I say lamely. I know little about the school except that it is the only one within an hour's radius and that the children's teacher-to-be, Sue, very much likes to sleep in caves.

'Come on, Mum, everybody likes their children.'

Not wishing to commit perjury, I refrain from answering. Jack proceeds to entertain himself the rest of the journey by perfecting his introduction.

'Hello, I'm Jack and I'm from another country.'

'Hi, I'm Jack. I come from England.'

Devil's Slide school turns out to be a collection of three mural-painted shacks, each smaller than the next, like an Ikea nest of tables which has been allen-keyed into the desert floor at the foot of a cliff. There is a parking area in front, and to the side a field of Indian grasses with the cadavers of six or seven mutilated cars nestled picturesquely amongst them. Behind the shacks gigantic tractor tyres have been imaginatively arranged for traditional playground games. 'The Swing' is a tyre suspended by three chains from a wooden construction. 'The Climbing Frame' – a bunch of tyres piled one on top of the other; and yet more have been placed at even intervals on the ground to make 'Stepping Stones'.

We're the last to arrive. As the door bangs behind us, faces turn. I count roughly twenty-five kids, ranging from Emmy's age up to around twelve years old. Apart from a couple of wildly beautiful Indian girls, the numbers are about 30 per cent Mexican to 70 per cent white. On the whole the younger children are neatly turned out, with combed hair and pressed jeans. Some of the older kids, though, are a rough-looking lot whose flinty eyes suggest they've seen the back of their daddy's hand more than once.

'Stetson, Wyatt, Carson, Jésus,' the teacher reels off names. Until this moment my biggest worry has been that the children are not going to like their school lunch. I'd warned them it could be bean-related, and in anticipation of such a crisis have armed them with baggies full of peanut-butter sandwiches. Now, as the inmates of Devil's Slide turn their old men faces towards us and fix us with curious if not downright hostile stares, I wonder what on earth I've got them into.

In the back row of the class, a pale boy with very

blond hair, pellucid blue eyes and a nose plug of crusty snot taps Jack on the arm with the end of a chewed pencil.

'Hey, you.' He eyeballs him up and down. 'How old are ya?'

'Eight,' Jack says.

'Oh yeah?' The boy looks sceptical. 'You're pretty short for an eight-year-old. What class you in?'

'I'm in PP2W,' Jack says politely, quoting his London classroom.

'Listen, pal,' the kid drawls, 'if you're eight years old, you'll be in third grade like me – you got that straight?'

Jack nods and squares his shoulders. There's not even the slightest question of me giving him a hug before I leave.

I drive back along the road and pull into the next gas station where, although not in the least hungry, I find myself buying something very nasty called a break-fast burrito – a cling-filmed refrigerated tortilla filled with scrambled egg, beans and onions – which, despite its fifteen-second sojourn in the microwave, is not adequately heated through.

Ten minutes later I stop the truck and throw up the wretched thing into the fishscale grass by the side of the road. For a briefly heroic moment I wonder about racing back to rescue the children, striding into the classroom and scooping them into my arms amidst wistful cheers from their fellow students and possibly an uplifting soundtrack, but I do not do this. I cannot do this. I've toyed with the home schooling option, of course I have. There have been moments in the Walton Household, when the lights are switched out one by one, when I allow myself to picture Jack and Emmy at the table, dressed in cotton smocks, clutching samplers and reciting the three Rs while I colour our winter butter with carrots and drink sarsaparilla, but this is not an option. The flat truth is we're broke, Robert and I, at least close to it. In the restaurant, Robert had pushed a piece of steak round his plate and tried not to cry. He was good at keeping balls in the air, he'd admitted, but all he'd really been doing for the past five years was juggling debt, and I knew then that I couldn't leave him. It's one thing kicking a man when he's down, it's another altogether to nail him to the floor. I might have had to settle for a more temporary escape but there is still only a finite amount of time, a finite amount of goodwill, and a very finite amount of money for this project. Credit a year of house rent while we're here and Robert's in Switzerland, credit school fees, credit not living in the most expensive city in the world, debit the living expenses in Temerosa and the loss of my meagre salary, still equals actual hard cash to renovate the town, to sell it on and justify my being here, giving it another name apart from self-indulgence or, scarier, trial separation. So yes, home schooling is out of the question and no, I'm not feeling good about it, but the changes in the children's lives are incontrovertible, and when I'm feeling more rational and marginally less sick, I will attempt to reassure myself that this is no bad thing.

In the sky above, a huge bird soars. I screen the sun with a hand. Its wingspan is enormous. A condor? A vulture? Definitely some kind of hawk anyway, and –

from the flashes of a white tail and head – I'd say an
eagle. Two ravens are swooping it repeatedly. The eagle
cuts and swerves, at one point narrowly avoiding death
by power line, but eventually surrenders and speeds off
at full tilt to the high rocks behind the school, its
tormentors in hot pursuit. I'm about to get back in the
truck when, from out of the blue, really quite literally, a
feather spirals slowly down from the heavens and comes
to rest briefly on the hood of the truck before fluttering
to my feet. I pick it up.

It's golden brown and about eighteen inches long. I
smooth the velvety tendrils against my cheek. It smells
musty, of bird, and it brings back a rush of nostalgia for
Scotland, the dank mud of the bog and the nesting
peewits in the marsh. Feeling tentatively pleased at what
must be a good omen I climb back into the truck and lay
the golden feather carefully on top of the dashboard.

Back in Temerosa, a long grey pickup has been parked
across the path to the cabin. I stare at it, weighing up
whether I can steer round without running into the twin
culverts of the drainage ditch, but the space is just too
narrow. At first I'm annoyed then it occurs to me the
truck's been left there on purpose and I begin to suspect rather belatedly that I'm being robbed. Killing the
engine, I climb out and sneak round the hill towards
the cabin, keeping low, out of sight of the windows,
eventually dropping down behind a boulder near the
back porch where I crouch and catch my breath like an
out-of-condition cat burglar.

'Morning.'

I peer over the stone ledge. Halfway up a ladder and fiddling with the pipe by the bathroom window is a man in a black cowboy hat. I stand up, hastily brushing down my jeans to cover my embarrassment. 'What are you doing?'

He continues fiddling.

'Excuse me.' I stomp indignantly to the foot of his ladder.

He glances down.

'What are you doing?'

'Your ventilator pipe is blocked.'

'My what?'

He holds up a piece of grey plastic piping. 'Ventilator pipe . . . maybe you noticed the smell?'

'The smell? The sulphur, you mean?'

'No, ma'am, I mean the shit.' He resumes fiddling, leaving me staring once again at his back.

'Look, who are you? Do you mind coming down, please.'

A pair of scuffed cowboy boots descends, then a pair of the filthiest trousers I have ever seen.

'This'll need replacing.' He puts the pipe in my hand. 'I'll bring you one later in the week, meantime don't use the toilet.'

'I'll be sure not to,' I say caustically, only too aware of the curdle of bad egg still in my stomach. 'And you are . . . ?'

'Duval,' he says.

He is not what I am expecting. For some reason, I had Duval pictured as one of the guys who worked in the hardware store in Ague; a skinny, dungareed, mountain-biking type with fuzzy orange facial hair measured in yards and a cloth pouch of tools round his hips. Duval is not particularly skinny, neither is he young. Late forties at a guess. Unusually for Arizona, where it is de rigueur to sport one of three moustache types – the 'walrus', a droopy style popular with those on the road to baldness and generally accompanied by a ponytail; the 'mariachi', a neat cube which bristles proudly on the upper lip of many local Mexicans; or the 'rodent', so named for its resemblance to some large piece of marsupial road kill which has been peeled off the tarmac and reattached to the face with no particular attention to form, hygiene or aesthetics – Duval is clean-shaven. In fact he looks more like a cowboy than a builder.

A cowboy builder then.

'Do you want some coffee?' I open the door into the cabin.

Duval shakes his head no, but I go to make some anyway in an attempt to buy a little time. Outside the kitchen window icicles drip and melt, shadows fall across the rounded contours of snow-covered boulders. Duval lays his hat on the table. Underneath it, his hair is dark and flattened down with sweat. 'These the plans?' He pulls the scrolls towards him and smoothes them across the kitchen table with a dusty forearm. He studies them briefly, then, taking a pencil from his shirt pocket, crosses out the entire back section of the boarding house.

'Feel free to write on those,' I say dryly.

He continues without comment.

'So you're the Duval who did all the original renovations on this cabin?'

'That's right.'

'You were contracted by the Toronto owners?'

He circles another section. 'You'll want to minimize grading here.'

If I knew what grading was, I might well want to minimize it, but I'm unwilling to yield the interview stage to design quite so quickly. I feel at a distinct disadvantage, caught on the hop by his unexpected appearance. Three weeks have passed since Benjamín gave up his name and promised to get in touch with him, and in the interim, I'd begun to get twitchy. I badly didn't want to blind contract a building company out of the sprawling air-conditioned horror of Phoenix or Tucson – the sheer travel alone would have made it inefficient and expensive. Besides, what work has been done on Temerosa seems to have been done well and, God knows, I didn't want a new lot of builders scratching their heads and gazing in mock horror at somebody else's work with the predictable, 'Oh dear, oh dear, call this a finished job?'

The problem was I had no way of getting in touch with Duval and Benjamín had been exasperatingly vague when questioned, pulling down on his mariachi and looking into the middle distance as though his errant foreman might appear over the horizon at any given moment, singing, 'If I had a hammer – I'd a-hammer in the mornings . . .' But still – I had wanted to know – where did this Duval live? Was he away on another job? And what kind of a name was Duval anyway?

In the end, though, I gave up and had preliminary plans for Temerosa drawn up by an architect who had

sounded, leastways on the telephone, adequately qualified for the job. He agreed to drive down from Tucson
to take a look, and turned up with both his wife and
an engineer in tow, the latter spending most of the afternoon complimenting his boss on his choice of headgear.
Surprisingly, the plans they'd sent had looked reasonably
good. Nevertheless Duval turns each page with quiet
disdain.

'How did they get on to you in the first place?' I ask.
It's essential that I muddle through all preliminary meetings without giving away that I am less than sure what
I'm doing. I began training as an architect, it's true, but
dropping out after three years to marry Robert meant
exchanging girders and foundations for flora and fauna,
a mistake I have regretted ever since and one that now
puts me at a distinct disadvantage. Once I have extracted
a quote from him, I'll feel more secure; until then there's
no doubt I'm an easy mark.

'Can't recall,' he replies. Duval speaks slowly, allowing a pause to lapse before answering. Everyone does
it round here – as though it's necessary to think long
and hard before producing the most unembellished of
answers. Granted this is not a part of the world where
the snappy rejoinder is celebrated, even so, it's hard to
get used to. I constantly find myself biting my tongue in
order not to start other people's sentences for them.

'And what were they renovating the town for?'

'Oh some kind of getaway for rich city folk.'

I take this dig with extremely good grace. 'Why did
they not get you to finish the job?'

Pause. 'Ran out of money.'

'Did you get paid at least?'

Pause. 'Yup.'

'You're lucky. The whole group went bankrupt – that's how we ended up here.'

There's no need for me to elaborate on my back story other than a desire to distance myself from any profligacy on the part of the former owners. To somehow illustrate to this man, who probably doesn't care one way or the other, that I'm different, that I'm going to be honest and fair and straightforward to deal with. You and me, mate, we're going to see eye to eye. It's a little sad, and don't I know it – but if my cowboy builder were a chippie from the East End, I'd probably be talking cockney by now.

Duval leans back in his chair as though to confirm that as far as he is concerned, one absentee owner is pretty much the same as any other.

'Do you know how much they spent?' I persist. 'Including everything . . . generators, utilities, the well?'

Such a long pause now, that I wonder whether he's adding it all up in his head, nut by screw by bolt. ''Bout three hundred thousand,' he says finally.

I whistle.

'It's an expensive business finding water in the desert, Mrs Coleman.'

As his expression betrays no trace of irony, I assume none is intended. 'Call me Alice,' I murmur.

He flicks through the rest of the drawings and I stare at his hands. His nails are black with dirt. A deep, partially healed cut runs through the middle of his index finger. 'So what is it you've got in mind for the place?' he asks.

'Oh, you know,' I lean back in my chair, 'some kind of getaway for rich city folk.'

For the very shortest second his eyes flick to mine. Gotcha, I think with satisfaction.

I scribble a figure on a piece of paper and push it over to him. 'This is what I have to play with.'

He studies it. 'I'll need to price the job up for you.'

'Ballpark, though? Do you think it can be done?'

'Maybe,' he says non-committally.

'Okay. Great. So . . .' I stare at him awkwardly. 'So . . . how many men do you have in your crew?'

Pause. 'Enough.'

'And they're local?'

'Mostly.'

'And they're good?'

Duval reaches for his hat and puts it on, giving it a quick anti-clockwise turn, the way everyone does round here, as though important to screw it directly into the scalp in case of high wind or a rogue bird swooping down to snatch it off.

'Why don't we go down to the town and you can see for yourself.'

I choke on my coffee. 'Now?'

'Now,' he says.

Men are swarming in and out of the bunkhouse, stripping the place clean like an army of red ants. One by one they push through the screen door carrying animal skins, galvanized buckets of stones, armfuls of cans and dismembered sections of rusted boiler. I count fifteen workers, the older men dressed in plaid shirts buttoned over jeans and slant-heeled cowboy boots, the younger men in faded sweatshirts, trainers and baseball hats. They're all Mexican, every one of them.

A boy no more than sixteen, with an angry red birthmark on the side of his neck, looks up as we approach. One or two others also glance in our direction but Duval shouts something in Spanish and they quickly look away, dumping their loads on the ground before heading once again back into the house. Duval watches the activity through narrowed eyes.

'Isn't it a little unusual to put men on a job before you've met the client?' I ask him.

Pause. 'Benjamín said you were in a hurry.'

'Well yes,' I concede. 'But how do you know I haven't contracted somebody else to do the work?'

Pause. 'I can have these men cleared out of here in ten minutes flat, ma'am.'

'Alice,' I correct vaguely, still playing for time. Short of a total miscommunication from Benjamín it's bizarre that Duval should have brought his men here and just started work. Bizarre and stunningly presumptuous, as though the idea that I might want to ask for references or get him to formally tender a bid was ludicrously nit-picky. Nevertheless the men were here. Moreover the figure I'd written down was 20 per cent less than the Tucson company had quoted for the job.

'Are they the same lot that worked on the town originally?'

'They're a good crew.'

'I'm sure they are, but are they . . . I mean can th—'

'Between them they can supply everything you need, from finished carpentry to roofing.'

'They're all Mexican.'

As I'm presumably stating the obvious, Duval makes no answer.

'So how would it work? Who would my contract be with?'

'You pay me, I pay them. Simple.'

At that moment one of the men struggles through the patio door, the base of an iron bed on his back. I watch him thoughtfully. It's late February now and, according to Benjamín, the weather will soon break. Sun up no longer guarantees a big blue. Dark clouds form and disappear, occasionally seeping a little rain in defiance of the sun. Rainbows come and go, throwing a yellow misty light over the town. A raw wind flips the hood of my jacket over my head and whips the cottonwood leaves into mini typhoons around our feet. Time is passing. Duval might be high-handed and he's certainly odd – but maybe round here it's as he claims. Simple. I need someone who knows the vagaries of this site, and he does. I need workers, and he has them.

'All right,' I say slowly. 'Fine.'

I start towards the boarding house. 'So will you introduce me to the men?'

'Not a good idea.'

I stop. 'I'm sorry?'

'You won't remember their names and besides none of them speaks more than a word of English.'

'How am I supposed to communicate with them then?'

'You don't have to. I'll communicate for you.'

I feel my face flush.

'And if you're not around?'

As I said, Mrs Coleman, it's very simple. You tell me what you need doing and I'll get the job done for you.'

7

I'm ten miles from the school when the big white Ford Explorer materializes out of nowhere and flashes me to a standstill. What is it with these patrol vehicles? Behind me the road is straight, the edges are flat and I do, I swear, occasionally look in the rear-view mirror – possibly not as often as specified in the highway code book, but enough to notice when there's a chunk of metal biting my ass. I watch with weary resignation which swiftly turns to disbelief as, with a twiddle of hat and gun holster, Winfred Tennyson advances the fifty yards to my car.

I wind down the window. 'Look, I really wasn't going that fast.'

'My machine says fifty-two, ma'am.'

'Well, there you go!' I say triumphantly.

'Speed limit is forty-five here, ma'am.'

'Oh, come on.' I bang the wheel in frustration. 'Just where is the sign that says that?'

'Ma'am, may I see your driving licence?' Then at my heartfelt sigh, he adds, 'It's an offence not to carry your licence, Mrs Coleman.'

'Yes, yes,' I say irritably, 'so I've heard.'

'Is this your truck, Mrs Coleman?'

'Dammit, you know it's my truck, Winfred. Come on, give me a break, will you? I'm on my way to pick up the kids from school.'

'Oh sure, the kids.' He casts an eye further into the car as if only just noticing their absence and once again I'm struck by his intonation. His words are shunted up together, the back end of one sentence bumping up against the next like freight carriages whose driver has braked suddenly.

'That's a big feather.'

'Yes, it is, isn't it?' I pluck the feather off the dash-board and again smooth down its tendrils. 'I think it's an eagle. A bald eagle, maybe?' I muse, seeking to distract him. 'It had a white head anyway and a huge wingspan.'

'Nuh-huh,' Winfred says. 'May I see it?'

'Sure.' I pass it to him. He turns it over in his hand.

'Eagles are protected around here, Mrs Coleman.'

'Well quite right, so they should be.'

'There are big fines.'

'Good, great. I'm all for it.'

'Thousand dollars, maybe more, maybe five thousand dollars. My sister Brunhilda, when she found a —'

'I'm sorry,' I interrupt, 'you have a sister called Brunhilda?'

'Yeah, and another called Moira, but she's pretty fat. She doesn't go out much.'

'Oh . . . I see.'

'So, okay, when my sister Brunhilda found out about

the fines, she buried her eagle feathers in the ground so she didn't get caught.'

Finally, finally, I hear the muffled clang of a warning bell. 'What exactly do you mean by *caught*,' Winfred?'

'It's against the law to take eagle feathers, Mrs Coleman.'

'Well I didn't *take* this feather, Winfred, it dropped out of the sky.'

'Mrs Coleman —'

'Alice, please.'

'You could be in big trouble.'

'Really? Well you know what? Maybe it's not an eagle's feather, after all. Come to think of it, I may have exaggerated the wingspan. It was actually pretty small. More the size of a pigeon, I'd say.'

'I'm not kidding, ma'am, I can impound your truck.'

'Oh really?' I'm beginning to get very annoyed with Winfred Tennyson. 'On what grounds?'

'The US 668 Bald and Golden Eagle Protection Act,' he recites flawlessly. 'All vessels, vehicles, aircraft and other means of transportation used to aid in the taking of any bird, or body part, nest, or egg or feather, shall be impounded.'

I look at him sceptically. Either he's bullshitting or Winfred has a truly impressive grasp of obscure prohibition acts protecting migratory birds of the USA.

'So what you're saying is that this eagle feather is protected *by* and is in fact the property *of* the US government?'

Winfred nods. 'Yes, ma'am, that's what I'm saying.'

'Well, Winfred, put this in your pipe and smoke it. This eagle feather landed on *my* truck. So the way I see it, this eagle feather is guilty not only of trespassing *on*, but also deliberately inflicting damage *to* my property and I'm going to have to seriously think about suing the US government, naming you as a co-respondent.'

Winfred considers this at some length. 'Mrs Coleman, I'm letting you off the bald eagle offence.'

'Very decent of you.'

'But I am going to have to fine you for speeding.'

'Oh, come on, Winfred!' I bang the steering wheel again. 'Considering that we're old friends, considering you've already had a hundred dollars off me, don't you think you should let me off this time?'

'You're a very funny lady, Mrs Coleman, and I like you, but you better pay me the seventy dollars anyway.'

'Oh, so it's seventy this time, is it?'

'It's ten dollars for every mile over the limit, ma'am.'

'Tell me something, Winfred,' I ask, clawing at the money in my wallet. 'How did you know I lived down the Temerosa road when you stopped me before?'

For the quickest second his eyebrows pull together and pucker up the smooth skin of his forehead. 'Hey, everyone's been saying how an English lady's bought up the town.' He tears off the ticket and hands it to me. 'I just figured out it was you.'

'Really,' I regard him doubtfully, 'you just figured it out.'

'Yes, ma'am, that's right.'

'I guess that was pretty clever of you then.' But as I

watch him making his leisurely way back to his patrol truck, I wonder, just as I had wondered with Benjamín, what reason Winfred could possibly have for lying.

Crawling along at the prescribed forty-five mph makes me late for pick-up. By the time I arrive, school is well and truly out and Emmy is swinging on the giant tyre, flirting languidly with a couple of older boys. As I hurry up to her, one tugs the shirt of the other and says darkly, 'So here's the mom now,' and they both nudge Emmy.

Jack is nowhere to be found.

Sue is at her desk in the main classroom reading a copy of *Defenders of Wildlife* magazine. 'Oh yeah, the little English boy, sure, sure.' She cocks her head to one side in faint recognition at his name. 'Funny little kid.'

'Well yes, maybe,' I concede, 'but I'd like him back nonetheless. Where is he?'

Sue is slight and almost pretty but I already suspect her of being one of those women who always manage to look at the world with weary eyes, irrespective of how much sleep they get. She rests her pencil on an article entitled 'The Air We Breathe' before looking up. 'He went home with Travis on the school bus.'

'He did what!'

Her neck snaps straight at my tone. 'Went home with Travis?' she hazards more cautiously.

'And you let him go, just like that?'

'Is there a problem?' She's now blinking out a hurt expression, but I'm in no mood for emotional Morse code.

'Yes, there is a problem. Aren't you supposed to keep

him here at the school – you know, till a parent or a *guardian* comes?'

'No, I don't think so,' she says, and looks so genuinely puzzled at this deeply foreign notion that my anger evaporates.

I break all speed limits following Sue's directions. What if Travis, right now, is helping Jack onto a wild stallion or letting him play with his pet rattler or just beating him to a pulp with a large stone? Travis's home turns out to be a car junkyard about five miles from the school. Two or three acres of cars and trucks in varying stages of dilapidation enclosed by a chain link fence. Jack is sitting on the gravel by a trailer in the centre playing with broken pieces of toys. He ignores me when I call his name. Next to him Travis is performing an autopsy on a dead bicycle.

'Hi. Travis, right?'

He nods.

'Are your parents here?'

'Nope.'

'Okay.' Jack's head is still down. 'Well . . . Jack . . . it's time to go home.'

Jack doesn't stir.

'Jack, I said it's time to go home.'

Jack acknowledges my presence with angry, glittering eyes. 'You shittin' me?' he says.

I steal a look at him on the way home. His face is set stubbornly and he lolls in his seat, body language indicating that right now, right this minute he'd rather move in with Travis and live in his nice trailer for the rest of his natural life than come home with his mother.

'Jack,' I say finally, 'are you cross I was late?'

Nothing.

'Did you think I wasn't going to turn up?'

Still nothing.

'I got stopped for speeding. By the same cop. I'm sorry I was late but, you know, you could have waited.'

No comment.

'Emmy waited.'

His eyes slide to the left just in case his sister dares to look smug.

'Didn't you wonder what might happen to Emmy if you abandoned her . . . don't you think she's too young to be left on her own?'

'Certainly am not,' Emmy says furiously. 'God!'

'What if something had happened to her?'

'What could have happened to me?'

'Anything, anything could have happened to you.' I turn back to Jack. 'What if a mountain lion had run up and bitten her head off?'

'Mummy!' Emmy cackles throatily.

'How would we have got her home again? How would we have got a seatbelt round just a head?'

'Mummy! How dare you?' Emmy is thrilled with this unexpected twist in the conversation.

'Think of the mess!'

Finally, Jack chances a look in my direction.

'Look, Jack, I don't want you going to a friend's house or anyone's house unless I know about it first.'

He nods.

'I need to know where you both are the whole time,

okay? Or I'll get scared.' I put my hand out to him and he touches the pads of his fingertips to mine. 'Okay?'

'Okay,' he agrees and I realize he was expecting far worse.

'Good.' I hand him the packet of biscuits I'd brought from home.

'So how was it?'

'Fine.'

'Come on, tell me what you did.'

Jack shrugs and bites into an Oreo.

'They didn't let me climb the rock,' Emmy says from the back seat. 'It's so unfair. Everybody else got to.'

'Maybe they thought you couldn't climb.'

'Of course I can climb,' she says scornfully. 'All children can climb.'

'One of the other boys only has one arm,' Jack says.

'What happened to the other?'

'Got caught in the reaper.'

'God. I look at him, horrified. How awful.'

He shrugs again. 'It happens.'

I study his profile for trauma from the day's events, but his expression is hard to read. I try to remember the last time my son really emotionally engaged with me and feel depressed when I can't. Maybe Jack's a particularly bad case but up to a point it's true of most children. Think of all the worry, panic and guilt you endure in the first years of a child's life. Think of all the bound-less patience, understanding and love you pour into the bottomless hole of their need. But say you were to die before they were seven or eight, would any of it really have made a lasting impression on them? Case in point, my mother left when I was six and I don't really remember her. Oh, I know that she had short hair and delicate features but only because I've looked at the photograph book my father keeps in his bookshelf. The day I was born, my father gave my mother a plover's egg. It was pale green and dappled, almost perfect except for the tiny pin hole in the top. She hadn't wanted an egg as a birthing present, though. She had wanted lilies. Something that smelt nice in the hospital, something that made her feel beautiful and special, but the thing is, you can't get fresh-cut lilies in the Orkneys.

8

Emmy has taken to school like a mongoose to crocodile eggs. Geography seems to be the only subject she's taught, but she can't get enough of it. Within the space of a week, she is impressively well informed about erosion and rock formation and piously instructing me in her new Margaret Thatcher voice not to tread on certain types of desert top soil (contains valuable oxygen) lest I irreversibly damage the earth and doom us all to never-ending drought and destruction.

At break, instead of the sedate game of hopscotch she might be enjoying at her nursery school, Devil's Slide kids scramble up the piñon and juniper of the rock face and throw stones at each other's heads – and Emmy, who, on flat ground, is the clumsiest thing imaginable, collecting broken toes and dents in her forehead like other children collect baseball cards, scrambles with the best of them.

'Today I cut my head so deep you could see my brain,' she says proudly.

'How great! What colour was it?'

'Mummy!'

'Are you trying to tell me you haven't checked it out in the mirror?'

More chuckling.

'Jack, get over here! Let's take a look.'

'I'm not looking at her disgusting brain.'

At bath time she presents me with her battle scars: arms decorated with a myriad of raw scratches, vermilion-coloured bruises like stepping stones up and down her legs, blackened torn fingernails caked in dust. 'School is cool,' Emmy announces. At lunch, older children terrorize younger ones with tales of 'Man corn' and the cannibalistic Anasazi who liked nothing better than to nibble on their fellow Indians in the fourteenth century, and whose remains are scattered around the desert caves. Devil's Slide itself is the cliff from where a group of Apaches, their weapons depleted, chose to freefall to their death rather than give in to the grisly torture of their enemies, all of which Emmy laps up with ghoulish fascination. Any day now, I expect her to arrive home flexing a tattoo of a fat green snake on her left bicep, sign of a newly minted member of the notorious Cobra gang, modern-day warriors who rule the darker areas of the Indian rez.

Instead of the grind of homework, I give the children Spanish lessons, courtesy of my Waterstone's tapes. Forget the blind leading the blind, this is the dumb leading the deaf.

'*El río está helado*,' I intone on the way home in the car.

'*¿Sí? ¿Qué?*' they reply politely.

Brilliantly, though, I have tricked them into believing

that chores – sweeping the deck, setting the mousetraps, securing garbage against the raccoons – are a legitimate fixture of their after-school curriculum. Woodwork, a particular success, takes the form of me lying on the sofa drinking margaritas while they struggle in and out of blistering winds fetching blocks of wood for the fire and scorching their little fingers on damp matchbooks printed with 'God Bless America'.

I don't immediately appreciate the effect all this is having on them until one night, after a tremendous crack in the sky, a storm breaks with such intensity it takes the power out with it. It's early evening and as the cabin darkens and I realize the lights aren't going to come back on anytime soon, I offer to take the children to Ague for a hamburger dinner. Both Jack and Emmy immediately begin synchronized wailing.

'It's all right, my chicks,' I say tenderly, 'I know it's scary, but we'll just throw on our boots and drive to town.' Renewed moans from the children.

'I don't want to go to bloody Ague.' Jack beats his fists against my chest. 'We want to have marshmallows for supper and light fires. Why do we have to go to Ague when this is the best day of our lives?'

'Best day of our lives,' Emmy gurgles.

Later, when I blow out the candles, I look at them, faces pressed against the window, looking at the orange mist outside and discussing what lies beyond, and I realize with a pang that they're beginning to change. Gone is the me, me, me of their former London selves; it's as if everything they are experiencing has jump-started their curiosity and suddenly the whole world is opening up to them. And, for the first time since we arrived, all the doubts and guilt I've been pushing down so hard slowly seep out of my body and I begin to feel cautiously optimistic.

9

The first thing I ask Duval to do is have the workers enlarge my bedroom window.

There's a grunt.

'What?'

Pause. 'Cabins out here traditionally don't have big windows.'

'Well I know, but then traditionally they don't have a view either.'

'There's a pretty fine view from the front deck.'

'Yes, I know that, but the thing is, I'd like to have a view from my bedroom so I can see it when I wake up.'

Pause. 'Those windows were built small for good reason.'

'Which is?'

'Keep warmth in, keep the sun out.'

'Well now we have a stove, so there's plenty of heat, and I come from a city that gets sun about three days of the year so . . .'

Pause. 'It might not be practical, is all.'

I mentally stamp my little foot. 'How about you cost it, then I can decide whether it's practical or not?'

'It's your dollar, ma'am,' he says mildly.

I move in with the children while the Mexicans work in my bedroom. Enlarging a window turns out to be a swine of a job. I had imagined it to be merely a question of hacking out the right-sized square and popping in a piece of glass. But no, apparently there are other considerations: structural forces, the re-cladding of walls, reframing, etc. not to mention placing a special order in Phoenix for a ten-foot piece of glass, subsequently delivered by a tough female driver who negotiated her way along the Temerosa road in a twelve-wheeler lorry. 'How on earth did you manage that?' I asked her. 'I would have given up on the first bend.'

'Women round here don't quit on a job,' she said bleakly, cracking open a Budweiser with her teeth.

As soon as the glass is fitted, Duval stands aside for me to take a look. The bedroom faces south and where before was visible the merest sliver of mountain, a smidgeon of tree and the thinnest slice of sky, like enticing thumbnail prints in a holiday brochure, there is now a stunning panoramic view.

I'm busy telling Duval what a success it all is, and suggesting, perhaps a touch patronizingly, that we opt for the same in every cabin, when there's a thud. A small bird smacks against the glass at tremendous speed and plummets to the deck below.

Emmy had been sitting on the floor organizing plastic tubes of glitter and nail varnish into pleasing colour coordinates, while Jack, bored, had been knocking them over with his feet. Now they both leap up and gallop downstairs. By the time I catch up with them, Jack's struggling to slide open the stiff lock of the back door and Emmy has hoisted herself up on the stove to see through the window. Outside on the deck, a beautiful jewelled hummingbird lies on its back, feet in the air, panting.

'Don't worry, it's only stunned.' I edge Jack aside, wondering whether mouth to beak is appropriate, but no sooner do I get the door unlocked than a raven swoops down right in front of us and snatches up the humming-bird in its claws. Emmy hides her face with her arm and forces a strangled noise out of her throat. Jack stares at the departing predator. 'That is so cool,' he pronounces, awestruck. Emmy looks confused. She blinks once then stills her oscillating lower lip. 'So cool,' she breathes.

The new window is a magnet for small birds. So much so that, morbidly, the children take to keeping a Chart of Death which they mark with gold stars as PAM! one after the other, starlings, hummingbirds, tiny blue-grey things I can't identify – even with the help of a bird book I buy in Ague – thud into the glass like feathered kamikaze pilots, blinded by the awful reflection of the sun. Under the watchful eye of ravens, which now con-stantly circle the perimeter of the cabin like grim reapers, we try everything – positioning hideous plastic owls from the hardware store on the outside rail, hanging bird feeders from the porch beams – but the birds are simply too stupid, too short-sighted, or both.

The systematic obliteration of Arizona's *petit oiseau* population is not the only window-related problem. By two o'clock in the afternoon, the sun, on its travels east to west, hits its highest point over the mountains and the temperature in the room soars to an unbearable level, only beginning to dissipate again around seven when the cool night air and the baking heat pass each other stealthily through the gaps between glass and wood. Duval does not comment on either the dead birds, the white sheet I eventually nail over the window to save them or the fluctuating temperature conditions in my bedroom. But then it doesn't appear to be in Duval's nature to comment on much. He listens, he responds in kind, but social chit-chat is not exactly his forte. Nevertheless we fall into some kind of modus operandi. Every morning at first light, Duval's truck drives along the windy path, tyres throwing up clouds of dust in its wake. In the back, the men sit hunched together, knees held tight to chests, heads down against the grit. By the time we leave for school, the beat of hammers and the monotonous whine of the drill has broken the peace and silence of the town.

Now that the children are at school, southern Arizona is my oyster. With a view to at least getting our own cabin together, I begin to explore the country, driving further and further afield, weaving around dirt roads, barrelling through tiny towns with no more than a post office and gas station to show for themselves. I stop in at yard sales and trawl through tables of dirty glass bottles, battered cowboy boots, boxes of naked Cindy dolls with tangled hair and missing limbs, jars of stewed apricots, embroidered dishcloths, lethal-looking knives and watches that no longer tick. I stop off at pawn shops and watch skinny teenagers racked with pustulating acne sidle round the counters where the guns are kept while

Mexican children offer flea-bitten kittens for sale for a dollar.

As the days fly by, the back of the truck begins to fill up with an eclectic assortment of 1950s furniture, frosted beer glasses, funky lights and box after box of unused linen sheets.

In a small antique shop, I find a cowhide stacked up inside a cupboard. Its white fur has discoloured a little, but nothing a dry clean wouldn't sort out. I ask the old lady whether she has any more. 'Sure,' she says, 'got some right out back here.'

I follow the hunched, achingly slow figure through the shop and into a stale-smelling living room where a wedding photo is prominently displayed on top of a cabinet filled with the gloomy knick-knacks of widow-hood, a porcelain sheep and shepherdess, a white bobbled punch bowl with glasses hooked to its side. The old lady pushes open the fly screen and steps out onto her porch.

'There,' she says.

I look for a rug on the sun-bleached wood, but she taps my shoulder and points to a small group of cows grazing peacefully in the distance.

'You can have Merleen or Lorraine or Eleanor.' She fixes me with watery eyes. 'Jest as soon as I git 'em butchered.'

My quest for kitsch results in two punctured tyres on the butterscotch truck, both of which I get fixed at the M&M, a truckstop west of Ague which has a sign offering 'A Square Meal and a Hot Wheel' and a con-stant stream of gleaming Mac trucks rolling in and out, with names like 'Road to Perdition' and 'Duel for Life' painted on their front cabs. The proprietor of the place is called Dud and has the smallest piggy curl of a tail growing from the back of a wide sunburnt neck. His face is deeply weather-beaten, and when he opens the customer hatch he reveals himself the owner of a massive pigeon chest which is thrust out in front of him as he walks me through to the workshop at the back. The mechanic I'm turned over to is small and sinewy, and wearing a peaked leather hat set jauntily over white hair, making him look like one of Santa's elves. A Dobermann pinscher playing with an oily cloth jumps at me, licks my fingers then bites me playfully on the calf. 'Ouch, hey,' I gasp. Blood seeps through my jeans.

'Jest a puppy,' the Santa's elf says and winks.

While in town I buy ingredients for whatever new foodie delight I have settled on for the evening. The irresistibly titled *Trials of a Wilderness Bride*, plucked from the shelves of a second-hand bookshop along with a grease-spotted copy of *The Joy of Cooking*, has useful recipes for things like corn bread and something called calf fries, which turn out to be breaded testicles. Much as I long to place a brace of fried testicles onto the children's plates in the evening just to hear them scream, it's surprisingly hard to find even such a thing as a leg of lamb round here, let alone the range of speciality cuts required for such an exotic dish. Even the Wal-Mart in Tucson fails me with its rows of homogenized geometric shapes which appear to bear no relation to any known animal. When I ask, adrift in aisle 101, whether they might have such salubrious a thing as an organic chicken, the helpful Wal-Mart lady adjusts her permed crown of hair with one six-inch nail, cocks her head to the side and muses, 'Organic chicken ... now then, would that be made of soy?'

Foolishly, I complain about this to Benjamín and, before I know it, a decapitated local lamb is delivered. 'You said you wanted fresh meat,' Benjamín says, dragging the carcass from his truck and tossing the saw down after it.

'How many more animals must die?' Emmy cries, although she doesn't really, but would I'm sure if she only knew that her mother has recently sanctioned the slaughter of an adorable little piggy who will shortly be taking up residence in our freezer in the form of buff paper parcels filled with bacon bits and shoulder roasts.

I'm like a secret drinker with my new cookbooks and instead of refining drawings, or musing on the volatility of cesspits, I find myself guiltily dipping into grills and steams and roasts. Jack and Emmy are appalled by my foodie volte-face and speak of the days of macaroni cheese like war children deprived of fresh eggs. I remain unmoved. Morally, of course, I have the upper hand, but geographically, too, I now hold the higher ground. It's either my cooking or they can go down the hill for Benjamín's legendary broth *de coq*.

'The choice is yours,' I tell them gleefully.

Usually when I get back from town, Duval and I meet for a 'walk-through' of the building site. Unlike the sometimes inane task of prettifying window boxes for capricious city dwellers, renovating a house feels intensely satisfying – taking something tired and broken down and restoring form and function to it. I've decided that houses are not unlike the women I've become so tired of dealing with. Both need constant primping, painting and good lighting. When they're brand new and prettily decorated everyone is in love with them but sooner or later they get old, their shine begins to fade, bits of them wear out and need replacing. Should they not be properly looked after they become susceptible to dry rot and during prolonged cold spells tend to freeze altogether.

As soon as they see us coming, the Mexicans stop work and break for lunch. Cans of soft drinks, thermoses of coffee and sandwiches wrapped in greaseproof paper all materialize from somewhere and are consumed in huddles, with only the occasional flicker of curiosity directed at me from under the brim of a hat. After my daily snoop is complete and I'm once again considered to be a safe distance away, the men trickle back into the cabins and the hammering and sawing begins afresh. Despite my friendly little waves, despite my jolly little '*Buenas tardes*', my cheery '*¡Hola!*' and perky '*Hace buendia ¿no?*', in fact despite all other salutational plums that drop from my mouth courtesy of my language tapes, no fruit of friendship has been tossed my way in return. Nevertheless I am starting to recognize my crew, if not by name, if not by face, then at least by clothes. Working the drill is red baseball cap, who is not to be confused with the Bank of Texas T-shirt guy, currently digging up the ground, who in turn looks alarmingly similar to, though a little older than, denim jacket man, who was clearly separated at birth from black jeans, black shirt, gold bling, who I swear I once heard addressed by the name of Ramon. Despite such promising anthropological inroads, it's hard not to merge these flashes of skin tones and features into one single airbrushed photofit of 'Mexican worker'.

I don't know why everyone's so unfriendly towards me. Maybe they're being relentlessly exploited by Duval, and hold me accountable, maybe they're just naturally suspicious because I'm a foolish gringa, but if I didn't think it fantastically unlikely, I'd say the real problem is that they're scared of me.

10

Duval is harder to fathom.

True, he's professional. He does what he says, when he says, and the job gets done – but that's about the sum of it. Meetings between us are strained. Usually when people are devoid of edge, when they don't employ the tools of sarcasm or have wit or irony at their disposal, you're left with a ponderous bore. Duval isn't dull, he's just pathologically unresponsive, and being one of those sorry people who tend to compensate by twittering into other people's awkward silences, the more taciturn he is, the more garrulous I become until I'm left with the humiliating feeling that it is I who have bored him and not the other way round.

When not discussing plans with me, or checking the Mexican's work, pencilling notes and measurements onto the walls of whichever cabin they've been assigned, Duval stations himself on the porch of the boarding house and works large blocks of wood, whistling softly under his breath.

I watch him from a distance as he runs long fingers over their surfaces, feeling for gnarls and splinters, and I wonder – is he without a sense of humour? Uninterest-ing? A little slow? – but every time I'm prepared to throw in my lot with one of these theories, some warning blips red on my radar. Some discrepancy or irregularity I can't put my finger on. Whenever we meet, I feel like I'm watching a faulty video on which the soundtrack has been badly dubbed and I just can't rid myself of the instinct that something about Duval is a little off.

And then the dog incident happens.

Since its arrival in our lives, the dog has taken to coming and going as it pleases. During school hours, it makes itself scarce, padding out of the door behind the children as though commuting to some smart job. In the evening, before darkness falls, it reappears. It no longer whines and scratches questioningly outside the door. Now it merely barks an order in full expectation of being obeyed. For the most part it lives under the kitchen table, its two-tone eyes fastened upon us in a myopic squint. During the night, however, it creeps stealthily up the wooden stairs and curls up to sleep at the foot of my bed. Despite such show of affection, which secretly I find endearing, it remains an aloof creature, summoning up a deep-throated snarl should anyone make the mistake of venturing too close.

On the day of the incident the dog had been unwell, coughing up, earlier in the morning, some disgusting fur ball of recent kill. Subsequently, I can only assume it called in sick to its day job because it remained under the kitchen table all day, feeling sorry for itself and ignoring my every attempt to force it outside until eventually, bored of trying, I forgot it was even there.

Later in the afternoon I'm sitting across from Duval at the kitchen table, going over pump-size requirements for the boarding house, when Benjamín opens the door and the children burst in from school. Seeing the dog in residence, Jack drops to his knees and propels himself across the floor.

'Taco,' he croons. 'Taco, Taco, Taco.'

Under the table, the dog pricks up his ears. Sure enough, as Jack completes his Torvill and Dean slide, it snaps viciously. Jack snatches at his hand and starts crying. For all his tough talk, Jack is a bit of an old woman. Last week, for instance, when I tried to remove a splinter from his foot, the operation took nearly two hours. Nevertheless, having reassured myself that his hand is still attached to his wrist, I turn my attention to Taco, determined to give the beast a good slap when I notice that Duval has dropped his fingers onto Taco's head and is absent-mindedly scratching the fur between his ears. Taco, in turn, pushes his snout upwards into the palm of Duval's hand in a gesture of total acquiescence, and suddenly the penny drops.

'This is *your* dog, isn't it?'

'This dog?' he repeats vaguely, as though somewhere in the room, an entire police line-up of *chiens méchants* awaits identification. 'Yes, he's mine.'

'His name is Taco,' Emmy says, appearing at Duval's elbow.

'It's a good name,' Duval says simply. 'I never got round to giving him one myself.'

I cross my arms in the manner of a fishwife and wait for an explanation. 'The dog needed a good home.' 'The dog got used to being here when I was working on this cabin.' 'The dog loves women and children, can't keep away from them.' Frankly, anything would have been fine, but Duval just carries on pencilling notes on the drawings and his silence makes me peevish.

'You know he's been sleeping here for nearly a month?'

'I'm sorry you've been inconvenienced, ma'am.'

'I haven't been *inconvenienced*, it's just – why is he here? Why have you never said anything before about him being your dog?'

'The dog comes and goes as he pleases. He's half wild.'

'You can say that again, he could have taken Jack's hand off!'

Jack helpfully ups the tenor of his wails a notch. Duval raises his voice over the noise.

'He's not used to children, is all. Doesn't mean any harm.'

'Oh, I'll try to remember that when his teeth are embedded in their skulls.' Then, because I feel the need to justify the dreadful fuss Jack is making, add rather testily, 'You really should have him neutered.'

'Oh, come on,' Duval flashes back, 'surely one of us needs to have a little fun!'

I open my mouth, then shut it again. My first instinct is that he's made a mistake and with a shock I see that Duval is thinking the same. It's right there in his face. His eyes cross with mine and behind the dead-end stare there's something else, like a door opening briefly onto a hidden passageway. A look of acknowledgement passes between us, then his eyes blank over again. He stands up and screws on his hat.

Pause. 'I'd better be going.'

'Yes, and your little dog too,' I say evilly.

'No!' the children shriek.

Duval clicks his fingers and heads for the door. Taco pads across the floor and obediently falls in behind him.

For the rest of the evening, the phrase 'out of character' keeps coming back to me but it's not until I'm groggy with sleep that I finally pinpoint why. If Duval's quip was out of character, then it implies that for the rest of the time Duval is *in* character and if he is *in* character, then by definition he's pretending to be somebody he is not. And once again the penny drops and this time it lands with a loud clanging noise. I shoot up in bed and feel for the light switch – then fumble in the bedside table for the little wooden box. Sure enough, it's gone. Of course it's gone. How could I have been so obtuse? Taco sleeping at my feet, Duval instructing the crew in Spanish. Duval who, in supervising the widening of the window, had plenty of opportunity to take back what was his. It's Duval who had kicked off his boots and lain on top of the shrunken wool blanket while the coyotes bayed outside the window. It's Duval who has been sleeping in my bed.

I say nothing.

Maybe it had been only the one night. Maybe his truck had broken down. Maybe he lives in a trailer home and simply wanted to take advantage of hot and cold running water while he could? While it's not an alarming thought, it is a puzzling one. Speaking both Spanish and

English might not be significant here on the apex of two countries, but the letter was headed 'The University of California' – and if Duval reads and writes fluently in two languages and has a university education then certainly he's not the monosyllabic hick he pretends to be – and if he's not? Well ... I don't know. I try to work through the other possibilities but, instead, other thoughts begin to creep into my head. What was he thinking as he lay in my bed? Did he wake early, as I do, and wait for the outlines of trees to appear in the dawn light? Had he ever wondered about me? Tried to put a face to my name? Imagined a life for me?

February turns into March. The sun rises noticeably hotter now. In the hills, one or two rogue cacti sprout early flowers. Work progresses on the town. Duval splits the crew into two groups. Half remain on the boarding house, the other half begin to strip out the rest of the smaller cabins. Duval is out of town much of the time, collecting supplies and returning at the end of the day, his pickup weighed down with sheets of drywall, slabs of stone, endless lengths of wood and rusted tin for the roofs.

When he's not around, the atmosphere in the town is noticeably less strained and whilst I'd be hard pushed to describe the relationship between myself and the workers as close, they've got used to my pottering around the building site. In an effort to keep one step ahead of what's going on, I spend many an illuminating evening boning up on Infestation, Insulation and Ventilation from *You Can Do It! The Complete B&Q Step-by-step*

Book of Home Improvement. Then there are the eight-inch-thick catalogues of fixtures and fittings picked up from the hardware store. For every wall plate, for every switch, for every plug or cupboard handle, there is a multitude of choices. You can buy any of them apricot with antebellum roses, you can buy them with intricately carved eagle heads, you can buy them in patriotic red, white and blue or with dramatic Arizona landscapes glazed over their concave surfaces, but the one thing you cannot do is buy them plain bloody white.

I've invested in a small camera from Wal-Mart and everywhere I go, I photograph stable doors, the shape of a window, the roof of an old barn so I can copy the details. More and more frequently, though, like a third-rate spy doing reconnaissance on a newly discovered military base, I find myself levelling the Olympus's powerful zoom at the town from behind the trunk of an oak tree or a strategic boulder – not because I want to catch the workers sneaking an extra break, but because the Mexicans are camera shy and it's only through subterfuge of this kind that I can keep some kind of record of progress. Every week I pin up 'before and after' photos and occasionally I get a sickening feeling in my stomach that if buildings really are women, then renovating the whole of Temerosa is going to be as tough as taking a group of abused and battered housewives and restoring them to their prom-night innocence.

It's late one morning, with Duval up in Phoenix, when I come across the worker I've christened 'Red Baseball Cap' kneeling on the ground by the cottonwood, trying to clean his hand in the murky water of the wash. He's cut himself badly; a deep incision running from the base of his thumb right through to the centre of his palm, and from the way his thumb is hanging backwards, it looks to me like he's severed the nerve. He's terrified to see me and scrambles to his feet as I approach.

'Escuse, please, sorry,' he stutters, backing away, all but brandishing the silver cross he's wearing in front of my face. Undaunted, I take hold of his arm, and in reciprocal stumbling Spanish, compel him to accompany me back up to the cabin where I hold his hand under the kitchen tap then find him one of Emmy's Blue Parrot plasters and a bandage to go on top. Throughout my Florence Nightingale routine, the boy refuses to look at me, instead staring intently at his hand as if willing a map of escape to materialize in its creases and curves. He's really young, no more than seventeen or eighteen, with baby-soft skin which looks like it has yet to meet the blade of a razor. The plasters and bandage are barely adequate and almost immediately the blood begins seeping through. I suggest driving him to the medical centre in Ague. *'Te llevaré al médico,'* I say, pleased to have an unexpected chance to practise the future tense of *llevar*.

He shakes his head violently.

'No, really, I'll take you.'

'¡No! ¡No al médico!' he says so vehemently that I let him go, whereupon he hotfoots it from the cabin like a teenager released early from school detention.

I think no more of it until a couple of days later when I'm walking through the town with Duval. The men are working on the roof, bending lengths of pale new wood like whale ribs across the top of the cabin's structure. Bank of Texas T-shirt is perched vertiginously on top, legs astride a cross beam, a nail gun in his hand. Duval's gesturing some instruction at him and he is nodding and pantomiming something back when Red Baseball Cap walks out of the door carrying the front end of a piece of plywood.

'*Hola*,' I call at him. A drill is reverberating in the background and the boy doesn't turn.

'*¿Cómo está la mano?*' I ask when he gets closer, and touch him gently on the shoulder. His head snaps round as though my fingers have burnt a hole in his T-shirt and I see with a shock that he is a different boy, equally young, equally mortified to find himself accosted by the English gringa, but a different boy nonetheless. At that moment Duval notices us. He shouts something and the boy hunches his shoulders around his ears and disappears back into the cabin.

'What happened to the other boy?' I ask Duval. 'Where is he?'

'Other boy?'

'The one who cut his hand?'

Duval looks blank.

'The one who normally wears that red hat?' I persist, despite realizing how silly the question sounds. There is surely no dearth of red baseball caps in this part of the world.

'I'm sorry,' Duval says, 'I've told the workers not to bother you.'

'He wasn't bothering me. *I* was talking to *him*,' I say levelly.

'If you have any complaints, ma'am, you should really talk to me.'

'I don't have any complaints,' I say, frustrated. 'I was just trying to—'

'Then if you have no complaints,' he cuts in with maddening composure, 'I'd appreciate it if you could let the men get on with their work.'

11

The confrontation leaves me oddly uneasy for the next few days and I'm still puzzling as to why exactly when I notice Jack wandering around the cabin clutching his homework, looking like he's carrying the weight of the entire US national debt on his shoulders. In truth it's taken a little longer for Jack to turn native. The Devil's Slide boys are a tough bunch. Most learned to ride at the age of two and by eight were sitting on a horse fully armed and running cattle. Stetson, the snivelly albino-esque boy who'd rattled Jack's nerve that first morning at school, has become his main enemy. One of four sons of the local jail guard, he's an accomplished bully. 'Maybe he pushes me round a bit,' Jack finally admitted, 'after school, in the playground, but I can handle it.'

'Did you tell the teacher?'

He nodded.

'And?'

'She told me not to give away my power. She's an idiot.'

I had every sympathy with this. Sue's head is a

bottomless well of new-age mysticism. When I told her I knew no one in Arizona, she replied, 'There are no strangers out here, Alice, only friends you haven't met yet.'

'Do you want me to talk to her, Jack?' I'd asked.

'No,' he'd said furiously. 'I'm dealing with it, okay? I'm not scared. I'm not scared of nuthin'.'

'So what's up now Jack?' I ask him.

No response.

'Come on, what is it?' Detecting a bulge in his trousers, I pat him down like a murder suspect. 'Why have you got an onion in your pocket?'

'So I don't get smallpox.'

'What?'

'I don't want to get smallpox,' he says in a very thin little voice. 'I don't want to get sick and die.' He rounds on me, fists clenched, and pummels my stomach. 'I want to go home. I want to see my friends.' Then he starts crying; big fat tears which splash onto the fleece and are quickly absorbed despite a label on the back professing the garment to be water repellent.

'Let me see that.' I prise the damp worksheet from him. 'Settlers' Ailments,' I read out loud. 'For rheumatism, soak half a bucket of rusty nails in vinegar. For teething pains, warm the brains of a freshly killed rabbit then apply to child's gums.'

Dear God. I close my eyes for a moment then open them to Jack's pitiful face. 'Go get your coat.' I tell him.

We sit in the M&M and look at the menus. The place is empty except for an old cowboy, alone in a booth, tobacco tin and packet of papers neatly laid in front of him, elbows leaning on the scratched surface of the table as he painstakingly rolls a cigarette.

'Okay,' I tell the children, 'no chilli 'n' beans tonight, no sheep's eyeballs. Have anything you want. Eat till you feel sick. My treat.'

'Why?' they ask guardedly.

'Because I'm adorable, that's why.'

'No, why really?' Jack demands.

'Because everyone's grumpy and sad and I dragged you both out here and it's all really different for you and you miss Daddy, and because there is stuff happening to you that shouldn't happen to you and I'm sorry.'

Jack stares at me suspiciously for quite a long time then drops his eyes to the menu. 'I'll have pancakes with syrup and bacon and a chocolate milkshake.'

Emmy lays her hand on top of mine. 'Don't cry, Mummy,' she says softly. 'It's not your fault.'

I blow my nose discreetly and spot Winfred Tennyson standing in the corner by the ice-cream chest, eating an Eskimo Pie. Reverently, he pushes the dark slab of biscuit and vanilla ice into his mouth using all eight of his fingers before his eyes roll back into focus and he sees me watching him.

'Hey, Mrs Coleman!' He wipes his mouth on the sleeve of his uniform.

'Hi, Winfred.'

'You having your dinner?' he says in his clipped accent.

'Pancakes, we just ordered them. Want some?'

'Sure.' He slides his robust frame in next to the

children and orders a chilliburger from Barb, the waitress.

'How ya do-in', kids?'

'Fine, fine,' Emmy pips.

'Fine,' Jack echoes eyeing up Winfred's holster.

'What about you, Mrs Coleman? Been obeying the speeding laws?'

'Oh sure.'

'It's pretty expensive to get fined, you know.'

I look at his fresh, open face. 'Gee, yes, Winfred. I know.'

He grins.

'So what are you doing in here?' I ask him. 'Are you off duty?'

'Oh no. I just picked someone up.' He nods through the window to the Ford Explorer. A skinny little Mexican is fidgeting in the front seat looking like a kid who's praying his mother will remember to buy a packet of crisps along with the petrol.

'Who's that?'

'Just some guy I'm taking back into Nogales.'

'Why?'

'José? Cos he's an illegal.'

'And you left him alone in the truck?'

'Sure, why not?'

'Isn't he under arrest?'

Winfred shrugs. 'Nuh-uh, he's been running drugs and needs a lift home.'

I study his face for signs of subversive humour, but Winfred just doesn't look like someone who knows how to take the piss.

'He's a mule. He comes across two, three times a week, gets rid of his load, then he goes back over the border. If I see him, I give him a ride, y'know, save him the trouble of walking.'

'Let me get this straight. You fine me a hundred dollars for driving ten miles above the speed limit, but you give a drug trafficker a free lift home?'

Winfred's smile is clean and white and might be graded as classic American were it not for his canine teeth, which have crept over his incisors, causing his upper lip to jut out somewhat. 'Hey, Duval said you had a temper.'

I stiffen. 'You know Duval?'

'Sure.'

'How so?'

'Oh, him and me, we're good friends.'

'Really?' I keep my tone casual. 'How did you meet him . . .? I mean are you both from round here?'

'Nuh, my home is in Utah.'

'And Duval?'

'I meet *him* all over the place. He's one crazy cowboy!'

'Uh-uh . . . what exactly do you mean by that? What kind of crazy?'

Winfred begins to look a little shifty. 'I dunno.' He reaches for a toothpick.

'So what brings you here?' I change the subject. 'To Ague?'

'Me? Oh, I got into a fight on the rez, and so I left.'

'Did you kill someone?' Jack asks.

'Are you a sheriff?' Winfred chuckles. 'Cos you don't look like a sheriff.'

'I'm a lawyer,' Jack replies severely.

I ask Winfred how he got into the Border Patrol and he tells me that after his fight he went to Las Vegas and drank heavily for a while, then got his act together and took the law enforcement exams.

'Is that where you learned to speak Spanish?'

'Yeah, I learn it pretty good at the academy but it's slipping away now.'

'You don't need it?'

'Sure, I need it. I need it to say – name, José? Stop, José! Sit down, get up, put your hands behind your back, José. I speak good enough for a *mulo*, but Mrs Coleman, don't you go giving anybody lifts round here, okay?'

'Why's that?'

'Two men, from the prison, they escaped a few weeks back and nobody caught them yet.'

'What were they in prison for, running a red light?'

'Ha ha, Mrs Coleman,' he wheezes.

'Alice,' I say automatically.

'There have been murders on the border so you got to be careful. Don't go picking up any strangers, you know what I'm saying, ma'am?'

'Have you seen *The Blair Witch Project?*' Jack interrupts.

Winfred looks to me for help.

'It's a film.'

'Have you?' Jack presses.

'Nuh-uh.' Winfred shakes his head.

'What about *The Exorcist?*'

'Jack,' I say warningly.

Jack, of course, has seen neither of these child-friendly films but nevertheless has a masochistic desire to be terrified. If I ever cave in to pressure and allow him to watch an even faintly scary movie, it's a disaster. He invariably storms my room in the middle of the night and refuses to go back to sleep until I have promised never to be so irresponsible again.

'I don't know nuthin' about movies,' Winfred says.

'They're about the devil,' Jack says.

'I've seen the devil,' Emmy says.

'You certainly have not.' Jack turns to Winfred. 'Have you seen the devil?'

'The dude with red eyes?'

'And horns,' Emmy corrects.

'Naa, I've seen skinwalkers, though.'

'What are they?'

'Spirits of dead Indians.' He lowers his voice. 'They're bad things. Everybody sees them, they're everywhere. They smell like rotting flesh. They run fast, really fast, they cover a lot of ground. They leave dust behind them and when you get close to them,' he snaps his fingers, 'they disappear.'

'Do they shoot people?' Jack asks.

'Yuh, man, all the time.'

Jack's eyes widen. 'Did they shoot you?'

'Sure, they shot me once.'

Emmy gasps. 'Did you die?'

'Of course he didn't die, stupidhead. Did they shoot you with a *gun*?'

'Naa, they shot me with a *bead*.'

'A *bead*?' Jack looks bitterly disappointed.

'In here,' Winfred touches the back of his shoulder with a hand. 'I had to get the witchdoctor to suck it out.'

'A *witchdoctor*?'

'It was an iddy-biddy bead with shells on it. Witchdoctor sucked it right of my shoulder blade.'

The children wriggle with pleasure.

'What else, what else?' they shriek.

'You know those coyotes you hear at night?' Winfred leans forward over the table. 'They're just skinwalkers. They can turn themselves back and forwards whenever they want. If you see a coyote track, don't step on it. It's dangerous.'

'Why?'

'You can get coyote sickness. Also you should never look into the eyes of a coyote. It's a bad omen.'

'What's an omen?' Emmy asks.

'It's a sign that something is going to happen,' I explain.

'If you look into the eyes of a coyote, you go crazy,' Winfred says.

'What else are you scared of?' Jack says. 'Snakes?'

'Naa, snakes, naaaaa. Owls. I'm scared of owls.'

'How can you be scared of owls?'

'They're a bad omen too. If you see an owl, someone close to you will die.'

'Is there any animal you can look in the eye without dying?' I ask drily.

'Yuh,' he says, 'snakes. But you shouldn't open your mouth when you see a snake, or it will jump in.'

'Hey, you don't scare me one bit,' Jack says scornfully. 'I'm not scared of nuthin'.'

We wind slowly around the Temerosa switchbacks heading home. My head feels heavy and woolly. Weatherwise it's been a strange day, muggy and close, a stormy tinge to the sky. I'm tired and strangely depressed. I close my eyes for a second, trying to squeeze out a headache, but as I open them again an animal darts in front of the car. A small white-tailed deer. Instinctively I slam on the brakes. The truck lurches sideways, glances off the rocky corner of the hill, spins then slides inexorably towards the edge and, for one horrifying truncated moment, I'm paralysed with fear, then I yank the wheel and ram my foot down on the stiff lever of the hand brake. The car spins in a circle then, oh merciful God, stops.

My heart pumps furiously. Any faster, a few more feet, and we'd have been over that edge and into oblivion. Shakily, I turn to look at the children. They stare back at me, white, speechless. 'It's okay,' I say as calmly as I can. 'It's okay. We're just going to get the truck on the right side of the road again and then we'll be fine.' I ease the gears into neutral and try the ignition, but the engine, apparently resentful of such unnecessary cardiovascular exercise at this late hour of the evening, gives a sickly cough then promptly flatlines.

The truck's bonnet opens via a lever underneath the passenger seat. I stare hopefully at the blackened greasy innards in case something wildly obvious presents itself to me, but it's a futile exercise. I have mastered petrol and windscreen-wiper fluid, but I am unable to tell a growling minotaur from a purring battery. I slam the bonnet shut again.

'What's wrong?' Jack is first out of the car.

'I don't know. It won't start.'

'Can't you fix it?'

'I don't think so.'

'Why not?'

'I don't know how.'

'Why not?'

I have no answer. Why can't I fix it? It's truly pathetic and don't I know it, but meanwhile, what to do? I have no idea how far we are from home, I can't even remember how long since we left the truckstop. 'You're always dreaming,' Robert liked to complain and he was right. Fuck. The children are already tired and the chances of someone coming down the Temerosa road at this hour are about zero.

'Jack, Emmy,' I take a deep breath, 'we're going to have to walk.'

'Walk!' Understandably, the children sound appalled.

'There's no other way of getting home.'

'Why can't we get a lift?' Jack says.

'Do you see any taxis driving by? Do you see a bus stop anywhere?' Jack looks subdued and I feel bad, but it's all I can do not to drop to the dirt myself and throw a good tantrum. What the hell are we doing out here in the middle of nowhere, where mobiles don't work, where there's no such thing as the AA, or a chirpy switchboard operator from Dial-a-Ride ready to direct a black cab in our direction? I want to be able to get on a tube or catch a bus or call a friend, then wait for them in Starbucks, surrounded by coffee and muffins and newspapers. How hopelessly irresponsible to be out here with two children and not have even the first idea how to change a tyre. I sift through the plastic container in the back of the truck. A road map, one of Emmy's mittens, some sticky sweet papers. No first-aid kit, no torch, no rope, no nothing. What if we had crashed? What if it had been storming, and how could all this only be occurring to me now?

An owl flashes across the road, the beat of its wings making a swishing noise. Emmy covers her eyes with her hands. 'Someone's going to die,' she moans. 'Winfred said so – Jack's going to die.'

'Why me?' he retorts. 'I bet it'll be you.'

Emmy starts to cry. I pull her close. 'No one's going to die. We're all going to be fine.' I wrench the car keys from the ignition, retrieve a phlegmy-looking bottle of water from under the front seat and set off, the children trudging beside me in stunned silence.

'How far is it going to be?' Emmy asks after thirty seconds.

I look at the road ahead. One curve of this hill looks very much like another and I'm not entirely sure where we are. The sky is black and glitters with stars. The silence is noisy with night whispers and I'm watching out for coyotes, for owls and snakes, for skinwalkers.

'I'm cold,' Emmy says.

I take off my fleece and pull it down over her head. The sleeves dangle almost to the ground.

'How far?' she repeats.

'I don't know, sweetie.'

'Oh, oh, oh,' she groans.

'Emmy.'

'I'm not walking.'

'Come on, Emmy, you have to.'

'I don't and I won't.'

'Then I'll have to leave you here.'

'Fine fine fine. Leave me then just leave me here to die TO DIE do you hear?'

'Listen, Emmy.' I drop to my knees. 'Think about it. You could be doing what every other five-year-old in the world is doing, you could be finishing your homework or having a bath or arguing about going to bed, you could be having a day like any other day, like everybody else's day and you'd never remember it. But today is different, so it doesn't matter if you get cold or tired because you'll be dry and warm in a couple of hours. You'll get home and you'll have hot chocolate and you'll remember tonight for the rest of your life, because tonight we had a big adventure.' This rousing speech nearly brings tears to my own eyes. Unfortunately, Emmy remains unmoved.

'A couple of hours!' she says. 'No way, no way.' She shakes her head slowly.

'Oh, God. Emmy, please.'

'Emmy, come on, I'm cold too.' Effortlessly, Jack raises her to her feet, then taking the limp end of her fleecy sleeve begins leading her along the road as though she were a small petulant donkey.

'There was an Iranian monk,' he recites, 'who went

to bed in a bunk, he dreamed that Venus, was tickling his penis —'

'Jack!' I say, mildly shocked.

'And woke up all covered in —'

'Jack!'

'Sweat!' he shouts.

'Jack! My God! Where did you learn that?'

'Jack said penis,' Emmy gurgles. 'Jack said penis.'

'That's unbelievable. Who taught you that?'

'Can't remember,' he shrugs warily.

'Well, it's *great*. Do you know any more?'

'Of course I do. I know lots.'

'There was a young plumber of Dee.' He begins reciting again. 'Who was plumbing a girl by the sea.'

'Okay, Jack . . . er . . . maybe that's enough. I glance at Emmy, who's now skipping happily along the road . . . 'but, you know . . . *thank you*,' I whisper.

'Whatever,' he says.

'Did you learn these at school?'

'No.'

'Where then?'

'Don't remember.'

'You must remember.'

'Don't.'

'Granny taught us,' Emmy pipes up.

'Wha-at!' My heart whacks against my ribs.

'You stupid!' Jack pinches Emmy's arm.

'I'm sorry,' Emmy begins sobbing. 'I'm sorry, I didn't mean to.'

I whip her round to face me. 'What do you mean, Granny! Which Granny?' But I already know which granny. Robert's mother, a formidable eighty-year-old Austrian, died several months ago, and it is only because Robert has finally begun unravelling the legal complexities of her estate that he cannot be here.

'Granny, my mother Granny?' I confirm.

Jack nods.

'But where . . . how?'

'She came to Grampa's, on the train. She brought us presents.' Jack hangs his head.

'I'm sorry,' Emmy says. 'I'm sorry, Mummy. I'm sorry.'

I slump down on a rock, stunned. I do not see my mother. I have never allowed the children to see my mother because I do not believe she's earned the right to her grandchildren.

'Mummy, please . . .'

I look helplessly at my daughter's ketchuppy face. As a child I thought my mother would love me because that's what mothers do in books. I struggle with indignant tears. How dare she think she can just slip into their lives, guilt free. How dare Dad let her?

'Grampa said you'd be angry,' Jack ventures.

'I'm not angry with you, either of you, I'm not.' I smooth my hand against his cheek, then grab hold of Emmy and squeeze her. My poor little Emmy who can't keep a secret. Emmy, who has said nothing for all this time . . .

'Mummy, stoppit.' She wriggles free. 'Look!' She twists my head and I stare, puzzled, into the night-time haze until I see them, just visible, two headlights dipping in and out of view as a car rumbles round the mountain.

'Oh, thank you, God.' I jump up.

'Yes, thank you, God.' Emmy puts her hand in mine. I put my other arm around Jack's shoulders and we stand in the middle of the road together as the headlights grow brighter and rounder and bigger and closer.

The children sit wordlessly in the back of Duval's truck. I take sips from the water bottle, my feet nudging Taco's back, while I try to think of something to say. Since the Taco incident, conversation between Duval and myself has become even more of a tightly scripted affair, based around the tangibles of light fixtures and electrical sockets, so after my 'thanks a lot, very kind of you' and his 'no trouble' we both fall mute. It's dark outside the window. The skeleton outline of the mountains just visible against the sky. In the Orkneys, I think, under this very same sky, people could be staring at the Northern Lights.

'What are you going to charge people to stay in that place of yours once it's finished?' Duval's voice breaks the silence.

'I don't know,' I answer, surprised at the direct question. 'Couple of hundred dollars a night, maybe.' There were health retreats and spas all over the west of America. I've done my internet homework. One, on the outskirts of Taos, New Mexico, offered peace, serenity and cyanide baths for $3,000 a week.

'Uh-uh. So people who drink too much, smoke too much, eat too much, will be able to pay even more to feel better about themselves.'

'There's nothing wrong with people who have money and are not starving,' I say coolly.

But I hear Robert's voice in my head. 'We must decorate it western style,' he'd shouted, tramping through the cabins, barking ideas enthusiastically into the mini disc recorder he liked to keep clipped to his shirt pocket. 'Horseshoes, bear heads, Indian prints . . .' and then he was off. As I listened to him crashing around, I stood on the deck outside and watched the early morning light wash over the hills. A hawk of some kind flitted between the rocks. Under my feet, the stones on the path were a mixture of browns and rusts, their edges glittering with pockets of quartz and I remember thinking that no one should ever be allowed to touch this place. Ever.

'Alice,' he shouted when he finally emerged. '. . . Oh, there you are . . . Was it the Sioux Indians out and about scalping around here, or the Apache? Check breed of Indians!' he commanded into his mike without waiting for a response.

'So what'll these people do once they're here?' Duval says.

'Oh . . . I don't know, the usual stuff. Go on diets, get healthy, have massages, go for hikes.'

'Hikes.'

'Yes, hikes.'

'Uh-uh.'

'What's wrong with hikes?'

'From April on the sun will fry these people like pieces of raw liver in hot fat.'

'That's okay, they can wear hats.'

'Uh-uh.'

I'm so sorry, I'm tempted to snap, but I don't actually speak grunt.

131

'What if they step on a snake?'

'Well, you know, hopefully they won't.'

'There are seventeen different kinds of rattlesnake around here. Diamond backs, sidewinders, mohaves and they're all lying around in the hopes that some fat city slicker will hike by close enough to get bit on the ankle.'

'A rattlesnake bite's not fatal, though, is it?'

'Not unless you're unfit or unhealthy or overweight.' He grinds his cigarette into the ashtray. 'A rattler will kill a child. Adults get about six hours. Snake serum costs around $5,000 a pop. Local hospitals don't carry it.'

'Why not?'

'Hard to say. Maybe they figure there aren't that many people round here worth saving for those kind of dollars.'

'Well, I suppose guests will just have to sign disclaimers.'

'And your kids,' Duval says, 'will you get them to sign a disclaimer?'

I turn round. Emmy has fallen asleep. Jack, eyes wide, is listening intently.

'You're scaring Jack.'

'Certainly is not,' Jack says, riveted.

'Look, other children have been brought up in Arizona and survived.'

'Local kids have the ground rules beaten into them from the day they're born. Have you taught Jack and Emmy to shake out their boots before they put 'em on? Do you sweep the beams over their beds? Do they check under their pillows?'

'You want me to check under their pillows for *snakes?*'

'Spiders.' He holds his thumb and forefinger and inch or so apart. 'Brown recluse, small, harmless-looking.'

'I'm really not worried about spiders.'

'A brown recluse bites you, you won't have any idea how much trouble you're in till you start getting feverish and vomiting and your flesh turns black.'

I look at him. 'Duval, I assume you're trying to make a point, I'm just not sure what it is.'

'Do you have any idea of the dangers out here? For a woman like you?'

'What's that supposed to mean – a woman like me?' Angrily, I screw the lid back on the water bottle. Under my feet Taco mutters in his sleep.

'You broke down seven miles from town. What would you have done if I hadn't come along?'

'You know what, we would have managed.'

'With a quarter litre of water? What if it had been daytime? Ground temperatures in summer reach well over one hundred degrees.'

I nearly hit him. I don't need Duval to make me feel guilty about this evening. 'Do you really think it's any more dangerous out here than in London, where they're asphyxiated by pollution? Where paedophiles lurk behind every post box?'

Duval doesn't take his eyes from the road. 'Take your children back home,' he says evenly. 'They don't belong here and neither do you.'

And in the dark cool of the truck I feel my cheeks begin to burn.

Later, once Emmy is safely in bed and asleep, Jack becomes my shadow, refusing to leave my side, not even for a second, going so far as to crouch by the basin while I'm having a pee as though I might suddenly disappear in a puff of smoke.

'I hate snakes,' he says.

'Me too.'

'I don't want to let you out of my sight,' he says, as we climb into bed.

'Okay, don't then.'

'Don't go anywhere without telling me, especially don't go anywhere after I'm asleep.'

'I won't.'

'Don't.'

'I won't, I promise.'

Under the covers, he wraps himself around me until every one of his limbs is intertwined through mine and I lie there, stroking his hair, wondering what Duval had intended with his warning. What had he been doing on the road so late in the evening and what is it that he's hiding? I'm beginning to understand that the south-west of America is a place grand enough to swallow the dreams of all kinds of people. Nature lovers, loners, drifters, man haters, dream chasers. There are those running to a better life, those escaping a bad one. There are philosophers looking for the romance of another culture, or wanderers satisfying their thirst for adventure. There are some who come to escape the cold and others who come to die – and then, I guess, there are the real fugitives, the unruly and the lawless, who see in this vast empty land a place where they can disappear forever.

Perhaps Duval is one of these, perhaps he's simply an arsehole, or maybe he's just being unwittingly woven into the complicated fantasy that I am starting to impose on this place – but whoever he turns out to be, I resolve to watch myself very carefully indeed around him.

It's around four a.m. when a coyote cuts loose with a long howling session from somewhere nearby. We both wake and in the utter blackness of the room, the final vestiges of Jack's bravado evaporate.

'Skinwalkers,' he moans and buries his sweaty head in the crook of my arm. 'You know,' he whispers, 'I told Winfred I was afraid of nothing, but the truth is I'm afraid of everything.'

'Snap,' I tell him.

12

Tucson is a strange and soulless city. It appears to be modelled on a grid system of sorts so it's easy enough getting in, but getting out is another matter entirely. The streets are so devoid of individuality or even discernible street names that there's no way of telling one from the other. I'm lost. And I've been lost for some time now. If this map is to be believed I'm supposed to be in the centre of town but I'm driving alongside nothing except seedy commercial buildings, tyre-shredding businesses, warehouses all battened up and deserted. It's mid-afternoon on a Friday, yet the place is as quiet as a mausoleum.

I don't know if it's just me, but there's an unfriendly feel to Tucson. With the exception of a lugubrious drunk who gives me directions to Wal-Mart and sends me on my way with the reassuring 'God is with you', and, in fact, the employees of Wal-Mart itself – the Daria Beths, and the Cindys who willingly propel their fourteen-stone bulk through the aisles in order to extract from the shelves the single can of pinto beans amidst 420 other varieties of beans on offer – people in this city take your money furtively as though it would make their day if they could only short-change you in some small way or break your eggs for no good reason.

My low-grade headache is now being joined by gum-ache as the novocaine in my mouth slowly wears off. A nagging toothpain I've ignored too long finally prompted an emergency flight to the dentist this morning. True, I could have gone to see Dr Adams in Ague, but then I've seen the state of people's dentures in my local town and they're not a pretty sight.

I finally leave the city centre behind me, but within minutes become embroiled in the mass of converging secondary roads which loop over and under but never actually directly onto the freeway heading south. Hoping for salvation before I hit Canada, I battle on through Tucson's suburbia, a nightmare sprawl of real-estate offices and Motel 8s offering cheap room rates and frothy Jacuzzis, before the system spits me out into an industrial zone and, shortly after that, a small town preceded by two signs, the first echoing Winfred's warning with the enigmatic 'Danger. Do not pick up hitch-hikers!' and the second, a mile on, the more explanatory 'Prison'. I stop the car. According to the map, I am now north-west of Tucson instead of south-east but there are precious few humanoids around to ask and the only sign of life is the coughing engine of a tri-coloured GMC with very bald tyres parked about a hundred yards away by the entrance to a Shell refinery. The Indians inside the car are big and scary and wearing cheap cowboy hats. All four of them are chewing something which has left a greenish layer of scum on their lips and when they direct me straight through the dirt track of the refinery, with a series of thumb jerks and grunts, I suppress the instinct to drive off at high speed in the opposite direction and instead, due to some innate English embarrassment about not wishing to appear rude, follow their advice to the letter. The first few miles are spent glancing twitchily in my rear-view mirror but after a while I relax. It's a beautiful afternoon, the sky blue and empty save for the odd white twizzle of an aeroplane that appears like some alien vessel coming from one world, on its way to another. I have a map, bags of supplies and a full tank of petrol. The truck is mended and working fine, the children are being fed and watered by Benjamín and I don't have to deal with any residual feelings of unease about Duval until Monday.

On either side of the road, the oil pumps of the refinery duck up and down with slow sinister inevitability, like giant storks feeding, or monster lobster claws digging in the sea bed. After five miles they peter out and the dirt track turns into a stretch of newly laid asphalt divided by a glowing yellow line which cuts through the eerie lunar landscape of the desert. The rock here is buttery gold and bulbous with not a jagged edge in sight. Now and again monoliths loom, some smooth and rounded by the elements, but others grotesque and deformed, like prehistoric beasts temporarily inert with sleep and so extraordinarily lifelike that I stop the truck to photograph them, imagining dinosaurs sweeping through this part of the world, nudging boulders aside with their tails before falling to the desert floor, exhausted by their efforts After an hour or so of this, landscape complacency sets in and I find myself zoning out and dreaming into the emptiness before me. How many bones are buried beneath this soil? How many ghosts haunt the ground above them? It strikes me that what makes this land so romantic is everything you cannot see, that which you can only imagine. The vastness out here is incomprehensible and absolute. It feels as though nothing you do could affect anyone or anybody. If a bolt of lightning were to smite the truck right now, I would turn to a speck of dust and nobody would be any the wiser. How different from existence in the city where everything you do impinges on someone else. You stall your car, the man behind bumps into you, five people turn to look, a passer-by becomes a witness and, before you know it, you've had an effect, a meaningless but nevertheless tangible effect on the lives of others. As a child, I was intrigued by this idea. I liked to think of people as snails, leaving a thin thread of life behind them, and every time one human being impacted on another I imagined these threads crossing, and the course of their lives becoming tangled forever.

The Mars landscape finally gives way to a drier, more desolate backdrop. I'm still unsure of where I am exactly, but the sun is dipping to the right, so I guess I must be heading south. This area is marked on the map as the Tohomo O'Odham reservation, and seems to be desert right up to the horizon. I come across a couple of yellow school buses disgorging Indian kids with backpacks onto the side of the road and I watch as, heads down against the dusty wind, they begin making their way along narrow paths to scattered trailer homes.

It's getting darker. Cool air filters into the truck. Clouds change from orange to pink. The sunset spreads quickly, infusing the pale sky with a sudden stain of colour like an anaemic receiving an emergency blood transfusion. I flick on the headlamps and something catches my eye. It's far off, no bigger than a dark thumbprint in the centre of the windscreen, and as I draw closer I see it's a dead animal.

Sue, Jack's teacher, told me this part of Arizona had, once upon a time, been overrun with an extraordinary variety of wildlife: 'I mean, before we hunted them to death there were jaguars, turkeys, armadillos, even little monkeys.' But this particular road kill is nothing more exotic than a dog – still, as I pass it, then glance at it again in the mirror, there's something about the way it's lying there, silhouetted against the burning sky, that induces me to brake the truck to a stop.

The dog is a big domestic animal with a smooth brown coat and the snub forehead of a boxer. Its lips have been pulled back as though it died with a snarl on its face and its top teeth have settled over the lower jaw in a clenched grimace. Its eyeballs have rolled back in its head and they stare up at the sky, opaque and pupil-less. I focus my camera, but as the shutter clicks there's a faint noise. It's no more than a rustle, a slight break in the current of air, but with a start I realize I am not alone.

I hear them most nights, of course, but I've seen only two since we arrived; one high up in the hills to the back of the house, the other at dusk, far, far away and crossing my eye line so furtively it might have been the shadow of a ghost. This is the first time I've seen one close up. The coyote stands motionless in the scrub, a mere four feet away, but it's not quite the ferocious beast of my imagination. It's a leaner, longer-legged version of Taco with a pointed face and a black tip to its tail. It eyes me insolently, as though issuing a silent order to relinquish my claim to the dinner which by all the laws of nature is rightly his.

'If you look into the eyes of a coyote, you go crazy,' Winfred had warned. 'You should never look into the eyes of a coyote. It's a bad omen.'

Very slowly, so slowly, I bring the camera up until level with the coyote's head and softly depress the shutter. The flash flashes. Startled, the coyote blows on its front legs then pushes itself round and vanishes into the desert, sending up small puffs of dirt in its wake. I turn the camera back to the dead dog and fire off a dozen or so shots in rapid succession. The light show in the sky is reaching a climax. The sun has melted out of the constraints of its circle and is arbitrarily shooting streaks of orange through the riot of violet and crimson clouds above. Then, as it drops lower, an angle changes. The pale milky film of the dog's eyes suddenly catches the light and the pupils begin glowing a deep molten red. I take a step backwards. The dog looks demonic. Supernatural. Like some terrifying pagan deity about to be resurrected by the power of the dying sun. Thoroughly spooked, I retreat a couple more steps, unwilling to present my back to the beast.

I do not see the Mexican until I turn. No intuition, female or otherwise, warns me that the real danger lies not in front, cold and stiff in death on the road, but behind, alive and very much human. Except that the man standing by the truck doesn't look dangerous. He looks scared. He stares directly at me, but how long he's been standing there, watching, waiting, I have no way of knowing. Certainly long enough to have swiped the shopping from the back of the truck. He holds all eleven of my Wal-Mart bags. Five hooked through the fingers of one hand, six more cutting into the wrist of the other. He steps backwards, feeling with his trainer for the edge of the desert, but all the while staring, almost as if waiting for an order to drop the food, and I think later that had I had the presence of mind to call out, he might have put the bags down, possibly even murmured an apology; but it doesn't occur to me and when it dawns on him that I am not about to make any attempt to stop him, he turns and scrambles down the scrub of the bank, melting away to nothing as the desert closes protectively around him. As I look after him the irony strikes me. That out here in the middle of this emptiness, not ten feet from the supernatural fantasy I was ready to lose myself in, exists somebody else's harsh reality.

His face comes back at me that night. Troubled bloodshot eyes, a broken front tooth. In retrospect, I realize I'd been lucky. He could have taken the truck. The keys had been in the ignition and he could have been long gone before I got anywhere near him. So why hadn't he? Enough basic humanity not to abandon a woman alone in the desert? Or had there been others, hidden away in the darkness – too many to climb into the truck without being heard? Or did it all just come down to a question of priorities? How close to starvation do you have to be to choose food over transport? I close my eyes, but his image remains. I've never seen this man before yet he seems so familiar to me. Something in his face strikes a chord. Then I realize it's not those hawkish features literally, but the expression in them. It's that look of fear and desperation I've seen before. I've seen it in the face of a Mexican boy holding an empty gallon water bottle by the side of the road, I've seen it in the eyes of people staring out of the windows of green immigration buses, and, God knows, in Temerosa, I get to see it every day.

13

A brand-new Chevy Silverado, unusually clean and polished for the area, draws up outside the cabin early Tuesday afternoon. My visitor is a lanky man of about fifty years old wearing denims with a pronounced crease down each leg and a pressed shirt cinched at the collar by a jewelled flag with two strands of black leather hanging from it.

'Mrs Coleman?' he queries as I open the door.

'Yes, hello?'

There's an initial look of surprise at the bare feet and cracked black toenails courtesy of a recent Emmy makeover, but he swiftly recovers.

'Jeff Hogan, ma'am.' He removes his hat. 'Your neighbour down the way.'

I'd been in the middle of a kitchen blitz, a weekly attempt to quell the anarchy of the tinned-can cupboard and impose a more militarized discipline on open packets of spaghetti, which most of the time tend to slouch untidily against the walls of the cupboard like soldiers on the verge of desertion. Every surface is covered with packets of cranberries, bags of flour and rice all waiting to be re-stationed, so it's with some reluctance that I shake his proffered hand and invite him in.

'How nice. I didn't know we had a neighbour.'

'Fifteen miles north-east, just past the turning to Fishsprings. You've probably seen it. Beautiful place, view over the Patagonia Mountains. One of the finest properties around.'

I murmur something appropriate. I have no idea what Jeff Hogan's business is with me, but I have a sinking feeling it's not going to be over nearly quickly enough.

He stands awkwardly in the kitchen. 'So, now, would Mr Coleman be in?'

'No, I'm afraid not.'

'Do you expect him back any time soon?'

'Actually . . . no.'

'I should come back tomorrow then.'

'My husband is in Europe.'

'Oh, that's too bad.' Hogan shakes his head. 'I'd have come sooner had I known. I've been neglecting you and I'm sorry for it.' He looks so genuinely remorseful standing there, clutching his hat, that I relent and offer him a drink.

'Why, that's kind, thank you, ma'am and I'll take a beer if it's no trouble.'

I fetch him a Budweiser and a glass. Then, because there seems no other option, we sit down and examine each other politely. He has a pleasant, rather earnest face and thick white hair which falls boyishly across his forehead.

'Hope it's no imposition coming in like this.'

'Not at all.'

'I hear you've been doin' work to the property.'

'That's right.'

'Bought it off those Canadian fellas, I understand?'

'Well . . . in a sense.'

'And your husband's not here to oversee the job?'

'He'll be in Europe for the foreseeable future.'

'That sure is too bad,' Hogan repeats. He gazes round the room, as though it must surely be Robert's absence which accounts for the domestic disorder.

'I like your neckpiece,' I tell him.

'My bolo tie?' He grips the metal flag and tightens it. 'Patriotic, ain't it?'

'It certainly is. I should get one for my son.'

'Why, certainly you should, ma'am.' He gazes round the room a little longer.

'So . . . you live at Fishsprings?' Reluctantly, I prolong the conversation.

'Yes indeed, ma'am, I own ten thousand acres of prime cattle land. Bought them back in ninety-six when I happened to be passing through with my wife.'

'You're a rancher then?'

'No, ma'am, a dentist. I have my practice in Houston.'

'Oh! What a pity you weren't here last week,' I say gaily and touch an explanatory finger to my mouth.

'I'm in the cosmetic end of the trade, ma'am.' He leans forward eagerly. 'There are dentists who'll give you a whole mouth of new teeth for next to no money but, heaven help you, you'll look like you've gone and got Chiclets stuck into your gums. You want work done, you'd better come to an outfit like us. Different ball game altogether. We charge, but we're worth it.' He coughs discreetly. 'My daughter always prided herself on having the best teeth in high school.'

midnight cactus

'That's great!'

We stare at each other a little longer.

'Mrs Coleman.'

'Call me Alice.'

'Mrs Coleman . . . ma'am,' he falters.

'Alice,' I say firmly.

The whole ma'am thing drives me mad. In Ague, where they address anything in a skirt as ma'am, Emmy bares her teeth like a weasel on hearing it. 'I'm not a mam,' she snarls. 'I'm a litttle girl . . .'

'Alice . . . ma'am, see here . . . I hope you don't think I'm speaking out of turn but, well, I . . . well . . . I understand you were involved in an er . . . well, an incident a few days back.'

'Me?' I frown. 'No.'

'Robbed I heard.'

'Uh . . . no.'

'Scared pretty bad too.'

'Nope.' I shake my head. 'Not me.'

'And well,' he persists, 'it made me feel all the worse for not paying you a visit sooner.'

'Look it's very kind of you, but it's simply not tr—' I stop as it finally occurs to me what he might be referring to. But how had he heard? I'd hardly mentioned it to anyone . . . well, except Benjamín, of course, who, as soon as I delivered the description of the dog, had sucked in his breath and put a hand to his jaw. '*Mal de ojo*,' he whispered awfully. '*Mal de ojo*.'

'What is that? What do you mean?'

'It is the evil eye. Is very bad, Alice.' He looked shaken. 'Very bad.'

147

'It was just a dead dog, that's all.'

'Noh, noh . . .' he said vehemently, 'the *mal de ojo* causes illness, Alice . . . sometimes,' his voice sank lower, '*la muerte* . . . death.'

However, I couldn't see Benjamín as a confidant of Jeff Hogan so it must have been Sue, to whom Emmy had blurted out, 'Mummy got burgled,' as soon as we arrived at school yesterday, whereupon I'd been obliged to tell the whole story.

'That's too bad,' Sue commented. 'But you know, Alice . . . all this used to be theirs.' She made an expansive sweeping gesture with her hand.

'All what?'

'Arizona, California, Texas, everywhere. It all used to belong to Mexico before we took it away from them. We stole from them, they steal from us.' She dipped her head. 'I believe it's fair that they should take back what's rightly theirs.'

'Well I'm not sure you could argue that my half-pound of Cheddar and that jar of pickles were rightly theirs, but let's not quibble about details.'

'Alice,' Sue said firmly, 'did you know that our government has never even formally apologized to the Native Americans? Chaos will endure as long as there is no proper stewardship of the earth.'

Hogan waits, twisting his hat nervously through his fingers.

'You're talking about my shopping getting stolen, right?'

'Yes, ma'am,' he says gravely.

'Okay, well, yes,' I concede. 'But it was no big deal.'

Hogan shakes his head. 'Mrs Coleman, you're being brave and I admire you for it but, believe me, I know just how frightening these things can be.'

'Really, Mr Hogan, it's fine.'

Hogan looks in no way satisfied. 'This is very awkward, Mrs Coleman, you without your husband and all . . . but my wife . . . she rang all the way from Houston and she said to me, "Jeff, they're your neighbours and you have a duty both as someone with standing in the town and as a leader of the community . . ."' On and on he stumbles and all the while I'm thinking – it's true, the snail's thread I spin out behind me has crossed with the Mexican's and here come the repercussions.

'Mrs Coleman . . . ma'am, what I'm trying to say is . . . well . . . were you in any way . . . well . . . *hurt?*'

'Hurt?' I say surprised. 'No. Not at all.'

'Well now that's a considerable worry off my mind . . . story I heard was that . . . well . . .' He shifts uncomfortably in his chair.

'What story?' I say, mildly interested.

'Folks have been saying that you were . . . *violated* in some way.'

I nearly laugh out loud. It's the look on his face. Fatherly concern mingled with agonizing curiosity.

'Well, in actual fact it was my truck took the brunt of the attack, but I'm sure, with counselling and gentle handling, it will recover in time.'

'This ain't no laughing matter, Mrs Coleman,' Hogan says solemnly. 'Next time it could be far worse, you could be harmed in some way.'

I shut my eyes. The Mexican's face looms.

'It was nothing, really, you mustn't worry.' In the pocket of my corduroys, my fingers close round a single Skittle, sequestered from Jack's private stash in the car. I set myself the task of getting it to my mouth without Hogan noticing.

'But I do worry.' Hogan's voice rises with indignation. 'Why, I'd never forgive myself if something were to happen. You here alone! No husband! Two small children! Ma'am, it's not right. It's not safe. Your property is no more than six miles from the border. The hills round here are overrun with illegals.'

The way he says 'illegals' makes it sound as though a new and ferocious breed of groundhog had been identified which was even now cavorting in the mesquite in their thousands, chomping on Indian grasses and breeding prolifically while horrified locals were forced to hole up in fortified cabins.

'The problem's not only here on the border,' Hogan is saying. 'My mother-in-law is up in a retirement home outside of Phoenix. They got Mexicans tending the lawns up there – like they got 'em *everywhere*,' he adds darkly, 'sweeping the trash and mopping the floors. Believe me, these people have no respect for the folk they work for. My mother-in-law has suffered terribly at their hands.'

'How dreadful.' It's my expression now that is surely one of agonizing curiosity. Had the poor woman also been violated?

'Yes, dreadful,' he echoes bleakly. 'She had her finest brooch go missing.'

'Ah, I see.' The Skittle is a tropical flavour. Mango? Kiwi? 'Well I'm sorry to hear it.'

'These illegals are everywhere.' Hogan shakes his head sorrowfully. 'They cross our land, stealing animals, threatening our people. My own wife lives in fear.'

'All the way from Houston?' I say gently.

Hogan reddens.

'Look.' Hastily, I try to make amends. 'It's really nice of you to be concerned, honestly it is, but the poor man was probably more frightened of me than I was of him.'

'Well that may be so,' he replies stiffly, 'but my wife insists we offer you our protection. Rest assured that I'm prepared to pass by this way every evening if it will give you some measure of peace of mind.'

Oh, God forbid. 'It's very kind of you really, but I have Benjamín.'

'That fella who caretakes the place?' Jeff Hogan splutters into his beer. 'You think he'd turn a gun on his own kind?'

'I very much hope he wouldn't turn a gun on anyone,' I reply primly, pushing back my chair and standing up.

He makes no move to go. 'Mrs Coleman, ma'am . . .'

'Mr Hogan.' Resolutely, I remain standing.

He sighs and scrapes back his chair. 'Mrs Coleman, I'd be grateful if you'd give me the telephone number of your husband. As a property owner he has an investment to protect, same way I do. The troubles are not good for business, not good at all.'

'They're affecting dentistry?'

Hogan appears not to hear. 'Tombstone ain't the only place around here that's got itself some history,' he says. 'A bunch of fellas and I have invested a lot of dollars into Ague. I don't know whether you're aware, but the fine hotel there, Prestcott's, is mine, the restaurant too.' He shakes his head. 'I was real pleased to hear your husband had taken over Temerosa. A commercial venture here will be beneficial for us, and a town near by with attractions and shopping and fine eating to offer tourists, well, I'm thinking that'd be good for your husband too.'

Something sour rises in my throat. I'm rapidly beginning to dislike this man with his faux folksiness. Any second now, he's going to start calling me little lady.

'So can I count on your cooperation?'

'For what?'

'There's a meeting in the town hall tomorrow night. I'm hoping you'll find the time to attend.' He looks towards the door as it opens and Duval comes in, a roll of plans in his hand. The two men regard each other with mutual dislike. 'Duval,' Hogan says disagreeably. He plucks his hat off the table.

'Jeff.' Duval leans against the door and eyes Hogan insolently as he walks past.

'Say, Duval.' Hogan stops and turns. 'Those Mexican fellas you got working here, they all legal, if you don't mind my asking?'

'Why, Jeff?' Duval says, smiling grimly. 'What would make you think they weren't?'

'No offence meant, I just think Mrs Coleman has a right to know. She wouldn't want to be getting into any trouble with the INS.'

'Trouble?' I ask quickly. 'What kind of trouble?'

Hogan puffs out his chest like a homing pigeon with a vital message to deliver.

'Well, ma'am, we have something here called a resident identification programme. It's a visa that allows Mexicans to move freely across the border for work purposes only.'

'And?'

'Every employer round the border area needs to have their paperwork in order.'

Duval holds Hogan's gaze effortlessly. He maintains his arms-crossed pose, the very picture of laid back, and my guess is, if there'd been a toothpick to hand, he'd be chewing on it.

'See, Mrs Coleman,' Hogan says as he turns back to me, 'if by chance your permits weren't in order and someone put a call through to the INS,' he pauses, 'why, ma'am, there'd be agents crawling all over this place within hours.'

'How are those fish of yours getting along, Jeff?' Duval interrupts pleasantly. 'Still having trouble with poachers?'

The veins in Hogan's neck stand taut. I lay my hand on his arm. 'Please don't worry, Mr Hogan, I've seen the permits and everything is fine.' I studiously avoid catching Duval's eye. 'Thank you so much for coming by. It was very nice of you.'

Hogan exhales noisily. 'Just glad to have been of service, is all. I'll get that number for your husband another time.'

'You do that,' I say soothingly and steer him to his waiting Chevy, feeling Duval's eyes drilling into my back.

'Can I expect you at the meeting then, Mrs Coleman?'

Hogan bends his long body like a folding ruler into the leather seat.

'I'll do my best.'

'Everyone round here has to pull together. We need to take care of our own.'

He yanks at the power steering and throws a wintry look at Duval. 'You should have come to me first before hiring that fella,' he says. 'You watch out for that man, Mrs Coleman. You watch out for him!'

Dust hangs in the air from the departing Chevrolet. I stomp back to Duval, brimming with self-righteousness. 'Why didn't you just tell him what he wanted to know?'

'I don't answer to Jeff Hogan.'

'So you just assumed I would back you up?'

'You don't answer to him either.'

'That's not the point. I don't want any trouble with the IN whoever it is.'

'Hogan's a fool,' he says mildly.

'Well that may be, but so would I be, if I was knowingly hiring illegals to work in the town.'

Duval smiles thinly. 'You think these men would risk their lives and freedom smuggling themselves backwards and forwards over the border every single day just for the privilege of working for you?'

'That's not —'

'So they can build a *resort*?'

I'm so angered and embarrassed by the contempt in his voice, I can barely get the words out. 'Do you have the paperwork, Duval, yes or no?'

'Why, I surely do,' he drawls, in full hick mode. 'Would you like to see it?'

'Yes, if it's all the same to you, I would like to see it. I'd like a copy, please, so I don't have to have my afternoons ruined by people like Jeff Hogan.'

Duval pulls a folded piece of paper from his shirt pocket.

'H2 work visa.' He hands it to me. 'There's already one copy in the back of your file with the plan revisions and a second copy pinned to your photographic "montage" in the boarding house.'

I scan down the tiny print. An official-looking seal is dated and stamped by USA Customs, Nogales. 'And this covers everyone?' I say lamely.

'Yes, ma'am,' he says. He folds the visa and puts it back in his pocket. 'Now, if that's everything, I'll leave you with these,' he hands me the rolls of plans, 'and be on my way.'

He ambles down the steps, tipping his hat, but I cannot curb a childish impulse to have the last word.

'Actually, there is one thing.'

'Ma'am?' He turns with exaggerated civility.

'If one more person round here calls me ma'am, I'll kick them in the fucking teeth.'

He stops for a moment, his boot on the bottom step, and into his eyes comes a flash of pure amusement.

14

Ague's town hall is a red-brick building set back from the main street by a flight of wide steps dividing two rectangles of all-year-round grass. Banners hang across the windows of the ground floor, presenting passers-by with those comforting reminders – 'United we Stand' and 'Proud to be American'.

Directions to the meeting are marked on paper with thick green arrows. I follow them up the stairs and into the main auditorium, a large characterless room with rows of municipal chairs facing a stage. It's only a few minutes after seven o'clock, the posted start of the meeting, nevertheless the room is packed, standing space only, and attention already focused on two men sitting at a table on stage, one in jeans and a flannel shirt, the other in the navy-blue uniform of US Customs. I edge along the wall and try to merge inconspicuously with other latecomers, wishing I was back in Temerosa with the children, watching Enunciada's descent into romantic purgatory on TV from the comfort of Benjamín's sofa; and up until a couple of hours ago, I'd had every intention of doing just that, with a shortlist of excuses including 'sick child', 'burst pipe' and 'uncontrollable vomiting' at the ready should Hogan ring and coerce me into attending. I'm a big fan of the last-minute excuse and in London used it as often as I dared for extricating myself from some of Robert's more turgid evening plans, taking a rather guilty pride in fielding the sympathetic follow-on calls – 'Poor old you, but you really shouldn't eat takeaway curry, everyone knows it's just boiled cat covered in cream' – and in spite of the fact that I can drink battery acid without any adverse effects, amongst Robert's cronies I've acquired a reputation for being of a delicate disposition. Still, I'd made the tactical error of mentioning Hogan's border troubles to Robert when he called to speak to the children.

'What kind of troubles?' he said, his radar flicking from green to amber.

'Oh, just something to do with his property,' I hastily backtracked. 'Nothing that concerns us really.'

'Well you should definitely go to this meeting,' he said. 'Get in with some of the locals. I bet there are some major property owners out there who could be useful to us.'

'Maybe . . .'

'How's it all going anyway?'

'Fine, it's going fine.' I was careful, as always, to keep the faintest tinge of ennui in my voice. *It's not so great that you'd want to be here, Robert, but then you don't have to worry about us either.*

'And how's that bloody lazy Mexican?' he asked, his voice slurred. It was midnight for him and the schnapps was kicking in. 'You're not letting him rip us off, I hope.

I don't like you being out there alone with him, anything might happen. I wish you would fire him,' he added for the hundredth time.

I laughed and pretended I thought he was joking. Then I promised to go to the meeting and make lots and lots of new friends. God forbid that Robert should come charging over to slay imaginary dragons for me.

Skimming through the sea of faces I'm surprised to find one or two I recognize. Towards the front is the owner of the second-hand bookshop, a Gulf War vet who dresses in brown polyester trousers with mustard-coloured knitted ties. Behind him, there's the sweet woman who works the till at the hardware store, dispensing change and information with breathtaking patience. 'That's two dollars seventy-seven, thank you, Babs. Door jambs, Steve? A-fourteen, middle aisle, next to four-inch brass hinges.' I'm interested to note that not every face in the room is white. Dotted amongst the largely blonde hair of the women, a few dark heads stand out like burnt flecks in oatmeal. Certainly, the customs man on the stage, with his swarthy skin and hooded eyes, looks Mexican, and in the back row a white woman holds hands with an Indian who is pouring sweat and transferring his weight from one leg to the other as though in the throes of a heinous attack of claustrophobia. Jeff Hogan sits quietly in the front row, his thin hands resting on his knees, his head tilted, listening intently to a man who has stood up in the centre of the room and begun speaking.

'Why does the INS not prosecute USA employers who encourage immigrants to keep on coming? Cochise county is the number one point for aliens crossing into our nation.' He points his finger accusingly at the stage. 'And for every one man intercepted there's five who get through. So I ask you again, Mr Chavez, what is the INS doing to stop this?'

'Yeah!' someone shouts. 'Our kids can't get a job in Burger King because the Mexicans got 'em all already!'

'They're draining our welfare system, hospitals, education!'

'Why can't you put troops on the border? Close it!'

The customs official holds up his hands for quiet.

'Some of you know me, but for those that don't, my name is Emilio Chavez. I'm border chief for the Nogales sector. Let me tell you something: it doesn't matter what you read in the press, there is no border that can't be controlled. Back in Vietnam we had extra-sensory equipment so sensitive that when somebody coughed three miles away you could hear it.' He pauses. 'Last time we had mass deportations in this country was in the Depression. Back then there was no electronic database linking immigrants to their whereabouts. Today all I need to track somebody down is their correct name and a date of birth. But let me tell you something, people: if we clamped down and removed all illegals from the USA, there would be economical implosion in both countries and a destabilization of our government. Now raise your hand, any one of you who wants to see ten million Mexicans crossing the border during the course of a single week.'

'Only if we get to shoot them as they go!' a voice rings out. There's a quick smattering of laughter which is quickly self-regulated. Nobody risks a raised hand.

'Yes! Over there, lady in the white shirt. Jeannie, ain't it?' The compère squints. 'Eyesight ain't what it used to be,' he apologizes. 'Jeannie Steves? That you?'

'Bob,' the woman acknowledges. She stands up and looks beseechingly round the audience. 'I have two boys,' she begins, barely louder than a whisper, 'Ray and Terry.'

'Speak up, Jeannie,' Bob shouts. 'We all need to hear what you got to say.'

Jeannie nods; a big woman with pretty features concealed by sun-aged skin, her fingers flutter at the turquoise belt buckle of her jeans.

'My sons, Terry and Ray, well they're good boys . . . real good boys and, as some of you know, they ain't always had it easy. Thing is, they're teenagers now and they're growing up real quick.' Her voice deepens with confidence. 'Now y'all remember what happened to my sister's eldest.' She looks around, acknowledging the collective murmur of the room. One or two people shake their heads and look at the floor. 'All our kids are at risk like Stanton was. I don't want my boys hanging around the border. Bars and clubs on the other side, they don't card the kids like they should. They'll serve 'em till they're stupid with liquor. Our kids can go into Mexican drugstores and get anything they want, twenty-four hours a day, no prescription, no ID and, Lord knows, the drugs over there are cheaper than candy. So what I want to know is what are the customs people doing about that, Mr Chavez?'

'Yes, sir!' Bob points from the stage. 'You have something to say about this?'

The hand waving from mid-field goes down and a jowled man stands up. 'I lived in Phoenix for forty-seven years till I came down here. Had 'em practically in my backyard. They lived like pigs. Didn't even bother to learn English.'

The hall is becoming hot and testy with emotion. Bottoms shuffle uncomfortably on seats.

'What about you, Doug?'

A whippet-thin cowboy with a long-boned face and eyes that have been beaten back to slits by grit and wind, stands slowly. Up on the stage, Bob strokes the air in a crowd-quietening motion.

The cowboy clears his throat. 'Folks, I've been ranchin' for forty-five years. I eat dust fifteen hours a day, seven days a week and it's back-breakin' dirty work. I got no pension, no social security worth nothing. I work jest about as hard as a man can and ain't got a nickel to show for it. But I ain't complainin', cowboyin' is a good life. Only life I ever known. Now we have Mexican fellas on the ranch from time to time and I have to tell you we was awful afraid of them at first.' He shakes his head. 'But I ain't got nothing against 'em, nothin' at all. You see one of them fellas up on a horse and there ain't a single muscle in his body don't know what it's doin'. They're good hard-working cowboys, jest like us.' He sits down carefully.

'Doug's right.' Another cowboy, with a white moustache that fans out from under his nose like the tail feathers of a dove, jerks up to his feet. 'No Mexican ever done me no harm.' His neck suffuses with blood as attention shifts his way. 'I used to keep goats and sheep,

161

and a while back a mountain lion got into my barn and killed all fifteen of them.' He snaps his fingers. 'Just like that. Had a Mexican fella at the time. It was his job to look after them goats. Wasn't his fault, mind, wasn't anybody's fault, but made him cry to see 'em like that, throats all ripped out an' bloody an' all.' He collapses onto his chair, retracting his neck into his shirt like a tortoise.

The mood softens noticeably. Several people, including the Indian man and his wife, nod in agreement with this.

'Jeff?' the compère says. 'I know you got something to say!'

Hogan stands up. 'Well yes, Bob, yes, I do.' Picking up the plastic bag at his feet, he walks up the steps and crosses the stage. 'Something to say, something to show.' He looks keenly at the audience then takes the bag by its bottom corners and tips it upside down, spilling rubbish onto the table. 'You know what this is?' he asks throatily. The assembly has gone completely quiet and suddenly, to my surprise, I notice Duval. He's slouching in the corner on the other side of the hall, his black felt hat obscuring most of his face as he works the dirt from his nails with the blade of his Leatherman.

'This is a tenth of the trash I pick up every day off my property.' Jeff's voice throbs with anger. 'Every damn day, I'm telling you, and the load never gets any less.' Everyone in the room cranes their head for a better look. Hogan pulls on a pair of Marigolds and begins plucking the garbage from the table, piece by piece. He holds up a milk carton and stabs a finger at the label. 'Mexican

162

brands. All of 'em.' He reaches for a ball of crumpled newspaper. 'And this,' he says, 'do you know what this is?'

No one speaks.

'It's newspaper.' Hogan has the full attention of the room now. 'Mexican newspaper and it's soiled with human refuse.' For a moment the silence is absolute before it is pierced by the odd manifestations of outrage which gather momentum until they swell into a single long expression of disgust.

Hogan unravels the newspaper, holding it up for everyone to see. 'This is Mexican shit,' he cries, 'and it's besmirching the face of our own president.' As one now, the entire front row leans forward to get a better look at the defecated-upon features of Mr Bush.

'If they would just pick up after them . . .' a woman in the front row pipes up. 'I'm sympathetic to their plight, but it ain't just that it looks bad – the cattle eat that plastic stuff.'

Hogan plucks the repacked rubbish bag from the table and walks round to the front of the stage. 'Here.' He thrusts it at the woman, who wrinkles her nose in disgust and quickly plays pass the parcel with the teenager sitting to her left.

'You want to appreciate what it's like clearing this day after day? No disrespect, ma'am, but see how you would like it.' He returns to the table as the bag is handed along and back through the rows like a church collection box.

I'm aware of my own nose wrinkling, yet I'm surprised by the strength of Jeff Hogan's invective. Texas borders Mexico as much as Arizona and I would have imagined that even up in Houston there would have to be a modicum of peaceful co-existence.

'It's time to draw a line in the sand!' Hogan cries. 'Either the government must keep these criminals off our private property or I say it falls to the property owners to do it themselves.'

There's a roar of approval. 'Who's for a show of hands?' Hogan says rousingly. A smattering of hands shoot up, quickly joined by others until the room is a mass of waving arms. I glance over to Duval, but he's looking to the back of the room where a dim murmur has begun and is rippling through the crowd row by row as a woman pushes her way to the front of the hall.

'Hey!' someone shouts. 'Who asked Nora?'

Powering on, ignoring the muttering and the catcalls, the woman elbows her way through the latecomers until she makes it to the foot of the stage. She's short, no more than five foot three, and near obese with the sort of excess flesh which suggests either a pack of doughnuts a day or an untreatable lymph disorder. A green baseball hat embroidered with the words Bass Buster is perched high on her head under which long grey hair falls in individual greasy points down her back. As she mounts the stairs, she plucks at the waistband of her trousers, which keep slipping down at the back, revealing a gaping expanse of soft white rump.

Ignoring the three men at the table, she kicks off without preamble, 'I'm here to raise support for the Humanity Patrol.'

'Get on home, Nora.'

'The Humanity Patrol leaves water and helps folk who get themselves into trouble.'

'Hey! We don't want no bleeding-heart liberals here!'

Nora pays no attention, simply amplifies her voice until it projects over the growing clamour of the audience. I steal another look over at Duval. He has finished with his Leatherman manicure and is watching the assembly intently.

'Every man has the right to feed his family,' Nora bellows. 'Dying of thirst is too high a price to pay. These people need protection, illegals or not.'

'Yield the floor, girl.' It's the same voice again, coming from somewhere in the back. I peer around the heads trying to identify the caller, as up on stage Emilio Chavez braves an approach. Nora swats him away like a bluebottle. Chavez, smile tightening, presents the audience with a helpless shrug.

'Now come on, people, be fair,' she shouts. 'Y'all are happy to have Mexicans sweep your porches up in those fancy houses of yours.'

'Yeah,' counters the heckler, 'they sweep the porches, then they case the joint and rob the place.'

Nora clenches her fists as though bracing herself for another bout in the ring, but who she thinks she might win round is unclear. The tenor of the meeting is vehemently against her. Some of the audience cup hands to mouths and boo, and that's when it happens. From somewhere deep in the back of the auditorium, a milk carton comes sailing through the air. With devastating accuracy, it hits Nora square on the shoulder, then ricochets up to her face before dropping to the floor with a soft thunk.

'People, people.' Bob the compère waves his arms ineffectually, but it's too late. There's raucous laughter as the crowd caves in to pack mentality and Nora finally cuts her losses. She fixes the room with a look of defiance then stomps offstage.

'Hey, Nora,' calls the persistent heckler, 'better not stick around in the hog season lest you git shot.'

This time I spot him. He's standing up, a thin feverish man in the back row who's taken possession of the rubbish bag. In his right hand he's now holding a crushed water bottle. He weighs it up, judging the length and power required for another shot, but as he pulls his arm back to make the throw Duval steps swiftly out of his corner, and seizing the man's wrist, twists it sharply behind his back. The heckler lets out a yowl and his face contorts with pain, but all eyes are on Nora as she heads down the aisle, the sheer vicinity of her menace opening up a path before her. On she goes past the rows of detractors, past Duval still holding fast to the heckler, until she reaches the exit doors at the back and punches through them using the flat palms of both hands.

'People, this is uncalled for,' Chavez is shouting. He waits for the room to settle. 'Look, I understand your frustration and I appreciate the problems some of you are having, but nobody wants to be taking matters into their own hands. Nora is entitled to her opinion as are all of you here, but understand this – the government sees its tolerance of illegal aliens as a form of foreign aid. We do what we can with the money we're given and the laws we live by. If you want things changed around here, lobby your county commissioner or write to your local senator. We need a bigger budget, more helicopters and more manpower. The border is nearly two thousand miles. You want to see a wall that long? You need to build it.'

Only now, as Chavez folds away his notes and shakes hands with Bob and Jeff Hogan, do the people in the back rows begin to pay attention to the mewls of outrage coming from somewhere in their midst. 'Did you see that?' The heckler stands shakily supporting his right arm in his left. His eyes dart from one puzzled face to another. 'Did you see what he did? Look at it!' His voice rises to a whine. 'My wrist, I think it's broke!'

The car park is empty. Most people have stayed behind for crisps and beer but I couldn't get out of there quickly enough. The townsfolk of Ague, lighting their torches in the darkened gloom of Mary Shelley's *Frankenstein*, and I want no part of it. I just want to go home, back to the children and the apolitical bubble of Temerosa.

I'm beginning to think that for all its beauty there's something mean-spirited about this part of the world. Maybe it's to do with the land, with its jagged and sinister topography, maybe there's a faction of the population that has become as twisted and burnt out as the trunks of the drought-ridden scrub oaks. Arizona is full of people who have drifted to the west for their own reasons: because it's cheap, because it's warm, because one day their trailer just broke down and they couldn't afford to fix it. People come to Arizona from all over, crawling out of the skin of their old lives and growing a new, tougher one. Nevertheless for those who have jumped a rung on the ladder there seems to be a tendency to turn round awfully quick and take a kick at those scrabbling just behind them.

I turn the corner of the building and head towards the commercial dustbins where I'd parked the truck. Then with a small jolt of fear, stop. The setting ahead could come from a Hopper painting: the blandness of a deserted car park, the reassuring shine of a street lamp. A scene of everyday banality, yet one suddenly full of threat and menace. In the butterscotch truck, plainly visible, is the silhouette of a man. My eyes drop to the licence plates. There's no mistake, it's my truck all right. I stand still, unsure what to do, then slowly force myself to breathe out. People who mean you harm do not tend to sit behind the wheel of your car in full view. Your traditional psycho prefers to lie low, only making his presence known once you are driving through the back-water roads of no safe return. Besides, only two people left that meeting before I did and only one of them had been wearing a black cowboy hat.

Duval winds down the window as I approach.

'Get in,' he says pleasantly.

'What do you mean, get in?' I say, much less pleasantly. 'It's my truck!'

'True,' he says, 'but I'm a lousy passenger.'

Slowly, I walk round to the other door, wondering whether this is a good time to resurrect my inner feminist or simply give in to curiosity.

'Where's your truck?'

Duval nods his head out of the window.

'What?' I identify his truck from the line-up of parked cars and squint at it. 'Oh.' The tyres are flat, all four of them. 'Wow . . . what happened? Did someone slash them?'

Just as a blind man develops an enhanced sense of hearing, Duval compensates for his lack of words with an entire range of shoulder shifts and head movements, all of which are variations on the theme of shrug.

'Nora?' I persist.

'Nora would never slash a tyre . . . a throat, maybe, but not a tyre.'

'She looked pretty angry to me.'

'Slashing a tyre is a fool's revenge.' He pats down his shirt for cigarettes. 'Kind of thing a weak person does.'

'What about wrist-breaking? What kind of person does a thing like that?'

The match flares in the darkness of the cab. 'I didn't like his manners.'

'Ah well, that's all right then.' I steal a look at him from the passenger seat as the truck grumbles into life, aware that I seem to be developing weirdly conflicting feelings about this man. I don't trust him, I can't even say I like him – all my instincts tell me he's up to no good, yet . . . I like what he did in the meeting. I liked it a lot. I had been fiercely conscious of his presence throughout the evening and now that he's here, in the car, well the truth is, I'm glad of that too.

'So where are we going?'

'Temerosa. I'll take Benjamín's truck on from there.'

I say nothing, disappointed not to have the opportunity to see where Duval lives, but this is soon superseded by increasing anxiety about his skill behind the wheel. Duval drives like someone who simply doesn't acknowledge the concept of traffic. He steers a haphazard line through every curve with a sort of lazy confidence, oblivious to the possibility that another vehicle might appear round these blind corners at any given moment.

'So why did you go to the meeting?' I ask, my eyes glued to the road ahead.

Pause. 'Curious.'

'And what did you think?'

'They made their point.'

'The people in the town?'

'Some of the men in that room have big cattle ranches on the border. They were plagued by Apache raids in the last century and now it's the Mexicans or the Bureau of Land Management or the government. They're tired of fighting. I can understand that.'

'Hogan's no cattle rancher, he's a dentist.'

Duval draws on his cigarette. 'Last year a nine-month-pregnant woman shot dead an immigrant who entered her house. He was starving and unarmed, she was terrified and alone. This is an emotive issue.'

'So who's side are you on then?'

'Nobody's.'

'But presumably you have some sympathy with people crossing?'

'It's not my concern.'

'How can it not be? Your entire crew is Mexican.'

'That's business.'

'I'm not really sure I believe that.'

'Believe what you like. Mexicans are cheaper and work harder than anyone else.'

'I see. So you're saying you don't care what their issues are.'

'I'm no politician.' He expels cigarette smoke into the night air.

'But you live here, you must have an opinion.'

Even as I say it, though, it occurs to me I don't have one myself. Frankly, I'd never given border crossings much more than a second's thought until this evening. Besides, nowadays it seems like the whole world is on the move. Hideaways, stowaways, refugees, asylum seekers. The terrible images wash over you until you don't even notice them any more: cities of camps built on slivers of boundaries between countries populated by misery. Sangatte, the Channel Tunnel. Destination UK.

Before first coming to Arizona, if I was ever to think about Mexico, it would be to conjure up images of mariachis in silver-threaded sombreros crooning mournful love songs, villains with pebbledash complexions blowing curling smoke from the top of guns, crosses atop churches in white sun-baked towns or braided virginal beauties fleeing banditos through verdant fields of tequila. Mine was the clichéd Mexico of Hollywood's hard-bitten romances: *The Magnificent Seven*, *A Touch of Evil*. Then I saw a movie, *Men with Guns*, in which a professor at a medical university in Mexico City dispatches a bunch of his best students, all filled with the milk of human kindness, into the poor rural communities in the Chiapas region. When they disappear he sets out to find them. His search takes him to sugar-cane plantations and tiny towns in the mountains, lost and forgotten communities where he is met with a world of oppression and hostility. It turns out that all his students had been murdered, the only woman doctor amongst them raped and crucified first.

Nevertheless Mexico looms invitingly on the other side of my mountains, a country to be dipped in and out of at will, but although I've a powerful curiosity to explore it, I've not yet done so, still awaiting I suppose some psychological visa that will allow me to embark on the great untapped adventure I know it represents.

Duval still hasn't answered.

'Come on, Duval.'

'Doesn't matter what I think,' he says finally.

'Why not?'

'Because it's not my problem and it's not yours either.' He stops the truck at the turn-off to Temerosa. 'Listen to me, Alice,' he says roughly. 'I don't know what it is you've come looking for, but whatever it is, don't count on finding it out here.'

I look into his face, but it's impossible to read anything in those dark eyes. It should make me angry, this second veiled warning of his, but it doesn't. I just feel triumphant that after all this time he's finally called me by my first name.

Benjamín has got the children into bed and asleep by the time we reach the cabin. I find him sitting in the corridor upstairs, where he has stationed a chair outside their room like a White House security guard in charge of high-risk diplomats.

'I'm sorry, Benjamín', I whisper. 'It's so late.'

'Noh, Alice, no problem.'

'Someone slashed Duval's tyres.' I squint out of the thin slit of the corridor window. 'He's taking your truck home.' Puzzled, I stare after the red tail lights. 'Benjamín, why is he going that way? Surely you can't get back to the main road that way?'

Benjamín moves away from the window. 'Maybe he left something in the boarding house.'

'Maybe,' I agree, but I go on watching until the tail lights disappear. 'So how were the children. Good?'

'Oh yes, very good.' He breaks into a grin. 'M-E bit me.' He holds up his finger. 'Little M-E,' he says fondly, as though the bite has been the highlight of his week. 'I go home now, Alice, thank you.' He lays his hand briefly on my arm.

'Benjamín, wait . . .'

He hesitates, foot on the top of the stairs, and I ask him the question I've been putting off for weeks.

'Benjamín, you have children, don't you? Children of your own?'

His eyes drop from mine. He touches his jaw then turns and walks slowly down the steps, and because I know the answer already I make no move to stop him.

The big window is shut in my bedroom and the air is dry and stale. The children have stripped off their pyjama tops and their bare skin shines brown against the whiteness of the sheets. They look like they're practising synchronized sleeping – right arms are thrown to one side, left hands shoved under pillows. All four knees are bent upwards and the pyjama shorts they both like to wear are hiked up, revealing one buttock each. Emmy has an eczema scab on her back which has leaked a smear of blood where she's been scratching it, and suddenly, from way out of left field, I feel turned inside out with loneliness. I creep into the bed between the children and hold their sweating bodies close. I blink out into the darkness and picture Benjamín making his way back to his cabin, replacing his children with mine; then, because I don't want to think about it any more, I shut my eyes, but it's no good, my head is filled with one sad image after another. Robert in the restaurant, his head in his hands; my father walking down the beach, a small hunched figure against the grey sea; fat Nora, alone somewhere, nursing a beer and probably minding the jibe about the hog season more than anyone could know. I think of Jack and Emmy forced to see their grandmother behind my back, of Duval steering his truck around the silent curves of the mountain. And right at this moment, the world does not feel like a place where anyone can find happiness. I think about what Duval said and maybe I don't understand what I'm looking for and maybe I won't ever find it here, but I am starting to believe that you don't need to know what you're escaping from to become a fugitive.

15

Jack sleeps like a dead man. If you were to chalk an outline around his body at night, he would still be lying precisely within its boundaries the following morning. Emmy, on the other hand, is not an easy child to share a bed with. On her stomach, her black hair spread across the pillows, her legs drawn up and bent, she is like a big black frog languidly scooting across the surface of a pond, using me as the rock from which, every few minutes or so, she painfully propels herself to a new position. By the time morning comes my eyes are scratchy with tiredness. Mechanically, I herd the children into the truck and off to school but afterwards I can't face returning. Twitchy and cabin-feverish, it's as though all my pioneering aspirations are today distilled down into one primordial urge: to go shopping and buy something I don't need; to do something urban-like and self-indulgent in an attempt to cut this lingering knot of loneliness down to a manageable size. It's not another human being I miss, although it would be nice to have a girlfriend to talk to, or even the moon face of Winfred to be annoyed by. It's this feeling of displacement and not belonging which makes life seem very empty all of a sudden.

Shops in Ague don't open till ten o'clock so I default to the M&M and while away the time before my coffee arrives watching the industrial choreography of trucks drawing in and out of the petrol pumps and feeling vaguely sorry for myself. It's later, though, in the washroom, splashing water on my face, that I see, to my horror, there is a much more immediate crisis to be dealt with. Somehow, I've managed to persuade myself that fresh air and lack of city smog have steadily been transforming me into a wild and natural beauty, a Barbarella of sorts, glowing with good health and youthful vigour – a fantasy easy to sustain on account of the detestable absence of mirrors in the cabin. Instead the face that looks back at me is positively Darwinian. It's taken only these few short months to bypass cave woman and mutate straight back to ape. My eyebrows have all but knitted together in a vicious tangle across my forehead. My hair is a snarled sub-tropical growth of outgrown roots and split ends. Only the skin on my face, now that I've stopped using sun creams so religiously, has lost its customary translucence and acquired a healthy pre-cancerous glow to it. I am less Jane Fonda and more Cousin IT.

'Sure, there's a beauty salon,' Sharleen from Prestcott's Hotel says. 'Other end of town, right by the feed lot.' She pats her own architectured locks coyly. 'Be sure an' ask for Missy.'

I'm dubious, but surely just a trim, and who knows, even a pedicure, might do the trick. The last time I was in Tucson, I actually tried to buy one of those hard-skin scraper things from the pharmacy section in Wal-Mart, but the girl behind the counter informed me they were illegal.

'Only registered podiatrists and pedicurists are allowed to carry 'em.' she said primly, before adding, 'They're very dangerous, you know.'

'*Dangerous?*'

'Oh yes, they're very sharp. We wouldn't be allowed to sell something like that here.'

'But you can buy a gun in this store, right?'

'Sure can,' she chirruped. 'Right over there by the hunting knives.'

'So let me get this straight. I can't buy a scraper, but I could buy a gun and shoot the dead skin off my feet, right?' But she'd looked so bewildered I hadn't the heart to take it further.

As I wrench open the door to Vanillaheads, a great mushroom of hair spray escapes, stinging my eyes and forcing my throat to constrict in protest. The two girls inside wear green pinafores and sport *Dynasty* hair and white stilettos, which add four inches to their height at either end.

'Help ya?' says one, carefully extricating her client from underneath the dryer. When I fail to answer, the other prompts, 'Here for a cut? We do hair and we do colour and we do manicures.' She flips a paw my way and I duly admire her nail extensions, which are exquisitely decorated with tiny star-spangled banners.

It's a small salon, with only four hairdressing chairs. Three of them are occupied, two with clients whose heads are encased in flesh-coloured rubber hats permeated with holes through which selected tresses have been yanked then smeared with bleach, making the women look like burn victims who've lost most of their hair but who are, at least, having a soothing salve applied to their scalps. I panic, and instead ask for directions to the first thing that pops into my head.

'What kind of church?' the girls chorus helpfully. 'There's a First Baptist right round the corner, or a Seven Day Separatist opposite, there's the Methodist over by the Ob/Gyn's office on Portal Street . . .'

'And what about the Church of Jesus Christ of Latter Day Saints, back on up the north side of town?' one of the poor burn victims offers up.

I cruise the streets aimlessly, eventually driving south out of town. A few miles later, I slow the truck down at the sight of an upside-down brown Cadillac and the whirring lights of an ambulance in front of it. A couple of Indians are being administered to by the edge of the road, surrounded by broken beer bottles. One is lying on his side as though fast asleep, the other is having a comical slow-motion fight with a medic who is trying to clamp an oxygen mask to his face. Gingerly, I steer the truck round them then, on a whim, transfer its bulky weight to a random dirt track leading into the hills. The rocks here are the colour of clay and look as though they've had their clammy surfaces scored by Emmy's fork before being baked hard by the sun. The track narrows further and just when I'm thinking it would be better to turn around than risk a quadruple puncture, it splits at a signpost for Wildcat Canyon and I stop the truck, remembering something.

The menu of the M&M is designed as a newspaper, its front page printed with dishes on offer and its inside section a mixture of articles, ads, and one cracking good story with the headline: 'Tucson Finds Hobbit Living in a Warren of Caves', which I had torn off to show the children. Now I pull the crumpled piece of paper out of my pocket and there it is, a tiny ad on the reverse side of the article for 'Wildcat Haircutting'. Out of mild curiosity, I drive on until the track dwindles to a dead end and a splintered B&B sign.

I can't see a Bed and Breakfast anywhere, but like a pig after truffles, I follow an overwhelming smell of frying food, eventually dropping down into a small clearing with two low bungalows and a wooden cabin. The bungalows are identical with four doors apiece and metal numbers nailed to them. There's a definite air of *Texas Chainsaw Massacre* to the whole place and if someone were to casually mention that the letters spelling out BAR above the door of the cabin had been daubed in blood, you wouldn't be in the least surprised.

Inside, a woman sits alone at a yellow formica table, an arrangement of plates in front of her. 'Yup?' she says, without looking up. She is larger than I remember from the meeting, but with the same Bass Buster cap perched high on her head. Her arms are white and blotchy as though they've never been exposed to a ray of sun. Purposefully, they work their way through a round of eggs and steak on a serving dish in front of her. A stack of hash browns as high as a woodpile sits in one bowl and a mountain of battered onion rings in another. Nora's small dimpled hands cut through the steak with ruthless efficiency. She swallows and replaces the cubes of meat in her mouth with unfaltering regularity as though her tongue is a conveyor belt continually transporting food from source to destination.

'A real semen-free zone,' I remember somebody snickering as she'd slammed out of the hall last night.

'You here to check the rooms?' She swings a greasy chin in my direction.

'No, don't worry.' I hover at the door. 'I was just passing by. Didn't mean to interrupt your breakfast.'

'This ain't ma breakfast.' Nora scrapes back her chair. 'It's ma lunch.' Above the door the Budweiser clock reads 10.30 a.m. She plucks a set of keys from a nail on the wall and pushes by me. 'B'sides you're here now, girl, so you may as well look.'

I trot dutifully behind her as she propels herself out of the bar and towards the first of the bungalows. Sticking out of her back pocket is plastic bag full of chewing tobacco. Underneath the baseball hat, Nora's hair reaches to her shoulder blades. Dirty though it is, it strikes me as a rather beautiful colour, pale grey lightened by streaks of almost pure white.

She opens the doors of 1–4 with the same key. The bungalows have been decorated in warm, earthy tones though possibly not at any point during the last thirty years. They smell of thrift shops and are superficially tidy but I notice the trash hasn't been emptied, and when

Nora thumps on the polyester coverlet to demonstrate the quality of the mattress, so much static is let loose I worry the bed might spontaneously combust. The rooms are all identical, notwithstanding small creative differences between the works of art hanging on the walls . . . room 1 has a picture of a startled deer printed on velour; 2, in the same material, an osprey plucking a fish from the rapids of the Colorado River; while 3 features a bobcat which looks as if it's wearing Sony headphones.

'This last one's the biggest.' Nora unlocks number 4. 'It's eight foot by ten, shower's three foot by two. Go ahead, take a look.' She sweeps back the shower curtain and gives the slab of greenish soap stuck to the tiled floor a kick with the toe of her sneaker before standing aside for me to pass. Very quickly, however, it becomes apparent that there is insufficient room for me to do so, thus with a tango of infinite grace and elegance, we both withdraw, advance and side-step until a clear view of the hellhole duly presents itself.

'Nice,' I comment.

'It's fifty-eight dollars twenty for two.' Nora stands, feet apart, hands on hips.

'Fifty-eight twenty. Wow.' I hedge a little longer, not wanting her to think I'm wasting her time. 'How did you arrive at that figure, I mean how did you decide on the twenty cents?'

'Tax.'

'Right, of course. So how much for one person?'

'Fifty-eight dollars twenty.'

'That seems awfully unfair.'

'So git yourself a partner.' She locks up the bungalow, then heads back up the slope. 'Wanna beer?' she throws over her shoulder.

Inside the bar, she plucks a beer from a crate on the floor and tosses it over. 'Shut the door, will ya.' She sits down at the table and gathers the plates of food towards her with both arms. I'm not a big beer drinker, especially at eleven a.m. in the morning, but I snap the can open and take a swig, unsure whether or not I've been officially discharged.

'You were at the meeting last night, weren't you?' I venture.

Nora's mouth opens like a trap door to receive a cold onion ring. 'Folks round here are ignorant and mean.' She chews methodically. 'They'll crap over anybody to keep themselves out of the dirt.' The next onion ring isn't large enough to necessitate the heavy artillery of her teeth. Nora swallows it whole and washes it down with beer. 'It'll come back on 'em, though.' She shoots me a look. 'Sit down, why don't ya? You ain't here for a room so what do you want?'

I slide into the booth. On the plate in front of me the remains of the steak have run aground in a black pond of stagnant blood.

'Well you probably won't believe it, but I was after a haircut.' I haul the M&M menu from my pocket and smooth it out on the table.

The sight of it provokes a snort from Nora. She grabs her beer and sucks noisily at the glass, then clears her throat and tweaks a small amount of escaped mucus from her nose.

'Let me see that.' She snatches the paper and laughs thickly. 'Girlie, I haven't cut hair for twenty years. Which is probably the last time they changed that menu.' She tosses it back across the table. 'Why, the green chilli burger has been special of the week for the last four.'

'I'm sure.' I shrug, feeling stupid. 'I just saw the ad, then I happened to see the sign for Wildcat Canyon and . . .'

'Something wrong with your life that you need a haircut?'

'No, why? Should something be wrong?'

Nora nudges some bread through the grease on her plate. 'I cut hair for fifteen years an' I'll tell ya one thing I learned. Women only cut their hair in times of crisis. Hell, you ever see a woman used to have long hair who gets herself a short back and sides . . . you gotta know she's in trouble.'

'Do you really think that's true?'

'Sure it's true.' She sweeps the dirty plates aside. 'It's somethin' a woman always has the power to do, even when she loses control over everything else. Cuttin' hair is a cry for help.' Nora's eyes thin. 'What is it? . . . Your man bin ignorin' ya?'

'I—'

She waves her hand dismissively. 'I don't wanna know.' She digs into the recess of her backside for the snappy bag of tobacco. 'Want some?' She pinches two fingers-full.

I shake my head. 'At the meeting you said you left out water for immigrants.'

Nora nudges a filament of stray tobacco from her lip back into her mouth then rubs her front teeth. 'There's misery everywhere you look,' she says eventually. 'People dyin', children sufferin'. You can shore up your country with trenches and barbed wire and walls and broken glass on roofs but it only ever leads to one thing and that's more death an' more misery. People need to eat and their families need to eat an' if that makes me a bleeding-heart liberal, so shoot me. Yeah, I put out water, I give medical help when I can and the rest of the folks be damned.' She spits the tobacco onto the plate. 'You Australian?'

'English.'

A small estuary of juice runs down the side of Nora's mouth. She blots it onto the polyester of her shoulder and leans forward across the table. 'I found one once.'

'Found what?'

'A Mexcin, an Indian. From Honduras or Guatemala, hell them brown folk all look the same from down south. He was sitting under a tree – legs all hiked up, elbows restin' on his knees.' Nora lifts the cap off her head, punches its cavity before putting it back on again. 'Jes' sitting in a natural position, head back against the trunk, like he was takin' a rest from the sun,' she laughs mirthlessly, ''cept out here in summer, there ain't no rest from the sun.'

'What happened? Did you bring him here?'

'Didn't seem to be no bones broken,' she says matter-of-factly, 'leastways not as far as I could tell. Didn't seem to be nuthin' wrong with him at all 'cept he'd tried eating cactus and his mouth was all bloody from the spikes, that and some kind of animal, mice or rats mebbe, had started eatin' away at his hands.'

'Oh.' I finally understand what she's saying.

Nora shakes her head. 'Buried him right where he died, under that tree.'

'So do you go out looking for people in trouble, or do they turn up here?'

'They're too scared to come here. Naa, I do shifts with my buddy Milt and some others. We find 'em, water 'em, let 'em do a bit of work round the place and mostly they're grateful for it, though I had one bunch turn up recently and flat demand I rustle 'em up some eggs. Had a good mind to call the Border Patrol,' her mouth turns down, 'for all the use they'd be. Bunch of cock-suckin' losers.'

'They seem pretty efficient to me.' It's my turn to snort now. 'They've had me up twice already for speeding.'

Nora's eyes narrow to nickel slots in her puffy face. 'Border Patrol?'

'Yes.'

'You sure of that?'

'Why?'

'Border Patrol ain't authorized to ticket people.'

'What do you mean?'

'Speeding's a cop's business.'

She sees the look on my face and guffaws. 'Girlie, there are more fun ways of gettin' screwed round here than handin' your money over to the Border Patrol.'

Goddammit, Winfred, I think wearily, is nobody out here what they seem?

'So what about that haircut of yours?' Nora is still wiping tears of laughter from the corner of her eyes.

I tell her I was only looking for a trim, mention split ends—

'Turn around, I'll do it for you,' she says then chortles at my expression 'I won't snip your ears off, girl, if that's what you're afraid of.'

It's exactly what I'm afraid of, but it's too late. Nora's already fetching scissors from behind the bar and when she starts to rake over my scalp with a manky comb, I don't query whether she oughtn't to wet my hair first, I don't demand a copy of *Vogue* to read, or check to see whether leave-in conditioner will be applied sparingly to my tips because, frankly, I'm thinking to hell with it – today just can't get any more Kafka-esque.

Nora combs and snips and combs and snips. And although I can smell the tobacco on her fingers, she's surprisingly gentle. My sleepless night begins to manifest itself as an ache behind the eyes so I close them – the smell of the food and the noise of the scissors and the mustiness of the air all having a strangely soporific effect.

'You asleep?' Nora taps the scissors against the side of my head.

I deny it but she merely chuckles. 'Always had a light touch,' she boasts.

'Why did you give up then?'

Nora tilts my head away from her. 'Saw a TV programme once about an earthquake in Turkey. There were hardly any survivors but they found one, a woman, still alive, buried under a concrete slab. So they cut away this slab real careful, then they dug with their bare hands till they could see her, an' there she was! Lyin' flat on her side, an' she was fine, jes' fine, not a drop of blood on her – but still they couldn't pull her out.'

'Why not?'

'Cos she had this long black hair and her hair was trapped. There was this old man helpin' with the rescue operations and he finds himself apologizin' to her. "We can't get you out, I'm sorry," – like he's gonna have to leave her there, so she gets freaked an' asks, "Why can't you get me out?" An' he says, "Cos your hair is trapped."

' "Go ahead and cut my hair," she says, but he says he can't. "I can't cut your beautiful hair," he says, and starts crying like a baby . . .'

Nora stands in front of me and squints at my face. 'Anyways, you're done and there's no charge for it. Now there's a haircuttin' place in town right close to the Baptist Church – ain't nothin' special, but if you git home and don't like what you see, you can go there and pay for a repair job.'

'Thanks,' I tell her, squinting into the circus mirror reflection of the kettle and amazed and rather grateful not to have a mohawk. 'Thanks a lot.'

16

Emmy wakes screaming in the middle of the night.

'Shut up, Emmy,' Jack is moaning as I reach her bedside. 'Shut up, shut up.'

'Shh, go back to sleep, Jack.'

'Oh, God,' he explodes burrowing under the pillow.

I put a hand to Emmy's forehead. She's burning up and the sheets are soaked. Worried, I carry her writhing body to my room and hold her fast while I grapple with the child-proof cap of the Calpol. I force the spoon into her mouth mid-scream and the sticky pink lava oozes out, hopelessly gumming up her hair. Most of the next spoon trickles down her throat and she momentarily stops crying in order to choke.

'What is it Emmy?' I whisper. 'Does it hurt anywhere? Is it your tummy? What is it?'

But she just starts screaming again. On the FeverScan her temperature reads 104. I sit, holding her on the bed, trying to keep calm. Children always have high temperatures, they can shoot up and down within the space of minutes. It means nothing. It's just a fever, flu . . . Dear

God, why is she still screaming? Her arms flail out and she clutches her head like a mad thing.

'Emmy, does your neck hurt?' I say urgently. 'Emmy.' I snap on the light, watching to see if she flinches, then pull up her nightdress to look for a rash. The one that either does or doesn't go when you press a glass to it. Oh, God, meningitis, whose symptoms are as well known to a parent as the Lord's prayer. This happened once before, when Jack was small. The doctor who came round had eyes rimmed black with tiredness. 'If a child's temperature reacts in any way to Calpol, it's not meningitis,' he'd said. 'It's the only way to tell.'

I sit through the next hour, biting my lip, holding Emmy close, trying to think of ways to endure the screaming calmly, praying for her to cool down, praying for her to suddenly pass out in the muck sweat of a fever peaked, but as the minutes tick by she becomes increasingly fitful. I put my hand on her head for the hundredth time. She's hot. Really hot. Each consecutive black square on the FeverScan lights up green and I try to quell my rising panic. If Calpol doesn't bring the temperature down within the hour, you're supposed to call the doctor. I look at Emmy and snap out of my daze. Right, I think. Call the doctor. *Call the doctor.*

But I have no doctor.

'What is it?' Jack is standing sleepily in the doorway. 'What's wrong with her? Why doesn't she stop screaming?'

'I don't know,' I say shakily. 'Look, stay with her, okay, make sure she doesn't fall off the bed.' I run downstairs and find the number for the medical centre in Ague, but it's answered by only the most cursory of messages. The clinic is shut until nine a.m. No night service. It's two a.m. I dial my GP's number in London and page the night doctor, but the system won't allow me to punch in an overseas calling code. 'Mummy!' Jack is shouting, near hysterical. 'Mummy, come back. Mummy, please!' I race upstairs, Duval's warnings flooding back to me. What if she's been bitten by that spider he was talking about, the brown recluse? What if, right now, her flesh is beginning to soften and turn necrotic? What if she has that mouse disease, Hunter's, apparently so prevalent round here? I remember the feel of the dead mouse under my foot our first night. How many times have I let the children scramble through the cabins, breathing in the deadly ammonia of stale droppings? Dear God, what if she's been bitten by a snake and no one noticed? Except I'm being ridiculous. I check their bedroom and mine every night. Of course she hasn't been bitten by a snake and I curse Duval for filling my head with so much paranoid terror I can barely think straight. In the bedroom Jack is staring down at Emmy on the bed. Her screams are shorter now, high-pitched, urgent. I strip off her nightdress. She's boiling.

'Go get a wet towel, Jack,' I order. He stands stupefied. 'It's okay.' I steady my voice. 'Use cold water, but do it now.'

I check her body, but who can tell if there's a rash amongst Emmy's plethora of scratches, her eczema scabs, her patches of dry skin and bruises? Who could say if she had a rash, had been bitten by a spider or simply neglected by a crappy mother? Jack races back with the towel and I sponge her down then wrap her loosely in the sheet.

'Turn off the sun,' she moans.

'It's just the light, baby.'

'Turn off the sun, the wolf is coming,' she screams, and then, without warning, she convulses, her arms and legs spasm and her head jerks from side to side.

'Emmy!' I shout. 'Emmy! EMMY!' I want to shake her, to restrain her, do something, anything to stop it, but I don't dare. Her eyes turn back into her head. She goes suddenly rigid then seems to relax in my arms, her eyes closed.

'Jack, get your shoes and a jumper.'

'No, no.' He stands white with fear, sobbing hysterically.

'Go!' I shout and he turns and runs. I throw on my own clothes and grab my bag. Benjamín will help us. Benjamín will know where to go.

Benjamín doesn't answer the door. I bang again, shout his name, but the cabin is silent, empty. Back in the truck Jack sits ramrod straight, holding Emmy in her blanket as though she is something putrid and dangerous which might explode at any given moment.

'She's going to die, isn't she?' he says dully.

I will myself to think straight. Tucson. I'll have to get her to Tucson. There'd be a hospital there, but where, in God's name? Tucson is seventy miles away and who to ask in those deserted streets? It would be better to drive to Ague and raise help there. I sit, frozen with indecision, and then it comes to me, the thread of a memory. Ague. The town meeting. I close my eyes; see the woman with the turquoise belt buckle, hear her voice. Her two boys, problems with the bars, problems with drugs. Yes. That was it! Mexican pharmacists were no better than drug pushers. Everything was available over the counter. Pharmacies across the border were open twenty-four hours a day – and where there were pharmacies, there would be doctors.

The Arizona sky is a navy blue, speckled with diamanté. I drive carefully, stunned by how unprepared I'd been for something to go this wrong. Every few seconds I look over at Emmy. Her head is sunk onto Jack's shoulder, her eyes still shut. At least she's conscious, making little mewling noises at regular intervals that tear my heart in two. Oh, God, how fragile life is out here . . . Oh, God, let it not be meningitis. Let it not be a brain seizure.

Nogales, Arizona, is deserted. The motorway flies over the top of the town, but I am the only moving thing on it. Below, billboards for the Holiday Inn Express and Best Western Hotels flash by. Doggedly, I follow the big green signs for Mexico, past a Burger King, a McDonald's, round a concrete-lined mini roundabout. I have no idea what to expect in the way of a border, but as I draw up to it I see it's a huge official thing. Five lines of car checkpoints and customs buildings on either side. To the left traffic is creeping into the US from Mexico. I veer right. Two uniformed officials stand at one of the checkpoints talking to a truck driver, and it's only now, right this second that it occurs to me that I do not have my passport and that I'm bound to need it, but before I have a chance to work out what to say, the car in front of me moves ahead through the barrier and I'm already winding down my window.

'Nationality?' the customs official asks; he casts no more than a routine eye over the children.

I gulp, say American, and I'm through.

Nogales, Mexico. Where am I? Where to go? The road takes me alongside a monstrous green wall – the border actual, I guess, made of corrugated iron, rusted and patched in innumerable places and crowned with two foot of wire netting angled inwards and held in place by metal rods, making it impossible to clamber over. One poster depicting white crosses and unmarked graves reads 'Don't go down a road when you can't come back'. Another with a skull and crossbones instructs 'Beware the "Polleros". *¡No les pagues con tu vida!*' written in Hammer Horror lettering with blood dripping from it.

There is nightlife in Nogales, Mexico. Men hang in doorways and step out of shadows. An emaciated drunk leans against a telegraph pole, drinking some home-made brew through a straw stuck into a polythene bag. A car stands stationary, its front door open. The toe of a white ostrich-skin boot taps on the dirt of the road. When I slow down to ask for directions a man looms out of the darkness and, startled, I accelerate again, down to the end of the street, turn right onto a main strip of restaurants and shops and there, barely half a block away, is the comforting white and green neon cross of a pharmacy.

The girl behind the counter is young and heavily made up. Underneath her white coat everything shines and flashes, the tiny sequins and pearls on her boob tube, the gold rings on her fingers. Even her crenellated black hair is covered in a glossy lacquer.

'*Hola.*' She smiles.

'*Necesito un médico.*' I hold out Emmy in my arms like a religious offering. '*Está enferma, una fiebre, muy alta,* a fever.'

The girl's eyes flick to the little television on which Tom and Jerry, dubbed in Spanish, are walloping each other with mallets.

'I need a doctor, *un médico.* Do you speak English?'

Her eyes focus on Emmy.

'Papa! she calls.

An older man, also in a pharmacist's coat, materializes from the back.

'*Necesito un médico.*' I pull a bundle of American bills from my pocket. '*Emergencia.*' I'm close to tears. The man listens to my strangulated Spanish then calmly picks up the phone.

'I will call someone.'

'You speak English!'

'Of course,' he says. He puts his hand on her forehead. 'She's hot.'

I tell him she had some kind of fit, but that I don't know what is wrong with her. Emmy is awake now and crying in a pitifully hoarse voice.

'Emmy,' I beg, 'what is it, where does it hurt?' I check her chest yet again. 'Do you think it's meningitis?'

'*¿La meningitis?*' The pharmacist makes a clucking noise against his teeth with his tongue. 'Noh, I don't think so.'

'What then?'

'The doctor will tell you.' He motions me to a chair and says something quietly to his daughter. I look down at Emmy fretfully, her skin has a greenish tinge to it, her eyes are two muddy hollows, then I catch sight of my own face in the mirror and realize it's just the harsh strip lighting of the pharmacy washing us both with its tubercular glow. Out in the street, music blares from a boombox. The pharmacist's daughter returns with two paper cones of Coke. She hands one to me and the other to Jack.

'It's going to be okay, Jack.' I give him a one-armed hug.

'Can I have a quarter to weigh myself?' Jack says.

The doctor is large and sweaty with a small moustache that curls under his nose and droops down either side of his mouth lending him a mournful expression. He shakes my hand limply and introduces himself as Louis. He makes little grunting noises as I relay each of Emmy's symptoms to him, examining her with an air of tired resignation. As a character in a movie, he is the abortionist who has been struck off, the alcoholic local doctor who digs bullets from the shoulders of heroes with a blunt instrument and a slosh of whisky to dull the pain. 'I also have two children,' he remarks conversationally, hooking the stethoscope into his ears.

'That's nice.'

'Yes, I like it,' he agrees amiably. 'My wife is a very good mother and an excellent housekeeper, she mops the floor five times a day.'

'Oh, well.' That's a lot. I can't take my eyes off Emmy's face.

'To me it looks clean after the first time, but I know

the rules.' He bends over Emmy's chest. 'Women are always right. Please . . . turn her round.'

'Is she okay?'

He puts a stethoscope to Emmy's back. 'Did you take her to the doctor before?'

I go through the whole saga. The medical centre had been closed, Tucson had been too far.

'Ahhh,' he says, 'you live in America,' and I'm reminded that I am now in a different country. 'You are very fortunate.' He pulls gently down on Emmy's chin to open her mouth. 'You know what they say, "Poor Mexico, so close to the US, so far from God."' He shines a torch into the cavity of Emmy's throat. His hands are soft and hairless, small as a child's. 'In America you make money but you're on your own. In Mexico you are poor, but you are subsidized.'

'You speak really good English.'

'I had US residency once.'

'So why don't you work on the other side?'

He sighs weightily. 'I lost it when they bust me for running drugs.'

'Oh.'

'Hey, it was only marijuana.' He looks affronted. 'Everybody does it, but I spent time in a federal prison. If they catch me on the wrong side of the border I go back to jail.' He leans his hands heavily on his knees to stand up, then says something to the pharmacist, who begins rifling through the stacked shelves of small boxes behind the counter.

'Is that it?' I look from one to the other. 'Are you finished?'

'Finished? Yes.'

'So what's wrong with her?'

'She has an ear infection.'

'An ear infection! Is that all? Are you sure?'

'Quite sure.'

'But it can't be – her temperature was so high, and the fit, I mean, it was really scary and I thought . . .'

Louis pats me clumsily on the arm. 'Fever is maligned and much misunderstood. The fever is to show you her ear infection, but the infection makes her dehydrated and dehydration forces up the fever. If the temperature is high enough she can have a little seizure, but I don't think she will have another.'

The pharmacist gives him a bottle of banana-coloured liquid.

'*Antibiótico*,' Louis says. 'She must take this three times a day, after she eats.' He smiles, seeing my hesitation. 'You can trust me. She will be all right. Can you pay me twenty dollars?'

'Of course.' I'd happily have signed over the deeds to Temerosa.

'If you need anything for your daughter, you can come back or ring me. We will post everything to you direct.'

I thank him and pocket the business card he offers.

'Take your daughter home,' he waves in the general direction of the street, 'and think of us over on the other side sometimes.'

I strap the children back into the car. For a second I wish Robert was with me, just to have someone to take responsibility, so I could sit in the back and hold on to my daughter and keep her safe, but at the same time I know he would never have agreed to crossing the border, there would have been exhaustive arguments and wasted minutes and who knows what might have happened, who knows . . .

I steer the truck across town following 'To the USA' signs but as I turn left to the border, I realize that while getting out of the USA might have been easy, getting back in is going to be another matter entirely. Instead of empty checkpoints, hundreds of cars are backlogged into six or seven lanes, creating not only a massive gridlock but also a raging night economy to service it. Street kids are everywhere, sidling through the gaps in the lanes, tapping on car windows and offering trays of gum and noxious-looking sweets in plastic bags. Some, so grubby it looks as if their bare skin has been rubbed with a dirty tyre, advance towards the windscreen, brandishing filthy cloths and mud-streaked water buckets. Parallel to the road, Mexican soldiers carrying rifles patrol the railway with dogs. Behind them the border rises up, green and menacing into the hills. There's an intangible crackle and sense of urgency in the air. A cripple in a wheelchair, head far too big for his wasted body, expertly manoeuvres his way through the aisles, one hand extended casually, as though money might accidentally drop into it from the Good Lord above. Street vendors offer slices of watermelon sprinkled with red chilli, bottles of Santa Maria purified water and plastic cups of Jell-O. Under the awnings of closed shops, hawkers sell garish velour towels printed with images of virgins and saints and the Last Supper. As I edge the truck into the queue, one beckons. 'Come on, baby,' he croons, 'everything you like is here, I bring it over?'

I shake my head.

'Noh?' He grins. 'Okay then, baby, I wait for choo all day then maybe you come back tomorrow, huh?' I give him a thumbs-up and swiftly wind up the window just as a girl's face appears, pale, Western-looking. Cautiously, I wind down the window again.

'Help me,' she begs. 'I've been robbed.' She holds up a bag with a knife slash through the bottom. 'They took money! My passport! I can't get across the border. I need to call the American embassy, get back to my children. Please, just a few dollars?'

It feels like a scam, but she's an American, and in trouble, no doubt about that.

'Look, I haven't got a passport either,' I say half-heartedly. 'You could come with me.'

The girl's eyes flick to the children. 'Just give me some money, lady.' She rakes her nails up and down skinny arms. An addict. I fumble in my bag and thrust a couple of dollars out of the window.

'That it?' Her eyes are flinty. 'Haven't you got more?'

I stammer an apology but she just spits on the ground and slips into the next lane.

Only three cars in front of us now. Papers and passports are being passed backwards and forwards, car trunks being opened and checked. If I hadn't been able to talk my way out of a speeding ticket, I haven't got much chance of getting through this. I think of Winfred ripping me off twice and, wondering whether a bribe might be in order, surreptitiously transfer my bag to my lap. I'm not exactly au fait with the going rate for bribing officials in Nogales, let alone the methodology, but surely it will need to be handled subtly, the money passed over with skilful sleight of hand and a knowing look. Already the car in front is being waved through the barrier and I'm so busy siphoning the last few bills out of my wallet and stowing them up my sleeve that I misjudge the distance to creep forwards and overshoot the line. It can't be by more than a few inches but you'd think I'd come roaring through the checkpoint with a hand grenade in my hand and the pin in my teeth for the reaction it provokes.

'Whaddayathink you're doing!' screeches the customs officer. 'Get back over the line, GET BACK!' He's a chunky American with freckled skin and bulbous eyes showing a little too much white around the pupil. I hastily reverse. 'No, not that far! Move forwards!'

I jerk forward again until I'm about an inch from where I first stopped.

'Do you think this barrier is a joke?' He punches a button and a line of spikes shoot out of the ground right in front of the wheels. 'Do you want to get yourself killed? It's dangerous up here! The line is for your own security!' He jumps out of his box and stalks over to the truck.

In normal circumstances such officiousness would have me giggling behind my hand, but with no passport, no weapon of identity and dressed still in my pyjamas with a sweatshirt on top, I cower behind the steering wheel while he takes a long stick with a mirror stuck at one end and pokes it up the truck's backside.

He straightens up. 'There's a lot of mud on this vehicle. Where have you been driving it?'

'In Arizona. I live—'

'Citizenship?' he interrupts.

'American?' I mumble hopefully.

'Passport.' He holds out his hand.

My heart sinks. 'Look, I don't mean my passport's American, I mean my passport is, in fact, English, it's just that I'm living—'

'Passports,' he repeats. 'All of them.'

I chance an explanation. I mention doctors and fits and spasms, reiterate just how truly close to life and death this whole episode has been, turn round and point at poor little sick Emmy who needless to say is now sleeping soundly, her fever making her look as pink and healthy as a baby flamingo.

'So that's why I haven't got the passports with me,' I conclude.

'Have you checked your bag?'

'No, but they're not—'

'Check your bag, please, ma'am.'

'Look, they're not in my bag, I know they're not there.'

'Are you saying you deliberately entered Mexico without a passport?'

'Well no, I mean, yes, but—'

'Mexico is an international border. Crossing an international border without a passport is a violation of US law.'

'I understand, it's just that – as I said – it was an emergency.'

'Ma'am.' He takes a step forward. 'You drive into Mexico without a passport – you don't come out again.'

'Look, officer, can I just give you . . . *this?*'

He looks at the crumpled twenty in my hand. 'What's that?'

'Oh, this?' I look at the note as though relatively surprised to see it myself, 'Well now, that's a . . . well, it's uh . . . money, actually . . .'

'What's it for?'

'It's, uh, well . . .'

'Ma'am,' he says very loudly, 'I hope that money isn't intended as some kind of bribe?'

I positively chortle with laughter and shrink further down into my seat. 'Goodness me, of course not! It's for, uh . . . you know . . . uh . . . for the toll!'

'Pull over.'

'Okay,' I say wearily.

I turn on the engine and press down on the accelerator. A hand slams flat on the windscreen. With a look of utter contempt, the guard backs into the booth, presses the button and the spikes disappear into the ground. He waves at another official. 'No passport.' He shakes his head, as though this is the most incredible thing he's ever heard in his career as a US customs official. I mean, problem with a passport! Geez, can you believe that such a thing could ever happen at an international border?

'What's going on, Mummy?' Jack says in a small voice.

*

'This must happen all the time, right . . .' Apprehensively, I follow the new official into the customs building, Emmy in my arms and Jack tagging along at my heels. 'There's a mechanism for dealing with this kind of thing, I assume? I mean, people must get their passports stolen every day?'

'No biggie, ma'am,' the new official says kindly. He presses a button and the elevator doors open into a waiting room of sorts. A long counter at one end is divided by a perspex barrier behind which more agents are rifling through filing cabinets and checking paperwork. 'Wait here,' he says, pointing at an unoccupied chair.

I look around. The walls are painted an anodyne cream, lending the room a hospital-like air. Pinned alongside framed pictures of Bush and Cheney are various notices on immigration, the simian features of an FBI most wanted and warnings of the dire penalties of drug smuggling. A dozen people are waiting to be seen, all Mexican. A young couple holding hands. Two wrinkled men in cowboy hats and a teenage boy who leers at us with the burning, unblinking eyes of a junkie. A thickset Mexican with a shaved head and ears like kidney bowls stomps by, trousers tucked into black military boots, his navy uniform straining over every inch of his body. A walkie-talkie strapped to his waist crackles with some kind of code. 'Three-twenty activity . . . south . . . two-seventy . . .'

Our friendly official reappears and asks me for picture ID and I go through the whole story once again. Agent Harrigan, I read off his badge.

'Not even for the kids?'

'Nothing. I'm sorry.'

Is there anyone I can call, he asks, who will bring the passports to Nogales? And I think of Benjamín, but even if I had the capability of reaching him, I have no idea of his exact legal status.

'No.'

He returns to the telephone. I haul Jack onto a chair and slump down in the empty seat next to him, Emmy heavy in my arms. I watch the clock as fifteen minutes pass, then another fifteen. Emmy's eyes flutter open. 'Mummy, Mummy,' she says, 'I want you to buy me a blanket a soft one for a five-year-old girl like me and I want you to give it to me so I can sleep with it and cuddle it and not be scared so much any more.' I look down at her dirty face, at the tiny clusters of broken veins visible beneath her skin and shake myself into action.

Agent Harrigan is still on the phone.

I poke my finger in his arm. 'Excuse me, what's happening?'

He holds a finger to his lips, but I am not to be shushed.

'Look, there must be a system for a situation like this. What do you do with people who've had their passport stolen, for instance?'

He places his hand over the phone. 'Your passport hasn't been stolen, ma'am. This is a case of wilful violation.'

Wearily I begin again. Emmy's fit, my headlong panic, the passports being left at home. I describe their exact whereabouts – on the bookshelf in the bedroom – hoping that the sheer mundanity of detail might reassure him. But no. I try to keep my cool, to control the prickle of sweat breaking out over my body. I try to convince him that if he will only let me go home, I can myself fetch the passports and bring them back later on in the day.

'But ma'am,' he says as patiently as he can, 'without a passport we can't let you go home.'

At which point, all the repressed fear and frustration of the night begin to rise uncontrollably through my veins like the mercury inside Emmy's thermometer, until finally I see red.

The man sitting behind the desk bears the faintest scars of teenage acne. His black hair is wavy and greying at the temples and he's handsome in an old-fashioned, rakish sort of a way.

'Yes, how many?' He speaks quietly into the receiver. 'Keep the men there for another hour . . . yes . . .'

Agent Harrigan herds us into the room then hastily backs out like a veterinarian assistant delivering some wild creature, a bobcat or deranged hyena, into the custody of somebody more qualified to use a stun gun. Still fired up, I'm tempted to deliver a parting snap, perhaps even sink my teeth into the beefy region of his upper arm, but I know when not to push my luck. The desk in front of us is ordered but not without personal touches. A photograph frame, a bronze statue of Degas's 'Little Ballerina', a gold name slide which reads Emilio Chavez . . . and suddenly I get a sting of recognition. Of course, Chavez, the Mexican-looking official up on stage at the Ague town hall meeting.

'No . . .' he sighs, 'I will speak to the family myself . . .' He places the receiver back in its station, then presses his fingers to the bridge of his nose as if to squeeze out a headache. 'Mrs Coleman . . .' he begins.

'Look—' I say aggressively, but he holds up his hands.

'You want to go home, I understand.' He studies the sheet of paper on the desk. 'Arlington Road, London.' He looks up. 'You're a long way from home, Mrs Coleman.'

I nod. Tears prick my eyes.

'This phone call concerned another young woman also a long way from home, an Ezme Santega?' he continues conversationally, as though I might have come across her somewhere, a dinner party perhaps. 'Ezme is an illegal immigrant who has been working in Tucson. In less than two years she earned enough money to pay a coyote fourteen hundred dollars to bring her brother across the border to join her but he never arrived. Instead the coyote contacted her and said her brother was being ransomed. She sent more money. Still he didn't appear. She eventually sent all the money she had earned or could possibly borrow from her family, her neighbours, from other immigrants who were prepared to help. Still he didn't appear. By the time she called us this evening, she didn't care about being deported, she just wanted her brother back. Two hours ago, I sent men to the safe house outside Nogales where he was being held. Inside we found Kalashnikov casings and pools of blood. I very much doubt we will ever find the body of Ezme's brother.'

'Why would they kill him if she sent the money?' It feels surreal to be having this conversation in the wee small hours of the morning with a Mexican who looks like Errol Flynn and talks like Tom Ridge.

'Who knows? Perhaps less trouble to kill him than deliver him.' He smiles at Jack who is slumped in his chair, raccoon-eyed with tiredness.

'People tend to think of us as the bad guys, Mrs Coleman, but the last thing my agents are here to do is to hound women and children. Unfortunately, this border – any border – is home to unscrupulous smugglers of both human and narcotic cargoes and it is our job to apply the law. In your case the law stipulates that you should stay in Mexico until you either get hold of your existing passport or receive a new one.'

'But that's ridi—'

'I'm aware of the irony of your situation,' he says gently. 'You cannot get your passport if we don't allow you access to it.' His fingers brush the photograph frame on the desk. 'A sick child is a frightening thing for any parent.'

'May I?' I turn the frame towards me. Three children, in Sunday best, photographed against a backdrop of an azure sky and fluffy cumuli.

'Ana, Rosa and Alfredo. They live with their mother in California.'

'Oh . . . I'm sorry.'

'Don't be, I see them quite often.' He indicates the sleeping Emmy. 'What was wrong with your little girl?'

'Just an ear infection, but she had a fit, I panicked.'

'She's pretty,' he says. He opens the drawer in his desk and brings out a sweet which he hands to Jack.

'I'm told there is nobody you can contact who will

bring your passport here, but do you have someone local who might vouch for you?'

I think of Duval, the heckler's wrist twisted in his hand. 'What about Jeff Hogan,' I remember suddenly, 'would he do?'

'Jeff Hogan?' Emilio Chavez looks surprised.

'He's my neighbour at Temerosa. He asked me to come to the meeting in Ague you spoke at last week.'

'So,' Chavez looks thoughtful, 'you are the new owner of Temerosa.'

'Do you know it?' I take the sweet from Jack, who is struggling to pull off the wrapper.

'I know it well. My agents used to drive up that road quite often before it was closed.'

'What road? The road isn't closed.'

'There's an old mining road out in the desert. It's not much more than a track, but it used to take you round the mountain and almost to the border. Unfortunately, a car was washed away by flash flooding a couple of years ago. A whole family died in the accident. They closed it after that.'

'How awful.'

'The road was treacherous. Built across several old mining washes. There were other incidents. It should have been closed years earlier.'

'And it originates in the town?' I try to picture where Chavez means, distractedly delivering the sweet back into Jack's waiting hand.

'Not any more. It's been reclaimed by the desert, but we think the mountain track is used by coyotes, drug smugglers —'

'Oh yuk.' Jack spits the sweet straight out of his mouth.

'Jack!'

I hastily pick the chewed mess up off the floor. 'Jack!' I hiss.

Chavez chuckles.

Emmy stirs and opens her eyes. 'My throat is wrinkled.'

Chavez pushes back his chair, his face softening. 'Take your children home, Mrs Coleman, and get some sleep. Please bring your passports, along with your green immigration forms within forty-eight hours.'

'Thank you.' I push myself out of the chair. Grab Jack's hand.

'Park in the gas station on the US side of the border, come through on foot and then ask for me downstairs.'

'I will. Thanks again.'

'You're a long way from anyone out there,' Chavez remarks. He hands me a card. 'If you need help of any kind, I want you to know that you can call me.'

17

It's nearly four a.m. by the time we pass Benjamín's cabin, but there is still no truck outside. I get the children into bed and throw myself down beside them, falling quickly into a fitful sleep. A face looms at the window of my consciousness, the American girl with her slashed handbag. 'I'm Ezme Santega,' she says, 'help me.' She drops her eyes with a shy smile, but when she looks up again her features have changed and now it's my daughter who is stretching out her arms to me. 'I'm Emmy,' she begs, 'help me,' then her mouth twists evilly and she throws a bucket of dirty water straight at my face. I wake with a start.

Emmy lies next to me, arms and legs spread across the sheets like a starfish on the beach. Her head is still hot to touch. I press the thin thermometer to her skin. The first few windows turn yellow then slowly green. The last square remains reassuringly black. I close my eyes again but the events of the night keep playing out behind them on eternal loop and eventually I give up and wander down to the kitchen, taking a blanket off the bed to keep warm.

midnight cactus

I wait for the water to boil, staring listlessly out of the window. How differently this could have all turned out. How close to disaster we had been. I press my forehead against the cold glass feeling numb with exhaustion and anticlimax then, for want of anything better to do, pull the brimming garbage bag from its bin and open the back door. The sky is the colour of pewter, the trunks of the trees like charcoal sketches beneath it. In an hour or so the sun will be up. I stow the bag in the big trash container and squash the lid back on top – and then I hear it. The growl of an engine. I stiffen, paranoid suddenly that we might have been followed home. Kalashnikovs, kidnap, blood on the floorboards and Emilio Chavez shaking his head sorrowfully: 'I don't suppose anyone will ever find the bodies of those poor Colemans.'

The noise of the engine grows louder. I press quickly against the wall as a truck rattles by then stare after it through the rising dust. Maybe it's Benjamín, heading home, a six-pack of beer on the seat beside him. Maybe it's Duval, once again steering along the curves of the Temerosa road at an unsociable hour. But either way, why from the direction of the boarding house? There is nothing beyond Temerosa but mountain and desert except . . . except, of course, that's not true, is it? There's an old road through those mountains, Chavez had said, one used by coyotes and smugglers, and I picture Duval's tail lights disappearing towards the boarding house the night of the Ague meeting. Maybe Duval had left something behind, Benjamín had suggested, and maybe he had, but in retrospect I wish I'd investigated further, taken action of some kind.

So now I do.

I pull on my gumboots and run after the truck, rank with suspicion. Round the first corner, then the second. I can taste the dust in my mouth, feel it stinging my eyes. The sound of the engine cuts out and I freeze then glance back towards the cabin. I dare not leave Emmy more than a few minutes, but I *have* to see, I *have* to know. I creep towards the next bend, keeping close to the trunks of the oaks, and peer round.

My heart pounds against my ribcage. The truck is at a standstill, its driver's door open and serving as a partial screen for the figures standing behind it. Two men, one wearing a cowboy hat. They seem to be arguing over something and I realize there is a third figure between them, shorter – a woman, I think instinctively. I strain my eyes to see better in the half light. Yes, Duval and Benjamín, unmistakably, and whatever their argument they appear to be settling it. Duval gently pushes the woman over to Benjamín. She stumbles, but Benjamín catches her arm and, pulling a backpack onto his shoulders from the bed of the pickup, he pushes the woman quickly in front of him along the track to his cabin. I wait, still motionless, until Duval climbs behind the wheel and rolls off, then I turn and run back along the road, my head whirling.

What the hell were they up to? Drugs? Prostitution? Smuggling? But apart from tonight's clandestine meeting, what was there tangible to go on other than the tension that has been building up in the town like a storm that will not break? It's the Mexican workers with their whispers and veiled looks that have made me the most uneasy. It's the fear of the boy with the cut finger. I close my eyes and remember touching him on the shoulder, my shock at the different face under that red baseball hat – and then something catches in my throat.

Back inside the cabin I check on the still-sleeping children, then scoop the packs of photographs from the kitchen drawer and lay them on the table, making a line for each individual worker. They're all there, Black Jeans, Gold Bling, Bank of Texas T-shirt, Red Baseball Cap, stacked in rows like a game of patience, all as normal and familiar as can be, except, except . . . not.

I begin to feel sick. It's not the fact that the faces of the workers have changed over the weeks. Builders come and go, different expertise is required, other jobs beckon. What's making my stomach churn is that the clothes these different men are wearing have remained steadfastly the same.

'*Ola*, Alice.' Benjamín hovers in the doorway.

My eyes graze over the woman standing beside him. She's short and heavy-boned, with a full mouth spread with red lipstick and a face directed at her feet.

'This is Dolores,' Benjamín says. Behind them the morning is hot, blue. The distant mountains blurred in haze. A bird is croaking somewhere near by. Upstairs the children sleep on. It's Saturday today. No school, no Duval, no workers.

'She is my cousin,' he adds, hopping from one foot to the other.

Of course she is, I want to say; and please refer to the 'Idiot' tattooed on my forehead.

'Alice?'

I've still not spoken at this point and Benjamín has noticed – oh, not that I'm angry and feeling betrayed by him, just that I'm not my regular nice-as-pie self, and it's making him twitchy.

'Dolores came on the bus yesterday!' He begins over-compensating furiously. 'She has been to see her family in Mexico! She lives in California!' He pulls on his moustache and scratches the back of his neck. 'But now she will stay with me for a while, and she will work for you!'

'I'm sorry, what?'

'Yes. In the cabin. For a while,' he confirms.

'Doing what?'

'She will clean for you.'

'I don't need a cleaner.'

'Ah, but she will clean, she will cook, she will work very hard.' Benjamín is stumbling a little now. 'Dolores is a good worker.' At the mention of her name, Dolores creeps behind his back.

'She has no English,' Benjamín explains.

'I thought you said she lived in California.'

'She is very timid. She doesn't go out much.'

'Uh-uh . . .'

'Yes, Alice, you can pay her four dollars fifty an hour.' He speaks quickly to Dolores who nods her head. 'And she can start now.'

'What a surprise!'

'Yes,' he agrees uneasily. 'She will clean the house today and cook something for tonight.'

'Is she as good a cook as you, Benjamín?' I say drily.

Benjamín forces out a laugh. 'Ha ha ha, Alice. You like my *sopa de pollo*, yes?'

But I don't laugh with him and Benjamín finally loses his confidence.

'There is a problem, Alice?'

'I came by your cabin last night, Benjamín, I tried to find you.'

Benjamín's mouth forms an 'oh'. When I tell him about Emmy, he looks appalled.

'She was sick?'

'Very.'

'She is okay?'

'Well now she is.'

Benjamín shakes his head woefully. 'Little M-E. I tell you bad luck will come.' He puts his finger to his eyes. '*Mal de ojo . . . Mal de ojo.*'

Dolores crosses herself and takes one superstitious step backwards.

'It wasn't the evil eye, Benjamín,' I say, deeply irritated. 'She has an ear infection. I had to take her to Nogales, to a doctor.'

Benjamín sucks in his breath. '*El médico?*'

'I told you, she was very sick.'

'You went to *Nogales?*'

'I came to find you but you weren't there.'

'I pick up Dolores in Nogales,' he says. 'From the bus station.'

'The bus arrived in the middle of the night, did it?'

'*Sí,*' he says emphatically. 'The bus was very late. I wait and wait. And when he doesn't come I go to the church and light a candle for Dolores.'

'So you were in Nogales and I was in Nogales, what a coincidence!'

He looks at me anxiously, not understanding the sarcasm, but recognizing the anger driving it. Dolores touches his sleeve and whispers something with a timid look to me.

'What is she saying?'

'She thinks you don't want her. She says she won't come if you don't want her.'

I know that Benjamín is lying to me, I know that Duval has been lying to me and I think of all the things I should do. Confront them both, ring Chavez and have him send a posse of his finest agents over to arrest everyone in sight, but I look at Benjamín's crooked face and I look at Dolores's shiny red lips and the pistachio nylon blouse which I know she's got herself all dressed up in to come over here – and the only feeling I can squeeze out is one of wretched middle-class guilt.

'No, Benjamín,' I sigh. 'Tell her she can clean for me. Tell her it's fine.'

I wait. For the dust to settle. For Emmy to get well. She's pretty subdued for a day or two, but once the antibiotics kick in, she improves fast, morphing in an inordinately short time from adorably wan Camille, stoically suffering life's injustices on her deathbed, to Idi Amin, issuing ever more outrageous demands and holding the entire household in the grip of a three-day reign of terror. I leave nice, mute Dolores to change her sheets while I take Emmy to the medical centre in Ague, where the cute bearded resident delivers exactly the same diagnosis as

Louis. Yes, she has an ear infection. No, it's unlikely she will have another fit. No, I'm not to worry, but she must be kept quiet and encouraged to drink plenty of water. I manage to purloin the doctor's home number for future emergencies then drive to Nogales and present Chavez with our passports. He makes a big fuss of Emmy, showing her his Degas ballerina and giving both her and Jack more of those little wrapped sweets which he keeps in his drawer and which the children again spit out, much to my embarrassment, straight into their hands.

Dolores cleans the house. She keeps out of my way and says little, and, except for *buenas tardes* and *gracias*, I say little back to her. As a housekeeper she's a disaster. Unable to grasp the idea that removal of dirt as opposed to relocation of dirt is where it's at, she pushes the broom in front of her as though it's a lawn mower that has run out of juice. She moves so slowly and dreamily round the house that having never had the least desire to become a domestic goddess, I itch to snatch the brush from her hands and furiously clean the floor with quick efficient strokes. I don't even bother to ask her to cook. She doesn't know why I'm angry. Possibly she thinks that all gringa employers are equally cold, unsmiling and ungrateful. Possibly we all are.

Of Duval and the workers, I see very little. I use Emmy as a reason for eschewing our daily meetings and I don't allow the children to go to Benjamín's cabin any more. When they ask why, I make up excuses. Benjamín is tired, he's busy, he's redecorating with a particularly noxious paint that's only poisonous for the under-ten age group. The children argue his case vociferously but

I'm adamant. There might be nothing but affection for them in his face, but I don't know the man behind that face any more. A little bit of suspicion is a dangerous thing; a drop from a pipette of poison into a bucket of otherwise clean water. Now, twitching at the curtains like the most busybody of neighbours, I watch with bitter suspicious eyes as Duval's truck drives in and out of town. I hate this new cynical reincarnation of myself, but I can't do anything about it because out here nothing and nobody holds up to close inspection.

As soon as Emmy returns to school, I begin searching the desert beyond the boarding house. Exactly what I am looking for – the old road, a secret shack, a car full of marijuana? – I'm not sure, but every day I throw a couple of litres of water into my backpack and head south out of the town. Dozens of trails look promising, only to peter out into dead ends. I hike deep into the hills, standing on different points and staring fruitlessly at the landscape until finally, one day, I spot something. A thin chalky line in the distance cutting through the green of the scrub. A road, indisputably. I try to trace it back to where I'm standing but am thwarted by the impenetrable expanse of oak that belts the town. Still, it occurs to me that if I were to cut round the mountain at an even steeper angle, circumvent the oak altogether, then drop onto it from above, it should be possible to follow it back to Temerosa.

On Thursday I inform Benjamín I'm going to Phoenix for the weekend. On Friday I ring Sharleen and Candy and arrange to drop Jack and Emmy off at Prestcott's after school – having promised the children a great deal of latitude with regard to hamburger eating and television watching – then on Saturday morning I set off.

I climb steadily for the first hour, zigzagging up the side of the hill, keeping the chalky line of the road in the corner of my eye. Climbing isn't so easy in spring as it is in winter. Plants and shrubs are sprouting everywhere and, wary of lethargic snakes and even warier of the spiky cactus cities dotted around underfoot, I keep my eyes glued to the ground, so much so that when I reach the cliff edge I nearly step straight off into the abyss. I walk along the spine of the mountain until the belt of oaks below me swings far to the right, then scramble down and set off again. I can no longer see the road, but according to the compass it should now be directly south.

Distance is misleading. It plays tricks on you. The sun, the heat, the sheer scale of the surroundings all conspire to swindle you out of your sense of time and perspective. I had figured on reaching the road within a couple of hours, three max, but after a further hour of flat hiking, I seem to be no closer. Uneasily, I check the compass, then shake it disbelievingly. Somehow I've lost due south and now appear to be heading west, with no way of judging how long I've been off track. It's getting hot and my backpack is rubbing against my shoulders. I stop and drink some water, shielding my eyes from the sun and for an instant, sensing that I'm being watched, check the immediate bushes, but there's nothing out here. Just a great stretch of rock and scrub. The landscape is empty of people, apparently empty of threat, but of course that, too, is just an illusion. Even with the glitch in direction I can't be more than a few miles off the Mexican border and where there's a line there will be people crossing it. At any moment our paths might meet and how safe will I feel then? Still, I bolster myself with the thought that this is merely a hike. No different from any other I've been on over the last few months. Just because it's a hike with intent shouldn't make it any more dangerous. I hitch up the backpack, correct course and press on.

Another hour passes, an hour and three-quarters then, abruptly, the ground opens into a gaping ravine. I stop in dismay and squat down, tired and disheartened. My throat is dry, my head throbbing. It's already two-thirty. I drink more water and eat the egg sandwich and apple from my backpack, minutely scanning the land on the other side. How could I have got it so wrong? The road should be there, it should be, but there's only more cactus, more rock, more bloody juniper and mesquite. I am just coming to the conclusion that I'm going to have to turn back when something catches my eye. A series of quick flashes then the sun moves behind a cloud and they're gone. I go on staring and slowly, slowly, as though drawn onto a treasure map with invisible ink, the road reappears. A rough winding track, cut into the opposite side of the cliff and, just below it, what can only be the tin roof of a cabin.

A spasm of nerves twists my stomach. Up until now this has been a hunch I've been close to dismissing as silly, but if this cabin represents what I think it does – a hiding place – then to continue would be to knowingly walk into danger. I vacillate for a bit but it's no good, curiosity has me in its grip, and besides, I can't bear to go on seeing my distrust of Benjamín reflected in his face. I walk the edge impatiently, looking for a way down, and am eventually rewarded by a break in the cliff, a wash of loose stones that looks as though it leads as near as dammit to the bottom. I start down tentatively, shoving my heel in hard with each step to keep from slipping, but soon default to sliding on my bottom. The wash becomes progressively narrower, finally tapering into a dead end between two jutting pieces of sheer rock above the canyon floor. I peer over the edge. It's only about five feet to the bottom, maybe less. A hand on either side of the rock and I should be able to swing through and land safely. I wait to catch my breath but again, irrationally, I get the feeling I'm not alone. This time I spin round quickly only to discover I'm playing grandmother's footsteps with a coyote. He stands at the top of the ravine, the remains of my apple core in his mouth. Reassured, I throw the backpack to the ground, then keeping my weight as evenly distributed as possible, swing through the gap in the rock and let go.

The nail protrudes at an oblique angle from a length of wood wedged into the canyon floor. The tip meets my leg about two inches above the ankle, and the force of the jump drives it straight through my calf. There's a searing pain. I look down in time to see the flesh closing swampily around the nail and realize with horror that a piece of wood about a foot and a half long is now attached to my leg. Instinctively, I take it in both hands and, with as much strength as I can muster, pull it out again. The tissue surrenders the nail with a sucking noise and the blood follows – at first in a great gush, then in long powerful spurts like the initial yield of an unexpected oil strike. I press one thumb on it, then the other, but the blood flows relentlessly down my leg, seeping into the white cotton of my sock like tomato juice into kitchen paper. Shocked, upping the pressure of my thumbs, I try to remember if there's an important artery there. One of those bleeding-to-death-in-three-minute ones. As an experiment, I let go. Sure enough the blood pulses steadily higher. Tourniquet! I think wildly, tourniquet! – And squeeze down as hard as possible.

Fuck. I am going to bleed to death at the bottom of this canyon and have my leg gnawed off by coyotes with cider breath. My children will be taken into welfare and Robert will say I told you so. Minutes pass. Pain begins to register in waves. I keep the pressure on until I can no longer feel my thumbs and still I hold them there until eventually the pulsing calms down. My panic subsides. I might not be about to die after all but I need to get out of here and quickly. My leg is tacky with blood from the knee down and stiffening up fast. I examine the nail. It's eight inches long and thick with flaked rust and God only knows what else. Tentatively, I put my foot to the ground. There's an unpleasant squelch. I unknot the laces with shaking fingers and ease off the boot. My entire sock is crimson with blood. I tip the boot's heel. Blood spills onto the rocks and spreads out in a dark pool, and without warning I'm overcome with dizziness. Black spots form before my eyes, the ground begins moving beneath my feet like a listing ship and the world tips sideways. I cast around for something to hold on to but there's nothing that isn't spiky or unfriendly. Still I stay standing, willing the faintness to pass, but it's no good; my legs and arms turn rubbery, my knees start to buckle as though somebody has thrust their hands into my body and whisked out all the bones, and now the black spots grow ever larger and begin to merge with one another until finally they block out the world altogether.

18

Consciousness returns in small fragments; sun creeping through gaps between logs; a section of corrugated tin roof; the itchiness of a blanket against my bare skin. There are men's voices, a murmur of Spanish, feet moving around. I can smell tobacco and burning cedar. Smoke drifts lazily through the light. I turn my head. Duval sits at a wooden table, scraping at a piece of paper with a standing knife. He looks up briefly as I stir, then bends his head without speaking. I, too, say nothing. After all, to the traditional first questions of capture, namely 'Who are you?' and 'Why am I here?' I already know the answers. After a while, though, my head begins to clear and I push up on my elbows.

'What happened?'

'You fainted.' He examines a piece of paper under the light.

'Certainly did not.'

Duval pushes back his chair. Under the table, Taco raises an enquiring head.

'It's nothing to be ashamed of. It's just not very

practical when there are so many sharp things to land on.'

'What do you mean?'

He picks up my hand. I look at it stupidly. Four neat red splodges have seeped through a white bandage.

'I don't understand. How did I get here?'

'You were carried.'

'By you?'

There's a theatrical bit of throat clearing behind us as Winfred eases his bulk off a stool in the corner.

'Hey, Mrs Coleman!'

'Winfred found you,' Duval says. 'He's the rodeo champion haybale tosser so he's used to hauling dead weights around.'

Winfred cracks a grin. 'How you feeling, Mrs Coleman?'

'You owe me a hundred and seventy dollars,' I say weakly.

'Ha ha, Mrs Coleman.' He chuckles nervously. Duval looks at him.

'Speeding fines,' he pleads half-heartedly.

Duval shakes his head. 'You can't help it, can you? At heart you're just a no-good thieving Indian.'

'Aw, come on, Duval,' Winfred says coyly.

'Give Mrs Coleman back her money.'

Winfred smirks and reaches into his wallet. Duval takes the bills from him and counts out $150.

'Deduct a twenty for your trouble. I'm sure Mrs Coleman wouldn't begrudge a little road recovery fee.' He hands me the wad of dollars.

'Were you following me, Winfred?'

'Naw.'

'I heard you.'

'Winfred's tracking is not what it used to be.' Duval flicks him in the gut. 'Too fat to be light on his feet.'

Winfred pushes out his chest. 'It's all muscle, bro, check it out.'

'Like hell – you only have to be downwind of the smell of food to put on weight.'

'It's true,' Winfred says proudly. 'If a truck hauling potato chips drives along my road while I'm asleep, I wake up two pounds heavier in the morning.'

Not prepared to be charmed quite yet, I tuck the money into the pocket of my shirt.

'What about all those other times in the car, Winfred? Were you following me then too?'

'Duval told me to watch out for you.'

'Why?' I look from one to the other.

'Ma'am, I mean, well . . . look at you. You're not bully-beef.' Winfred sounds in no way apologetic. 'Duval was worried you'd be a magnet for every weirdo in this state.'

'Really,' I say drily. 'Well, seems he was right.'

Winfred chuckles and slaps Duval on the back. 'I'll come back later.'

'Oh, sure . . . go.' Duval grins. 'Leave when the going gets tough.'

I look at him curiously. This Duval is so utterly unlike the Duval of the perpetual frown and disapproving comments. One of the Mexicans passes Winfred in the doorway. He's wearing a grubby Guess USA T-shirt and a University of Wisconsin baseball hat. He's new on the site, well . . . at least the hat and shirt are. Silently, he hands Duval a white cloth and a bottle of witchy purple liquid then retreats awkwardly, knocking his hip against the door frame on his way out.

I take a look around the long narrow room.

'So this is where you live?'

'Some of the time.'

'And the rest of the time?'

'There are other places I go.'

'Where you leave boxes and cigarettes in bedside tables?'

'Yes, I'm sorry about that. I had meant to remove them before you arrived.'

'Why didn't you then?'

'Minor change of plan.'

'I see.'

'As you've found out the hard way, life in the desert can be a little unpredictable.'

'I guess,' I say ruefully, then fall silent as he sets the bottle on the table and unclips his Leatherman from its leather pouch. 'So what is this cabin?'

'It's an old schoolroom.'

'Part of the town?' I'm surprised. There is no mention of a schoolroom on the Temerosa deeds.

'Built between Temerosa and Black Mesa – another ghost town. Shared by the two.'

The long pauses that have always characterized Duval's speech are gone, and without them it feels like he's finally talking in sync. 'You realize your accent's slipping, don't you?' I tell him. In answer he pinches out the blade of his knife.

'Sanchez,' he shouts.

'Who are you? Is Duval even your real name?'

'Roll up your jeans.'

I look at the approaching knife. 'You're not going to use that on me, are you?'

'Roll them up.'

I do as he says. The blood has dried, dark and thick on my skin, like a layer of Marmite or congealed redcurrant jelly. Duval cuts the cloth into three strips, then he takes the bottle of water off the table and sloshes it up and down my calf. Using one of the strips, he starts daubing at the blood around the general area of the hole. I bite my lip. He moves to the second cloth. Clean, the wound looks disappointingly pedestrian, no bigger than the head of a drawing pin. Duval squints at it with a certain forensic detachment then squeezes it open and shut.

'Ow,' I say crossly, 'that hurts!'

'Good. Now I know I'm in the right place.'

'I might have thought the hole was an indication of that.'

'Nail?'

I nod.

'Had a tetanus shot recently?'

'No.'

'Pity.' He trickles more water into the wound, then pokes at it with his finger. 'You need water pressure to get this clean. Unfortunately, as you may have noticed, our amenities here are a little basic.' He digs in deeper with his finger. I wince.

'Sanchez!' he shouts again.

This time Sanchez appears. Duval says something to him in Spanish.

'What? What did you ask him?'

'Hold the leg like this,' Duval instructs and Sanchez takes over the opening and shutting routine as Duval reaches for the bottle of purple brew.

'Hey! What's in that?'

'This might hurt a little,' he says gently and sloshes the liquid straight inside the hole.

A line of fire burns through my leg as if someone has shovelled smouldering coals along its length. Duval quickly lifts my foot by the heel and pours on another shot. I buck against Sanchez's hand, but the Mexican holds fast.

'Oh, fine,' I grit my teeth, 'just shoot me now.'

Duval chuckles. 'Not plan A but I might reconsider depending on how much of a pain in the ass you are.'

Nauseous, I hold on to the edge of the cot. Fainting once is excusable, fainting again, particularly in front of Duval, would be downright humiliating.

'Put your head between your knees,' he suggests, kneading his fingers up and down the flesh as though making home-made bread. The feeling of unreality is overwhelming. What time is it? What would the children be up to? Would Candy and Sharleen be bouncing off the walls? I try to picture Robert sitting in some legal office in Geneva, bored, tapping his leg while the lawyers pore over the legal minutiae of trust documents. By the time my head clears Sanchez has left and Duval is slowly winding a bandage round my leg.

'Here,' he hands me a mug, 'drink this.'

'What is it?'

'Tea.'

I sniff it. 'I hate tea.'

'Don't be so ungrateful.'

'What happened to good old-fashioned whiskey?'

'This isn't *High Chaparral*. The tea has sugar in it.'

I take a few sips. He's right. It's thick with sugar, and its milky warmth is strangely comforting. The fire in my leg begins to subside and I remember for the first time why I came.

'What are you running here? You, Winfred, the workers? A drug-smuggling operation?'

'Living in these conditions?' Duval looks amused. 'I can't be very good at it, if that's the case.' He finishes with the bandage and tucks the edges in.

'So it is people then,' I say flatly, and the feeling of disappointment is almost crushing. I hadn't wanted to believe it of him but it's the only explanation. Bringing Mexicans over the border, moving them through the town. Men slipping in and out of the clothes left by the workers before them, using the building project as a cover before disappearing on and up into the north.

'You're a coyote,' I say hollowly.

Duval scratches his stubble and adopts a drawl. 'Well, what with the increase of upwardly mobile immigrants, we in the coyote business prefer to be called guides.'

I look at him in disgust. 'You trade in people. You make money out of their misery.'

'And you, I presume, armed with self-righteous zeal, have taken it upon yourself to come up here and stop me?' He unzips the top of my backpack and takes out the contents. 'You're not exactly well equipped for a citizen's arrest, are you? One bottle of water, inadequate. One plastic compass, useless. One penknife, blunt. One map, tourist, and let's see . . .' he digs down to the bottom, 'one Powerbar. "Made with love and soya",' he reads off the back. 'Personally, I'd be tempted to shoot someone who offered me love and soya in the same sentence.'

'How dare you patronize me?' I say angrily. 'You've been using the town as cover, using me . . . How can you possibly justify what you do? How can you?'

An unreadable expression passes over his face, then he rolls the leg of my jeans down. 'I think you'll be fine to go home now. Winfred will take you.'

'I could call the authorities, turn you in.'

'Yes.' He takes his cigarettes out of his shirt pocket and shrugs one out of the packet. 'You could.'

'And you think I won't!'

'I think you're a fugitive, Alice,' he says quietly, 'and therefore not much different to the rest of us.'

The cabin is still and quiet. Thank God for Sharleen and Candy, thank God the children are at Prestcott's trashing bedspreads and stealing mini soaps, and I have nothing more taxing to do than hobble upstairs and fall into bed. The leg burns but the shooting pains have stopped. My hair smells of tobacco and wood smoke. I lie drowsily under the covers, trying to arrange my thoughts and feelings into some sort of order, but my head just grows heavier and heavier. I dream I am running along the white beaches of the North Orkneys, in the middle of a pack of wolves. I run at great speed. The sand feels firm under my paws. A cool wind rushes past my face as my skin turns to bristle. I let my tongue hang down to catch the splatters of sea spray. Eventually the rhythmic pounding of feet gives way to a more localized pounding in my left leg and I wake. The hands on the clock read five. It feels good to lie in bed for a while, listening for the creaks as the mining ghosts tread the floorboards, but in the end I get out of bed to join them, hauling my stiff leg down the stairs like a new prosthetic limb I haven't yet mastered the technique of using. In the kitchen I crunch up coffee beans and shake the leg around, trying to loosen it up while water heats in the saucepan. Taking a blanket off the sofa and carrying the mug of steaming coffee outside to the butterscotch truck, I hoist myself up into the flatbed and lean against its cold metal side, waiting for the sun. The sky is still grey over the mountains, the echoes of night not yet entirely receded. I love these moments just before dawn, when you're the only person awake and the whole world belongs to you. In the twin beds of Prestcott's, the children, still in the grip of their night-time blackout, would be throwing their limbs about like double-jointed zombies. In the secret schoolroom, the Mexicans would be shifting and turning on the floor. And Duval? Well, who knows . . . 'There are other places I go,' he'd said and I picture him in the dark confines of a woman's bedroom, watching her silently as she sleeps.

I pinch myself. There can be no romanticizing the situation. Duval – trafficking in people, using the town as a cover. I know perfectly well I should call the Border

Patrol and yet . . . I sip the burning coffee. 'After you left Temerosa that first time I never thought you'd be back,' he'd said as he helped me up into Winfred's truck and I'd looked at him, expecting to see the same mocking smile, but his eyes had been serious. 'I never dreamed you'd come to live here. Not on your own, not with two small children . . .'

The longing for escape began as a slow burn. Other people's dissatisfaction had names and they certainly all had cures – Prozac, Botox, Valium. Hey, call my therapist! Join my Pilates class! Listen to my whale music! But I held on to that picture of Temerosa. It stayed stubbornly with me almost as if my head had become a viewfinder for which all other slides had been lost. And over the following months, as emotionally I found myself dropping down to the same latitudinal line as Alaska, the flame of escape stayed lit, warming at low level, like a pilot light in my heart, stopping it from freezing over altogether.

Like Duval said, I was a fugitive, just like the rest of them.

Benjamín is walking up the path to the cabin. He walks slowly, turning his head this way and that as though conducting a heated rhetorical debate with himself. In his hands he carries a loaf of bread and a jar of apricot jam.

'¡Hola, Benjamín!'

He jumps. 'Ohh, Alice.' He looks at me, then to the front cab of the truck as though expecting some unseen chauffeur to fire it up and drive off. 'What're you doin', crazy Alice?' he says with an attempt at levity that seems to have quite the opposite effect on him, for he bites his lip and looks totally wretched as I slide down off the flatbed.

'Oh noh, Alice.' He fixes his eyes on my leg, then on the ground, looking for all the world like he's going to burst into tears and then – before I know it – he does. Tears wash out of the corner of his eyes and he puts his hands on my shoulders, still holding the bread and jam, then clasps me roughly to him with a jumble of Spanish until the two of us become one great big teary wet sandwich.

'*Perdóname*, Alice, *lo siento*.'

'Benjamín, it's okay.' I hold on to him clumsily, comforted by the soapy smell of his shirt. 'It's okay.'

'Why do you say it's okay?' His nose drips. 'Something bad could have happened to you. Real bad, worse than your leg.'

'Yes, but it didn't,' I reassure him. For a place with scattered telephone coverage, the grapevine is certainly very efficient round here. 'I'm fine.'

But Benjamín is not to be cheered. 'Everything is bad. Everything is changed.'

'Nothing has changed,' I lie.

'It's my fault.' He's let go of me now and distractedly blots his nose on the bread instead of his sleeve.

'It's my fault you don't let M-E come to house any more, it's my fault you don't trust me.'

'I do trust you. I do,' I protest feebly.

'No, Alice, you send M-E and Jack to the hotel.'

'Benjamín,' I say, a little exasperated, 'look, you have to understand, I need to know they're safe. At all times.'

'I never let something bad happen to the children,' he says fiercely and makes the sign of the cross. 'I swear on the soul of Our Lady of Guadalupe, I will die for Jack and M-E.' He squeezes my hand. 'Yes, Alice?' he petitions. 'It is okay, yes? You let me take them to school again, you let little M-E watch television with me?'

I look at Benjamín, at those features I've come to know so well. The downward eyes, the wayward jaw. The peppershot of grey in his sideburns. Today he is wearing a baseball cap with cheap wrap-around sunglasses clamped above the peak. His pale denim shirt is meticulously pressed and snapped up to the last button and its precision almost makes me want to weep as well.

'Benjamín . . .' I turn up my hands helplessly.

'And Duval,' he persists, 'he is a good man. You can trust him.'

I shake my head violently. 'No,' I tell him. 'I'm sorry but I can't. Your countrymen, people who are desperate or in need of work, I can understand, but a man who makes his money exploiting them?'

This notion elicits an unusually elongated denial from Benjamín. 'Noh, Alice,' he repeats emphatically, 'Duval does not take money!'

'Oh, come on, what does he do it for if not for money?'

But Benjamín merely shakes his head. 'Alice, it is not for me. He must tell you.'

'Benjamín, I can't let him go on doing this here,' I plead, 'not in Temerosa. I have to call the Border Patrol. I do.'

'Noh, Alice, no! You must speak to Duval.'

'Well, fine, here I am. I mean if he wants to talk to me, he knows where to find me.'

'Yes, good,' Benjamín says eagerly. 'You must talk to him, you must wait for him to come back.'

'What if he doesn't?'

'He will come, Alice, I swear to you.'

'Well, okay, fine, but when?' I press, then experience a moment of acute déjà vu as Benjamín rubs his jaw and stares into the middle distance.

'Soon,' he says, 'he will come soon.'

19

It's a mere thirty-six hours since I last saw the children, but that's plenty of time for them to have switched their allegiance to Candy and Sharleen. As soon as they hear my voice there's a stampede along the upstairs corridor of Prestcott's Hotel as they make off in the opposite direction. Blood might be thicker than water, but it's still very much thinner than an evening of television and room service combined and the children have apparently never known joy like it. Sharleen, on the other hand, wears the shell-shocked expression of someone who's just been presented with an accumulated thirty-year tax bill. She stands outside the swing doors of the hotel's saloon and waves us down the street with small flipper-like movements of her hand.

'Why are you walking like that?' Jack asks as I lift Emmy into the truck.

'I hurt my leg.'

'Really? Is it bad? Can I see?'

I pull up my jeans. The children are duly impressed by the crisp new layers of bandage, administered earlier, along with a vicious anti-tetanus shot, by the cute doctor in the medical centre.

'It looks really bad.'

'Why, this iddy-biddy little thing?' I say nonchalantly. 'Shucks, it was nothing.'

'Did it bleed?'

'A bit.'

They summon forth a vaguely sympathetic grunt.

'Actually,' I say, piqued to have lost their attention so quickly, 'it bled a lot, I mean it was pretty deep.'

In the revisionist version of this incident, exaggeration is already hardening to fact and, as recounted first to the doctor and now to the children, the quantity of blood gets measured in litres rather than pints, the eight-inch nail grows exponentially, and the hole it makes widens to the length and depth of a mine shaft. All mention of fainting and sobbing has been ruthlessly exorcized in favour of a story about courage in the face of adversity. In reality the leg underneath the bandage had been something of a let-down. The flesh had been pleasingly swollen and pink, but without the pulsing blood, without the stained and grimy bandage, it looked curiously dead – a limb that had been allowed to wallow in the bath, or a shank of mutton left to unthaw in the sink. It's hard to sustain a tale of courage against adversity about sitting in the bath too long, but that doesn't mean to say I didn't give it my all.

'Mummy?' Emmy says from the back seat.

'What?'

'I would hate it if you died.'

'I'd hate it too.' I sneak a hand through the seat divide and find hers. 'So don't worry, I won't.'

'Imagine if you were in an orphanage and you were

the only one there. You were the only one whose mother and father died.' Tears fill her eyes and her voice cracks. 'That would be so unfair.'

'Oh, Emmy,' I say.

'Actually, I love death.' She stuffs the end of her braid in her mouth and sucks on it thoughtfully.

'Emmy!'

'I'm so evil.' She sighs, and after a further minute of reflection adds, 'You know I don't really care if Jack dies because I don't really like him but if you died, Mummy, I would keep all your jewellery in a bottle so I wouldn't forget you.'

'How were people invented?' Emmy asks later when I put the children to bed.

'Big Bang,' Jack says, spitting toothpaste into the sink. 'Some people believe in the Big Bang and some people believe in those naked people.'

'Adam and Eve?' I offer helpfully.

'Adam and Eve,' Jack repeats. 'They had children, then the children had children and the whole world got born.'

'Who invented the naked ones?' Emmy asks.

'God.'

'So who did the Big Bang invent?'

'Apes.'

'Apes,' Emmy shrieks. 'That's so funny! What's the point of inventing apes?'

Night lightens to morning, morning stretches to noon. Shadows lengthen and afternoons linger on as the sun works harder and burns longer. The pain in my leg collects in a solid block between knee and ankle and, for a couple of days, keeping it horizontal seems the best option so I pass the days sitting at the kitchen table, ears like tuning forks, waiting for the vibration of an engine, or languishing on top of my bed, eyes straying from my *Plumbing Manual*, Volume 11 to check for the headlights of a truck swinging through the turn. I wait for Duval, because I know that he will come and I want him to come because . . . well because he damn well owes me an explanation. While the children are around, I hide this strangely mercurial mood of anger/anticipation but once Benjamín has got them off to school, I find myself unable to focus on anything much and eventually give in to a sort of helpless daydreaming, which though very pleasant is not the slightest bit constructive. Still, all the anxiety and suspicions of the last few weeks have gone and whatever Duval's so-called reasons turn out to be, it's as though someone has lifted a great rock off my chest. Instead, I feel more like the child who has set fire to the bathmat out of nothing more than curiosity and my only real fear is how strongly and out of control it will burn.

20

The morning kicks off a deep cobalt blue. A clear sun shines down on a landscape of wild flowers. I sit on the ground, back against the cabin wall, and look out over the hills. It seems almost impossible that everything before me, Mexican gold poppies, purple scorpion weed, the tangled lupine and desert marigolds, germinated on their minuscule ration of water from last fall's rainy season, have now sprung up as potent and lovely as any rain-drenched English rose.

It's only early, but already I'm hot and thirsty. Ten minutes ago my hair was wet from the shower and now it's as brittle as the brush of the broom leaning against the wall beside me. I still can't get used to it. I spent a whole childhood working out ways to keep things dry. Hanging clothes on a line in the salty wind, laying wet socks on the Aga, stuffing newspapers into gumboots. Nowadays, I've taken to not flushing the loo unless it's absolutely necessary, unable to handle the guilt at five gallons less in my well. In Scotland, where rain and damp are the enemy, 'wringing every last drop of water out of something' means actually getting rid of the stuff. Here in Temerosa it means the opposite. Conserve is what nature must do to survive. A cactus needs only a centimetre of water a year to flower. Those little hairy chipmunk-like things that are forever scurrying beneath the wheels of the butterscotch truck live on only a few drops, and every time I see one I have a vision of it holidaying up in the Orkneys, drunk and happy, lying in a bog nursing a bloated belly full of brown peaty water.

'Hello.'

I'm startled into spilling my coffee.

Duval is standing above me, shading his eyes from the sun.

'How's your leg?'

'My leg?' To my mortification, I feel blood suffusing my cheeks. 'Fine.'

'You sure?'

'Yes, I'm sure.'

'Let me see it.'

'No!' I'm annoyed to be caught unawares like this, barefoot, dreaming. I had wanted to be prepared, my line of questioning probing and focused, the presiding judge on the Duval case, deliberating whether or not to grant bail.

'Come on. Let me see it.' He squats down and I've no option but to pull up my jeans. He unravels the bandage slowly, while I become more self-conscious by the second. The leg is actually in pretty good shape, the bruising dying down, returning the skin to its unattractive pasty white. Duval turns my heel this way and that as though inspecting a prize parsnip at a country fair.

'Nice scab,' he says eventually.

'Thanks.'

'Don't pick it, will you?'

'Why not?'

'It'll be another few days before it's the right consistency. You want it that nice chewy quality which makes it stick to your teeth.'

I hide a smile. 'It looks disappointingly small for all that fuss.'

'So do bullet holes.' He presses the pads of his thumbs gently along the length of the bone. 'Does it hurt?'

'No.'

'Liar.'

'Well maybe. A little.'

'Can you ride?'

'Ride?' I look up, thrown by the non sequitur. 'No.'

'Too painful? Or because you don't want to?'

'Because I've never been on a horse.'

'Never been on a horse,' he says slowly. 'Now that's something you don't often hear in this part of the world . . . Well, well, well! He looks thoughtful. 'Want to try?'

'What?'

'Riding. Want to try it?'

'Now?'

'Yes, why not? If you're up to it.'

'Give me one good reason why I should go anywhere with you.'

He stretches out his hand. 'I absolutely intend to.' And when I still hesitate, he takes my hand anyway and pulls me to my feet. 'Come with me, Alice, there's something I want to show you.'

Two of the boniest horses I've ever seen, one a

chestnut, the other a pale grey, stand nuzzling at the ground just beyond the cabin deck, their narrow backs covered in blankets and saddles.

'Indian ponies,' Duval says.

'Are they yours?'

'Winfred's brother's. They've come up off the reservation.'

The horses snatch at the new shoots of oily grass poking through the gaps in the deck.

'Poor bastards have been living on dust the whole winter. Talk about pigs in clover.'

I touch my fingers to the soft muzzle of the chestnut and stroke the hollow cavities on either side of its nose. I'm actually a little nervous of horses.

'Now, you know something about these creatures, right?' Duval says. 'The section with the teeth is the front, the tail is the back.' He steers me round. 'This middle bit is the seating area.' He laces his fingers together. 'Think you can get up there?'

'I think I can manage,' I say archly. I put my good foot on his hands and he throws me up as if I weighed no more than a pencil.

'This is a Mexican saddle.' Duval moves my ankle forward and adjusts the straps. 'Not as comfortable as an American saddle, not as much leather. Pretty, though.'

'It's beautiful.' I smooth my hand over the rough white stitching.

'It belonged to an old farmhand I used to know. He left it to me when he died.' He unknots the reins. 'Hold these loose, through your fingers, like this.'

'Okay.' I take them from him. 'Then what?'

He swings up onto the grey. 'Then nothing. The horse knows what to do.'

As instructed, I keep the reins loose in my hands, but I don't really need them. The chestnut walks sedately along behind Duval, his nose an inch from the grey horse's swishing tail.

We walk for an hour or so. Duval says little and so do I. The questions I have for him are piling up, one on top of the other, but I've realized I'm not going to extract any information out of him by force, so, holding all curiosity at bay, I concentrate instead on the scenery.

The horses pick their way over every colour of rock. To the north long thin grass shimmers on the plain. Beyond runs the roller coaster of the Santa Catalinas.

Duval stops his horse. 'If I was at all religious, I'd say that God had smiled on this country.' He twists in the saddle. 'Recognize where we are?'

I steer my pony alongside his and look around.

'The schoolroom is just over that ridge.' He turns his pony with a slight movement of his wrist. 'It's built right into the cleft of the mountain, virtually undetectable unless you know exactly what you're looking for.'

'How come I saw it then?'

'You came an unusual way.'

'What do you mean?'

'You followed your gut.' He nudges the horse and we walk on. The sun disappears behind sporadic clouds. Nevertheless I can feel the dry air sucking the moisture from my body. I take surreptitious swigs from the water bottle in my saddlebag. Duval, I notice, leaves his untouched.

'How's the leg bearing up?'

'Fine,' I tell him, but when he's not looking I slip my foot from the stirrup and prop it up on the saddle to alleviate the throbbing. Still, it's strangely hypnotic riding a horse and as time goes by I begin to zone out and am almost disappointed when the chestnut breaks rhythm and tosses its head. Duval has stopped again.

'Where are we?' I ask.

The desert looks different under cloud. Unfinished. As though all associated plant life has been designed specifically to require the sun on its face before revealing its true colours, and without it there's no shimmer from the garnet crystal in the rock and no spiky shadows to bulk out the cacti. Even the flowers look like they've had all their brightness washed out of them. Nevertheless the three crosses in front of us rise stark against the sky like bone-white sentinels. They're only crude – painted pieces of wood nailed together and jabbed into the earth. Two are unmarked except for a date but the third is inscribed with a single name:

Estella.

And beneath it: *en la paz.*

Estella, in peace.

Duval leans back in the saddle, the reins slack in one hand. 'You asked me why I do what I do,' he says. 'Well this is why.'

21

'Why are you having a romantic dinner?' Jack asks.
He scrunches up pages from the *National Enquirer*
into tight balls and builds a teepee of logs around
them.

'I'm not.'

'Why are you lighting candles then?'

'I like candles . . . and, um, they save on electricity.'

'Okay, I'll turn out the lights,' Emmy offers.

'No, don't do that,' I say quickly. 'I mean not yet.'

'Why not?'

'Because we won't be able to see.'

'But we'll have the candles!'

'Yes, but they won't be enough.'

'Wait a second,' Jack re-examines, 'did you or did
you not claim that the candles in question were to be lit
in order that electricity might be saved?'

'Yes, but . . .'

'Just answer the questions yes or no, Mrs Coleman,'
he says wearily.

Obviously, I take the fifth.

'Mummy's having a romantic dinner, Mummy's having a romantic dinner,' Emmy chants.

I sigh. When did my children get so savvy or do all kids, from birth, have some extra-sensory perception that informs them of an approaching opportunity for blackmail? I look at them suspiciously. They're both wearing that familiar expression, the one that invariably precedes public parental humiliation and is usually adopted on aeroplanes or in the confectionery aisle of the local supermarket checkout. They smile back sweetly. They fully recognize the signs of distraction and know full well how to exploit them.

'Can we stay up, Mummy, can we? Jack, ask Mummy . . .'

They go on, cawing away at me, but I cannot keep my mind from wandering back to those white crosses in the sand, back to Duval and his story, back twenty years to the desert one hot and terrible June . . .

Benjamín had left the body of the girl where it lay. He'd taken the strip of cloth El Turrón had torn from the hem of her dress, then in one swift, agonizing movement, lifted the loose shelf of his jaw back into place and tied it with the cloth, knotting the ends on top of his head. Looking like an old-fashioned ad for a man with a toothache, he headed north, or his nearest approximation of it, the stabbing pain in his relocated jawbone keeping him conscious, keeping one foot in front of the other, keeping him alive. Eventually, when he could walk no further, he leant against a rock and closed his eyes. He slept fitfully through the night and part of the morning until the buzz of the helicopter entered his brain like a wasp, and when he opened his eyes the first thing he saw was a pair of black shiny boots. The cop shouted something then knelt down in front of him and put a bottle of water to his cracked lips. Two hours later he was back on the other side of the line. And that had been only the beginning . . .

Years passed and Benjamín crossed the border in every way imaginable. Under the wire, over the fence, along the tunnel, through the river – just another peripatetic soul, drifting like a phantom in the dust of the desert, not dead, but yet not alive either, belonging neither to this country nor to any other – simply going round and round, back and forth through the revolving doors from Mexico to the US. It was a life of relentless low-intensity conflict with the authorities, a deadly serious game characterized by childish names: Touch Tag, Hide and Seek, Snakes and Ladders, Cat and Mouse.

In the spring he worked picking citrus fruit out of the irrigated desert of Phoenix. After the season he headed south like some weary migrating bird, back over the border, through the turnstile, down the street to the bus station, and from there, the all-night drive, with its comforting whispers as it bumped along whatever road would lead him home, to Nopalillo, to his wife and children.

But his broken promise to the dead girl haunted him. How it had happened, he wasn't sure, but sometime during that first night, with his mind drifting in and out of consciousness, she had become an emblem of his survival. Of the two faces forever branded into his consciousness, it was El Turrón's that kept his anger hot, but it was Estella's that softened his bitterer moments. Her face became more familiar to him than even his own wife's. Once or twice when the trickle of work swept him further west, out of Arizona and into California, he'd thought about delivering the letter. Tried to imagine himself walking into the University of California, but then what? Without the child, he would be no more than the bearer of bad news, yet he could not bring himself to throw it away. Instead he rolled it like an ancient archaeological map, secured it with the strip of Estella's dress, and placed it in the wooden box at home where he kept things he valued the most.

There were constants in his life: men he got to know from the orchards, the better farmers who employed them, a coyote he fell in with en route and came to trust. And if he knew that life was difficult and lonely for him, he knew, too, that it was just as lonely for Marie Elena waiting back in Mexico with only a wire transfer once a month to keep her company. So he kept his aspirations low. To earn enough money for his wife to be happy. To return often enough for his children to recognize him. For these reasons he tried to find work as close to home as possible. He hugged the line, picking avocados, melons, lemons, inhaling the *pesticidas*, sleeping on the ground, avoiding the thorns, because even in one short season he could make more money than any of his sisters' husbands could in a lifetime.

Then one day he returned home and it was all over. Maria Elena waited for him no longer. She had taken the children, moved to another village, gone with another man. Cuckolded, his jaw beating with rage and humiliation, Benjamín sought her out. He stood on the cobblestone street in front of her new house and screamed bitter abuse. Now she would never have a refrigerator or shop for groceries in an American supermarket or own a car. Now their children would be as poor and ignorant as their forefathers and all because she couldn't wait, all because she was a *puta* to end all *putas*. So he left the dustbowl of Nopalillo, walked away from the only things worth staying alive for. He left his children and climbed back on the rattling bus to *El Norte*, vowing never to return.

That time, appropriately, he crossed the border curled up by the engine in the front of a Ford whose battery had been removed and jacked up underneath the car to make room for him. The heat and the dirt and the burns served to stoke the furnace of his anger, but he was nearly asphyxiated by pollution travelling through south LA. Still, he held it together long enough to find a job on a rose farm. For a month he put on a leather apron and picked flowers till his hands bled, but on his first payday he went on a wild drinking binge and was eventually picked up by the police.

It was 1996 then and the border was no longer just an ideal. It was a hard tangible thing, forged out of steel, barbed wire and intolerance. It had become a politicians' tool, a $235 million sop to real Americans, the ones with a vote. Following the devaluation of the peso, 1995 was a year of economic crisis in Mexico and the floodgates opened. In came Operation Gatekeeper, Operation

Safeguard, Operation Hold the Line. Under the new crackdown everyone got scrutinized, employers and illegals alike – and what, the police asked Benjamín, was a *campesino* doing with a letter from the University of California if not being offered work of some kind? Benjamín couldn't remember what he answered, but maybe in his drunkenness, in his numbness, he boasted of friends in high places – thinking anything was better than having his ass dumped ninety miles south of the border again. So the police contacted the INS who contacted the head of staff at the University of California – and finally, finally, this particular deus ex machina, thirteen years in the making, came full circle.

'Mummy. For God's sake!' Jack's voice finally breaks through. He wipes charcoaled hands on his jeans. 'You're so unfair.'

'Yes, you're so unfair,' Emmy echoes. 'You always tell us we don't listen to you, but you never listen to us. Never.'

'I'm sorry. What were you saying?'

'We want to know if we can stay up.' Jack might not have graduated onto pro-bono work, but he's perfectly willing to support a class action.

'Mmm. For a bit.'

'No, *not* just for a bit,' he says with infinite patience, 'for dinner.'

'Not for dinner, no . . .'

'Why not?'

'Because it'll be late.'

'So . . . ?'

'So . . . you'll be tired.'

'Certainly won't. Besides, we can sleep late in the morning. It's the weekend!'

'Jack, I said no already.'

'But why? What possible harm can it do, what would *actually* happen? I mean, would the world *actually* come to an end?'

'Probably not, but you'd be bad-tempered which is more or less the same thing.'

'I wouldn't be bad-tempered. If I slept late, I'd get the same amount of sleep.' His voice rises imperiously as he counts hours on fingers. 'One, two, three . . .'

There's no arguing with either the mathematics or the logic of this, it's just a question of who can sustain the debate the longest.

'Maybe you're right,' I concede, 'but I'd be bad-tempered if you stayed up late.'

In the end we cut a deal. The children agree to go to bed on time in return for a cup of hot chocolate with real melted chocolate pieces which they are to be allowed to drink in their bedroom. I listen to them slurping and giggling, as I stand in front of the cupboard, suddenly insecure, wondering what to wear, wondering why I care and if Duval is the kind of person who will notice anyway. In the small tin mirror I'd hung there, the face that looks back at me is pale and English, so different from Estella's striking beauty.

He'd met her in Guanajuato. She was seventeen with slim brown legs and a mouth that didn't quite close over her teeth. He had come to Guanajuato to look at an eighteenth-century Jesuit seminary he had heard people talk about. She was selling arts and crafts in the square. He watched her through the window as she did a little dance around her rug of dolls when she thought no one was looking. She came from a small speck of an Indian town fifteen miles to the south where at nights the streets are empty save for the dogs scavenging for rubbish.

Duval had been born on a cattle ranch in New Mexico. His father was a tight-lipped but upstanding citizen who'd inherited the property from his own father, a conservative east-coast businessman who'd decided in a single act of spontaneity to take advantage of the free market and availability of public lands for the grazing of livestock in the west and headed there with his twenty-three-year-old bride. Every skill Duval truly valued he learned from the cowboys, both Mexican and English, who worked on the ranch. He had these old boys to thank for being immensely practical with his hands, for breaking in a colt, speaking Spanish; but he told me later that everything he learned about fighting he taught himself. He'd been schooled locally and post-college had applied to the University of California, which he got into on the quota system before spending a year cowboying down in Mexico – more than anything to escape his father's overbearing personality.

Mexico changed him. Its utter corruption, its relentless poverty. Disenchanted with the greed and privilege of developed America, his sympathies lay increasingly with the people of its peripheral borders. Once he was in college their faces came back to him like black and white photographic stills. Farmers in the strawberry fields. Indian women on street corners. Children sleeping under blue tarpaulins. He wrote to Estella as a form of absolution for the first love affair, the one that carries so many hopes and expectations but eventually comes down to the memory of innocence lost – a feeling of guilt for promises made and forgotten. He'd never known for sure whether she received it until the day he'd walked into that INS office and found himself face to face with the small Mexican with the broken jaw who'd stared at the floor as Duval read the fading piece of paper. He'd never known about his son until Benjamín raised wary eyes to his. 'You help me,' he'd whispered, 'and I will tell you about the child.'

I shake myself. The house has been quiet for a long time. Downstairs, I open the oven and haul out the heavy skillet. A shoulder of pork has been slow-cooking all day. Underneath the lid, the liquid bubbles gently. The fat from the meat has melted into the juices and the onions and chillies have caramelized at the bottom of the pan into a sticky delicious gunge. Dolores's *puerco con poblano*. I put it back in the oven and look out of the window in the direction of the schoolroom where the workers would also be hungrily waiting for their food.

Estella's story had been harrowing, shocking. I had so many questions, but it hadn't seemed like the right time. I'd turned the horse away from the grave, not knowing what to do, what to feel.

'What is it that you want from me?' I'd asked Duval.

'Fair warning.'

'For what?'

'Oh you know . . . if I'm to send the men into hiding. Post Winfred as lookout on top of the hill to decipher

the probable danger of every approaching dust cloud.'
He drew alongside me and I could see he was smiling.

I nodded my head slowly. 'Okay.'

'In that case,' he led the chestnut on, 'I think it's time
you finally met your crew.'

There had been around fifteen Mexicans in the schoolroom. Some I recognized from their building-site clothes,
others were strangers, obvious newcomers, streaked with
dirt and sweat, their clothes dirty and crumpled. All
talking stopped and curious eyes flicked to us as Duval
showed me into the low-ceilinged shack adjoining the
schoolroom. '*Compañeros*,' he said, 'this is Alice.'

He went on to introduce each man as though hosting
some professional dating party at a smart Phoenix venue.
Joaquim, this is Alice, two children, temporarily separated from her husband. Alice, this is Joachim. He lost
his brother in a border accident some years ago. One by
one they told me their stories. Almond growers, peach
pickers, porch sweepers, janitors, each a tiny cog in the
wheel on which Wall Street and the price of frozen OJ
turns. And what I began to understand that afternoon
was that if America is the land of opportunity, a country
where perseverance and hard work is rewarded by recognition, then an illegal harbours the opposite ambi-
tions. His greatest reward is anonymity, invisibility. Aided
and abetted by market forces and the laws of supply and
demand, he hones his skill to stand up but make sure
he's never counted.

The men shook my hand, some smiling, most sombre,

shy. Of all of them it was Dolores, the only woman, who found it hardest to face me straight on. She stood at the makeshift stove stirring a frying pan of beef and chillies, a high stack of flour tortillas on a paper plate at her elbow. Duval said her name twice before she reluctantly turned. She raised big oval eyes to mine and blurted out something.

'What did she say?'

'She says she thinks she's a lousy housekeeper.'

'Oh no, she's great,' I lied.

Dolores muttered again, rubbing her fingers fretfully over the tiny red roses embroidered on the pockets of her apron.

'She says it's better she doesn't clean the house any more.'

'Okay, sure, whatever she wants.' There were beads of perspiration on Dolores's upper lip. '*Está bien*,' I said to her and, equally embarrassed, made to move on.

'*¡Espera!*' She laid a timid hand on my arm, then – plucking a tortilla off the pile and cradling it into a half shell – she spooned in meat from the pan. The rich smell of beef had been intoxicating and I realized I hadn't eaten all day.

'*¿Te gusta?*' she asked and I nodded, mouth ablaze with chilli.

Duval chuckled and leant in to hear what Dolores was saying.

'She says, if you like, instead of cleaning your house, she will cook for you.'

I looked at the faces of the men then back to Dolores's

own, questioning, anxious, and I felt the warmth and the smoke close round and found myself overcome with a sort of heady acquiescence.

'Yes,' I said. 'Tell her, yes, please.'

Duval lays his hat on the table. He looks round the room and gives a low whistle. The cabin looks pretty in candlelight, and despite my protestations Emmy has laid the table with her favourite mismatched booty from the yard sales. Duval picks up the frosted glasses one by one, examining the painted Indian chiefs on each. 'Sequoyah, Geronimo!' He looks up. 'These are wonderful. Where did you find them?'

'Apparently, they were given out as freebies in the sixties by the oil companies.'

He laughs. 'So no irony there then.'

'No, I guess not.'

He puts the glass carefully back on the table. 'This was Geronimo's territory, you know.'

'Really?'

'He was an Apache. In fact the only interesting thing about Tombstone, a town beneath contempt as far as I'm concerned, is that it hosted a baseball team which was interrupted by one of Geronimo's raids.'

'Somehow baseball and Geronimo don't feel like they belong in the same century.'

'They don't, hence the tragedy. When Geronimo was eventually exiled to Florida, a newspaper man asked him if it broke his heart to leave his people and he apparently replied, "I had no heart left by the time I got to Florida."' He lifts the lid off the pork and the sweet smell of spices and cilantro fill the room. 'So how's Dolores's cooking?'

Dolores is a wonderful cook. Benjamín told me she comes from his home town, that her husband died in an oil rig accident in the north. The other men wanted her to stay in the schoolroom, a Wendy to their Lost Boys, but Benjamín didn't want to risk her being alone there, not when the men were up working on the town.

'So where is she sleeping then?' I'd asked him, and Benjamín, turning a reddening face to the wall, admitted she was staying with him. Now every morning when she covers her pistachio shirt with a checked cotton apron and gets cracking at the stove, I worry about where she does her laundry and how she applies her red lipstick with only the reflection of the tin St Joseph to peer into. I wonder whether to offer her a change of clothes, a hot bath and some soothing Burt's Honey Bath Milk to go in it, but I don't because I'm guessing she'd be mortified. I'm guessing that Dolores still believes, despite Duval's protestations that I am a friend and will not turn her in, that she is working in the lair of the she-devil. So, to date I have offered her no more than fatuous compliments about her food in my dire Spanglish, but in answer to Duval's question, the stuff she makes is incredible. *Tostadas*, *chilaquiles*, *albóndigas*, and the children's favourite, *cajeta de celaya*, a fudge sauce made of goat's milk which they eat straight from the pan. The truth is, Dolores doesn't seem to mind what she cooks as long as she gets to use the Magimix. No matter how small the quantity to be chopped, no matter that it takes her longer to wash the machine than to do it by hand, if something needs grating, slicing, or even hacking in two, into the Magimix it goes while Dolores stands, finger on the pulse button, a beatific smile playing about her full lips.

Duval looks amused. He takes the plates I hand him. 'Well certainly this is a lot more elegant than we're used to – isn't it, Taco?' He nudges the dog affectionately with the toe of his boot. 'I usually eat straight out of a frying pan, and Taco, whose manners aren't nearly as refined as mine, prefers to eat off the floor.' At the mention of his name, Taco settles himself under the table with a wheezy yawn. 'Although last night, as it happens, we ate like kings.' Duval takes the matches from my hand and relights the spluttering wick of one of the candles. 'We built a fire outside and grilled fresh fish.'

'Fresh fish?' Having lived on nothing but red meat since January I feel quite giddy at the thought. 'There are nights I dream of fresh fish.'

'Well, stick around long enough,' Duval says casually, 'and I'll make sure you get some.'

He catches my eye and, self-conscious suddenly, I turn and busy myself with oven gloves, then hoist the skillet on to the table.

'So how did you end up in Temerosa, you and Benjamín?'

'Benjamín stumbled across it on one of his crossings. It was owned by an old man up in Bisbee.'

'And he didn't mind?'

'He never bothered us. No one bothered us until those Toronto sharks of yours bullied him into selling.'

'How inconvenient for you.'

'On the contrary, it was wonderful. It was a miserable little cabin before they paid us to put in electricity and water.'

'You fleeced them, I suppose.'

'Of course, but don't think they didn't deserve it. They didn't have the first idea what they were doing.'

Like me, I think. I spoon the pork onto plates. The meat is soft and falls apart to the touch. 'So you squatted in a town that didn't belong to you, you used other people's money to make yourself more comfortable, then, as thanks, you bankrupted them.'

'Oh, I can't claim all the credit myself,' Duval replies cheerfully. 'There were other like-minded people fleecing them all over the States. They owned dozens of towns like Temerosa. Bought them up with the idea of renovating them and selling them to – and I quote – "The New Pioneers of the West", for which read a bunch of white bigots living in exclusionary gated communities.'

'And then we came along.'

'Yes.' He pauses. 'Then you came along.'

I look down at my plate, feeling awkward, a little angry. No wonder Duval had always seemed so scornful of the plans for the town.

'I used to think about you, you know,' Duval says quietly. 'I'd lie upstairs, stare at the moon through that rotten little square of a window and wonder what you were doing on the other side of it.'

I look up to see him smiling and remember his resistance to widening the window.

'And what was I doing?'

'Well, to be sure, I fell asleep before I got that far.'

I laugh.

'I had it all worked out you know – you, your husband, your London life.'

'My London life,' I repeat and the words sound far away and unfamiliar coming out of my mouth.

'I imagined you ruthlessly efficient by day, juggling children, housekeepers, shopping, lunches . . .'

'Ah . . . that sort of woman.'

'Don't interrupt.'

'Sorry.'

'At night you would get ready to go out in front of a long mirror, frowning at invisible worry lines. Then you would stop in to kiss the children good night before stepping out to meet your friends to discuss over expensive bottles of wine which part of the world you would next choose to turn into your playground.'

'So a spoilt, shallow socialite then,' I say lightly. 'What a contrast to your Zorro; Duval, the quixotic smuggler of men, selflessly sacrificing your creature comforts for a life helping the poor and the desperate.'

He laughs at the pique in my voice. 'First of all, very little I have ever done is selfless; secondly, I now had all the comforts in the world thanks to your timely UPS shipment.'

I pick at a shard of pork on the side of the pan. 'And she was happy? This pampered soulless creature?'

'She was bored, lonely.'

I look away. 'Not the world's most flattering picture.'

'Ah, but I didn't need to flatter you. You were merely a figment of my imagination.'

'And now you're faced with the disappointment of flesh and blood.'

Duval knocks a cigarette out of his pack. 'All those months I imagined you dissolute, perhaps snobbish, certainly a little spoilt, but at no time did I ever picture you guzzling pork with your fingers at the kitchen table, barefoot, in some torn gypsy dress, with a great big dirty Band-aid on your calf.'

I feel the heat in my cheeks. The dress is dark green, fitted around the bust, with a skirt flared to just below the knee. I could never bear to throw it out because it was my favourite. I always thought the tear wasn't noticeable.

'Why did you come back, Alice?'

I push away from the table and gather the plates. I don't know how to answer him. I've not been able to explain it, either to Robert, to my children, or even to myself. God knows, I wish I had something tangible to run away from. An abusive husband, a crime I'd committed or a court order to defy, but there had been nothing like that. How can I explain that I left London because I felt numb, because I couldn't breathe there any more?

It's hard to admit you're not happy. Surrounded by so many 'good things' – nice house, healthy children, a decent father for them – it seems almost churlish to be discontented. You're not supposed to complain so not only are you dissatisfied but you find yourself feeling guilty about being dissatisfied. It's a bad thing to have feelings you're not allowed.

'Perhaps there should be a witness protection programme for people on the run from bad marriages,' Duval says. 'Leave your life behind, change your name, slip into anonymity.'

I nod. Anonymity. A clean slate. How tempting. Mrs R. Coleman could once again become Alice Porter, all baggage emptied and gone. I have a sudden flashback to the day I met Robert. He'd been laughing, at the top of the world, literally, 10,000 feet up a mountain in Switzerland, ready to launch himself down a lethal black run. I'd married him for that energy. A sporty daredevil, there was nothing in the world he seemed afraid of, and it took a long time before it occurred to me that this bravery was arrogance and that what I'd taken as intelligence turned out to be an almost biblical conviction about his own ideas. Age lent his boyish enthusiasm a faintly boorish edge and, with it, he became louder, more emphatic. He wanted everything bigger, better, and he became obsessed with getting it.

'I think women sign on for some ideal when they get married, and when they realize they haven't got anything close to what they want, they bury their disappointment. Discontented women are like pressure cookers. The steam rises and one day they just reach boiling point.'

'Have you ever been married?'

'Yes.' He uses the word deliberately. As full stop, and obediently I change the subject.

'So how did it begin . . . the schoolroom, the workers? How do people find you?'

'I keep a radio on, I get tip-offs from the Border Patrol.'

'From Winfred?'

He nods. 'In the beginning I just wanted to under-stand. Estella, all the others, how it could have happened, why it still happens so often. I began to stumble across people and I realized they had no idea what they'd let themselves in for. Men who'd never before left their home town. Women crossing in high-heeled shoes. Chil-dren. Not enough water for even half the journey they were undertaking.' He shrugs. 'I took to keeping supplies in the schoolhouse and after a while Temerosa became an open secret, a place people could head for if they got into trouble.' He collects his cigarettes off the table. 'The problem was I started to see the same faces, over and over again. So many of them got caught and sent back. The greener they were, the more they stood out. Out of frustration more than anything, I taught them a few words of English. I got rid of their Mexican clothes and dressed them in more invisible American ones. I gave them a background, a home town in the US, a sports team they could root for. They earned a little money working on the town and sometimes that was all it took for them to stay under the radar.'

'So, a one-man rescue team—'

'One man? No.' He shakes his head. 'For every law-abiding American citizen who believes the most construc-tive use of their firearms is to shoot a Hispanic, there are others who know they can't get by without their Mexi-can workers. There are ranchers who cook up pig roasts to welcome them back and help them fill out applications for US citizenship. There are people dotted all along the border who build water towers and worry themselves sick about doing the right thing.'

'Nora?'

'Nora, yes.' He hesitates.

'What?'

'Border politics comes in murky shades of grey. The good, the bad and the ugly can all end up on the same side at different times. Nora's well meaning, but she's a wild card. There's something not quite right.' He shakes his head again. 'I tend give her a wide berth.'

'Not the most fortunate choice of words.'

He chuckles. 'They say she used to be a great beauty.'

I picture the mottled flesh of Nora's backside spilling over her trousers, the tobacco-streaked teeth.

'They say unrequited love put paid to Nora. Someone broke her heart and it never got put back together again.'

'Not you, I hope.'

He laughs. 'That's one sin I don't need laid at my door.' He reaches for his hat and I realize with a start how late it is. He stands up and we face each other a little awkwardly. 'Well, thank you for dinner, it's always nice to have a fellow fugitive to break bread with.'

'Maybe, but the trouble with fugitives is that they get caught eventually.'

'Ah no.' He smiles. 'Some die a bloody death in the desert and have their bones picked clean by buzzards.'

'I owe you an apology, Duval.'

'No. You don't.'

'I thought pretty bad things of you.'

He puts on his hat. 'Don't be fooled, I'm here only until I find what I'm looking for. The same will be true for you.'

'And what if I never find what I'm looking for?'

'Then you'll stay lost,' he says lightly.

'Sounds lonely.'

'Can be.' He rests his hand on the doorknob, a quick flash of a smile behind his eyes. 'Goodnight then, Alice Coleman,' he says and, touching the brim of his hat, steps out into the black night.

part two

22

'Now this one is my favourite,' Helen Hogan confides, hands fluttering along the wingspan of a large bronze-coloured eagle. 'But of course each piece is so special, so absolutely *unique*.' She turns and glances mistily back at a stallion on another side table and then to a more recently admired wall plaque, which appears to depict a horse's head dissolving into cloud. 'They all come from the same gallery in Austin. The artist in question specializes in the *wilderness*. Look at the detail! The beak! Those eyes! So realistic, don't you think?' She angles the sculptured head towards me. 'Go ahead, touch it! It won't bite!'

Obediently, I turn the bird by its beak. It moves surprisingly easily over the polished surface. 'Whoa there!' Helen chuckles, and I get the feeling that this is a party trick she has played often before.

'So light!' I exclaim dutifully.

'Well, see, that's the beauty of them!' she says excitedly. 'They *look* like they're made out of bronze, but in fact they're made out of composite! Isn't that clever? We're travelled people, as you can see, bin all over the

Midwest, but I can tell you, I've never found this artist's equal anywhere.'

'I can imagine.'

'Of course *you* can.' She lays a hand on my arm. 'Coming from London an' all, but out here it's real hard to find people who appreciate good taste.' She glances across the room to where the other wives are sitting and drops her voice even lower. 'They do their best, 'course, but I guess they just lack the . . .' she gropes for the right word, 'well you know . . . the sophistication.'

The sculptures are ugly and pretentious and in keeping with the rest of the house, through which I've just been led on a painfully intimate tour, encouraged at every opportunity to be touchy-feely with a variety of objects from the scalloped bound edges of the apricot towels to the gold taps on the matching Jacuzzi. Worse, the entire thing had been punctuated by a loud roaring as the Hogan teenagers circled the house on quad bikes like latter-day Indian braves rousting a covered wagon.

'Tucker and Cody,' Helen had mused, 'why, if it's not the quads, it's the snowmobiles. Jeff bought 'em horses, but the boys took one look and said, "Ma, if those things ain't got an engine, we don't want to ride 'em." Teenagers, huh? But then I guess you got all that still to come.'

I'd clucked something empathetic, cursing myself for caving in to Robert's pressure and accepting a tea date with the Texas Family Hogan.

Back in the main room we join the wives of Jeff's two business partners, who are crouching underneath a massive chandelier constructed from intertwined antlers and hooves and suspended from the ceiling by a thick brass

chain. Everything in this house is equally super-sized.
The chocolate chip cookies which Helen is now pressing
upon the women are too big for the plate, the studded
red-leather sofa on which they're sitting is too big for the
room, and the room itself, too big for the house.

Jeff Hogan's 'ranch' is 10,000 feet of new-build vertical log home. 'Finished only this summer, and quite our
dream project,' Hogan had said, although one might
imagine a little less dreamy for the two building companies he boasted of putting out of business during its
construction.

'The landscape artist comes from California,' Helen is
still puffing up to the wives, 'so she has that "big picture"
mentality but then Ague is still such a small town, isn't
it?' She points through the window at some cabbagy-
looking shrubs. 'She landscaped the whole of our garden
with native desert vegetation. They attract these big ol'
colourful butterflies in the spring.'

'God sure has blessed Arizona with extremely di-verse
landscapes and creatures,' one of the wives whispers and
I look through the window, wondering how on earth to
escape.

April has turned into May and spring is giving way to
summer. Today is another big blue. Outside the air is
hot and dry. Through the swagged curtains the sun winks
and beckons. Inside the air-conditioning is on full blast.
I pull my fleece around me and gnaw away at the biscuit,
my mind drifting to Temerosa. I hear the familiar echo
of the hammer, the distant whine of the drill. The first
phase of work on the town is nearing completion: the
boarding house and even some of the smaller cabins

awaiting only their doors to be finished. I picture Duval planing them flat on the worktable, his shirtsleeves rolled up. Now when I walk down to the town each morning, I watch for the smile in his eyes.

I've found there is another Arizona to be seen apart from the border. Duval takes me riding through hills covered in morning glory, up narrow mountain passes where long thin Douglas firs look like forests of unopened umbrellas. He weaves his pickup round serpentine roads, climbing to a vertiginous 9,000 feet in the Santa Catalina Mountains from where the world looks like it's been created by some God playing whimsical balancing games with stalagmites and boulders. In the high desert, he lowers me down into the narrow confines of slot canyons whose towering stone walls are indented with the fossils of strange prehistoric sea monsters. And here is the West I have dreamed of exploring, one of such bewildering scenery changes and harsh beauty that sometimes I feel that to surrender to it completely, to one day curl up and die here, might not be such a bad thing after all.

'Go on, take another one.' Helen is again bearing down upon us with the plate of biscuits. 'They're fresh out of the box, arrived FedEx only yesterday from the Gourmet Bake Company. They do bread, pies, glazed hams, even meatloaf, all home-made.' She whips a catalogue off the table. 'Jeff's an investor; he always saw a big future in mail-order food and he was right!'

'He sure is a fine man,' the wives echo dutifully.

'Hell, yes he is,' Helen says gaily. 'Sometimes you have to kiss every frog in the world to find your prince!' And I have to bite down on my lip not to laugh.

'Say! Talk of the devil!' Helen brushes the clinging crumbs off her velour tracksuit and springs nimbly to her feet as Jeff, rival tour completed, enters the room flanked by his investors. Neither are local. Lane, a stocky man from Albuquerque, seems terminally ill at ease with himself and had earlier mumbled an introduction from the corner of his mouth. The second man, Selby, is all bone and sinew and nerves. He stares at me curiously as Hogan advances towards us mid-anecdote.

'. . . so I'd been meaning to get the number off Mrs Coleman for an age.' He bestows a genial wink on me. 'Then last week I found myself at the realtor's office and Cathy just happened to mention she had a contact number for Mr Coleman in her documentation, so I said to myself, "Jeff! Seize the moment! Give this man a call!" ' He breaks into a snowy-capped smile. 'And real glad I am, too, cos if you don't mind my saying, Mrs Coleman, your husband sounds like a fine fellow.'

'Who exactly is this guy?' Robert had demanded on the phone. 'What's his business? What does he own in the town?'

'Why?' I hedged. Hogan's most recent contribution to Ague was a large poster outside Prestcott's which offered visitors a chance to 'Step back into the Bygone days of the Old West.' I'd been furious that he'd managed to get hold of Robert behind my back. Furious and deeply apprehensive.

'Alice,' Robert said, 'he offered us a *swap*!' And a nasty fibrous knot began to form in my stomach.

I was already in a tailspin of confusion about Temerosa. Now that reality has crashed headlong with my fantasy of the place, I couldn't see how I could possibly go ahead with plans for a retreat. I couldn't see how I could ever have come up with such a stupid idea in the first place.

'Don't be so hard on yourself,' Duval had said. 'The world exists on thousands of different levels and just because some are more tragic than others, it doesn't make them any more valid. You fall into that way of thinking and you become Nora, so overwhelmed by the world's suffering, you go mad. Besides, the border has always been a place where crazy ideas flourish and a retreat is nothing if not a crazy idea.'

Unfortunately, Robert, as I knew only too well, was an entrepreneur whose business strategy was built on crazy ideas. Anything that required a punt he was prepared to consider – and when I say anything, I'm not exaggerating. Robert laughed it off. Bravado had always been his calling card and, to begin with, I loved him for it. His conviction always enthused others but he had no patience for follow-through. Sooner or later money for every one of his projects drained away and he was left grasping at ever thinner straws. Each new idea was the angioplasty balloon that would unblock the clogged arteries of our debt and make the heart of our ailing finances beat healthily once more. Temerosa had been no different. For a while after we got back from that first trip, Robert was Bugsy Siegel and Temerosa his Las Vegas. Then the ghost town became just another piece of paper lodged with the lawyers. A ghost project, buried and forgotten, its potential scattered to the four winds of the Sonora. Six months ago Robert couldn't believe my resurrection of the Temerosa plan, and now here he was, thoroughly overexcited about the idea of a *swap*.

'Alice, what if this is the opportunity we've been waiting for? Hogan thinks that if we're ambitious enough for the project, it could attract some serious investment.'

'Robert, trust me. You do not want to be in business with Hogan.'

'Just hear him out, Alice. What harm can it do? Look . . .' He tailed off and I knew then what was coming. 'Maybe I should find a way to get over there.'

He'd said it before, but he didn't really want to come any more than I wanted him to. Our unspoken separation suited both of us and we knew it.

The silence down the line thickened.

'Alice, I want to see you.'

'Robert . . .'

'I miss you, I miss the children.'

Guilt washed over me. 'They miss you too.'

Sooner or later I'd have to let him come. Of course I would, just not yet. Please, dear God, not yet.

The investors join their wives. Hogan chalks up some small talk while I sink ever further into the sofa, squeeze my eyes shut and try to remember what the sun feels like on my face.

'Open your eyes.' Duval had closed my hand round something smooth and cold.

'What is it?'

'A fossilized leaf. I found it by the schoolroom.'

I traced my finger along the thin indented spine. 'So fragile.'

'Except – think of the unimaginable pressure it's had to withstand. It's been burnt by lava, flooded, crushed and yet it's still survived. It's an incredibly romantic idea . . .'

'Gentlemen, ma'am,' Jeff is saying pompously. 'To business.' He hands Selby a piece of paper. 'This is a US state department warning issued to tourists this week. Numbers of muggings and abductions are rising. Numbers of illegals crossing this year are up ten per cent on last.'

The two investors exchange a look. 'Jeff,' Selby says and his voice is pitched low, 'you promised us the situation would improve.'

'And so it has! Everywhere that Ranch Rights has patrolled, that is,' Hogan says. 'Security is tight on our own property lines, but gentlemen, geography is not on our side.' He spreads a map on the table. 'This is Ague,' he circles it, 'and this is where we are now.' He joins the two circles with a thick black line then taps the map with his pen. 'And this is where you come in, Mrs Coleman, because right here in the middle sits Temerosa.'

All three men look at me. 'We need to join forces, ma'am,' Hogan says emphatically. 'Take a share in each other's business. One investment to protect.' He rakes the felt tip across the map. 'One line to close off.'

'One twenty-mile line, Jeff,' Selby reminds him. 'How in God's name are we going to protect something that long?'

'Recruit more people, that's how.'

'Ain't this whole thing best left to the Border Patrol?' one of the wives asks nervously.

'Ma'am, I salute the valiant efforts of the Border Patrol to enforce the law but they don't have the men or the motivation to keep these criminals off private property. Why do you think we formed Ranch Rights in the first place? Think about it: the desert between Temerosa and the border is some of the meanest, most scorched ground in the whole of the west, so why do people continue crossing there?'

The two men look at him expectantly.

'Because someone is making it easy for them,' Hogan says.

'That's what folk are saying.' Selby nods.

'My guess is it's one of those middle eastern fellas,' Helen offers.

'Whoever it is, it's someone who knows the terrain round here like the back of their hand.'

I close my eyes again. See Duval leaning on his horse.

'If you want to teach your children something about this place, you should take a small patch of land no bigger than twelve foot square, and watch it every day. Look for changes in the leaves, the prints of animals, study their droppings, see what they eat. If you can do that for a whole year then you'll understand how the desert works.'

'So what's that then?' I'd pointed at a scrubby pine-looking thing.

'I haven't the faintest idea.'

'You're a complete fraud!' I'd laughed.

'I'm not really up on my conifers,' he said. 'Test me on cacti if you like. I'm brilliant on cacti.'

'Okay, give me your top ten then.'

'My top ten.' He looked thoughtful. 'Let me see now, would that be rated for personality or best in a swim-suit?'

'I'll settle for overall winners.'

He slapped a fly on the horse's neck. 'Well in no particular order, the saguaro, because they're so human. Drive through northern Arizona and the hills up there are choked with them. You can find ones that look like grizzled old men, or cowboys ready to draw a gun. Some look like Chinese priests or lepers. On a good day you can find one that's a dead ringer for your father.'

I laughed up at him.

'They have endearingly human qualities too.'

'Really? Like what?'

'They get thin in a drought and fatten up when it rains. They can live on a centimetre of water a year but if they don't get that much the older ones fold up and die and leave the water for the younger members of their family . . . Then there's cholla, which have wonderful names – Beehive Nipple, Strawberry Hedgehog, Teddy Bear.' He pointed at a bushy-looking cactus. 'Those are cholla there, but watch out for them. Their spikes detach very easily; if you brush against them they hook into your flesh leaving only the thinnest hair above the surface of your skin. Very hard to get out. In Spanish, the word means annoying small-town gangsters. Ask Benjamín about his various spats with the cholla. He believes they jump out at you out of sheer malice.' He pointed at another plant which looked like the padded end of an ogre's club. 'That's barrel cactus. Any minute now it'll sprout a pink or yellow flower on top of its head which makes it look exactly like a southern black woman going off to church in her best bonnet . . .'

Selby fixes me with his probing stare. 'Ma'am, you've been living in Temerosa for over four months now. Have you seen any of those 9/11 type people around the place?'

'None at all.'

'You spotted any aliens coming through town?'

'Apart from the little green ones?'

'Mrs Coleman, we appreciate your European sense of humour,' Hogan says heavily. 'Really we do but—'

'Jeff tells us you have a local builder handling the works,' Lane interrupts.

'Duval!' Hogan says with distaste. 'The man's a drifter, a liberal. He only hires Mexicans!'

'Mexicans, huh?' Selby's eyes narrow with suspicion. 'All legal, I assume?'

'I certainly hope so. At least Mr Hogan was kind enough to check their work permits for me.'

In the quiet of the schoolroom, I see Duval's head bent over the fake ID cards, a frown of concentration on his face.

'Just the same,' Selby is saying, 'you can't be too careful. Mexicans are Mexicans.'

'I don't know how you sleep at night.' His wife shudders. 'They say Temerosa is haunted.'

'Well I guess you can't have a ghost town without ghosts!' I say cheerfully.

'But it's so remote down that road!' she persists. 'You must dread those endless evenings.'

'Oh there's always something to do,' I murmur. Now,

when night closes in and the moon rises, when the children have fallen asleep and Benjamín takes up position outside their bedroom, Duval comes to the cabin. Through the window I watch for him to step out of the shadows, the reins of the horses in his hand, and then we ride out to the flap of a bird's wing, the swishing of tails and the tap dance of hooves on rock . . .

'We must get you more involved in our social life,' Helen is saying. 'In fact why don't you come to my pot-luck dinner next Thursday?'

'You're very kind,' I thank her, wondering what fresh hell a pot-luck dinner might be, 'but there's always masses to do, climbing, hiking . . .'

'Not around Temerosa!' Helen's agitation jiggles the rhinestones on her tracksuit top. 'Not so close to the border! Tell her, Jeff, please!'

'It would be extremely foolish,' Hogan says thickly. 'Now that the weather's so much warmer, the number of crossings will rise with every passing day.'

'First thing tomorrow I'm signing you up for the Happy Hikers club.' Helen pats my knee. 'It's all women. We use only well-marked trails. It's wonderful exercise.' She gives my leg an extra squeeze. 'I told Jeff it wasn't right, what if something should happen to you? What if you should meet one of those Mexicans face to face? These people are desperate. There's no saying what might happen.'

'It's time you and the kids came under the protection of Ranch Rights,' Jeff says. 'All of us here are members and there are like-minded people signing up with us all the time. Let us patrol Temerosa and the land surrounding it. If we come across anyone who shouldn't be there, you can be sure we'll catch 'em.'

'And then what?' I ask.

'We turn them over to the proper authorities.' Hogan clears his throat. 'Of course.'

'Hold on now, Jeff,' Helen says. 'Mrs Coleman's not comfortable with this, I can tell.' She makes a grab for my hand and clasps it between hers. 'I can see you're a compassionate person, same ways I am. Hell, I understand what you're thinking. Sometimes I sit and look at these people through Jeff's binoculars and I feel so sorry for them. They don't have a damn thing. We have our sympathies, we find it heartbreaking. Believe me, I want to take them all home and give them fried chicken, I want to give them my guest room.'

'But . . .' I ease my hand out of hers, 'you don't.'

'Alice, you keep on inviting people into your house, soon they'll be sleeping in your bed, eating your food, using your shower. The house won't sustain the people. The house isn't big enough for all the people and the house will eventually fall down.'

'Like my wife says,' Hogan has on his pulpit voice now, 'we're all caring souls, but our compassion stops at the border. Once these people cross the line, they're criminals and I have no sympathy for criminals. My duty is to American citizens. I have no choice but to turn these people back.'

'Won't they just try to cross again?'

'We convince them not to.'

'I see . . . How?' I ask quietly.

Selby and Lane look at each other uneasily.

'Ma'am, no disrespect, but this is a man's conversation and one I'd prefer to have with your husband.'

'Yes, of course.' I push up from the sofa. I have to get out of here. I make my goodbyes and promise Hogan I'll pass everything on to Robert when we next speak.

'Or if you prefer,' he offers, 'I'll call him myself.'

'Mr Hogan!' I curb a strong impulse to squeeze my hands round his throat.

'Ma'am?'

'May I speak frankly?'

'Of course. You're amongst friends here!' Helen says.

'Robert's mother has just died and this is a very difficult time for him and though he would think it rude to say so himself, being English and all, I'm sure you can appreciate he needs to be left alone to grieve. Actually, we both do.'

'Why, you poor things.' Helen looks mortified. 'I'm so sorry for your loss. Were you very close to her?'

'Very.' I contort my face into an expression of pious sorrow then canter towards the emergency exit. Hogan follows close behind. At the door he shakes my hand in his ponderous way and I can almost taste the fresh air when he implores me to wait and disappears into the hall cupboard, re-emerging with a plastic bag of fawn-coloured caps with 'Ranch Rights' printed on them.

'Take a couple for the kids as well,' he says, beaming, 'After all, one size fits all!'

23

'Why do people like Jeff Hogan move here if they feel it so beneath them?' I say irritably. 'And what's with the ghastly Betty Crocker wife? I mean, where do you find women like that these days?'

'e-Bay, probably,' Duval says, scanning the breakfast menu, and I laugh. 'There's money to be made on any border and Jeff Hogan thinks he's the man to do it.'

'And is he?'

'Look around you,' he says. We're sitting in a corner booth in the M&M waiting for Winfred to show. Apart from the usual disparate characters snatching a moment's refuge from life, the place is empty. Barb, the waitress, hovers by the serving hatch staring vacantly into space. Two truck drivers are simultaneously smoking and forking eggs into their mouths. In the M&M it's business as usual, it's all dreams and desperation, washed down with cup after cup of weak percolated coffee.

'See that guy?' Duval nods at a gimlet-eyed man sitting alone at a table, mopping up yolk with toast. 'He's fifty-two, looks seventy. See his boots? They're bound with duct tape where they've worn through. He lives in a cabin with no heating and no water and looks like he's a dollar away from destitute. In fact he owns a hundred and eighty thousand acres of deeded land and another three hundred thousand acres in leases.' He points to another table where an immaculately groomed cowboy studies the menu with the intensity of a college professor editing his lecture notes. 'That guy is a horse trainer. Good one too, but the locals are scared of him. He's a wild son of a bitch with two brothers in the state penitentiary and his wife's lover buried in his backyard. I bet if you were to look in his pickup outside, you'd find a pearl-handled colt forty-five in the front passenger seat and a couple of rifles in the back. You know,' he adds wryly, 'for the dangerous business of shoeing a horse.'

I look quizzically at the cowboy's ramrod-straight back.

'People fare better on the border when they're not all they seem. Hogan, however, is exactly who he seems and those who flash their credentials around as readily as he does tend to be stripped of them.'

'By you?'

'No, not by me. I have no interest in Hogan. But by someone.'

'And if not?'

'Then he'll make his fortune, sell that log monstrosity of his and upgrade to an expensive white stucco build with wrought-iron fencing, a bougainvillea-filled patio and a house alarm system with armed response in Scottsdale. He'll spend his retirement showing off to the rest of the community, congratulating himself on getting out of Houston and realizing too late that his new-found freedom in the desert extends only as far as the power of his air-conditioning unit.'

'If you ever forsake your life of crime, I think you should consider writing a column.' I sweep a by-line in the air with my hand: 'Great Stereotypes of the West.'

'And I think you should eat your bacon.' He's looking at me in that curious way he has and I drop my eyes for fear that he will read what's inside them. During these last few weeks I've been road-testing feelings that have been dormant for so long I scarcely remember what to do with them. All I know is that the more time I spend with Duval, the more it feels like the missing pieces to some emotional jigsaw are being slotted back in place, and I should probably stop right now, before it's too late, before the picture is complete and there, apparent for everyone to see.

'Why? Are you intending to pinch it?'

'It had crossed my mind.'

'Give me a low-down on the huntsman at the till and it's yours.'

Duval starts to twist round.

'No.' I touch his hand lightly. 'Without looking.' Underneath mine, his fingers are long and brown. A pianist's hands. I look down at them. I've wondered before how it would feel to have them curve around the edge of my ribs. To brush over my skin. I take my hand away.

'Okay.' Duval plucks a toothpick from the holder and chews on it. 'Camouflage hat, worn high on head, matching trousers, bunch of keys attached to belt loops. On his face, a look of bovine stupidity. IQ guaranteed slightly lower than room temperature and a propensity to spit. He's got a knife at his waist modelled on his favourite action-movie star, which only now he's discovering doesn't actually do the job. Boots are splattered with blood. Too bad a shot to kill the animal outright, so he's had to stomp it to death after a minor flesh wound to the leg. How am I doing?'

'I think he looks charming.' Over his shoulder I watch as Barb hands the huntsman a pile of cardboard take-out containers. As he heads towards the door, she takes a tortoiseshell comb from her apron pocket and draws her thin hair up into a bun. 'I mean, don't you think that for a man of such dubiously elastic morality, you're being a little judgemental?'

Duval just looks at me, the smile back behind his eyes, and begins counting. 'Five, four, three, two . . .'

Outside the hunter looks up at the sky then spits on the ground twice.

Duval grins and forks the bacon off my plate. 'So what was your answer to Hogan's little business proposition?'

'I said I'd consider it.' Through the window I watch Winfred's car pull in. It's his civilian ride, a stylish rezmobile, crouched low to the ground, with flaking green paint and a speaker wired to the top. The first time I'd seen him drive it, he told me it had won competitions. I never dared ask for what.

'And will you?'

'Of course not.'

'You'll have Hogan on your back till you do.'

midnight cactus

'Do you have to use "on my back" and Hogan in the same sentence?'

Duval laughs but I think of Robert, on the phone now almost every day.

'Hogan's offering us a stake in a business that's already up and running. How can this not make sense, Alice? Tell me how this can not be a good idea.' And I wonder just how much longer I can hold them both off.

'Hogan's a fool,' Duval says again.

'Maybe, but he's a fool with an army, and he's suspicious of you.'

'Yes,' he says quietly. 'I know he is.'

'Duval, sooner or later they'll come looking for you, and if I can find the schoolroom, anyone can.'

'Perhaps.'

'You're not worried?'

'I'm counting on not everyone having your combination of luck, perseverance and blind disregard for personal safety.' He signals for more coffee.

'What if they catch you?'

'Who they? Border Patrol or Hogan?'

'Either.'

'Well, Hogan is your average "shoot on sight, string 'em up from the tallest tree" kind of a guy.'

'Well that's okay then – and the Border Patrol?'

'Oh, you know the kind of thing. Jail. An orange jumpsuit, a long-term contract with one of those chain gangs you're so intrigued by.'

Riding through the desert one morning, I'd been profoundly shocked to come across a chain gang of women, digging graves in the county cemetery, not far off the road. They'd been padlocked together at the ankles and were wearing striped uniforms, in a scene more resonant of the deep south at the turn of the century than of contemporary America.

'Who are they?' I'd asked Duval. 'Serial killers or something?'

He'd shaken his head. 'Most of them are in there for minor infractions, cheque forgery or violating their probation. Some of them probably just couldn't make bail.'

I couldn't believe you get put on a chain gang for forging a cheque. But then Arizona is not exactly the most liberal state in the union. According to Duval it only got a Martin Luther King day after tourists threatened to boycott the golf courses.

Duval peels another toothpick from its plastic casing. 'If you like I'll apply for litter clean-up on the rez and you can wave at me next time you drive by.'

'What makes you think I won't be hammering rocks on the other side of the road?'

Duval's face turns serious. 'Alice . . .'

But we're both distracted by the sight of Winfred rumbling through the restaurant towards us. He's out of uniform, and looking a little unkempt in a Hawaiian shirt and jeans. 'Hey, Winfred!' I say, expecting his broad grin in response, but he gives only a perfunctory smile before easing his bulk along the bench.

'Duval, listen to me, man,' he starts. 'I got some news.'

Duval puts up his hand and Winfred stops questioningly.

'You can trust me, you know,' I say, unable to keep from bridling.

'It's not that.'

'What is it then?'

'Alice,' he says, his voice low, 'it's one thing drawing a line in the sand but it's another thing to cross it. I won't risk turning you into a real fugitive.'

I look at him and I think maybe he doesn't realize it, or maybe he wants no part of it, but whatever that line is, I have already crossed it. Whatever normal life used to be, I have lost all sense of it. I am an English woman living in Arizona in a ghost town, allowing Mexicans to slip in and out of the shadow of the law while I pull the wool over my children's eyes and keep my husband at bay with secrets and lies, and who for? Who for, if not for him?

24

Through the open window of Emilio Chavez's patrol truck, a rush of hot air picks up the flyer from the top of the dashboard. Small feet kick the back of my seat as the children scrabble to catch it.

'Ro-do,' Emmy spells out.

'Rod-e-o, dummy,' Jack says.

'What is a rodee-o anyway?' Emmy asks, signalling the end to her morning's sulk.

I twist round. 'You know, lassos, bucking broncos, fun stuff like that.' In the back seats, the children are strapped neatly into their seatbelts. They're not exactly appropriately kitted out for the day's outing. Jack is clad entirely in faux army gear from Wal-Mart. Emmy is wearing the pair of lizard-skin cowboy boots that she'd found in the thrift shop, and subsequently barely removed from her feet. These are teamed with her tartan kilt and a machine-shrunken woolly thing, far too hot for the weather but which I've nevertheless sanctioned as thanks for her having graciously agreed to forsake her new orange Mexican embroidered dress – the one Dolores had given her.

midnight cactus

'But why can't I wear it?' she had wailed. 'Whywhy-why? It's so unfair! You get to wear what you want so why can't I . . . oh, God, I hate being a child,' she roared. 'I want to die DIE do you hear then I won't have to be a child any more.'

'Exactly, you'll be a dead child,' Jack pointed out placidly. 'You still won't be a grown-up, so what's the point?'

'I don't care if I'm a dead child.' She punched him in the arm. I'd rather be a dead child than be bossed around all day long. Bossed around my WHOLE LIFE.'

I tried to explain, but what to say? Please, Emmy, try to understand. Your mother is harbouring an undocu-mented worker in the cabin and a dozen or so more down the road – oh, and also, pretty much on a daily basis, she's aiding and abetting a habitual felon so, you know, your cooperation in this matter would really be greatly appreciated. Sure, I could claim that Duval, his comings and goings, his sympathies and morality had nothing to do with me. Hear no evil, speak no evil, see no evil. But my blind eye was all-seeing, and, poor little thing, how could she help but give the game away? Emmy, who's passionate about all things Mexican. Emmy, who has taken to printing off little white ticker tapes of Spanish translations and sticking them onto random household items . . . lamps, blinds, tables, even the orange slab of Monterey Jack cheese in the fridge, so she, too, can learn the language. Emmy, who on some days follows Benjamín around so closely you'd think she'd grown out of one of his legs.

She'd cried for a full hour about the dress. I gave it to

her straight. 'We don't want anyone asking us questions about where it came from. We're not allowed to talk about Dolores. Dolores is not really allowed to cook for us. She's not really allowed to be in America. If she got caught, it would be really bad. She'd get into trouble. She'd have to go back home!'

'That's not bad!' Emmy howled. 'Why is that bad? I want to go back home too. I want to go home all the time. ALL THE TIME, do you hear?'

'Do you, Emmy?' I looked searchingly into her face. 'Do you?'

'No, not really.' She scratched a spot on her arm distractedly. 'Not all the time, just when I'm tired. And when Jack hurts me.'

'So don't tell anyone about Dolores, okay? Promise me?' I knelt down and held her shoulders. 'And I know you can keep a secret because . . . well because . . .' I wondered what to say which would adequately impress upon her the gravity of the situation, and then it came to me, 'because you kept the secret about Granny, didn't you?'

It couldn't have been a more direct hit.

'Mummy,' she whispered awfully, 'I said I was sorry.' Then she looked up at me with an expression of such remorse that my heart contracted with guilt. Making Emmy cry, making Emmy lie. 'I won't tell anyone about Dolores.' She drew a zipper over her lips with one grimy finger. 'Jinx personal padlock, I swear.'

There was a reason we'd gone through all this. Dolores had only just arrived for work when the familiar white patrol vehicle had driven up the track to the cabin.

midnight cactus

I stopped at the window, relieved Winfred would have news of Duval. It was three days since breakfast in the M&M and there had been no word from either Duval or Benjamín since. But it hadn't been Winfred adjusting his shades and hat in the wing mirror of the patrol truck, but Emilio Chavez. For a short moment I stared at him in surprise, then I bolted down the stairs to the kitchen.

Dolores was dreaming at the stove, her head in a cloud of cinnamon and chillies. The whole cabin was steamy with the visceral smell of frying meat.

'Quick!' I'd whispered and she turned in alarm. 'Go upstairs. Hide! *¡Escóndete!*' But she merely shrank against the counter and it wasn't until I'd uttered the magic word '*migra*' that she straightened up and her limpid brown eyes began to churn with fear.

A few minutes later Emilio Chavez was sitting at the table and I was wondering whether this was a social call, or something more sinister. I bustled round the kitchen as noisily as possible, crushing coffee beans, clanking mugs in and out of cupboards, worried that at any moment Dolores's not inconsiderable body mass might induce a telltale crack in the ceiling boards, and knowing that with both children at school any noise coming from upstairs might be construed as suspicious.

Chavez had been meaning to come for some time. He wanted to be sure we were okay.

'Yes, of course we are. Why wouldn't we be?'

'Alice, there has been an incident on the border.'

My heart started beating a little faster.

'Yesterday we received a tip-off. A truck, abandoned

in the desert. We quickly dispatched officers with water and medical supplies.' Chavez shrugged wearily. 'It's always this time of year, with the temperatures rising, that these "trucks of death" are found.'

I nodded. I'd read about this in the papers. Mexicans abandoned by their smugglers. A dozen, fifteen people left to die of heat exhaustion and suffocation. 'In this case, though, there were only two individuals locked inside,' Chavez said.

I started to feel sick. 'Who were they?'

'Smugglers. A coyote and his driver.'

Benjamín and Duval. I stared fixedly at a knot of wood on the table's surface. Why else would Chavez have come?

'Were they . . . dead?' I could hardly bring myself to say it.

'Dead?' He sounded surprised by my concern. 'No. In need of water? Certainly.'

I raised my head to find him looking at me keenly.

'Are you okay? You're very pale.'

'Yes, sorry, it's just a little hot today. So what happened?' My heart was still beating at 78 rpm instead of 33.

'We interrogated the coyotes. When the truck broke down they were worried that with so many people the heat sensors would be tripped and the Border Patrol alerted, so they locked them inside, *hijos de puta* . . .'

His mouth twisted, and I thought no, thank God, not Duval, not Benjamín . . .

'The last thing the coyotes remember before waking up in the truck themselves was heading back across the border on foot. They never saw who attacked them.'

'I don't understand. What happened to the people they deserted?'

'Gone.' He blew on his fingers. 'Vanished. There were seventeen people inside that truck. My men have searched the area, but not a single one has been found.'

'I see . . .' I waited for him to go on.

'It's a twelve-mile walk to the nearest town. They had women with them. Two elders. It's impossible that they could just disappear.'

'I'm sorry,' I told him, 'I still don't understand what this has to do with me.'

He leant his elbows on the table. 'Temerosa is the nearest town, Alice.'

I permitted myself an inward smile. Duval had them safe then. They'd be at the schoolroom or already on their way north.

'Folks who live on the border are essentially decent, well-meaning people.' Chavez was still watching me closely. 'They understand that Mexicans who try to cross the desert do so in their ignorance and sadness. They understand that the border exacts an agonizing toll on human life, but Alice, harbouring these individuals is against the law.'

'I understand.' I met his gaze directly. 'But I've seen no one.'

Chavez nodded as if this was the answer he was expecting. 'I must talk with your foreman now.' He glanced at his paperwork then back to me. 'Duval, isn't it?'

I wiped my expression carefully blank. Duval wasn't around, I told him, Benjamín neither. I offered up something about lumber yards and supply stores, but in truth I can't remember the exact excuse.

'In that case,' Chavez plucked his hat off the table, 'we will go and talk directly to his men.'

He waited by the cabin door. I held back, fussed over the whereabouts of shoes, sunglasses, trying to quell the nerves building up in my stomach. I liked Chavez, his quiet seriousness, his old-fashioned manners, such an entirely different thing to Hogan's gauche, vulgar hospitality, but as head of the local Border Patrol, he was the natural-born enemy of Duval and thus mine by proxy. It was one thing fooling the self-righteous Hogan with forms, but I imagined Chavez had a far beadier eye for a forgery.

Outside, light struck like a camera flash. It was that time of day when the sun has total control, when it establishes itself so fierce and high in the sky that it's inconceivable to imagine it ever being defeated by a weak curve of moon. I walked as slowly as I dared. The leaves of the cottonwood threw spots of dappled shade across the path. I was barely able to field Chavez's questions – How were the children? Were they enjoying Arizona? Not too hot for them? – trying instead to think of a way to put off the inevitable moment when the workers would glance up and see me approaching with this stranger in his hated uniform of the *Migra*. I could picture it clearly. The indecision in their eyes. Both Duval and Benjamín gone and far longer than they should have been. Their trust of me, a white woman, tentative at best. What if they didn't hold their nerve? What if they dropped their tools and bolted for cover? The noise of hammering and sawing echoed closer and closer, and out of sheer desperation I bent down to tie my shoelace, and that's when I saw it – somewhere in my peripheral vision – the waxy yellow flower of the whipple cholla. 'Watch out for it,' I heard Duval's warning. 'Ask Benjamín about his various spats with the cholla.'

Chavez stopped beside me. 'Those shoes are no good in the desert. You must buy boots. I will take you to a good place in Nogales.' I mumbled something and made to stand up, then executed what must have looked like the most pantomime of stumbles: avoiding Chavez's hastily outstretched hand, I squeezed my eyes shut and threw myself into the barbed embrace of one of Benjamín's so-called annoying small-town gangsters.

'Mummy,' Emmy moans from the back seat of the truck, 'I'm bored.'

I open my eyes. My arm had been a pincushion. Several of the cactus spikes had also impaled themselves through the soft half moon of flesh between thumb and forefinger.

'Don't touch them!' Chavez said at once. 'You mustn't leave the tips in.' And taking me by the elbow, he helped me to my feet. 'We must get you to the doctor.' But as he'd said it, he'd directed a long hard look at the town over my shoulder.

'How's your arm?' Chavez asks now, as if on cue.

'My arm?' I pull up my shirt sleeve. 'Oh, it's fine.' The cactus spikes show up as a smattering of red dots, like a minor outbreak of chicken pox.

In the medical centre, the cute doctor had pulled out the sturdiest barbs with a pair of tweezers then reached into the cupboard behind him for a bottle of Elmer's glue.

'And what are we making today?' I asked facetiously. Emmy had several half-dried bottles of the stuff in the cabin, which she used for constructing origami paper animals.

'We're making you better,' the doctor said severely. 'I've never seen a more accident-prone family.' He squeezed the thick white glue onto my arm, waited for it to dry, then peeled it off again like a face mask, and the rest of the tiny spikes had come out with it.

'I'm sorry,' Chavez apologizes again.

'Hey, I can hardly blame you for tripping over my own shoelaces.'

'Even so,' he says stiffly, 'I feel responsible.'

'Ah, so this is your penance? Taking us to the rodeo?'

'Of course not.' Finally, there's a glimmer of a smile. 'It's my pleasure.'

'Why do we have to go to a rodee-o anyway?' Jack grouses.

I want to tell him that partly it's because it's prudent to keep your enemies close, however friendly they might be, and partly it's because poor Chavez had insisted, and I couldn't really come up with a plausible excuse not to.

'Kids.' It's Chavez's turn to crane his head round now. 'This will be a fun day out, you'll see. Rodeos began as informal competitions among cowboys to show off their skills with roping animals and stuff. They're a big deal round here. Today is the International High School championships. A kid that wins today gets three maybe four years of free school.'

'Three or four years of school?' Emmy squawks, horrified.

'Bummer,' Jack agrees.

The rodeo is in full swing by the time we arrive. In the car park, music, pounding from speakers lashed to a telegraph pole, competes for supremacy with the thud of electrical generators. The entrance is through an enormous tent selling western wear. Chavez, citing official business of some kind, furnishes us with a meeting place, then disappears into the crowd leaving Jack, Emmy and me to explore. Here are accessories from another world. Saddles, stirrups, reins, leather chaps, walls full of tough, wicked-looking lassos; in fact pretty much anything that can be attached to a horse is on sale. The aisles are heaving with people. Families with small children clutching cotton candy and bags of fritos. Packs of slim-hipped teenage girls, identically dressed in high-waisted jeans and checked shirts knotted under their breasts; their hair either combed up into elaborate sugar confections or let loose to cascade down their backs like shiny gold ribbon. Every man, woman, child, old, young, fat and thin alike, wears a cowboy hat. Even babies in strollers have red bandannas knotted round their throats. The place is thick with the smell of leather and the chick-chack of spurs clattering by. Counting out dollars and cents, two old men hold out arthritic hands to each other and proudly compare loss of digits as though competing at a leprosy convention. 'I was roping a steer,' I hear one say to the other, 'thumb came right off and rolled in the dirt. Every one of them dogs was sniffin' and scrabblin' for it but Tom's big ol' sheepdog snapped it up.'

I stop for a minute, feeling almost surreally out of place. There is something so self-contained about this world and those who belong to it. I try to imagine any single one of the people in this tent transported back to Camden High Street, but it's hard. In London, a West Papuan in full ceremonial dress complete with nose horn would probably incite less finger pointing than a cowboy, and as they split and pass around us, I wonder if they too can tell, just by looking, that there are interlopers in their midst.

Emmy finds a jewellery stand and inveigles me into buying her a turquoise necklace and I talk Jack into trying on hats. The smallest is still a little big for his head, but he looks good and there is a definite strut to his walk as we leave the tent and head out into the glare of the main event.

A mismatched band of musicians is stationed in front of the food stands. The lead singer looks as if she's been teleported straight from Carnaby Street circa 1965. A thick hair piece falls asymmetrically over one ear. Her lower body is shoe-horned into a red mini skirt and as she stamps from one chubby white leg to the other she croons 'Take Me to the River' with great gusto. Her guitarist strums away, apparently on a different hit, while an even funkier-looking back-up singer, with a lopsided afro and fuzzy sideburns, swings his hips not entirely in time to either beat.

I clutch the hands of the children and look around for Chavez. There are faces I recognize in the crowd. Sue,

Jack's teacher, some children and parents from school, the arts and crafts lady from Ague. It's only eleven-thirty but people are already eating at trestle tables piled high with food. Catfish hoagies, quesadillas, curly fries, hamburgers, buffalo wings. A couple of benign-looking old-timers are selling cobs of roasted corn which get spat, blisteringly hot, out of a huge tombola-style grill. At a funnel cake stand, an Indian woman dunks patties of batter into boiling oil. Next to her a fit-looking Navajo, wearing a baseball hat emblazoned 'Desert Storm', sprinkles the golden pillow with icing sugar and hands it to Jack in a crenellated box. The air is so clogged with the smell of fried food I think that if I can ever bring myself to leave this place, this will be the scent I'll have to bottle for nostalgia.

Chavez is sitting with one of the cowboys from the town hall meeting. He's a tall gangling man, his shirt starched to attention and a grey felt hat pulled low over his face. Chavez beckons us over. 'Alice, Jack, Emmy! Come and say hi to Moss Adams.'

'Ma'am.' The cowboy touches his hat creakily, then places an enormous chapped hand on top of Emmy's head. 'Now you're a fine little lady. What are you going to be when you grow up?'

'A hit man,' she says.

The cowboy looks taken aback, then grips his knees and wheezes out a laugh revealing three ochre-coloured teeth staked precariously in his gums like loose fence-posts.

'Moss, let Emmy pull your moustache,' Chavez says noticing Emmy eyeing up the man's full Walrus, which is thick and wide and a superlative six inches long. Obligingly the cowboy bends his head. Emmy's hand remains resolutely in her lap. 'C'mon, girl,' he whispers, 'no need to be shy.' Emmy looks at me for reassurance then, reaching up, curls her hand around the bristly tail of hair and gives it a tremendous tug as though it's an old rope door-pull she's been warned doesn't work terribly well. The cowboy straightens up very quickly, his eyes smarting with tears. Chavez chuckles and introduces the girl sitting next to him as Moss's granddaughter. 'Ima's a big champion,' Chavez says. 'A national champion.'

'What event?' I ask her.

'Go-tang.'

'What?'

'Go-tang.'

'I'm sorry, what?' I know what she's saying is a close approximation but it just isn't English.

'Go-tang,' she repeats politely but firmly enough for me to lose the required confidence for further questioning and it's only when she bursts out of the stalls a couple of hours later on her horse, lasso in hand, corkscrew hair flying under her hat, and bearing down upon a skinny little goat at the other end of the field, that I realize, silly me, Go-tang is obviously Goat Tying.

Chavez makes his goodbyes and is herding us towards the sale tent when, to my surprise, I see Nora a little distance off. She seems to be heading our way, parting the crowd effortlessly before her, her streaky grey hair splayed across her shoulders under the familiar Bass Buster cap. Before I get a chance to wave she's already bearing down on us, but instead of stopping, she simply rolls on through us like a bowling ball scattering pins. 'What on earth was that all about?' I pull Emmy up off the grass.

Chavez stares after her as she powers on through the trestle tables. 'Poor Nora,' he says, shaking his head, and I wonder whether anyone ever uses Nora's name without attaching poor to it.

Inside the sale barn, old metal cinema seats have been racked up on three sides and the giant propeller fan fixed to them is so efficient that it almost blasts the hair off the skulls of people sitting closest to it. There's a children's auction in progress. A wide-eyed, gawky girl leads her sheep around the sawdust ring. 'These are all ranchers' kids,' Chavez explains. 'They raise these animals themselves. Money goes to charity, in case you're tempted into buying anything.' The gawky girl goes to sit down in the stalls. She watches her sheep, knobble-kneed in the ring, and crosses her fingers behind her back. The auctioneer calls the auction as if he's speaking double Dutch on fast forward. Emmy giggles. Jack imitates him in a Disney voice: 'Gobbledee, gobbledee, gobbledee.' 'Hyperbole, hyperbole, hyperbole,' the auctioneer reciprocates, and in the choked dustiness of the tent I find myself searching faces for Duval. Where was he? What really happened out there in the desert? That Duval was responsible for locking the coyotes in the truck, I had no doubt. But that he had intended them to die? I don't know; and if not, how could he have been so certain the Border Patrol would release them in time? Questions spin around my head. How many men had Duval killed? Was he any better than a vigilante himself? Then I began to picture it. The blackness in the truck. The fearful heat. Seventeen people with nothing left to them but to measure the pounding of their hearts as the temperature kept on rising. Had they waited quietly, conserving oxygen? Or had they struggled, panicked, tried to beat that door open? Seventeen human beings. Two old men, and women, amongst them, and I think I would have locked the coyotes in that truck had it been Emmy or Jack. And hadn't this been how Estella's journey began?

Duval told me he came to the border to learn the truth, but he'd found more than that. There were two truths: what had happened to Estella and her son, and the reality of what was happening every day. Despite everything, he had fallen in love with the border. For its beauty and its ugliness, for its passion and all its secrets. And in his more philosophical moments he persuaded himself that in staying he'd found some measure of purpose.

'Helping people or looking for this El Turrón character?' I'd asked him. 'Looking for revenge?'

'You don't think revenge is a good enough reason?'

I'd thought then of all the reasons people give to justify decisions that ultimately trap them. Security, money, children, fear, and I decided that revenge was as valid a rationale as any.

The night following Chavez's unannounced visit I hadn't been able to sleep. I stood out on the deck long after the children were in bed. The stars were so dense it looked like someone had spilt salt over the sky. Somewhere under this same lemon slice of moon, the workers slept, holed up safely in the schoolroom, the children turned and muttered, and Duval rumbled to a place unknown with his charges. I was forced to admit to myself that whatever he was capable of, whatever he had done, I didn't care. I stood there, a blanket round my shoulders, dreaming of his skin touching mine; and at the thought, a pain shot through to the pads of my fingers, a surge of electricity so strong that I reckoned I could light up a bulb simply by cupping my hands around it, or power one of Jack's toy trains along its track with the touch of my finger, and I knew then that I had never been as hungry for anyone as I was for this man.

'Well yihaw!' The slam of the hammer brings me back. The auctioneer has knocked down a big steer for $800. On the other side of the ring, Jeff Hogan stands up and receives a round of applause for his philanthropy.

'That shaw iz one pretty dumb-looking animal,' I drawl in my best Arizonian. Next to me, I feel Chavez stiffen. 'The one down there,' I add sweetly. 'Look, Jack! Emmy!' A small boy is leading an emu around the sawdust ring. It bucks its head coquettishly and purses its lips in a broad come-hither to the auctioneer, who holds out his hands in exasperation.

'Will somebody *please* find out whether you can eat these damn things,' he drawls to general laughter.

'Well, folks.' Hogan sits down behind us. 'I just bought myself one hellova steak dinner.' He shakes hands with Chavez, claps me on the shoulder. 'Ma'am, kids, good to see you here. Enjoying your day at our little fair, I hope?' He shakes his head sorrowfully as the emu is led out of the ring. 'Some damn fool thought it a fine idea when they bought it for two thousand dollars and now they're having to sell for a hundred.' He pulls down on the corners of his Waylon Jennings waistcoat and slides a quick look in my direction. 'It's a cautionary tale you could apply to most border economics, wouldn't you say, Chavez?' He beckons to a girl, who approaches brandishing a clipboard. 'Time to pay for my sins.' He rises from his seat. 'Mrs Coleman, ma'am, I'm thinking you and I need to get together.' He stoops closer. 'Real soon.'

I watch him in mute anger as he squeezes his stone-washed derrière between knees and the backs of the racked seating.

'There's talk of you going into business with Hogan,' Chavez says.

'You know I always wondered what "there's talk" actually means.' I turn to him disagreeably. 'Where is there talk? Is it just out there somewhere, like radio soundwaves, floating by on the breeze for everyone to hear?'

'I can see you're not used to small-town life,' Chavez says gently.

'I guess not.'

He rotates his hat in his hands. 'Don't misunderstand me, Alice, I support neither vigilantes nor any of this white supremacist craziness, but if you join up with Hogan it would give both your investment and your family some level of protection.'

'I don't want men with guns around my children.'

'I appreciate that,' he says in a low voice, 'but if that's the case I must ask you to promise me one thing.'

'Of course. What?'

'That you come to me personally. If there's trouble of any kind. If you feel scared or threatened by anybody in any way. I want you to promise not to hesitate and not try to be brave. You call the Border Patrol.'

I turn to look at him but there is nothing but reassurance in his serious brown eyes.

'Thank you. Of course I will,' I tell him gratefully. 'I promise.'

'And the rockets' red glare, the bombs bursting
     in air . . .
Gave proof through the night that our flag was
     still there . . .
O say, does that star-spangled banner yet
     wave . . .
O'er the land of the free and the home of the
     brave?'

In the rodeo ring a former Miss Arizona finishes a wonderful rendition of the national anthem in a quavering soprano voice. Everyone sits and the action begins.

Bull Riding, Bareback Riding, Steer Wrestling, Calf Roping, the children watch it all, rapt, teeth chewing on straws poked inside gallon-sized buckets of lemonade. Tirelessly, Chavez explains the rules. Cowboys must ride one-handed. To avoid disqualification they must keep their hand above a certain level. Cowboys may not touch their body, the animal, or the saddle. They must stay on for seven or eight seconds in order to get judged.

'See those two?' He points at the men on horseback waiting by the starting gate. 'If the cowboy does manage to stay on his eight seconds, they'll come alongside and hoist him off the bronco and get him safely to the ground.'

After the boys we get the girls and it's Ima out of the stalls first. She thunders across the dusty ground, the poor goat shivering in horror at her approach, looking for all the world like it's about to burst into tears. Snap, Ima's lasso is out and whirling. Snap, she curves her spine over the saddle and throws. Snap, she straightens up and the noose tightens around the goat's neck. I watch in awe as she sails off her horse without worrying about which side to dismount or getting her toe snagged in the stirrup, and pounces on the hapless panting goat, gathering its four legs together and whipping rope around them. Her fingers fly nimbly over the animal's hooves, and having secured the final knot she raises an arm in triumph as though having delivered a faultless performance of Rachmaninov's Third, which I suppose in go-tang terms she probably has. Like old pros the children look to the clock and wait for the rumble of the loudspeaker to announce her time.

Jack is desperate to pee. He hops from one foot to the other, clutching his pants. I drag him off, entrusting Emmy to Chavez. We make our way past melting ice creams and squelched corn dogs to the foot of the stands and duck under the raised wooden structure to short-cut through to the portacabins. They're all occupied. Jack's feverish to get back to the action but I make him wait. Underneath the stands it's shaded and cool and there's a pleasant smell of sawdust and horseshit. Jack holds on to his crotch and presses his nose to a chink in the seats, unwilling to miss anything. I follow the fortunes of the next competitor from the 'Oofs' and 'Aws' coming from my son then peer through a rival gap trying to pick out Emmy, finally getting a glimpse of her up on Chavez's shoulders, her cowboy boots pressed into his ears. I smile and shift position. She's waving her straw in the air like a flag. 'Now, folks,' the commentator booms, 'the Rodeo is about more than just a Bronco Buster trying to stay on an angry bull, am I right?' The crowd roars. Another boom. 'It's about Courage, it's about Character, it's about . . .' The crowd sways in agreement and I lose sight of Emmy. When I spot her again Chavez is bent over talking to another man, their heads close together. Suddenly, unexpectedly, they both look in my direction and for a split second the cold shadow of foreboding passes over me and I'm back outside the cabin, the night Emmy had been sick, watching Benjamín and Duval whispering under the oak trees. Then the crowd roars yet again, a leg blocks my view and I shake myself. It's absurd to always see dark conspiracy in everything and I resolve to stop. Jack pulls his head out of the gap.

'This is so cool.' His eyes are shining. 'Isn't this cool?'

'Yes!'

'Do you love me?' he demands.

I grin at his pink sunburnt face. 'Uhhhhhhh, gee, let me think.'

'Mum!'

'Hey, it's not like this is an easy question or anything.'

'Mum!'

'Just give me a minute, okay? Jeez! The pressure.' I make a great pretence of thinking. 'Now do I love you or do I not?'

'Mum!' He remembers himself. 'Hey, look, just a simple yes or no, okay?'

'Well, if you're going to rush me, then no, sorry, I don't love you at all.'

'You're so mean.' He writhes with delight. 'You're such a witch.'

'Yeah, well, it's a witchy world, dude.'

His response is drowned out by the noise of the crowd. I lean closer to him. Spontaneously, he turns his face up for a kiss but suddenly his new, too-big-for-him cowboy hat slides over his face and he finds himself with a mouthful of brim instead. Surprised, I look up and there right in front of me stands Duval, his hand holding Jack's hat down on his head.

'Mu-uum,' Jack is protesting in a muffled voice.

I say something but my voice also sounds muffled and far away.

Duval wrenches up the sleeve of my shirt. 'So Sanchez was right.' He stares at the cholla punctures on my arm. 'You crossed the line and now there's no turning back for either of us.'

And I feel the warmth of his hand on my wrist and know it's true.

'Goddammit, Alice.' He raises angry eyes to mine.

'Goddammit, Mum!' comes the stifled echo. Jack is still struggling. Duval releases him. Poor Jack finally gets to grips with his hat. He lifts it off his forehead and rakes his sweaty hair up into a peak. I look back to

Duval but he's ducking under the wooden stalls and vanishes into the blinding sunlight. Jack screws the hat back on his head, then notices I'm laughing. He fixes me with a suspicious look and demands crossly, 'What's so funny, girl? I'm still bursting to pee.'

25

'Hungry?'

'Starving!'

Duval catches my eye and smiles.

Behind us the sun is dipping. Filaments of orange and pink shoot across the sky then gradually dissolve like streamers of smoke. Back in the cabin the children would be still high on the day's quota of lemonade and even now chewing their way through a packet of strawberry twizzles under the benevolent eye of Benjamín. I lean out of the open window feeling almost giddy with freedom.

'Where are we going?'

'Oh, little place I know.'

'Round here?' I look at him with suspicion. 'A restaurant?'

'Well, I wouldn't go that far.' He continues whistling tunelessly until we eventually draw up to a ranch heralded by two soaring vertical logs carved into a wishbone shape with a horizontal log jammed across the middle. Landowners round here seem to favour these OK Corral gateways even when the property behind them consists of no more than a single acre. This one is more pretentious than most. The logs are stained a lurid orange colour and an intricately carved name sign has been suspended from its centre. It's also curiously familiar. 'Wait a minute.' I scrutinize the writing. 'This is Hogan's Ranch!'

'Good Lord,' Duval affects surprise, 'so it is.' He noses the truck down the drive.

'Duval, what are you doing? He'll be back any minute.'

'He'll be drinking his own health at the rodeo shindig until long after we're gone.'

'But he's got people watching the property. He told me.'

'Better keep your voice down then.' He takes the left-hand fork away from the house and pulls up on a low wooden bridge built over an ornamental lake. He climbs out of the truck and peers over the edge.

'What are we doing here exactly?' I follow him onto the bridge, keeping an uncertain eye on the house.

'You said you wanted fresh fish.'

'You've got to be joking!' I lean over the stone ledge and peer down at the flat greasy water below. 'Is anything actually alive in there?'

Duval takes a crust of bread from his pocket and tosses it in the water. Instantly there's a frenzied thrashing.

'Yikes!' I pull back involuntarily. 'Frankenfish.'

'Hogan's pride and joy. He far prefers them to his children. Feeds them by hand so they're practically tame and very fat.' Duval fetches a net out of the back of the truck then stops when he sees the look on my face. 'You're not going to make much of a fugitive if you baulk at a little poaching. Besides . . .' he hands it to me, 'it's one of the few crimes in this country that doesn't carry the death penalty.'

'Tell that to the fish.' I lean over the bridge and swipe the net towards the water. It barely ripples the surface.

'What a shame.' I hand it back with a grin. 'Handle's too short.'

'You're too far away. I'll lower you down.'

'I'm sorry? Lower me down?'

'Well you can't possibly expect me to do it,' he says indignantly. 'I'm no good with heights.'

'Let me get this straight. You want to dangle me head first off the bridge?'

'Not if you're scared.'

'Are you trying to goad me?'

'I'm trying to feed you.'

'Well can't you rope a steer or cook beans like a proper cowboy?' I hoist myself onto the stone surface.

Duval lays another piece of bread on the ledge beside me. 'You'll need to be quick with the net.' He puts his hands on either side of my legs. 'Ready?'

He's smiling down at me and I'm smiling too. 'This is silly, Duval.'

'I thought you were hungry.'

'Really silly.'

'Push away from the bridge with your arms.'

'And if someone comes?'

'I'll shoot them.'

'You'd better,' I say with feeling.

He lowers me slowly until my head is a foot clear of the water. The bread comes sailing down past my face and lands with a plop. Again the water froths and boils. I take a great swipe and feel the net almost jerked out of my hands. Through the pounding in my ears, I can dimly hear him shouting.

'Keep the net up!'

'Easy for you!'

I grip the handle, blinded by splashing water. My head feels swollen fit to explode. Inexplicably, I get the giggles. 'Pull me up,' I shout. I can see the fish in the net now, three of them, flip-flopping over each other in oxygen-deprived desperation.

'Pull, for God's sake.' I'm laughing so hard that choking threatens.

Duval gives a bark of laughter too, as hand over hand he hauls me up. My elbows graze against the stone of the bridge but finally the inside of my knee connects with the ledge and I wrap my legs around it. Duval shifts one hand to my waist and with the other grabs my arm and yanks me over the edge. I collapse onto the ground at his feet, soaked, hysterical with laughter and clutching, for dear life, the net with its wriggling contents.

Duval rests his boot against a rock and scrapes at the flesh of the trout with his knife.

I sit close to him on the sandy ground and feed the fire. A ball of brush catches alight and shoots sparks into the sky like fireflies on a mission to space. We're far from Hogan's ranch now, high up in the mountains, camped out on a wide flat ridge overlooking the desert below. The panorama from up here is so enormous that each slice of the sky has its own competing weather. To the east, grey clouds close over a remaining patch of blue, to the west a solitary needle of lightning flickers. Above us, the first stars wink anaemically.

'My father used to take me sea fishing.' I position the metal grille over the flame. 'It's just like netting, you know, requires no skill at all. When you go sea-fishing you catch monsters, quickly, any number of them.'

Duval looks up and smiles. He lays the gutted trout on the rock and takes a second from the net. 'There's a pack of Dolores's tortillas in there if you want to get them out.'

I reach into the canvas bag. The tortillas are freshly made and wrapped in cloth. There are two limes and a bag of finely chopped chillies to go with them. 'We went with Roddy, the local fisherman. He had a rowing boat with a tiny outboard motor and I was always terrified it was going to run out of juice and leave us stranded in the middle of the ocean.'

The flames of the fire dance in the blade of his knife and I fall silent, remembering the hours spent in that boat. The sea was so black and deep and the wind so cold you'd wish yourself back home, but suddenly there'd be a tug on the line, then another, and you'd pull it up eagerly, one hand over the other, until you saw them – four or five, sometimes more, their silver backs glinting like swirls of mercury. Then my father would heave them over the side and rip out the hooks because I was too squeamish, and out the lines would go again.

'What were you fishing for?' Duval asks.

'Mackerel, mostly, but lythe and saithe as well. Some-times, though, you'd be out there and catch nothing. It was like someone had stolen all the fish in the ocean and you'd just sit there, hauling the line up and down till your fingers blistered and your face was raw from the saltwater spray. Then the weather would turn nasty and these huge waves would swell and roll towards you and the boat would rock madly.'

'Were you scared?'

'Not really. I sort of loved it.'

'Why am I not surprised?' He holds out his hand for the third trout.

As a child I was scared of touching the fish once they were dead and, knowing this, my father would look into the baleful eyes of each and give it a personality. 'This one is a bully who has learned the error of his ways. This one is too shy to speak to girls. This is Macbeth after killing Duncan.' Afterwards he would take me home and comb the mackerel scales out of my hair. He tried to be gentle, but he always pulled the knots too hard.

'You're looking very pensive all of a sudden. What are you thinking?'

I glance up to see Duval smiling quizzically.

'Oh . . . nothing really.' Actually I'd been thinking that it was a mother's job to pick mackerel scales out of her daughter's hair but it only sounds self-pitying when I voice it out loud.

'Children expect their mothers to love them, no matter what. Those who don't get this tend to feel cheated the rest of their lives.'

I prod the fire with a stick. The wood has burnt down and the embers glow red.

'I just think that if someone really has to leave, if they

really feel they have no choice, then why does it have to be forever? Why does it have to be all or nothing?'

Duval lays the filleted trout in the pan. 'Sometimes extreme choices are the ones you get faced with. All or nothing. Life or death.'

'You think like an outlaw.'

'Maybe,' he agrees.

Or maybe, I think privately, it's mutually exclusive to have a great passion for a man and give unconditional love to your children. Maybe every woman secretly wonders whether – if it ever came down to it – she'd be capable of walking away, leaving everything she loves behind, but dismisses the idea because she knows she will never be tested. An enduring passion is rare, like a shark bite or a plane crash – and pretty much just as devastating.

The trout spit in the pan, their skin shrinking and curling, releasing a skein of greasy smoke. Duval flips two of the tortillas on to the metal grille.

'In the world I live in,' I watch as the surface of the tortillas blackens and bubbles up, 'people aren't often asked to make life or death decisions. There are no causes to die for. You can go through life never knowing which of your friends would really come through for you.'

Duval touches the tip of the knife to my arm. 'You, however, bled for every man in Temerosa.'

'That's different.' I fiddle self-consciously with my sleeve. 'That was hardly life or death. If it had been a rattlesnake, believe me, I wouldn't have stroked it.'

'If the stakes had been high enough you might have.'

Duval lifts the pan off the fire, then opens two bottles
of Dos Equis XX and hands me one.

I lean back against the rock. 'Can you remember
when it was,' I ask him curiously, 'the moment you first
decided to run?'

He looks into the fire and for a long moment I think
he's not going to answer.

'I was sitting in the INS building in Los Angeles,' he
says eventually, 'and on the other side of the table was
this stranger, Benjamín, and he was wearing one of those
shirts he likes so much, you know, the ones that are too
tight for him? And it was covered in dust and stains
from whatever fruit he'd been picking and Benjamín
himself was a mess – his hands torn up and ingrained
with pesticide but in them he held this letter, *my* letter,
which he'd been carrying around for thirteen years and
yet it was in perfect condition . . .' He shovels some of
the cooked fish into a tortilla and squeezes on some lime
before handing it to me. 'He sat there, at rock bottom,
no money, about to be deported, and yet there was
something about him, God only knows what, that represented freedom to me.'

'That makes no sense.' I sprinkle the chillies into my
tortilla and take a bite.

'I know. It made no sense to me either.' He wipes
grease from his chin and grins. The smile leaves faint
lines in his jaw like crevices in a rock, and aware
suddenly of how close he is, I'm overcome with a desire
to touch them. Then I feel the heat in my face and am
thankful for the half light.

'The INS dumped him over the border and I waited

on the other side. Four, five hours I sat in that car and then finally there he was, scrambling underneath some straggly piece of barbed wire with this surprised look on his face when he saw I was there.' He breaks off with a laugh. "Toribio Romo!" he shouted.'

'Toribio what?'

'Santo Toribio Romo!'

'Who's he?'

'Ah well, since you ask, he's the patron saint of migrants.'

'Benjamín called you a saint?'

'Ironic, I agree, considering I'd never had even a vaguely altruistic notion in my life . . . But apparently the man was astonishingly handsome, so you can see how there might be confusion. Anyway, Santo Toribio Romo, or Holy Illegal Alien Smuggler, as Benjamín likes to call him, is quite a legend round here.'

'Tell me.'

'Well, he was a cleric murdered during the Cristano war in the late twenties. He lay low on his saintly duties for a while but popped up about thirty years ago and has been helping people ever since.'

'Ghostly apparition, white wings sort of a thing?'

'Not at all, he shows up in flesh and blood, dispensing water, food, dollars and even job information. People think he's a bona fide nice guy.'

'Until . . .'

'Until in return for whatever help he's given, he asks them to go to Jalostotitlán, his home town, to pray for him – and Mexicans, being obedient, religious people, do exactly that. When they get to the town, they're directed to a little church and there, lo and behold, they find his picture above the altar and his bones lying in a casket.'

'Great story.'

'It is a very good story,' he agrees.

'So Benjamín canonized you and you decided to lay your bones in Temerosa.'

'Well as we apologists are so fond of saying . . . seemed like a good idea at the time.'

'What about your old life, your real life?'

'My real life?' he repeats.

'You know, family, friends, a weekly pay cheque.' I toss it out lightly enough, but I know nothing about Duval's former life except that when Benjamín found him he'd been teaching Latin American studies back in his old university where he believed that with enough passion and energy he could put the world to rights.

'And you?' He kicks a piece of wood back into the fire. 'What precipitated your flight from London?'

I shake my head. 'I can't tell you.'

'Why not?'

'Too random. Too prosaic.'

He takes a swig of beer. 'Tell me anyway.'

It had been the maraschino cherry. For some reason I wanted to put it on top of my ice cream in the cinema but it had cost ninety-five pence and I didn't have enough change. It had been the last one and it glared at me out of the confines of its perspex box like a bloodshot eyeball.

'You're really asking me to pay you the full ninety-five pence for that thing?'

The man behind the Baskin-Robbins counter was

loosely oriental. His English was none too good but he got the gist of my irritation.

'Yes, please, ninety-five pence,' he repeated nervously.

'Come on, how long has it even been in there?'

He shrugged miserably, a sheen of sweat on his jaundiced forehead, and for no good reason I saw red.

Of course it really wasn't his fault. Someone in Baskin-Robbins Sales and Pricing had sat down at a table with someone in Odeon Cinema Marketing and come up with the price for fruit addendum on top of a double scoop. It wasn't his fault either that I had finally got to the point where I found myself enraged by small and unimportant things. He couldn't have known that I was using all these small unimportant things as buffers against the big significant things I hadn't the courage to put a name to. It was just bad luck his snail's thread crossed mine on the night when I reached an advanced stage of life fury. The one when if anybody had dared look sideways at me, I would have killed them.

'The city can do that to you,' Duval says. 'Ten million angry people all with their own grievances and those grievances all with problems and frustrations of their own.'

'Do you think you could ever live in one again?'

He shakes his head.

'Say you had to, though, what would it take?' I lick my fingers greedily.

'Too much.' Duval passes me the last of the tortillas.

'Okay, say you had to, but you could have three wishes,' I amend. 'Three things which would make it bearable – what would they be?'

Duval lies on his back and puts his hands behind his head. 'Let's see, I suppose . . . a woman I couldn't stay away from, a half-blind dog and maybe a lucrative commission to pen a tome on the shattered heart of America. Oh, and obviously the ability to write it.'

'That's four.'

'So it is.' Duval nudges Taco fondly with the toe of his boot. 'Sorry, fella, but all good things must come to an end.'

I laugh.

'And you?'

'Live in a city?'

'In Temerosa.'

'I'm already here, aren't I?' Smoke from the fire rises upwards in fine wisps.

'For now, sure. You'll stay a few months, maybe a year, but eventually you'll get bored with this place, it'll lose its romance for you and you'll go back to the safety of your husband and your life in London.'

I stare into the fire. 'Why do you say that?'

'Because you can't make your escape your reality.'

'You can't make your escape your reality,' I repeat.

'No.'

I turn to look at him. 'But this is reality. This is real, isn't it? Right here, right now?'

'No,' he says. 'This is a dream,' and a hard edge creeps into his voice. 'And one day you'll wake up and find you crave the smell of tarmac and throngs of people, in the same way you once sought space and solitude.'

'No.' I stare into the fire, upset.

'These few months here, tonight even, will become a memory, an amusing story to tell at dinner parties. Your year out in the Wild West.'

'That's unfair.'

'Is it?' he says evenly.

'All I know is that the whole world over, ordinary people feel trapped – imprisoned by fear and loneliness, shoring up a crumbling business, holding together a bad marriage; every tired housewife unloading her dishwasher dreams of escape. And they don't have to be driven by poverty, they don't have to be in danger and they don't necessarily deserve your contempt.' I get up angrily and walk to the cliff edge but his footsteps are close behind me.

'Alice . . .'

'It's as though you want to believe it,' I say, and I can't keep the hurt from spilling into my voice. 'Why do you want to believe it?'

He spins me round. 'Because there's no return from a woman like you. Don't you understand? You'll take me and change the course of my life. You'll fill every gap and hole I've opened up to lose myself, and then what?'

I look at him helplessly.

'Then what?' he says fiercely and pulls me to him.

His lips are dry, cool. I close my eyes. I'd forgotten. A woman leaves a man by degrees and I stopped kissing Robert a long time ago. Now I feel like a linnet who has cleared the winter twigs and cobwebs from her mouth and found she can sing again.

26

The road ahead is straight, empty. I lean my head dreamily against the window as mile after mile of shambolic dereliction flies by. Every so often, out of the sheer nothingness of the desert, something looms: a giant car-crushing business or an abandoned mining operation. A sign flies by. BUMP. It registers as a mere hiccup under the big truck as we roll on, east along the border to Douglas, a town about thirty miles from Nogales.

Duval drives with his customary one hand on the wheel, elbow resting on the ledge of the open window. He's been quiet for some time now, equally lost in thought. Every so often he glances at me and smiles and my heart twangs noisily like a guitar string that has been plucked and won't stop reverberating. Under my clothes I feel the imprint of his hands like burn marks against my skin. I close my eyes and feel my cheek pressed against his back as he sleeps beside me. Through the windscreen, the sun rules a cloudless sky. There's a succession of near-blinding flashes as it glints off the sides of hundreds of mobile homes, parked together in neat rows like a metal matchbox city. 'Wow.' I stare through the glass.

'Desert rats,' Duval says.

People are moving between the trailers, engaged in some activity or another. On the edge of the road, a man lies on the hot earth looking up the backside of his motorbike.

'How do they lead their lives? What do they do all day?' It's surely awe-inspiringly optimistic that humans should congregate and settle in such an inhospitable place.

Duval shrugs. 'They wake up every morning and go and see if they have any post or see if their disability cheque has come in, then they go back and have break-fast and a couple of cigarettes, maybe they fix something on the RV, a tube, a piece of exhaust, the feed for the propane.' He winds up his window. 'After that they doze in a nylon deck chair that they bought at a yard sale and soak up the reflected light from the sides of the RV, their feet up on all-weather green mats nailed down with spikes. They start drinking cheap beer at lunch. In the evening they do a little gambling, cards or bingo. Politics they talk about in terms of which ethnic minority they'd blow out of the universe if they had their finger on the button.'

'Oh come on!'

He glances in the rear-view mirror. 'Trust me. You wouldn't want to be a black guy in one of those places. You see them west of here, whole communities of these guys over in the yellow sands of Yuma; they roll up and down the dunes all day in those buggies, flying their American flags and waiting for some poor bastard to stumble over the border from Mexico so they can chase him till he drops in the sand.'

'Jesus, Duval!'

Neither of us speaks for a few miles. Then Duval reaches for his cigarettes off the dashboard.

'I should never have let you come.'

'I wanted to.'

'What if I can't keep you safe?'

'If safety was what I was looking for, I wouldn't be here.'

'What are you looking for?' Against the glare of the sun, his eyes look like black discs.

And I think to hell with it. Why is it we all spend so much of life subjugating every emotion, always covering ourselves? For what? To prove we don't care? So that ultimately we can applaud ourselves for feeling less?

'I think you know,' I say and his eyes hold mine for an instant before he turns back to the road.

Unlike Nogales, an all-singing, all-dancing border drama, Douglas, Arizona, feels like a town close to death. The streets are quiet except for an old campesino poppered into a vibrant striped shirt and a couple of nervy-looking youths bouncing on their hightops. Nevertheless we find La Mariposa almost immediately, a dark, low-ceilinged restaurant full of working Mexicans in cowboy hats. A sluggish wooden fan circulates cigarette smoke and coffee steam into a general feel-good haze. I stand behind Duval in the entrance and peer through the fog. In front of us, eight policemen are eating enormous platefuls of *enchiladas* smothered in sauce and cheese.

'Over there.' Duval's gaze has settled on a table far to the back where a middle-aged man in a caramel-coloured suit is scanning the newspaper. 'I'll cut off my pinky without anaesthetic if that's not the guy.'

'What makes you so sure?'

'Winfred mentioned he was something of a snappy dresser.' It had been Winfred's voice that had woken us this morning, hissing with static on Duval's radio. He'd finally set up a meeting with the informant he'd been so excited about finding and we'd barely had time to sneak back to Temerosa and grab a change of clothes.

I follow Duval's bemused glance down to the man's feet, which are encased in a pair of two-tone shoes that look suspiciously like spats.

'Good day, my friends,' he says as we sit down, and if there's an imperceptible raising of eyebrows at my appearance, they're lowered quickly enough. He folds his paper with precision, laying it to one side and shaking our hands then motioning to the waiter for coffee.

Post-introductions, Esteban segues easily into the familiar conversation of someone catching up with old dear friends after a prolonged absence. Life? Yes, well it wasn't so bad. His family was healthy, and his job (quality-assessment manager for a medical supplies company) kept him busy. Politically, his country was even more isolationist since 9/11, and his hopes for Fox working some kind of economic magic were fading. While he talks, he studies us with small, inquisitive eyes and I get the impression he's sizing us up, deciding just exactly how much information to divulge.

'I hate Douglas,' he confides. 'Oh it's no worse than any other border town but I hate it all the same. It's dirty and disorganized, the population is always in flux.' He waves at a couple of tourists through the window. The woman's dimpled legs merge under her beige shorts. She's wearing a canary-yellow sweater tied round her shoulders and a white sun visor. Her husband is equally ubiquitous. Bald, bland, a hand held protectively to his money belt, a pair of taupe chinos belted loosely under an unmistakable all-American gut.

'Mexico produces twice the national product it needs and yet our people are starving.' Esteban regards the Americans sorrowfully. 'Corruption in my country is so pervasive we now are forced to rely on tourists like these for our legal economy. If we want our children to attend the local school, Americans are the ones who pay for it. Look at them! Searching for cheap souvenirs to give their grandchildren. Maybe they don't even know there is another Mexico to be seen. Maybe this dirty little *ciudad* is all Mexico will ever represent to them, a big plate of guacamole, a mediocre margarita, and the homeland of their hired help. "Hey, those Mexicanos," ' he tries an American accent, ' "they sure know how to sweep!" ' He moves his elbow as the waiter puts a plate of *huevos rancheros* in front of him. 'But, hey, what do you expect? Mexicans are no good. Our police are corrupt. Our officials are on the take, border bandits rob and kill their own people. We are drug dealers, people smugglers and murderers. The rich live in splendour while the stomachs of the poor burn with hunger.'

'Not your stomach, though,' Duval remarks.

Esteban laughs throatily. 'Food is my religion.' He wipes egg from the corner of his mouth with a paper napkin. 'Do you believe in God, my friend?'

'No,' Duval says flatly.

'And you?' Esteban addresses me directly for the first time.

Do I believe in God? The children are constantly asking me the same question. 'I don't know,' I always tell them, and I don't. I am religious up to a point. For instance, when I think of the Father, the Son and the Holy Ghost, I can picture God with his great flowing beard and long robes and I have no trouble picturing Jesus suffering on the cross, but when it comes to the Holy Ghost all I can think of is Casper, the friendly ghost, white, rotund, and happily whizzing round the room like a balloon from which someone has just released the air.

'Who is more powerful,' Emmy likes to ask, 'God or the Queen?'

'I don't know, who?'

'God,' she squeals delightedly, 'because God saved the Queen!'

'I, myself, am a man of faith,' Esteban is saying. 'The gospel decrees if you have two coats and a man asks you for one because he's cold – give him your coat! Not a bullet in the back!'

'I understand you know someone I should talk to,' Duval says.

For the first time Esteban looks cagey. He glances round the restaurant, then leans forward and lowers his voice. 'This Mexican you're looking for . . . El Turrón. He has been in prison for the last six years. He's been gone from around here a long time.'

'And now he's out,' Duval says flatly, 'a free man.'

'A free man, yes, but an angry one. Someone is interfering with his business. One of his men, a *narco-traficante*, has been using young girls to smuggle drugs. Unfortunately, two of them died. Two sisters. The drugs burst in the stomach,' he explains for my benefit. 'A month ago, this *narcotraficante* was also found dead. Now, only a few days ago, two of El Turrón's coyotes were ambushed and locked into their own truck.' He looks pointedly at Duval. 'Perhaps you heard?'

'What I heard was that the border was a better place without them.'

'I might think so, and you might think so but not everyone would agree.' Esteban takes a slim box from his jacket pocket and offers it to Duval.

Duval puts up his hand.

'My friend, you must be careful.' Esteban holds a match to the end of his cigar. 'You don't bait the bear unless he's chained. El Turrón is not a forgiving man. Find him before he finds you.'

Duval looks at him coolly, then nods.

Esteban sighs. 'There's this little *mulo*, Reuben. People have heard him talking.' He turns the palms of his hands upwards. 'People say he talks too much. Still, I believe he has other information you might be interested in hearing.' He leans on his elbows. 'Nogales. In the plaza. Can you be there this evening?'

'What time?'

'He will come around seven o'clock.'

Duval nods his head. 'How will I know him?'

'There is a small *iglesia* on the north side of the square. Sit on the bench closest to it. But don't worry.

Reuben will find you. Reuben can smell *dólares Americanos* from many miles away.'

'Speaking of which,' Duval reaches into his pocket and draws out a small roll of bills, 'let me pay for your breakfast.'

'No, no.' Esteban waves the money away.

Duval looks at him enquiringly.

'You help my people,' he says simply, 'and I'll help you.'

Ahead of us a mini twister moves across the road, leaving tumbleweeds spinning in its wake. On the back seat, Taco stirs. As I turn round to pinch his ear, he fixes me with his myopic squint, sucks in his tongue then drops it from his mouth again, where it hangs unnaturally long and thin, like a slice of carpaccio. The heat is intense, cloying. In the distance a lazy mist hangs over the Patagonia Mountains. I look for some orientation in the landscape; something to mark this mile from the last. We pass an iron bed, the remains of a fire, a charred shack.

'It's spooky here. Where are we?'

'Parallel to the border.' Duval turns the next corner then hits the brakes. The truck judders to a stop but it's only when the dust begins to clear that I see why. The road ahead is blocked by a crude length of tree trunk acting as a barrier. Next to it, a military truck is parked.

Half a dozen soldiers in green uniform slouch around in lackadaisical ennui. A couple are smoking cigarettes, leaning their shoulders against a tree. Only mildly interested at our approach, they toss their stubs carelessly, stretch an arm for their guns, then swiftly turn and point them straight at us.

'My God,' I say, alarmed. 'Who are they?'

'Mexican Army,' Duval replies briefly. Up close, the soldiers are startlingly young, their hair close cropped. 'Military service,' he adds, as though reading my thoughts. The soldiers keep their rifles trained on the dusty, smeared windscreen of the truck.

'What do they want?'

'Oh, I expect they just want to tell us a good way of getting that squished insect paste off the glass.'

'Duval . . .'

'Just follow my lead,' Duval says and winds down his window.

The first soldier steps round, his gun still raised. '¿*Tiene marijuana?*'

Duval says something rapidly to them in Spanish.

The soldier's eyes flick to me, then back to Duval, uncertainly. The second boy starts probing under the truck with his rifle, then pokes it through the back window. Suddenly, Taco, who up until this point has seemed content to sleepily follow the action from a seated position, lunges towards him, barking ferociously. The boy jumps back in alarm.

'Oh, man! Does he bite?' he asks in good English.

'Sure,' Duval says, 'but usually just babies and old people.'

Involuntarily, the boy laughs.

'¿*Qué dijo?*' the other demands suspiciously.

'*Dijo que muerde sólo a los bebés y a los ancianos.*'

The first soldier lowers his gun and now regards Duval with rank curiosity.

'*Usted habla inglés,*' Duval says.

'*Sí,*' the boy acknowledges without explanation. 'So where you going? Nogales?'

'Eventually, but we were about to stop and have something to drink on the way. Here . . .' Duval hauls a six-pack of Coke from the back seat and casually hands it through the window. 'Go ahead, take it, we have plenty.'

The boy glances behind him. A little way off, an older soldier, and one of higher rank as evidenced by the insignia on his jacket, is following the proceedings closely from under a pair of sunglasses and a beret pulled over his forehead.

'*¿Su sargento?*' Duval asks.

'*Sí.*' The soldier waits for the nod from his superior then loops two fingers through the plastic casing of the six-pack.

'So,' Duval says with studied casualness, 'are we okay?'

Again the boy looks to his superior and waits for the nod. 'We're okay,' he confirms and signals at the soldiers behind him to move the tree trunk. '*¡Buena suerte!*'

Simon and Garfunkel are playing on the radio. Duval whistles along under his breath.

'Why *buena suerte?*'

'You know,' he muses, 'I never understood the lyrics to this song. Am I supposed to lay me down *on* the bridge? *Under* the bridge? *Be* the bridge?'

'Good luck with what?' I press.

'And why is the poor water troubled? What could possibly be troubling it?'

'What did you say when they asked if you had any marijuana?'

'Is it perhaps a song about poaching off bridges, I wonder?'

I punch him in the arm.

'All right!' he says, mock offended. 'I said why would I need marijuana when I had a beautiful, albeit vicious, English girl to keep me high.'

'So chivalrous . . . What were they looking for, do you think?'

'Oh, just rich tourists to rip off.'

'And we didn't fit the bill?'

'Apparently not.'

'So . . . good luck with what?'

He sighs. 'If you must know, I told them I was out scouting for a suitably romantic location to have my wicked way with you.'

'And are you?'

'Let's just say it's not the furthest thing from my mind today.' He pulls the truck sharply off the track ignoring a bilingual sign commanding all vehicles stay on the road. 'But right now, I want to show you something.' He climbs out of the truck and I follow him to the edge of the hill. 'See that clearing on the mountain?' He points to a bald spot on the carpet of green in front of us. 'Temerosa's on the other side of that.'

'It is?' I stare at the horizon trying to make sense of the geography.

'About fifteen miles if you were to walk straight over the top.'

'Can you do that? Can you cross from here?'

'People try. People die trying.' He narrows his eyes against the sun. 'Looks almost easy, doesn't it? And it should be. There are no heat sensors, no fences, no motion detectors, not even the BP like to come out here. It's a nasty, near-impossible bit of desert unless you know the way.'

I stare at the great wall of mesquite and suddenly understand why he's showing me. 'This is where Benjamín crossed, isn't it?'

'At the beginning of the century ranches round here were immense old cattle outfits, both Mexican and English. They endlessly raided across their neighbours' lands and shot at each other whenever anyone could be bothered. They stole cows, horses, women, and used a secret track through the mountains to escape with them. God knows how, but Benjamín stumbled on it during the course of one of his crossings. He's the only one who knows it, but it takes you to the other ghost town that used to share the schoolroom with Temerosa – Black Mesa. There's nothing left of it now, but in the last few years there have been so many casualties in this bit of desert that the Humanity Patrol put up a water tank there. If you can get to the water, it's possible to make it on to Temerosa.'

'And if you don't make it to the water tank?'

'Well . . . then you pray for a miracle.'

'Why do people cross here if it's so dangerous?'

'Why do people move to a different country in the

first place? Why do they leave their families behind only to end up being exploited or victimized, and why do they still decide to stay even then? For a Mexican with no money and no work in his own village, that "Help Wanted" sign is pretty hard to ignore. The paradox is that there comes a point when the desire for a better life far outweighs the instinct for survival.'

I go on staring at the horizon. In spite of everything there's something compelling about it, seductive almost, as though it's willing you to cross.

Duval touches my cheek. 'You weren't scared back there with those army kids, were you?'

'No . . . yes—' I break off, unwilling to answer. I had been scared, but I'd been excited too, close enough to danger to feel the living, pulsing heartbeat of it.

'You weren't scared that day Winfred found you either. I saw it in your face. You don't care if the cholla shreds you, or you drive a dozen nails into your leg. That's what you came here for, isn't it? The blind step in the dark and the freedom to take it. You came because you felt nothing any more, and feeling nothing is scarier than any number of Mexican soldiers with guns.'

'Yes.'

He takes me roughly by the shoulders. 'And now?'

I want to tell him that so much of my life I've felt numb, but that now I feel everything. I want to tell him that if he asked me to take off my shoes and follow him barefoot through the desert, I probably would. I want to tell him I'm in love with him, but then I look into his black eyes and I see he already knows.

*

In Nogales we drive back into the US and leave the truck in the car park opposite Burger King, where an ancient-looking Mexican attendant accepts Duval's $20 bill to keep an eye both on it and Taco. We cross back into Mexico on foot, along the wall, past the officer on duty, through the turnstile of the port of entry and into town. No one takes the slightest notice of us. No one asks my nationality or demands to see my passport, zippered safely into my combats. On the Sonoran side, the white concrete channel is daubed with bright religious graffiti, as if someone has bought one of the street vendors' more lurid velour towels on their way out and iron-transferred it onto the wall on re-entry.

'It was a school project,' Duval says, 'supposed to make the border look all warm and welcoming, not that anyone's actually fooled.'

Nogales by day – a different town from Nogales by night. Gone is the unease of that night with Emmy, but the crackle of energy is still there. The main strip of souvenir shops acts like a welcome mat for tourists beyond which the goods on offer become more functional: clay pots and copper pans, multi-coloured Tupperware in every conceivable shape and size and an astonishing number of shiny bridal gowns displayed in dusty boutique windows. Duval stops to look at some pot-bellied plastic figures with shanks of orange hair in the window of a toy shop. 'That's the Mexican interpretation of a typical tourist.' He points at the USA stamped on their foreheads. 'So who says bigotry isn't alive and well and on both sides of the border?'

It's close to six-thirty by the time we reach the plaza

and the light is softening. The fierce char-grill burn of the afternoon has dissipated into a more benign warming-oven kind of heat. We sit down on the bench nearest the church and wait.

Nogales is a people-watching town. You watch them. They watch you. A solemn group of school children pass by in grey kilts and bright red sweaters. A couple of prostitutes are loaded into the open back of a cattle truck by the police. A boy with a club foot makes his way across the square in a T-shirt so baggy it drops almost to his ankles. On a neighbouring bench a woman in a striped *reboza*, sitting with her child, dictates in short animated bursts to a man with pen and paper next to her.

'He's a public letter writer, an *evangelista*,' Duval explains, then smiles when I come over all dreamy at the idea. 'It's nowhere near as romantic as it looks. Her husband has probably been seduced by the extra green-backs and decided to stay in *El Norte*. He's written to tell her that he has a brand-new American family and he's never coming home, and she's writing to tell him to rot in the hottest part of hell; but yes, I like it too.' And I look up to find him smiling down at me.

'I love this town!' I say. 'I love the border. I may easily live here forever.'

Duval takes a strand of hair and tucks it behind my ear. 'And you wouldn't be bored?'

'I'd have my three wishes, remember? I'd be painting giant masterpieces or composing symphonies.'

'And you wouldn't be lonely?'

'I'd have a lover.'

He raises an eyebrow. 'What kind of lover?'

'An elusive one. One who'd turn up from time to time, when I least expected him.'

'Wouldn't that be very inconvenient?'

'Not at all.'

'What if he turned up at a bad moment – say, when you hadn't washed your hair or the house was untidy?'

'My lover would have impeccable timing.'

Duval smiles. 'And what would he be doing, this elusive and punctilious lover of yours, when he wasn't with you?'

'Oh, you know, riding across the land, a fugitive, an avenging angel, doing what he had to do to feel free, but from time to time he would dream of hearth and home and then he would come to me and he would take me riding at night and instruct me in the curious ways of cacti.'

'But what if he is doomed always to be a fugitive?'

'Then he risks being lonelier than I ever could be.'

'Poor man.' He takes my hand and examines the end of each finger. 'If only he had the memory of last night to live on, he might never be lonely again.'

I smile and I think of all the things I want to say to this man and I try to work out why I feel the way I do about him, but it just seems easier to sit there, our shoulders touching, his hand heavy over mine, as the light deepens then fades and the shadows lengthen.

It's well after eight o'clock when a wiry little Mexican of incalculable age sidles through the encroaching dusk towards us. He sits down on the far end of our bench, bouncing his knee up and down with such vigour it looks as though he's in danger of pogo-ing off across the square again.

'Reuben,' he announces finally, packing so much nervous intensity into the one word I worry he might have no energy left to speak ever again.

'How are you doing?' Duval asks him.

'*Así, así,*' Reuben shifts his legs on the bench, and risks a look in our general direction. 'Listen, we can speak English, you know; Reuben speaks great English.'

'Okay,' Duval agrees.

Reuben makes a sucking sound between his teeth. 'This is not a good place.' He jumps off the bench and heads down a succession of side streets, ducking and diving, hugging the walls and checking over his shoulder to see if we're following him. Finally, he rounds a corner and disappears.

Duval stops. 'Where'd the bastard go?'

There's a low whistle from a doorway. Reuben beckons us close. 'Look, I know the man you're looking for, sure.' His eyes flick this way and that. 'But first I have to give some money to a friend.' He unfurls his fist. Two dollar bills are screwed up in his damp palm like spent tissues. 'I'm short. Eighteen dollar.' He turns out his pockets to prove he's in good faith and I notice he's a little deformed with arms unusually short for his body and a monkey head too swollen for the emaciated frame it's perched on. 'Help me out, okay, man?' His eyes are ancient in a youngish face.

Duval hands him a twenty. Reuben's mouth splits into a grin. He claps Duval on the back. 'You're a good guy! I knew I could trust you! You can wait here for me.'

'How long?'

He shrugs. 'Maybe one hour, but no more than two.' He attempts to break through us, but Duval catches his arm.

'We'll wait, but not here. Give us the name of a bar.'

Reuben runs his tongue round his mouth. 'Okay, dude, sure. Why not?' He cocks his head to one side. 'Go to the Alubia. There is a *chica* there who likes Reuben. Tell her I sent you.' Then he ducks out of reach and scurries off.

The Alubia is on the east side of town where the houses are built on the steady incline of a hill. Down at the bottom stands the wall. A double layer of corrugated green steel which slices the rival citadels of Nogales Sonora and Nogales Arizona and their inhabitants into two halves. Those with the jam, and those without. I want to go down and take a look at it but before we even get close we're surprised to run into Reuben again. This time he's coming up the hill towards us, dancing on the toes of a rasta dressed in a sleeveless camouflage vest with body mass to equal a submarine and great muscled arms hanging by his sides like polished black torpedoes. Undaunted, Reuben talks animatedly up at him but the rasta merely flicks his dreads in irritation and lengthens his stride, causing Reuben to redouble his efforts not to be trampled underfoot. He passes us like this, apparently unaware of our presence, and we're staring after him unsure whether to laugh or race to his rescue when he shoots back round the corner and blags another $3, explaining that someone, though of course not the guy he's with right this second, is hassling him to repay a debt and will surely break his legs if he doesn't show.

'He's not the only one,' Duval says, handing over the money.

'Hey, man, relaaax,' Reuben wheedles. 'I'll show up, don't worry, you can count on Reuben. Everybody can count on Reuben.'

The Alubia turns out to be a reasonably civilized place. Dark and atmospheric with a narrow bar down one side and a band playing to an audience of largely middle-aged men and their women, who are dressed to kill in leopard skin and heavy lip liner. Three old men in black suits and fedoras stand absolutely motionless and unsmiling as they sing. We find a table near the back. A waiter brings an ice bucket full of beer bottles and places it on a stand next to us. The three old men troop off and are replaced by a group of mariachis resplendent in burgundy and gold outfits. First out is a Mayan-looking guitarist, with cheekbones sharpened into scythes and a long sloping forehead, followed by four Mexicans who sing a medley of songs from exuberant to soulful, conceding the microphone to each other in order of seniority and all equally adept at singling out the women who seem to crave their attention the most and crooning just for them. The Mayan doesn't sing but instead makes eyes at a pretty girl with a long plait and a chipped front tooth, who stands at the bar shyly fingering the frilled sleeve of her red blouse. At the table next to ours, a woman strains towards the youngest mariachi, a sultry baritone. A single tear coasts down her cheek then rolls onto her neck. Her husband puts his arm round her shoulders and squeezes her mournfully.

'What are they singing?' I whisper.

'I am still a man ... I am a free man ...' Duval translates, 'I still have the stars above me.' He looks down at me and his eyes are laughing and I laugh back at him, feeling heady from beer and happiness and overcome with a fierce longing to lay my head on his shoulder, to slow the world down to a crawl and stay forever here in this muggy, smoke-filled room with its murmur of Spanish, the smell of cigarillos, with the tears and passions of the women and the splendid pumping of mariachi trumpets.

A hand appears on Duval's shoulder. Reuben, grinning, bumptious. Much of his nervous energy seems to have dissipated but that might be because he's taken a huge hit in the eye. Beneath his swollen lid an eyeball peeps out, bloodshot and weeping. Nevertheless he seems in excellent spirits and waves away all enquiries as to what happened with a contemptuous flick of the wrist. 'This? Oh this is nothing, not important.' He edges onto the spare seat and looks hungrily at the melting bucket of beers. Duval hands him one along with a cigarette which Reuben fumbles into his mouth, veering into tourist patter as though he's completely forgotten why we're here.

'So how long are you in Nogales for?' He sucks on the cigarette. 'I can show you plenty of things, take you anywhere you wanna go. Nogales is a great little town.' He leans into Duval. 'Listen, bro, I mean it, whatever you want. Drugs, scrips, a clean hotel, Reuben is the guy to get it for you.'

'I'll settle for the information, thanks.'

'Sure, and I have your information so relaaax, but I also have Prozac, Valium, Phenterime.' He sends a sly look in my direction. 'Viagra too . . . very good prices, you know? Just tell Reuben what you need.' He swigs expansively on his beer.

Duval just waits, a muscle working in his cheek.

'Okay, okay.' He caves in grudgingly – 'So how much information do you want?' – as though preparing to whip out a pair of scales and weigh it by the kilo. Duval lays two $20 notes on the table and Reuben's good eye flickers greedily. He looks quickly round the tables then back to us. 'El Turrón is a powerful man, many men work for him,' he begins.

Duval listens expressionlessly.

'He was born in Nogales, but he works mostly in Tijuana. He has a lotta business there. He has not been working here in Nogales for many years.' He fingers the ceramic medallion around his neck. 'He has been in prison in the US.' He looks at Duval expectantly. 'For the drugs,' he adds, somewhat put out by our lack of reaction.

'I know all this.'

'Okay, so you know that, fine, fine.' Reuben adopts crafty expression. 'But did you know El Turrón has a brother?'

'I couldn't be happier for him.' Duval puts his fingers on the edge of the dollar bills.

'Wait, my friend, wait.' Reuben is breathing hard now. 'His brother is a man with authority. A powerful man. More powerful even than El Turrón.'

'What do you mean exactly?'

'He has many contacts. He helps Turrón but Turrón is afraid of him. It was the brother who sent Turrón to Tijuana because he didn't like the mess he was making here.'

'Why not?'

'It was very bad for his business.'

'What is his business? Drugs? Who is he?'

'This I don't know.' Reuben's eye is now sealed together with a yellow caterpillar of mucus. 'No one knows, but if you find him, I guarantee you will find Turrón.' He leans even closer. 'But let me warn you too, *amigo*, if you get too close to Turrón, the brother will make it his business to find you first.' He puts his hand on the other end of the twenties and Duval releases them. In a shot, he's up and out of his seat, zigzagging his way through the tables to the door and out into the shadows.

We walk slowly towards the edge of town. It's late and there are fewer people around. A couple kiss languidly in a doorway. A bunch of kids run across the street. Duval stops, his eyes passing fleetingly from one to the other. I watch his face, suddenly overcome with sadness for him. 'You're still looking for him, aren't you?' The boys disappear round the corner and Duval stares after them down the empty street.

'I must have looked into the face of every child in Nogales and wondered whether it's him.'

'But he'd be older, right? Eighteen or something?'

'Twenty-one ... if he made it that far. If the street has been his life he might be consigned to Reuben's fate, living some totally predatory existence in the shadows, ending up face down in a ditch because he can't pull together the five bucks to pay off a scam.'

I want to offer some comfort but there is nothing to say that doesn't sound completely fatuous. 'Maybe he's been brought up by a Mexican family, gone to a good school.'

'He's almost certainly dead,' Duval replies bluntly. 'And maybe that was the best escape for him.'

He sees my expression. 'Alice, I tried everything. Social services, Border Patrol, the Mexican authorities—' He breaks off. 'I got the feeling they could have helped but they weren't that interested. For a while I hung around with the tunnel kids in the hopes of the older ones remembering something but...' He shakes his head. 'I had very little to go on.'

I've read about the tunnel kids. The two Nogales might be separated by the wall, but they are forcibly linked by a sewage system, a great long metal pipe that snakes underneath the two cities. It's a route to the other side for pretty much everyone, coyotes and smugglers alike, but it's also home to the vagrant kids of the town who consider it their patch and exact a pretty heavy toll from anybody trying to pass.

'And nothing?'

'I followed a few breadcrumbs. Got hopeful once or twice, but nothing led anywhere. It was always going to be impossible.' He shrugs. 'It's not like they put missing Mexican kids on the back of milk cartons.'

'I'm sorry. Really.'

'Ironic, isn't it?' He smiles but it doesn't reach his eyes. 'It's the mundanity of life everyone tries to escape from but it was the ordinary stuff I wanted for him. The-sit-at-a-table-and-do-homework stuff.'

I think of Jack and Emmy with Benjamín, how I wouldn't be there when they came home from school. I think how easily I'd deserted them at the merest whiff of adventure.

'And this El Turrón? What would you do if you ever found him?'

Duval's face is impassive. 'Kill him.'

We've rounded the corner now and the kids are still loitering at the end of the street, kicking a rolling beer bottle to and fro across the road. A Border Patrol vehicle cruises slowly into view and a guard jumps out. The kids split and swerve round either side but the last one is too slow and, like a seasoned mountain lion picking off a baby goat, the officer pounces.

What happens next happens fast. The guard gets the boy down on his back, whacking him round the legs and letting loose a stream of 'goddamns' and 'stinkin' beaners'. Then a boot cracks into a rib and before I know it Duval's over there.

He shoves the man hard. Taken by surprise, the guard loses his balance and drops to his knee, somehow managing to keep one arm pressed into the neck of the squirming child. His other hand scrabbles for his gun. 'Fuck you . . . who the fuck?' he splutters, but Duval doesn't hesitate. He grabs the man's arm and yanks it behind his back with such force that the gun flies out of his hand and slithers along the road towards me. Unexpectedly freed, the boy hightails it back to his friends, still jeering and screaming encouragement from the sidelines.

'Beat it,' Duval shouts, 'all of you. *¡Lárguense! ¡Qué se pierdan!*' And they scatter. I stare at the gun lying in front of me on the cobbled stones and feel scared, unsure whether to pick it up or kick it into the gutter. The border guard gets to his feet shakily and I think that's the end of it, but it's not. In his hand is a knife. He thrusts it towards Duval in a series of short chopping movements.

'Back down,' Duval says. In answer, the guard lunges once more, drawing his arm back and striking with a trajectory that for one terrible moment looks like it will end with the knife plunged into Duval's neck, but Duval moves like a fighter. Quick, light, he sidesteps the blow effortlessly, and bringing his fist up to his shoulder he strikes the man once with the point of his elbow, and this time the guard goes down for good. For a frozen second no one moves. Not the guard, slumped on his belly, nor Duval bent over him. Then I sense something, some movement out of the corner of my eye, and I turn in time to see a car, headlights off, rolling slowly backwards down the side street until it disappears from view.

'You okay?' Duval takes hold of my wrist and gently removes the gun from my hand, which is just as well as I am barely aware of having picked it up.

'Duval . . .' My heart pounds uneasily.

'What?'

I glance again at the side street. 'I think someone's watching us.'

Duval narrows his eyes, but the road is empty, quiet. 'Let's go.'

'What about him?' I look back at the unconscious guard.

'He'll be waking up soon.' He slips the gun into his pocket. Come on, I want you out of here.'

He grips my elbow and we hurry towards the border like Reuben's disciples, hugging walls and looking over our shoulders until we merge with the hustle of the main strip and beyond that the reassuring exodus flowing unremittingly into the US.

The only sound in the truck is the death rattle of the air-con unit and the dry panting of Taco, who crouches precariously on the worn upholstery of the back seat like an only child starved too long of attention.

'Alice,' Duval says and I turn to him.

'Don't go home. Stay with me tonight.' He touches his hand to my face and I feel hopelessly torn in two. I think of the children asleep in their beds and I think of Benjamín, loyal Benjamín, dozing upright in a chair outside their rooms, and part of me wants to go home, to crawl into Jack's bed, to curl up beside the inert form of my son and hold him close for all life's worth; but a bigger part of me wants to stay, and I know that it will be Benjamín who will take little M-E onto his lap when she stumbles from her room with a bad dream, Benjamín who will stroke away her fears, and Benjamín into whose

midnight cactus

neck she will whisper, 'I love you, I love you with the guts of my heart,' because I'm looking at Duval's face in the blackness of the truck and I want to feel the heat of his skin against mine, I want to feel him inside me again before it's too late, because tonight an invisible hand has flipped the hourglass on our time together and the sand is fast running through.

27

My heart feels enormous and swollen in my chest, like someone has put a bicycle pump to its main valves and blown it up out of all proportion with the rest of my body. I move torpidly through the cabin, a conscious sleepwalker, a dreamer, only partially following the progress of Emmy's drawings and Jack's cardboard box fossil dig, all the while thinking that if I pinch myself hard enough I might wake again to the sun rising and Duval kneeling on the hard ground by the fire, the smell of ashes and coffee pungent in the morning air. So when the telephone rings the noise barely penetrates my brain. Nevertheless I pick up on automatic pilot and it's only when I hear my name for the third time that the real world comes sharply and sickeningly back into focus.

'Alice! Alice, can you hear me?'

'Yes . . . yes, I can hear you.'

'Where have you been! I rang all last night, earlier this morning even!'

It's the words 'this morning' that jar. 'What time is it with you?' I feel around for my watch in my trouser pocket.

'Same time as you,' Robert says. 'I'm in Ague, Alice. Ague!' he repeats and a cold hand squeezes my heart back down to size, smaller and smaller it shrinks until it's no bigger than a tiny unyielding pip.

'I flew into Tucson last night, I've been calling ever since. Where the hell have you all been?'

I picture the phone ringing to an empty cabin, the children in a messy jumble of legs and cracker crumbs on Benjamín's sofa. 'In the end I thought I'd better jump in a taxi. Ridiculously expensive,' I can hear Robert saying, 'and then of course I couldn't remember exactly where the turn-off was so I came here and by the time I checked in, well . . . it was late and I didn't want to wake you.' He carries on talking. About the hotel, something about the room. I manage to ask him where he is and he confirms Prestcott's and instructs me to come and pick him up and all the time there is this lump forming in my throat.

It's not tears, though. It's more like a cat's hair ball, or undigested pig's fat.

'Daddy, Daddy!' Emmy and Jack hurl themselves into their father's arms. The children jabber at him excitedly. There's a lot of delight and disbelief, a lot of kissing. I watch them giving him all the unconditional love and affection that I don't feel and it's so painful that I have to look away. Afterwards it's my turn. We embrace each other with stiff robot arms, then veer clunkily away from a kiss on the lips. Robert smells of aeroplanes and London pavements and a life I thought I'd left far behind.

In the truck he leans his head against the window with an epic sigh.

'Are you okay?'

'Fine. Tired. Long flight, long drive, you know . . .'

'You should have told me you were coming.'

'It was all a bit spur of the moment. I called you as soon as I landed. Where were you last night?'

'In Mexico!' Emmy pipes up from the back.

'Mexico?' Robert looks confused.

Mindful of the children's Spock-like ears, I come up with something vague. Pots and pans for the cabin, late-night shopping in Nogales—

'So who was looking after the children?'

'Benjamín.'

'The Mexican? On his own?'

'Of course on his own.'

'Alice . . .' he starts uncomfortably.

'What?'

'Daddy, I want you to come and see my bedroom,' Emmy butts in. 'I painted it all by myself. Daddy, I painted the whole house by myself!'

'Did you, darling?' Robert presses a handkerchief to the sheen of sweat on his neck. 'Well done you!'

'I helped too,' Jack says. 'We all did, even Benjamín.'

'Benjamín, eh?' Robert says with forced heartiness. 'Benjamín seems quite a favourite round here.'

'Oh, Daddy, I love him most outside anyone in my family. He's my best friend.'

'That's great, Emmy,' he replies hollowly. 'I want to talk to this Benjamín.' He turns back to me. 'Where is he?'

'Picking up building materials,' I lie effortlessly. 'He'll be back later.' Benjamín had taken Dolores to the safety

of the schoolroom, to Duval. 'Tell him my husband's
here, tell him . . .' I'd faltered under Benjamín's expression and suddenly pictured him shouting bitter words at
his own faithless wife as he stood on the doorstep of her
lover's house.

'I'm sorry, Benjamín,' I said quietly. 'You must think
I'm a terrible person.'

'Noh, Alice, noh. I will take Dolores.' He took my
hand and briefly held it to his ruined jaw as though it
were a comforting ice pack. 'Be careful, Alice,' he'd said.

'I don't like the idea of him alone with the children,'
Robert says and there's a throb of aggression in his
voice. 'I don't trust him, I never have, right from the
word go. Hogan says—'

'I'm sorry, but I have no interest in anything Hogan
says.'

'Well he's been my only means of finding out what's
going on here,' Robert says robustly. 'In fact I get to
speak to him more than I get to speak to my wife these
days.

'Hogan's a dentist from Houston. He has no clue
what's going on anywhere.'

'He says Temerosa is being used as a smuggling route,
that somebody local is helping bring Mexicans, drugs
and God only knows what else across. He says unless we
act now it's going to wreck the value of the property.'

'Well, he's wrong.'

'He doesn't seem to trust this builder of yours, Duval,
or whatever his name is. Says he's dishonest, says he's
been ripping you off—'

'Robert . . . enough, please!'

'Alice, don't you understand? I've been worried sick! You and the children here on your own. That's not unreasonable, is it? Surely that's not unreasonable. Anyone would be worried. It would have been thoroughly irresponsible not to have come.' He looks at me beseechingly now. 'I didn't warn you, because I knew you'd just put me off. I'm sorry.' He stretches out a tentative hand.

I take a deep breath. Of course it's not unreasonable. Not only is everything he says perfectly reasonable, it's also true. But it changes nothing. I take his hand in mine. His palm is soft, clammy. I close my eyes, try to find some thread of decency to hang on to, but it's no good. It's Duval's hand I'm holding. Duval's rough, dry fingers intertwined with mine.

'Look, Daddy!' The children point out landmarks as the butterscotch truck winds its familiar way along the mountain road. The mess of fallen rock. A deadly looking bayonet plant. The small khaki-coloured shrubs on the roadside, their leaves made brittle by the sun. 'Nearly there, nearly there,' Emmy crows with excitement as the cattle grids rumble beneath us.

'What if he's right, Alice?' Robert asks.

I ease my hand free. 'Why don't you just wait and see for yourself? And for a glimmer of a moment, I try to imagine a way for this all to work out: Robert will come, Robert will be reassured, Robert will quickly have his fill of the children and return home. There will be other nights to follow and other fires to build.

Outside the cabin three Border Patrol trucks are parked in front of the deck.

'What the—?' Robert squints through the cloudy windscreen. 'Who's this?'

'It's Winfred!' Emmy shouts.

'Who's Winfred? Who are all these people?' Robert strains against his seatbelt and I begin to feel sick. None of these cars belongs to Winfred. I slow the truck down. *Dolores*, I think irrationally. *They've come for Dolores.*

'Who are they? Why are they here?' Robert knuckles his eyes as though the strangers might disappear with a blink.

'I don't know.' *I don't know.* I cut the engine and help the children out of the car. If the Border Patrol had found out about Dolores, they surely wouldn't have sent three cars with a posse of six, no . . . seven armed border guards. I count them, two on the deck, three tramping along the path from the boarding house and two more approaching us from the side of the cabin, and it's only now that I picture the guard lying prostrate on the cobblestones of a Nogales street and suddenly remember the weight of his gun in my hand.

'Mrs Coleman?' The nearest man approaches.

'Yes.'

'I'll handle this.' Robert steps in front of me and holds out his hand. 'I'm Robert Coleman,' he says, 'owner of this place.'

Inside the cabin they ask questions. Do I know where he is? Do I know where he lives? 'He's been supervising building operations on the town for over four months but you don't know where he lives?'

'No.'

'Do you have a number for him?'

'No.'

'How do I get in touch with him then?'

I tell them I've never really needed to, that he shows up when he says he will, that he's very reliable.

'Then why isn't he in the town now? And why isn't there any work going on in the town?'

'Because there's a break in the schedule,' I say charily. 'Look, what's going on?'

'Did you see him yesterday, ma'am?'

I try to think straight. Had anyone seen us together apart from Reuben? Esteban?

'No,' I say and my mouth feels as dry as the desert.

'What about this morning? Did you see him this morning?'

'This morning?' I repeat the words as though they were a century ago, another lifetime. My fingers touch the edge of the flint, still in my pocket. I shut out the faces of the men in front of me and instead see Duval's.

'Look.' He'd put the piece of flint in my hand.

'What is it?'

'An arrowhead.'

'It's broken,' I'd said, disappointed.

'They're so fragile they'd break while the Indian kids were carving them.' He had run his finger along its sharpened edge. 'This one was probably thrown away in disgust by some neophyte teenager.'

'How long did it take to make one?'

'A real goody-two-shoes Indian, one who practised and listened to his elders, would probably be able to knock one out in about fifteen minutes.' He'd closed my hand around it. 'Keep it safe. It'll make a handy weapon one day . . .'

I open my eyes to the expectant faces of the Border Patrol.

'Look, please just tell me what's this is all about.'

'Yes, what's this Duval character done?' Robert says loudly.

Agent Butterfield and Agent McArthy look at each other.

'Henry Duval is wanted for murder, sir.'

'*Murder!*' Robert paces the kitchen floor. 'Wanted for *murder*! And all this time he's been here, in the town, with my children! It's fucking irresponsible of you, Alice. This is exactly what I was afraid of, exactly what Hogan's been warning you about, but would you listen? No. You had to have your own way. You *always* have to have your own way.' He smashes his fist on the counter but it's all white noise in my head and I block it out while I rake through the possibilities.

What could have happened? The guard had not been badly hurt. It had been a punch, no more. Had somebody taken advantage of him being down? Had the street kids returned to lay into him? If so, could Duval still be held responsible? I look over at the telephone. 'Promise me,' Chavez had said. 'If there's trouble of any kind, you'll call.' Why hadn't he come himself? Did he even know? I want to call and tell him there'd been a mistake, tell him I'd been with Duval, but it's not the thought of Robert that stops me, nor the questions which would inevitably follow, but something else. A fleeting uneasiness that leaves traces of acid in my stomach every time I picture it – the image of the car on the side street, silently rolling back out of sight . . .

'Alice, tell me you haven't become so removed from reality that you fail to understand the seriousness of this? You've been employing this man for five months. This could rub off on all of us. Make any potential investor run a mile.'

'Robert, please, stop being so melodramatic.'

'Am I, though, am I? Where is he then?'

'Who?'

'This cowboy builder of yours.' His voice rises with exasperation. 'I mean he's supposed to be your foreman, running your project. So why isn't he at work? It's not like today is bank holiday Monday – or is it bank holiday Monday? Is it, Alice, *is it*?'

'I don't know where he is. I told you already. He comes and goes.'

'And that doesn't seem a little suspicious to you? Oh, dear God!' he explodes.

Emmy materializes in the doorway. 'Mummy, why are you fighting with Daddy?' Her face puckers. 'He's only just gotten here today.'

'Emmy's right.' Robert knuckles his eyes again then stretches out his hand to me and when I don't go to him, he comes to me and determinedly gives me a hug under the raptor eye of our daughter. 'Look, I'm sorry,' he mumbles to the top of my head, 'this isn't your fault, you weren't to know. Of course you weren't to know.'

His skin smells oddly sweet and I hold my breath. 'How in your wildest dreams could you have imagined such a thing?'

After lunch, without asking first, Robert drags his suitcase up the stairs to my bedroom. 'Maybe I'll take a quick shower.' He yawns. 'Might wake me up.'

I try to think it's not his fault. *He doesn't know who I am any more.*

Robert has put on weight. When he takes off his clothes, I look away.

'What are these?' He peers at one of Emmy's ticker-tape labels on the light. '*La lámpara.*' He peels it off. 'You know the glue will stain it, don't you?'

'Leave it,' I tell him. 'Emmy likes them, she's learning Spanish.'

'As if she'll remember one word in a month's time.' Robert snorts.

He wanders round the room picking up objects, fingering the books in the shelves, and I'm overcome with an intense wave of possessiveness. I'd forgotten what it feels like. The welling depression – when you hate the way their hair sits over their ears, when you hate the way they walk and talk. When the sound of their footsteps makes you want to curl up in the most hidden corner of the house. When finally even the smell of their skin repels you. That's when you know love is dead.

'I mean, thank God for Hogan,' Robert is saying. 'If he hadn't been so bullish, I wouldn't be here right now, and how would you have handled this mess then? I mean his instincts turned out to be completely right, you've got to give him that.'

'Robert, please . . .'

'I'm just saying we should hear him out, okay:'

I stiffen. 'What do you mean, hear him out?'

'He's coming over.'

'He's doing what!' I stare at him aghast.

'Look, I rang him as soon as the police left. I thought he might know what to do about this Duval character and he does. He's bringing his investors and a bunch of local people he wants me to meet.'

'Robert, do you understand who these people are? They're vigilantes!'

'Vigilantes?' He laughs. 'Now who's being melodramatic? Besides, he's bringing a hired car. I'm not driving in that truck of yours again.'

'Robert, listen to me.' I lay a hand on his arm. 'You don't understand what it's like round here, who people are, it's . . . complicated.'

'Well, actually, I don't think it is. This is private property. We have every right to defend it. At least the law in this country is on our side.'

'The law is the job of the Border Patrol.'

'Then where are they?' He pushes open the big window and waves his hand at the mountains. 'I don't see them out there looking for this murderous builder of yours, do you? Christ alive, Alice, you've put so much time and money into this project already. Do you really want to see it all lost?'

But I can't answer him.

'It's all very well putting your head in the sand, but what are you going to do when this place is up and running and a group of these wetback people barge in on your guests?'

'Wetbacks, Robert? *Wetbacks?*' I hold my temper in check. 'Well, how about we offer them a prize – you know, for the lucky few who don't die on the crossing – a massage on arrival and the chollo spikes picked out of their toes?'

'Don't be flip. Besides, if this man is guilty of murder, if he really has been using our property for smuggling, then don't you want him caught?' He looks at me strangely. 'You seem so . . . not bothered by any of this.'

'I want you to ring Hogan and tell him not to come.'

'No, Alice, I won't.' He sets his jaw. We stare at each other and it's as if the Atlantic and its windy waters still stand between us for all the chill in our silence.

It's still light outside when Jeff Hogan drives up the track in his big Silverado followed by Lane and the weaselly Selby in a hired car. They clatter up to the cabin, shaking hands with Robert, and exchanging backslaps as though enjoying their first college reunion in twenty years. From the safety of the doorway, I throw Hogan a look of utter loathing then compose my features and dutifully fetch beers from the fridge. On the deck I shake hands with Selby, I shake hands with Lane and I even allow Hogan to press his thin lips to my cheek because all that matters now is finding a way of getting word to Duval before the other men arrive.

Robert and Hogan are in prime schmoozing mode. They exchange expansive gestures, mutual flattery and

cigars. Hogan is magnanimous in victory. 'Mrs Coleman
. . . ma'am,' he says, looking up. 'Don't mistake my
meaning. We're not saying you haven't done a fine job
so far, but if you want to see a return on your money,
then you're going to have to secure this property once
and for all. We throw out a big enough net, who knows
what kind of fish we'll catch?' He lowers his voice to
Robert. 'I blame myself for not being more forceful. To
think of your wife here, in danger, day in, day out. Why,
if a man is capable of murder there's no saying what he's
capable of.' He shudders. 'I wouldn't want someone like
that in such proximity to my own dear wife.' And, in
spite of everything, I snort as I picture Duval reduced to
a state of priapic longing at the thought of Hogan's wife,
supplicating and twinkling in her rhinestone tracksuit.
Hogan mistakes the noise for an exclamation of horror
and pats my arm clumsily. 'That was insensitive of me,
I'm sorry. I forget this must all have come as a real shock
to you.'

I'm saved by Emmy racing out of the cabin with Jack
in hot pursuit. He catches her, puts his hands around her
throat and lifts her up by the neck till her feet dangle off
the ground like the victim of a rough-justice hanging.

'OwOwOW!' Emmy howls.

'Stoppit, Jack! You're behaving like a yob!' Robert
thunders.

'But she's already had three!' Jack yells back. Silently,
I pluck the bag of cookies out of Jack's hands and empty
it into the crisp bowl on the deck.

Emmy takes refuge in her father's lap. 'You're going

down down down,' she spits at her brother. 'To hell and back!'

'Like I care!' Jack retorts.

'Say, little lady.' Hogan bends down, seeking to distract her. 'What are you going to be when you're all grown up?'

'Oh, Godddd,' she groans. 'Not again.'

'Emmy, don't be rude!' Robert scolds.

'Fine!' she snaps. 'I'm going to be a teenager.'

Hogan laughs a great big Father Christmas laugh. 'What about after that?'

'Divorced.'

'Oh, come now, you don't want to be divorced.'

'Yes, I do.' She giggles wildly. 'Then I can sex someone else.'

'Emmy!' I say. 'That's enough.'

'Good job on their manners,' Robert hisses.

'Daddy?' She wriggles round on his lap. 'You know Enunciada?'

'Is she a friend from school?'

'No, silly. Enunciada! On Benjamín's television.'

'Oh . . . I see.' Robert is unable to keep the disapproval from his voice. 'Well what about her?'

'She's been down there.'

'Down where?'

'There.' She widens her eyes into a blink-free stare and directs them at the ground.

'Where?' Robert says.

'To hell,' she breathes with awe.

'Oh. Right . . . well that's very bad.'

'No, actually it's okay, cos Enunciada's going to get resurrectioned!'

'Oh. That's nice.'

'Benjamín says he's been to hell too. In fact he says he's been to hell and back.'

'Really,' Robert quips acidly, 'let's hope he enjoyed it.'

'Daddy!' Emmy says, disappointed. 'You're not listening. It's hell, okay? How could he enjoy it? Plus it was probably *really hot*.' She eases herself off her father's lap.

'Now where are you going?' Robert sighs.

'To sharpen my toes,' she answers coquettishly.

'Little fireball, ain't she?' Selby watches her flouncing off. He helps himself to one of the cookies out of the bowl and breaks it in half. 'Hey, these are *galletas de azúcar*. Mexican sugar cookies. My mother had a maid who used to make these.' He looks at me closely and too late I realize my mistake in bringing Dolores's biscuits out. 'Who's the baker in the family?'

'Benjamín, probably,' Robert says belligerently. 'The man seems to do everything round here except the one thing we pay him for.'

'You mean the little Mexican with the broken jaw?' Hogan says. 'The one that's supposed to watch the place for you?'

'You can't trust a Mexican to watch out for other Mexicans.' Selby laughs humourlessly.

'I'd trust Benjamín with my life,' I snap then immediately adopt a more measured voice. 'I'd have been lost without him.'

'Seems to me, he's the one who's lost,' Robert says waspishly. 'I thought you said he'd be back by now.'

'He'll be here soon,' I reassure him smoothly, but with every passing hour Benjamín's return looks less likely and I'm thankful for it. Duval must have heard about the murdered guard and kept him in the schoolroom.

'It's not like we don't pay this man a decent wage. I'm sure it's a lot more than he'd get in his own country, so is it really so unreasonable that we should ask him to account for himself? Because my wife seems to think it is.'

'*Mummy!*'

I look up sharply. Emmy's voice comes to me so faintly, it might have been the whisper of the cottonwood trees.

'*Mummy.*'

There it is again. Jack is kicking a ball around moodily. I touch him on the arm. 'Jack, where's Emmy?'

'Up my bottom.'

'That's a good place to keep your sister,' I say vaguely, then, keeping an eye on the men, mutter something about further refreshments and move towards the cabin. In the doorway I can see a corner of Emmy's dress, fluttering like a handkerchief held out in surrender, and my heart beats a little faster. Now her face appears around the door frame, serious and pointed. The keeper of grown-up information. She puts a finger to her lips and draws me into the cabin and there, gripping her other hand tightly in his own, stands Winfred.

28

The clearing beyond the deck is now packed with SUVs and pickup trucks. There are eight further conscripts in Hogan's army, including his two hefty offspring, but apart from Bob, the town hall compère, and one of the ranchers from the meeting, the rest are strangers and I can do little more than stand helplessly on the deck and watch as they mill around the open backs of their vehicles preparing for battle.

'Can't you talk to them?' I'd begged Winfred.

'Mrs Coleman, for one I'm off duty,' he said indicating his clothes. 'For two they got your husband's permission. They're within their legal right. Nothin' I can do.'

'Can't you radio Duval? Tell him what's going on.'

Winfred shook his head. 'Everybody is on the radio today. Everybody is looking for him.'

'Then I'm going to call Chavez. Tell him about the guard, tell him the truth.'

'Duval will go to prison anyway. So will Benjamín and it will be bad for you too.' He glanced towards the deck and I knew he was talking about Robert.

'I don't care! Chavez is a decent guy, he'll put a stop to all this.'

'No,' Winfred said stubbornly. 'No Patrol. It'll only make things worse. Hey, Mrs Coleman, don't worry. Duval is smart. Hogan's men won't find him.'

'You have to warn him, Winfred.' I laid my hand on his arm. 'Please, you have to do something.'

Winfred glanced towards the deck. The frown between his eyes was fixed and set. 'I'll go out there. Take my own car.' He shot another look towards the deck. 'Keep them here, Mrs Coleman, long as you can.'

So I had. At the arrival of the troops, my smile had been charm itself. I tied on an apron and, like a Tupperware Queen, began tossing steaks and potatoes into a frying pan, opening doors to let the smell of onions and beef create its own temptations, and as the evening dragged slowly and painfully on, Winfred's window of opportunity had opened ever wider.

But now the dirty plates are in the sink, the crate of beer finished and the men ready for their after-dinner games. Most are dressed in their camouflage. All of them are armed. Hogan thrusts his arms into a padded vest, jamming a flashlight and strips of plastic ties into the multitude of breast pockets stitched onto the front. Into a further drop-down pouch below the waist he slides a handgun, then Velcros the lower straps of the vest tightly over his stomach. On the arm of his shirt, yellow embroidery patches have been sewn, their titles – Operation White Mouse, Operation Tumbleweed – broadcasting the success of previous missions. If Robert is taken aback by the show of fire power, his natural bullishness doesn't allow him to acknowledge it. He looks from Hogan to the other men as trousers are tucked into boots and floppy hats are wedged on heads. 'This is quite a show you're putting on here, Jeff. I'm not sure I was expecting—'

'Why would you be?' Hogan comments genially. He hands Robert a pair of night-vision goggles. 'Seeing as you come from a civilized kind of a country. You don't have our border issues.' He waves at one of his boys, who lumbers over. 'Tucker, this is Mr Coleman. He owns this property here and tonight he is an honorary member of Ranch Rights. I want you to take him to Bob and let him choose himself a decent weapon.'

Bob grabs Robert's hand and gives it a good shaking. 'You're doin' the right thing, Robert. We're all neighbours here, local landowners. Trust me, this has worked on my property, it's worked on other properties nearby. Now,' he hands him a gun from the back of his car, 'try this on for size. It's a high-powered huntin' rifle, with high-impact bullets.' He lets Robert handle the gun for a minute before exchanging it for another.

'This here's the Bushmaster, an AKA2. It has a nice chrome-lined barrel. Expensive gun. In fact my daddy uses this gun, but some folks prefer the Mossberg Tactical.' He produces a long-barrelled shotgun. 'It ain't as precise as the Bushmaster, but it's sure a lot cheaper. Go ahead, try it. It's tricked out with some pretty little features.' He watches approvingly as Robert discovers the quick-release button. 'Take whichever floats your boat, pardner.'

'Cool.' Jack has made his escape from my side. He snatches at the gun. 'Let me try it!'

'Jack!' I shout after him.

'Mum, come on,' he wheedles.

'Jack, stop being silly.' Robert lifts the gun out of his son's reach.

'Is this what you want?' I hiss at Robert, the shine on my Best Supporting Wife medal growing more tarnished by the second.

'Mrs Coleman, please, ma'am,' Bob says hastily, 'you're worrying unduly. We're dedicated patriots, all of us, and we're here to secure America's boundaries and safeguard its good citizens. These guns are for protection, nothing more. Our aim is only to apprehend these individuals.' He pats the radio in his belt pouch. 'All we do when we come across one is radio the Border Patrol and get them to make the pick-up.'

'Dad says we can make a game of it,' Hogan's youngest chips in. 'See who can catch the most!'

'Cody, that's enough,' Hogan warns, joining us.

'Look, most don't give you any trouble,' Bob intervenes soothingly. 'They're pretty traumatized and they have respect for a uniform. That's why we wear it. It confuses the hell out of them. They don't know who we are but they know we're authority and that's good enough.'

'Hell, some of them even lie down on their stomachs without us having to ask,' Cody boasts.

'I want Daddy to catch the most,' Jack chants. 'I want Daddy to catch the most!'

'Go inside, Jack,' I snap. 'Right now.'

'And what about the ones that don't lie down on their stomachs for you?' I say. 'What about Duval?'

'Henry Duval is another matter,' Hogan says self-importantly. 'The man's wanted on a murder charge and if he's out there it's our duty to bring him in. One way or another.'

'Alice, they're right.' Robert pats me heavily on the shoulder. 'We can't leave this man on the loose. I mean, think about it. Of course you feel safe now, with all of us around, but imagine if we don't catch him. Imagine how you'd feel then, in the dark and sleeping alone in your bed. Do you really want to wake up and find this Duval standing over you?' He looks at me almost entreatingly. 'Well, do you?'

I go on staring down the path until long after the dust has settled and the noise of engines receded. Jack is surprisingly pliant about bedtime but Emmy decides to stage a protest which quickly escalates into a one-child riot.

'I'm not tired. I don't want to go to sleep. I want to stay up till Daddy gets back I want Benjamín I want a biscuit I want Daddy,' she screams. 'You're so mean I hate you. I'm going to rip out my guts I hate you so much.' And when I move her to my bed to stop her keeping Jack awake, she strikes out at me with her hand, catching me sharply on the side of my face.

I get angry then and we fight for a while. Emmy holds strong but eventually throws herself back against the pillows weeping piteously.

'It's okay,' I say, prising her face off the damp sheets, 'it's just that you can't always lose your temper like that. What will people think of you if they see you losing your temper all the time?'

'They'll think I'm a bad person.'

'Not a bad person, no, but they'll think you're spoilt and not very nice.'

Her face crumples. Two enormous liquid pear drops roll down her cheeks in faultless synchronicity and I wonder why children's tears always seem so big and round and single until it strikes me that adults, adept at hiding their misery, cry with their hands over their faces.

'You don't see grown-ups screeching and hitting people and beating their fists against the pillow, do you?' I wonder why on earth I'm bothering with this but it just seems better to go through the motions of normality.

'But grown-ups are all nearly forty and I'm only five . . . just turned five,' she whispers.

'Well that's old enough to learn to control your temper.'

'I'm trying to, Mummy, but I've only just started and I'm not very good at it yet.' She lays her head on my shoulder, her face red and raw. 'I'll get the hang of it soon. I will. I promise.'

'Is your face stinging, Emmy?' I ask. She nods and I fetch a damp flannel and hold it to her eyes. 'Better now?' She smiles and settles back against the pillows and I stay with her, holding her hand till she falls asleep.

The night drags on. Restlessly, I pace the room, do my teeth, move objects from one place to the other. I lie on the bed and listen to the ticking of the watch on my wrist, but every few seconds I find myself looking up and out of the big window as though the black screen of glass might spontaneously fizzle and splutter into a picture of what's happening out there. My stomach dips and steadies as I veer from one extreme to another. Duval and Benjamín will be caught. Duval and Benjamín will slip through the desert like phantoms. Hogan and his vigilantes will never find the cabin. Hogan's men have night goggles, radios, torches. And there are so many of them – well . . . only twelve. Twelve people spread out over a huge expanse of land. Their net would be thin at best and surely full of holes big enough for two men and one woman to slip through. I look at my watch for the hundredth time.

'Mummy,' Emmy calls drowsily. 'I want to sleep in my own room.'

I scoop her up and put her in her own bed.

'Mummy . . .' she holds on to my arm under the covers, 'aren't you happy Daddy's here?'

'Of course I am, darling, of course I am.' Mindlessly, I stroke her hair until my hand feels unbearably heavy and the darkness of the room sweeps over me like the blue-black of a raven's wing.

I wake to a halo of red light on the horizon. It's three-thirty. Extricating myself from Emmy's octopus-like grip, I hurry to the big window in my room. In the east, a gibbous moon throws a hazy light over the escarpment of the mountains. The reddish glow is coming from the south. From the direction of the school-room. I jackknife with fear. Fire. It looks like fire. I stand fixated, in an agony of uncertainty, until the growl of a truck jerks me from numbness and almost immediately a pair of headlights swing round the corner from the direction of the town. Duval! Benjamín! The engine cuts, a figure jumps out, but there's no mistaking the heavy set of the shoulders and the square-cut silhouette of his head.

'Robert, what happened?' I say, but he pushes past me through the door and collapses onto the sofa. He puts his head in his hands.

'What is it?' I say urgently.

He groans.

'Are you hurt? What happened?' I kneel beside him and drag his hands from his face. 'Robert, talk to me!'

'Alice, oh, God.' He fumbles me to him. His breath smells sour. He groans again. 'What have I done? What have I done?'

'Yes, what *have* you done?' I ask sharply, and when he still doesn't answer, shake him. 'Robert!'

'I had no idea.' He raises tormented eyes. 'I should have listened to you. Why didn't I listen to you?'

'For God's sake. Just tell me what happened.' Struggling not to beat him with my fists, I take his hand and squeeze it and finally he starts talking.

They'd driven as far as they could in the vehicles, then continued on foot. Robert had been uncomfortable, in the wrong clothes – in the wrong shoes, but eventually Hogan had stopped and made everyone take up a position in a line, each person finding cover a few hundred yards beyond the next. It was to be like a stake-out, Hogan explained. They would rest up a couple of

hours and see what moved. And at that point, everything
had seemed fine. In fact it had been exciting, a bit like
deer stalking, except . . . well, except Robert had been
close to Tucker and had been worried that the boy was
secretly drinking . . .

'And . . . ?'

'Eventually, we spotted a group of people in the da—'

'How many!'

'I don't know. I saw them through the night-vision
goggles. They were walking one behind the other and I
thought *this is it, this is it.*'

'Yes, but how many were there?' I say, sounding
almost as agonized as he does.

'What does it matter! I don't know.' He cries.

'Okay, okay,' I try to calm him, 'just tell me what
happened.'

When the line of Mexicans got close enough, Hogan
and the others revealed themselves. They stood up and
produced their weapons, forcing the illegals first to their
knees, then down on their stomachs. 'It was all going
according to plan,' Robert said, 'they were no trouble.'
In fact he'd been surprised at just how subservient they
were – all except one. Bob was having difficulty securing
the plastic tie around the illegal's wrists and the Mexican
had begun swearing and shouting.

'I don't know what he was saying, I didn't understand,' Robert says, but it was at that point that everything started to unravel. Tucker shot his gun into the
air . . . a woman screamed. 'A woman, Alice. I hadn't
thought . . .' He tails off and my fear overspills again.

'What did she look like? Who else was with her? How many people exactly in the group?'

Robert looks up at me with a sort of tired frustration, as though I have completely missed the point. 'Why does it matter? I don't know, nine, ten, eleven maybe, I couldn't see properly, none of them dared look us in the eye and besides they were all on their stomachs . . .'

And I'm thinking ten people. Not Dolores, not Benjamín or Duval, just another random group of strangers shackling themselves to fate.

'Tucker struck the Mexican with his gun. He went down, but before I could move, something came out of the dark, like a ghost.' He shudders. 'I suppose it was one of the other wetbacks but it was all so confusing. Bob got pulled off his horse right in front of my eyes . . . there were more shots, then all hell broke loose and I . . . I . . .'

'What, Robert, what?'

'My gun jammed.' He looks incredulously at his hands, as though he was seeing the Mossberg still in them. 'I never meant to fire it in the first place.' His voice rises. 'I wasn't even aiming it, I swear – but there was so much happening and everyone was so jumpy . . . I panicked, I just panicked . . . Bob threw me his knife . . .' He covers his face again and grimly I realize there's worse to come. 'Alice, I think I may have killed someone.'

The words slam into me. I fight for breath, stand up. Robert grabs at my hand.

'Don't look at me like that, Alice. Please don't look at me like that. I don't know – I can't really remember, there were others close to me, people were shooting, there was a black car driving round in circles, everyone running all at once, but then someone came straight at me and I don't know . . .'

'Robert! Oh, God,' I whisper, and I cannot keep the disgust from my voice.

'Alice,' he pleads, 'the last few months have been torture. You and the children gone, I felt so . . . I don't know . . . rootless, flying backwards and forwards from London to Switzerland, those interminable legal meetings, nothing but that grungy rented flat waiting for me, every business collapsing around my ears, so when Hogan called me and offered me this deal, it seemed like light at the end of the tunnel. I always knew there was opportunity round here.' He balls his hand into a fist. 'I could smell it, right from the start and, God knows, Alice, I thought it was a chance to escape, leave all our problems behind and start over again but then Hogan told me what was going on and well—' He laughs bitterly. 'I know you, Alice, you have all these funny ideas, you're a dreamer and I thought you might do something stupid, irresponsible, ruin it for both of us.' He looks up at me in total misery, all bravado stripped away and in an instant I see my son in his face and I remember Jack that night, his arms wrapped tightly around me as he'd listened to the coyotes howling out their secret trysts to one another.

'I told Winfred I was afraid of nothing,' Jack had said, 'but the truth is, I'm afraid of everything.'

'Oh, Robert.' I hold him to me and when I feel his shoulders slump, I hold him closer still. 'I'm so sorry.

I'm so sorry.' But even as I'm mumbling it over and over again, I realize he cannot understand what I'm apologizing for.

Robert stirs. 'We have to leave. We have to get out of here.'

'What do you mean?' I release him.

He pushes up off the sofa. 'It's not safe, we should pack the children's things and just go.'

'Go? What are you talking about? . . . Go where?'

'Home!' he says, and still I stare at him, unable to grasp what he means. *I am home.*

'We'll drive to Tucson,' he says wildly, 'to the airport. Get on the next flight.'

'But our tickets are from Phoenix,' I say stupidly.

'To hell with that! We'll buy new tickets.'

'Robert, no!'

But Robert has thrown off his shock and awe. He paces around the room, talking, making plans. We will camp in his rented flat, he will speak with the agent, see if we can get our house back early. We'll pick up the threads of our old lives. Our London lives . . .

'Alice, we never have to come back here,' he says emphatically. 'Don't you see, it's perfect! We'll sell this place to Hogan if he wants it so badly and in a few months we'll look back on this terrible night and it will just be a bad dream.'

I turn my head and see Duval's face in the flickering light of the fire. 'These few months here will become a memory, an amusing story to tell at dinner parties. Your year out in the Wild West.'

Robert grabs me by the shoulder. 'Alice, it's okay. Together we'll get through this. I'm here now, you don't have to think any more. We must do what's best for all of us, you, me, the children. You want that, don't you?'

And when I still can't answer, it's his turn to shake me. 'Don't you, Alice?'

'Yes,' I say mechanically. 'Of course. What's best for the children.'

I move around the house, finding passports, opening drawers, folding great piles of clothes into cases without knowing or caring to whom they belong. The children sleep on and I can't stop thinking ... What if it's Benjamín lying in the desert with Robert's knife inside him? What if it's Duval? I should have rung Chavez, I should have done something, anything, and I have to call on every ounce of self-control left not to run down the path and along the track towards the schoolroom.

Finally, the packing is done and the hired car loaded. 'Wake the children,' Robert says.

Jack is lying on his back, his hand curled protectively around his balls. Emmy is rucked up on her stomach, her mouth open, a circle of damp on the pillow beneath her. I kneel between them and slide Emmy's hair out of her mouth, then I lay my head on Jack's chest and inhale his sweet smell, thinking that if I can just breathe deeply enough, maybe a part of him will stay inside me forever.

'Can I sit in the front?' Jack asks.

'Course you can.'

'Why can't I sit in the front?' Emmy says. Jack always gets to sit in the front, it's so unfair.'

'Emmy, shhhh,' Robert soothes, wearied already by the tears, by the exhortations, by the patience and the sheer imagination required to explain to two children why they are being woken at dawn and suddenly, bewilderingly, going home.

Real home. London home, was how Robert kept putting it, and Emmy's initial wails had turned to joy at the prospect of a reunion with squirrel, rabbit and other lesser members of her Camden High Street stuffed-animal family.

'No one's sitting in the front except Mummy,' Robert says.

'But Mummy said she didn't mind,' Jack says resolutely. 'And it's her decision, isn't it, Daddy?'

'Mummy can sit in the back with me.' Emmy sweeps her pink backpack to the floor.

'Oh, for goodness sake,' Robert says querulously. 'As long as Mummy doesn't mind.'

'I don't mind.' I shake my head, smiling at all of them.

'Right! Everyone happy now? Can we go? . . . Alice?'

And still I'm smiling.

'Alice?' Robert presses evenly. 'Can you get in the car, please?'

'You know, I was just thinking . . .' I speak in a bright normal sort of voice, as though we were negotiating arrangements for a picnic in the park, 'why don't you all go now and I'll follow you later?'

Robert decides not to hear me.

'Please get in the car, please, Alice.'

But I go on shaking my head.

'Get in the car, Mummy,' Jack says. 'You'll only end up arguing with Daddy.'

'No, really, why don't you guys go on ahead?'

Robert turns off the ignition and gets out. 'What are you doing?'

I tell him I can't go. I promise to come later. 'I can't leave all this,' I say. The children's faces are pressed to the windows.

'All what?'

'Everything. Temerosa.'

'Temerosa!' he says incredulously. 'Alice, this is a war zone! This is a place of hell! What do you mean you can't go? You can't stay!'

'I have to.'

'Why?' he asks desperately.

'Don't ask me to explain. I can't explain.'

'Alice . . .'

And I turn away, too spineless to face the pain in his eyes.

'Alice . . .' Robert takes a huge breath. 'We. Are. A. Family.'

'I know.' Of course I know this is my family, but a man I love is out there somewhere and he may be hurt, and he may be dead and I need to find him and hold him, otherwise all the days I have left in my life will stack up one after the other, grey and pointless except to torture me with what ifs.

'Alice, unless you get in the car right now, this marriage is over and, so help me God, you'll never see me or the children again.' White spittle has collected in the corners of his mouth.

384

'Don't be silly, Robert.'

'Alice, for God's sake, don't do this.' He grabs my arm. 'Get in the car.'

The children are watching. They know we are fighting. I bathe them in a dazzling smile of normality as I yank my arm free.

'Then none of us will go,' Robert changes tack. 'I simply won't allow you to stay behind and that's all there is to it.'

I harden everything left in my heart and turn my back on my children.

'And what if you *have* killed someone, what then?'

The remaining spots of red anger fade from Robert's cheeks.

'You go round knifing people, even Mexicans, and the police tend to want to talk to you.'

'Alice . . .'

'Listen to me. You have a chance to get out now, probably one chance only. I think you should take it.'

'Alice, I'm begging you —'

'I'll come later. I promise.'

'No,' he says flatly. 'You won't.'

The children stare at me as if I've decided to speak in another language.

Very slowly, Emmy's mouth twists, her brow puckers and she's off. I hold her through the window, kiss the tangled hair on her head, reassure her with everything I have left, but nothing is big enough to stop the flow of her misery.

'Mummymummymummy,' she wails and clings to my

arm and I know it's only a matter of time before I lose it too. 'Emmy, my darling . . . please.' But my resolve is nearly spent.

'Emmy, let go, for God's sake!' Robert utters in desperation.

'Let go, Emmy,' I say gently. 'Please . . . let go.'

'It's all right, Mummy, let me talk to her,' Jack says. He climbs over the divide into the back seat and shuffles in close to his sister, then puts an arm round her shoulders and starts stroking her hair, smoothing it down on either side of her blotched, teary face over and over again. 'It's okay, Emmy,' he says quietly. 'It's okay.' He pulls a strand of hair out of her mouth with infinite tenderness. 'Jack is here now, Jack will sit in the back with you.'

29

I make it upstairs, throw myself onto Emmy's bed and shut my eyes tight, but they're still there, like ghostly negatives, Jack biting down on his lip, Emmy mouthing my name, Benjamín's name, her fists banging against the glass. The tears come then, in great gulping sobs. I beat my own fists against Emmy's pillow, find a small hole and rip into the cotton in a fit of rage and guilt. When it's over I give way to some kind of semi-conscious paralysis and lie there in a fug of self-loathing for what seems like hours until, finally, I become aware of a sound. A scraping noise then another, coming from the stairs.

I push up off the pillow and listen. If you live in a house built of wood you become an expert on its idiosyncrasies. A sort of Miss Smilla of the creak, able to identify every sound it makes. Apart from the fact that every floorboard takes it upon itself to moan at will as though the breaths of the miners' ghosts are forever blowing on them, there are other noises I've come to recognize, a shudder prompted by wind, a stingy little protest induced by the unrelenting dryness. I have tried to exorcize the children's night fears, explaining that it's only when we're asleep that the house gets to relax and succumb to its aches and pains – but the creak on the stairs has a furtive, dishonest quality to it, that of footsteps being deliberately suppressed – and it scares the hell out of me. I grab the small fire extinguisher from the corner of the room and, raising it, step out into the hallway.

He stands motionless at the top of the stairs and there's something so fragile in the way he's holding himself that I stop dead. 'Benjamín!' I put down the fire extinguisher and take a step towards him, fearing the worst, fearing that any closer might somehow send him spiralling backwards and down. For a second he looks straight through me, then he collapses – slowly, almost neatly, the way a building falls during demolition when its central structure has been removed.

'Benjamín!' I crouch down beside him. 'Are you all right?' He nods his head almost imperceptibly but his eyes are dull and his skin a flat grey colour. 'Benjamín!' I fetch a toothmug of water from the bathroom and hold it to his lips. He coughs and shifts position. Under the harsh light of the naked bulb, the dark patch on his shirt reveals itself bright red.

I help him onto Emmy's bed. My attempts to unpopper his shirt elicit a weak protest. 'Oh, come on,' I say feverishly, but he pushes my hand away and eases his shoulder out of the sleeve. I suck in a breath. Just below his armpit, running up to his collarbone, is a yawning gash.

'Wait there,' I instruct him, then race down to the kitchen, fighting mounting panic. What to do? What to get? Boiling water? Clean towels? But this isn't a pregnancy, dammit. Nevertheless I fill a bowl with hot water, grab a clean dishcloth along with the first-aid kit from under the sink and race back upstairs.

I daub away at the soft edge of the wound, biting my lip, because what do I know about knifings? What do I know about gunshots and vigilantes and the murder of Border Patrol guards? The gash is uneven, the flesh on either side shredded and raw. I flash back to the weaponry of Hogan's army, to Robert's stumbling confession and feel a white-hot rage. Tiny fragments of shirt are embedded inside the wound. The gash is deep but from Benjamín's breathing it doesn't appear to have punctured his lung. He can move his fingers, he can lift his arm. He raises his eyes to mine. 'You have to go to the Border Patrol, Alice.'

I draw back and stare at him. 'Benjamín, no!'

'If you don't, there will be people killed tonight.' He winces as he claws the shirt over his shoulder.

'Benjamín, what happened?' And he starts talking.

He and Dolores had made it to the schoolroom. In spite of the Border Patrol, Duval had intended to take Dolores north then and there, disappear for a couple of days until he could figure out what had happened. But when Winfred came and Duval learned about Hogan's men, he knew it was too dangerous. They'd decided to stay put and trust that the tortuous geography of the schoolroom would prevent them from being found. They waited and waited. Everything had been quiet until a radio flash had made Benjamín jump. Ten, twelve people coming through. The *Migra* had tracked them over the border but lost them as they'd slipped in and out of the tight ravines.

'*¡Por todos los santos!*' Benjamín mutters. *¿Por qué esta noche?*' He shakes his head despairingly.

'I tell Duval we can do nothing to help, but then we hear gunshots.' He shrugs. 'So of course Duval went.'

It hadn't been hard to find them. Torches were dancing all over the sky. There was fighting and yelling. The *Americanos* had looked like monstrous insects in their night-vision goggles. In the confusion he'd heard someone shout his name. He'd ordered Dolores to wait in the schoolroom, but she must have followed him because when he turned he'd seen her struggling in one of the rancher's arms. He'd run towards the man, and the next thing he felt was the punch of a knife in his shoulder. After that, a kick to the head catapulted him into oblivion.

'Chavez will listen to you, Alice. He will send his men.'

'Winfred said no. He said don't call the patrol.'

'Winfred is dead, Alice.'

I clamp a hand over my mouth.

'He was trying to help us. His car went over the cliff.'

'I saw the fire,' I whisper. 'Benjamín, I saw it out of the window.' I cover my face with my hands and rock backwards and forwards.

'I will go to Chavez with you,' Benjamín says simply. 'We will go together.' He looks around the room, as if aware for the first time of his surroundings. 'Where is M-E?'

'Gone,' I say, my eyes sliding from his. 'Robert took them to the airport.'

He turns his head to one side. 'Little M-E,' he says brokenly. 'My little M-E.'

'You'll see her again, Benjamín,' I say feebly. 'I promise.' And he looks at me then as though we live in parallel worlds – mine is one where people are free to move across land and water and borders. A world where children go to school and do their homework and hop on planes any time they want to see their friend Benjamín. And his world? . . . Well, a door has opened into Benjamín's world, a door I have now stepped through and I feel a shiver of fear at the possibility of it closing behind me.

We park the truck in the gas station on the US side of the border and walk over to the customs building where Chavez's offices are located. It's only when we approach the two officials, a short compact woman and her male colleague, that it occurs to me Chavez might not be there. It's close to seven a.m. and what if his shift was over and he'd gone home? I briefly imagine him closing his curtains to the giant orb of the rising sun and climbing into bed, his heart heavy from another night sullied by the perfidy and greed of mankind.

'Is he expecting you?' the male official asks.

'Yes.'

'ID?' His eyes flicker over Benjamín.

I hand them my passport, explaining in a haughty, brittle voice usually reserved for British Telecom customer service, that Benjamín is an American citizen, currently in my employ and—

'Are you okay, hon?' The female peers closely at me.

I give her a funny look as, by now, it must obvious that all is not entirely well with my world. She turns my blood-spotted sleeve towards her colleague.

Ah yes. I explain very calmly that Benjamín has been knifed and reiterate my desire to see Chavez.

'*¿Necesita un médico?*' the man asks Benjamín, his tone considerably softer.

Benjamín shakes his head at the ground. The agents look at us and then back at each other as though they've never before been confronted by such an odd couple, as though, even here on the very axis, the blood meridian of the great ethnic divide, it was impossible to understand how this white English woman and the brown Mexican could be together, despite the blood ties splashed across our clothing, apparent for one and all to see.

In the customs building we're taken to the same room as before – and it's the same scene. A family of Mexicans on the hard plastic chairs under the watchful eyes of Bush and Cheney. An agent with a notebook asking questions. *¿Nombre? ¿Domicilio?* Another agent on the telephone: '. . . just a routine sweep . . . cleaning fluid . . . yeah real strong odour too . . . the truck showed signs of tampering.' Then we're in front of Chavez's office with the door opening and there he is, looking up from behind his desk, his grave intelligent face filled with concern.

'Alice,' he says, and stretches out his hand.

*

I do all the talking.

I tell him about Hogan, Ranch Rights and their exaggerated fire power.

'Alice, we have very little jurisdiction on private property. Not if they have permission from the owner.'

'They don't have my permission and they claim they're doing this on your behalf.'

When I tell him about the Mexicans being detained at gunpoint he picks up the telephone and says something in Spanish. He listens quietly then replaces the receiver.

'Yes, we had an earlier report of illegals in the area. A group of twelve. My agents lost them.'

'Well, Hogan found them for you.' I describe the fight in the dark, Benjamín being stabbed, and I look to Benjamín, expecting him to present his wound and corroborate the story, but his eyes are locked on his feet as though he is unwilling or unable to meet the eyes of authority.

'The Border Patrol doesn't condone anyone taking the law into their own hands. Alice, we don't want their help any more than you do.'

'Then send your agents back out there before somebody else gets killed.'

Chavez picks up a pencil and balances the point and rubber between his forefingers.

'Alice, if Henry Duval is involved, it won't make any difference if it's one of my men or Hogan's who finds him. The man's wanted for murder. One way or the other it's likely he'll find himself looking down the barrel of somebody's pistol.'

'Not if you call off the "dead or alive" edict.'

He leans forward and puts his elbows on the desk. 'What is it you're not telling me?' he probes gently.

So then I tell him mostly everything else. How we'd gone into Nogales for dinner, how we'd witnessed the patrol guard beating up on the kid and how Duval had tried to stop him but done nothing worse than bloodied the man's nose. I tell him that the guard had been alive when we left.

'Why didn't you inform my men of this earlier?' Chavez asks and for the first time I falter. 'Your husband was here this morning, I believe?' he adds almost conversationally.

'Yes.'

'And where is he now?'

'He took the children home. To England.'

'But you stayed?'

'Yes.'

'Alone?' He sounds surprised.

'Yes.'

'I see.' Chavez taps his pencil against his lower lip. He picks up the phone. 'Alice, we know Duval has a safe house in the desert. If you show us where to find him, we'll bring him in and talk to him. That's as much as I can promise you.'

He waits for my nod, then taps in an extension number. 'Come,' he says into the receiver, 'my office.'

Relieved, I lay my hand on Benjamín's arm, but still his head remains bowed. At the knock on the door Chavez excuses himself.

'Benjamín,' I whisper. 'Are you okay?' Chavez is

talking to another agent at the door. I squeeze Benjamín's arm and finally he raises his head. His eyes slide over me to the two men and then, as though an invisible fist has delivered a punch straight to his solar plexus, his face freezes.

'Benjam—?' I start, but his eyes flash back to me with such wild intensity that I clamp my mouth shut and twist in my chair. The agent talking to Chavez seems innocuous enough in his ill-fitting uniform. A middle-aged Mexican, nominally overweight, the soft mushroom of a belly pushing against a standard-issue black leather belt. He's about the same height as Chavez and stands close to him, arms crossed, and chewing audibly. Later, and long after the possibility of doing anything has passed, I wonder why a number of clues don't instantly broadcast him as a fake: the trousers, a good inch short of his ankle, the absolutely non-regulation gold chain around his neck. But what should have struck most forcibly was that someone on duty, taking instructions not just from a superior but from his head of sector, should be chewing with quite such gusto. It smacked of . . . well, gross overfamiliarity, I suppose; but in this moment I figure only that he is someone with whom Benjamín has had a run-in on a previous border excursion and I'm about to reassure him when the agent drops his hand. A sweet paper flutters casually to the floor and my brain, as if playing picture dominoes, links this image directly to another. The bowl of nougat squares in the cabin cupboard, the ones Chavez is always giving the children, The ones he keeps in his desk drawer. Stuck to the front of the bowl is one of Emmy's Spanish ticker tapes printed with *El dulce*. Next to the bowl stands a can of beans, duly ticker-taped as *Los frijoles*.

So?

Unable to make the connection it seeks, my brain ricochets round the cabin highlighting one ticker-taped object after another – *La mesa*, the table, *La silla* the chair, until finally it's Jack I'm looking at. Jack dancing around in front of the kitchen table, pressing the thin white strip to his forehead because it won't adhere properly to skin. *El hermano*, it reads.

El hermano, the brother.

Now through the smoky haze of the Alubia I see Reuben's fingertips on the edge of the $20 bill. 'El Turrón has a brother,' he is saying. His brother is a man with authority. A powerful man. If you find him, I guarantee you will find El Turrón.'

Back in an office in the US Customs building I look at my friend and protector, Chavez, a powerful man with both authority and contacts, and I think, *El hermano?* The brother? No. Impossible, absurd. A wild presumption based on what? I look from one to the other – a similar height and a preference for the same sweets? No. No. No. Still impossible.

'Mrs Coleman will take you to Duval,' Chavez is saying to the agent. He smiles at me and I smile back, determined to hold on to the idea of safety and help that Chavez has always represented, but the sharp claws of suspicion will not release their hold on my tired head. 'People fare better on the border when they're not all they seem,' Duval had said. Above the noisy hum of breakfasting Mexicans, I hear Esteban's warning: 'Find him before he finds you.' And as the hairs begin to rise on my arms, once again, on a dark side street in Nogales, a car rolls slowly out of sight and back into the shadows. 'Alice? . . . Alice!' Chavez says. Next to him El Turrón crosses his arms. I drag my eyes to his, determined to make contact, but I have to struggle to keep them there – such is the lazy contempt radiating from them. 'My agent will accompany you,' Chavez says. 'Right now we're between shifts, but radio position when you get there and the others won't be far behind.'

I want to stay in the chair. I want to glue my hands to the seat and nail my feet to the floor. Benjamín's head is down again. I will him to leap up or strike out, do something, anything to stop me feeling quite so helpless.

'It's okay, Alice,' Chavez says gently. 'Just take us to Duval and then you too can go home. You *must* go home,' he says with meaning. He puts out his hand to raise me off the chair and I take it in a daze, hearing the knock on the door and only barely registering the presence of a third agent.

'Sir.' The man addresses Chavez. 'The group of illegals you were enquiring about earlier?'

'Yes?'

'We've just had a report in. The situation is under control. A dozen individuals handcuffed in the area.'

'Have them picked up,' Chavez orders without missing a beat.

'Sir, the guy who radioed in – says he wants to speak to you. Says it's important.'

'Not now.' Chavez says sharply.

'But it's Jeff Hogan, sir. Says you asked to be informed if Duval was one of them.'

For a comical few seconds there's a real honest to God Mexican stand-off. Everyone looks at each other. Nobody moves.

'And is he?' Chavez enquires evenly.

'No, sir, he isn't.'

I move then. And quickly. I yank Benjamín to his feet and start walking. I thank Chavez, smile at the other two men, thank them for their time. I mumble something about getting Benjamín to the medical centre but all the while I keep going, herding Benjamín in front of me until I'm out of the office and halfway across the waiting room with the heady thought that we're going to make it – and then I feel it – jabbing into my ribcage, and I know it's too late. El Turrón's hand closes round my elbow and I'm overcome by an immense loneliness as the door to Benjamín's world slams shut somewhere far, far behind me.

I turn. Chavez stands watching us. 'Good luck, Alice,' he says. '*Buena suerte.*'

30

A gun in the back. I've seen it in every movie but I've never thought about how it feels. Well, it feels like this: like I've drunk a shot of distilled fear. Like I want to squeeze my eyes shut, put my fingers in my ears and block out this harsh new world until a safer one comes along. Down we go in the lift. Out of the building and into the butterscotch truck. Nobody speaks. Benjamín seems near catatonic as he climbs stiffly into the back. El Turrón pushes me into the driver's seat. His breath is hot and too close as I step up onto the worn metal step.

I sit behind the wheel, hands in my lap.

Lounging against the window of the passenger seat, El Turrón keeps the gun on both of us. 'Turn it on,' he orders me and obediently I fire up the ignition.

'Turn the truck around.'

'No.' In the rear-view mirror Benjamín's head is finally raised. His eyes stare back at me; hard, steely. 'It's better the other way,' he says and there's something in the timbre of his voice that lights a small match-flame of hope.

'Into Mexico?' Turrón's vowels are rounded with Americanese.

'It is the quickest way.'

El Turrón's brow furrows with suspicion. 'She said go through the town.'

'*Es una mujer, una gringa*,' Benjamín says contemptuously, '*Ni siquiera sabe cómo llegar a su propia casa.*' She can't even find the way back to her own house.

Still Turrón looks suspicious. He extends his arm until the barrel of the gun is an inch from my temple. 'You said it was through Temerosa, right?'

Yes, right. Of course, right. Gringa or not, I know there is no road to Temerosa through Mexico. 'It's a nasty, near-impossible bit of desert,' Duval had said.

'I don't know,' I say. 'I'm not really sure—'

'Hey, go through the town if you want,' Benjamín says and I hear the studied shrug in his voice. 'But we will have to walk maybe two hours. Go from the Mexican side and we can drive. *No quiero morir desangrado porque la gringa se ha perdido.*' He speaks slowly enough for me to understand. I don't want to bleed to death because the woman gets lost.

El Turrón looks from Benjamín to me and sneers, 'So it's like that, is it?' He grazes the gun against my cheekbone and sniggers when I flinch. 'Hey, girl, don't expect your house pet Mexican here to take a bullet for you!' He waves his gun towards the checkpoint, 'Go . . . go then,' and winding down his window he holds out his badge as we drive through.

On the Nogales main strip, it's business as usual. A hard orange sun is already roasting the bare arms of tourists, the air is rich with the smell of frying meat, of jasmine and hot tar. I'm overcome with a sense of unreality. It's barely four hours since the children left. They could be in the sky, or waiting to board the plane, perched on the plastic booths of the airport's food emporium, gobbling down warm cinnamon rolls. My stomach turns hollowly. I haven't eaten since lunch yesterday. A half-full water bottle is wedged in the truck's centre divide but I am unwilling to draw attention to it. I'm not sure what Benjamín has in mind, but if the day promises to be as hot as it looks, it won't help to have Turrón pouring what's left of our supply down his own throat.

I drive. Left out of the port of entry and up into the hills of Nogales, left again, and along the road to Douglas. The atmosphere in the truck is jumpy but, far from noticing it, Turrón seems almost bored. He drums his fingers on the dashboard, he fiddles with the radio. He takes another square of nougat from his pocket and pushes it into his mouth, dropping the wrapper out of the window. Every so often I feel his eyes roaming over my body with a lazy insolence that makes my heart somersault and I'm tempted to say his name out loud if only to relieve the tension, but I stop myself, remembering that he has no idea of what we know. Certainly, he hasn't recognized Benjamín and therefore right now we are only dealing with his desire to reach Duval, and the longer it stays that way, the safer we will surely be.

'Turn left,' Benjamín says eventually and I veer clumsily off the main road.

The truck judders over weeds and shrubs, bushwhacking on a barely visible track, kicking up dust alongside. I know where we are now and I know where we're heading and once again I feel hope burn inside.

'This is the way?' Turrón leans his head out of the window. In the rear-view mirror Benjamín catches my eye and quickly draws his seatbelt over his lap. Equally quickly, I do the same. At the click Turrón pulls his head back in. 'I said, you sure this is the right way?'

'This track leads to the old mining road, and from there to the town,' Benjamín says.

'Oh, and what makes you the tour guide?'

Benjamín says nothing.

El Turrón snorts. 'Once an illegal always an illegal, huh?'

'I'm an American citizen.'

'Sure you are.' Turrón laughs mirthlessly. 'So where are you from, Mr American Citizen? Los Angeles, New York, Chicago?'

When Benjamín doesn't answer, Turrón turns the gun on him. 'I said, *where are you from?*'

'Nopallilo.'

'And that's where you'll always be from, a shithole town in the south. You'll never be an American citizen. Look in the mirror, border bunny; unless that's fake tan on your face, you're not the right colour. Brown people work for white people. Isn't that right, Alicia?' He slides his tongue around my name and, despite the heat, I feel bumps rising on my skin.

I've never felt threatened by a man before. Oh, sure, there's always some guy opposite you on the underground or eyeing you up in a deserted petrol station, but this fear is corrosive and it eats away at my insides.

'You *pollos* are all the same.' Turrón sucks air through the gap in his front teeth. 'You think that's what it's all about. To be an American citizen! For what? So you can go to the United States and scrub toilets? Me, I am proud to be Mexican. And now your friend, Signor Duval, I hear he wants to be a Mexican too. Isn't that right, A-lic-ia? He wants to be a coyote!' He laughs bitterly. 'Americans!' His mouth twists in disgust. 'You steal our land, you use our people to clean up your mess, and now you want our jobs too.' His voice takes on a reedy edge. 'You think I couldn't have dealt with your professor a long time ago?' He strokes my cheek with the gun. 'Oh, any time, baby, any time. But I have respect for my brother, I tried it his way first. Oh yes, and you know why? Because I have respect for other men's work, that's why.'

In the back seat Benjamín's eyes are closed. I worry the bumps and potholes are taking their toll on his wound. Panic wells up again. Why has he brought us this way? Surely it would have made more sense to head straight through Arizona? There would have been other cars then and the possibility of help. Surely anything would be better than this utter isolation? I hug the cliff wall as the track winds it way down deeper into the canyon. El Turrón seems almost as agitated as I am. 'This way is no good.' He leans towards the windscreen, eyes thinning as they scrutinize the blankness of the landscape ahead and suddenly there's a flash across my peripheral vision as Benjamín makes his move.

He yanks on the steering wheel and spins it out of my hand. The truck lurches sharply towards the edge.

Instinctively, I grab at the wheel. The truck veers back towards the middle of the track but it's too late, the next switchback looms at an impossible angle.

'Brake!' El Turrón yells. 'Stop!' The gun is so close I can see his finger begin to close around the trigger but it makes no difference. The truck has had enough. Tired and old, its brakes are arthritic and its clutch not what it used to be. It shoots off the edge with the gay abandon of an octogenarian whose dying wish to take up paragliding has finally been fulfilled, and the last thing I remember thinking is that Benjamín and I are both wearing seatbelts but Turrón is not, and though it may not seem like it right this very second, perhaps this is a very good plan indeed. Then the bottom falls sickeningly out of my stomach, the truck connects with hard earth, my head slams against the steering wheel and we begin rolling. There's a cacophony of mashing metal and breaking glass and after that, silence.

My eyes open to a world slanted very oddly. Instead of throwing Turrón through the windscreen, as Benjamín presumably planned, the truck has landed on its side at almost a forty-five degree angle, leaving him relatively unscathed, but trapped by gravity in his corner.

'You fucking bitch!' he says, when he sees I'm conscious. '¡*Estupida!*' His struggle to raise himself ends in collapse back against the window.

'Open the fucking door,' he orders, but there's no way. I haven't the strength. My hand drifts to my forehead and comes away sticky with blood.

'Benjamín?' I croak.

'¡*Puta*! !*Estupida*! Shut the fuck up.' Turrón has his gun back in his hand. 'Open the door!'

I can barely breathe. Dust whirls in through the broken window. Even if I could find the strength, I cannot move close enough to the door to get any leverage and Turrón recognizes this.

'The window!' He shouts. 'Use your feet.'

I hold on to the seatbelt with one hand and grab the leather strap with the other, laboriously turning my body until it's possible to reach the side window with the soles of my sneakers. The shattered glass gives way easily.

'Now get out,' Turrón orders. Totally compliant, I plant a foot on the central divide, and, hanging on to the leather strap for dear life, terrified of falling onto him, unclip my seatbelt. I get my feet through the window and drop down onto the desert floor.

I think about running, but Benjamín lies unconscious in the back of the truck and, besides, my legs are shaking. 'Open the door,' Turrón shouts again and I open it. Noisily, he begins his climb out. Blood spots through my trousers. Something sharp is cutting into my thigh. My fingers close around Duval's arrowhead, still in my pocket. I work the sharpened end upwards until it pokes between my index and middlefingers, then ball my hand into a fist. Turrón lowers himself stiffly to the ground. The left side of his face is swelling grotesquely. His ear is torn and bleeding. 'Fucking bitch,' he says. His eyes are burning and I know that right now, with this man, anything can happen.

He takes a step towards me and I lash out. The tip of

the arrowhead slices open a long red line across his face. He looks at me in astonishment, then fury. He grabs my hair and twists it round in his hand, dragging me away from the truck, and my fear becomes a solid thing. It rises up from my stomach and collects in my throat. I turn my head and retch it out on the desert floor, but there is nothing there, just saliva and bile. Turrón regards me with distaste.

'Wipe your mouth. WIPE IT!'

I use my sleeve. I find a scrubby-looking plant on the ground and focus on it, trying to look as submissive and unthreatening as possible. Turrón wrenches my head back by the hair. 'You stink.' He mashes something against my mouth. When I turn my head, he slaps my face. My teeth clamp down on my tongue and my jaw opens involuntarily with pain. Turrón seizes his chance and presses the square of nougat into it. I gag, then with rising panic feel myself choking. Irrationally, I have a vision of Jack and Emmy spitting out the sweets in Chavez's office and I know it's because they're fussy and unwilling to try anything new, but the idea that my brilliant children sensed something I did not makes me smile. Turrón doesn't like the smile. His hand whips across my face again and this time I go down on my hands and knees.

It's not the fear and it's not the pain, it's the claustrophobia of utter helplessness that's so unbearable. Turrón's knees are concrete blocks on my legs. He squeezes my breasts and I go berserk. I claw at his arms, twist my neck from one side to the other, try to headbutt him. When he clamps his hand over my mouth I grab at the soft flesh with my teeth. He screams and snatches his hand away. I jab at him with my elbow, jerk my knee into his back. Something connects and his balance wavers. For an incredible moment I think that I can get him off me, that I can beat him, then the adrenalin drains away and, with it, the last of my strength. He growls something, pinning me down tighter. I feel his body hardening and I know with absolute certainty that I am going to be raped.

I start pleading then. Unconnected random pleadings. For mercy, for my children, for him not to hurt me. He puts the gun in my mouth and after that it all becomes about survival. My world shrinks to him and me. I acquiesce, go soft. Everything to do with rape I will accept and will therefore ignore; the pain, the crushing weight of his body, the dirty fingers scrabbling inside me. It's the smaller things I'm aware of, the sting of dirt in my cut lip, a stone under my head, the grate of the metal against my teeth; and I can't help it, I think of Estella and I wonder how hard she fought for her life and her child.

'¡Pinche, puta!' Turrón is swearing. He wants my trousers down now but he doesn't know to depress the elastic clips at the side. He takes the gun out of my mouth and fumbles with the small button at the top, but he can't undo it. The buttonhole has always been tight. Frustrated, he raises his arm again, a great swinging movement. The sun glints off the metal in his hand. I turn my head away, and I try to think that death is only pain, it's only pain. I wait for the blow, but it doesn't come. Instead a shadow passes across the sun as the weight is dragged off me, and unexpectedly I experience a strange insecurity. The two men are flailing in the dirt close by and I feel a sort of weary anger directed at Benjamín because it's no longer as easy as acquiescing any more. My world has broadened again to include the three of us and this means I must take action, help Benjamín in some way, but then I realize that it's Benjamín's arm and not Turrón's raised high and poised. Down it comes, again and again and again and again. The rock in his hand glistens with blood. And he is not my Benjamín but some freakish creature, lips drawn back in primordial animal rage, and still the rock comes down, smashing skin and bone until Turrón's face begins to disappear altogether in a mess of gristle and blood and I've never seen anything more frightening in my life.

Benjamín falls off the body, his eyes closed. When I crawl towards him, I feel like I am rising up and stepping out of Estella's dying body. Benjamín tries to hold me but collapses sideways against the rocks, and shivering uncontrollably I take him in my arms as though he were one of the children. His heart is pounding, his every breath rasps through burning lungs, and how much time we stay like this, together against the rocks, the sun beating down on our heads, I have no way of telling, but I do know that in this moment there is a large part of me that would stay forever. Then I cough. My throat feels like sandpaper. I try to find enough moisture to swallow but there is none and some spark of a warning connects.

The metal of the truck is scalding to touch and any hope of finding shade quickly fades. The temperature is higher in than out, but the bottle of water is there, loose in the corner, still half full. I grab it then crawl over the seats and feel around in the flatbed for the plastic tote – the one bought by the old Alice, a girl who had broken down with her children at night on a mountain road with no provisions and wrung her hands in horror. Now, I do not allow my hands to so much as shake as I separate the lid from the base. Inside lies salvation of sorts. No hats, no satellite phone, no sunscreen and no more water, but a snake-bite kit, two Powerbars, a flashlight, bandages, a box of Band-aids and half a dozen sachets of antiseptic.

I stuff half the provisions into pockets, knot everything else into the sleeves of my shirt and climb out of the truck. A half litre of water. I swill it round the bottle. It will not do. Doggedly, I cast around for a stick then lever up the bonnet. I no longer look at the workings of the engine as though it were some architectural model for the Pompidou centre. I know my spark plugs from my pistons. I know my alternators from radiators and radiators have water in them. I remove the cap and then I remember. Sailors go crazy from drinking salt water, those jail escapees hiding in the desert had died drinking anti-freeze from a car radiator. Anti-freeze in the desert. The irony strikes me, of course, but my sense of humour is not up to dwelling on it.

Benjamín is where I left him. He looks grey and near to death himself. I give him as much of the water as I dare and force the Powerbars down both our throats. This time he makes no protest as I undo his shirt and unravel the bandage. The wound has opened up and is oozing blood and pieces of liverish-looking clots. I press the squares of antiseptic wipes against it, wondering how Benjamín could have possibly found the strength to beat a man to death and praying he has kept enough in reserve to carry on, because sooner or later that's what we will have to do. My shirt provides some shelter over our heads but the sun bores contemptuously through the thin cotton and after a while I give up and sit there, waiting for Benjamín to recover.

I'm dozing when the noise wakes me. A hiss, a crackle. A rattle? I open my eyes with a start, thinking I must have imagined it, then I hear it again, and this time louder. The third time has me jumping back, sick with a whole new fear. The warning rattle is coming from somewhere close and Benjamín stares in horror at El Turrón's inanimate form. '*El diablo*,' he breathes and crosses himself. The crackle is more insistent now and I freeze. I can see nothing, but I imagine everything. The evil coil, the head held aloft – and I know enough to keep absolutely still; but the next rattle has Benjamín babbling, '*La serpiente del diablo se ha despertado*,' and it dawns on me it's not the snake he's frightened of, but the more dreadful possibility of El Turrón raised from the dead.

'Benjamín, shhhh, it's okay.' I try to calm him.

'Noh, it's the devil,' he insists, and right then, as though having received its cue from the wings of a theatre stage, comes a man's voice.

'*Habla*,' Benjamín shrieks. '*¡El diablo habla!* He is the devil, Alice, *lo juro*.'

'No, Benjamín! No.' I grab his hand. 'It's the radio!'

He stares at El Turrón's body then back to me.

'We have to turn him,' I say.

I've never before touched a corpse and I'm scared to do it now. The man's dead. I know he's dead, like the dog on the road had been dead in spite of his red satanic eyes, but somehow El Turrón's presence seems no less threatening now than in life. Gingerly, we push him over. No longer depressed by the weight of his body, the radio is mute. I ease it from the pouch on his belt and allow him to roll back without once looking at the mess of his face.

Like a miner who's stumbled upon his lost pan, Benjamín examines the piece of equipment in his hands, fiddling with the volume and switching between different channels.

'Wait.' I stop him. 'What are you going to do?'

'Duval has a radio.'

'Yes, but so does every man with the Border Patrol.'

'There are good men with the Border Patrol, Alice.'

'What if those aren't the ones they send?'

Benjamín holds the radio limply on his stomach, then leans back against the rock and closes his eyes.

Infuriatingly, I start crying then, just one or two small careful tears before I remember about conserving water. 'Why did you crash the truck, Benjamín?' I ask pitifully. 'Why here? There's nothing here. Nobody will find us.'

'Don't cry, Alice,' he says helplessly. He hesitates then depresses the speak button.

'Benjamín, no . . . don't!' I try to grab it.

'Toribio Romo,' he whispers into the rubber grille, 'Santo Toribio Romo. Come to us.'

411

'Benjamín, *what are you doing?*' I look at him, scared that the sun has already baked him dry of all lucid thought.

'Toribio Romo,' he intones. 'Come to those in need.' And this time I remember. Duval's murdered cleric, the patron saint of lost migrants. Holy illegal alien smuggler.

'We will go to the place only Duval knows. There is water there. Duval will find us there.'

'What if he doesn't hear?'

'He will hear,' Benjamín says, struggling to raise himself. 'But now we must walk.'

I follow Benjamín. Foot after foot, eyes trained to the ground, watching for cactus, watching for snakes. My heart beats unnaturally fast, my head throbs in time with some imaginary clock which ticks by the seconds, the minutes, the hours. How long have we been out here? How long since the children left? How long can we walk without water? The blisters come quickly. At first I stop and take off my sneakers and stick the small strips of Band-aid onto the raw skin, but they keep rubbing off and after a while there seems little point in bothering.

Information runs through my head, jumbled, conflicting. People can survive for days without water – dehydration can kill in hours. You should walk at night when it's cooler. Except at night the desert belongs to its creatures, scorpions and tarantulas the size of a man's fist. The thorns of the ocotillo will tear through your flesh like razor wire. Inside cactus there is life-saving water. I have a flash of Nora's Mexican leaning against the tree, his blackened lips and tongue lacerated by spikes. I see Emmy's pale face in the back of the car, speeding further and further away. Is it possible that my children are asleep in the vacuum-packed safety of their aeroplane? Is it possible that elsewhere in the world life could really be that normal?

The time passes, the heat intensifies. We walk, we rest, we walk again but nothing ever gets any closer. The mountains taunt us in the distance. Behind us the desert stretches out, infinite and unchanging. My throat is dry. It feels as though something is caught in my windpipe. I try to swallow but it gets harder and harder. Every so often Benjamín fiddles with the radio and I whisper along with him. 'Santo Toribio Romo. Hear our prayer. *¡Ayúdenos!*' Once in a while he turns and I'm comforted to see his face, so achingly familiar to me now. He peers at me questioningly and I reassure him with a smile but it hurts to talk, so we don't do it very much and soon it hurts to blink. I rub at the grit in my eyes then I realize there is no grit in them, they're just dry, out of moisture, out of tears.

We're zigzagging now, heading down deep into another arroyo, which means sometime soon we will have to climb out again and every muscle quails at the thought. There are black specks in front of my eyes. When I dare to look at the sun it sizzles angrily back at me like a burning cigarette tip.

Finally, I sense a break in the rhythm. Benjamín has stopped. Ahead of us, balancing on a rusting tripod of legs stands a blue tank with the word *Agua* painted on the front. I have a moment of wild joy, and then I see them. Bullet holes. Dozens of them.

Benjamín says nothing, so neither do I. Instead I try the radio again but now there's no static, no noise, nothing.

Benjamín takes it from me and fiddles with the knobs. 'Dead,' he says.

In the spartan shadow of the water tank we wait for Duval, for Toribio Romo, for someone to come. One hour, two. After that I stop counting. Benjamín's shoulder looks no worse, but I wonder how much more quickly the body dehydrates when wounded. How much further he will be able to go because today there is to be no miracle.

'How long to Temerosa?' I say eventually.

Benjamín doesn't reply. Very slowly he pushes back onto his feet.

'How far?'

'Not far.' He lies and smiles his broken smile.

Foot after foot. Step after step. I start to think about Estella and the baby and how it ended for both of them. For a surreal and muddled moment I think I must surely be the reincarnation of this girl. How else can the two of us be in love with the same man, be led over the border by the same man, be raped by the same man, and I wonder why fate has sunk her teeth into my ankle with such an obdurate bite . . . Then I pull myself together. I am not Estella and I will not lie down and I will not die here in the desert.

Things unseen tear at my legs: burrs, seeds, thorns.

I barely notice them any more. With every step, I walk closer to my children. There are tricks you can invent to keep your feet going. I find rhythms, random beats of songs. I mark the ground from one desiccated clump of mesquite to the next and start counting them, twenty clumps to the mile. I cross-reference footsteps with miles with mesquite bushes, looking for some neat algebraic answer which might lead to survival but the only thought that keeps coming to me is how vast the world is, and I feel lonelier than I ever thought it possible to feel.

My mind begins to wander. It tortures me with watery images. A dripping tap. The mellifluous trickle of a brook. Above a choppy sea a gannet folds in its wings and dives into the waves. My hand dips into a rock pool for an orange sea shell. When I take it out, it's cold from the water, then I realize that it's not cold, but hot, burning hot, and stow it once more inside my shirt. I hear the cry of a greater black-backed gull and look up, hoping to find shade under its majestic wingspan, but there's nothing up there, nothing except that sun, white, merciless and lethal. Dear God, if I come out of this alive, I will be a good mother.

My sweet Emmy, Jack – I promise I will never leave you again.

'Alice,' Benjamín says urgently. 'Alice.' His voice is barely a voice at all. 'Are you okay?'

I look at him like he's bonkers. Of course I'm okay. I'm actually doing pretty well. Considering.

'You've stopped.'

I shake my head. My body is on fire.

Suddenly, he's very close to me, his worried eyes looking into mine. I reach out towards his face. His skin is blistered. How drawn he looks, how ill. Oh, God, how much blood has he lost?

'We must rest,' he says.

I blink at him. Yes, of course we must rest, then I discover that I am resting already, leaning against a rock and Benjamín has come back for me. Rest. I pretend to consider the idea. Should we or shouldn't we? After all, it's important to put up a good show. Why? I don't know. Maybe because there's a small stubborn part of me that wants Benjamín to tell Duval I was brave. That I tried. Big comfort that will be to Jack and Emmy.

'Rest, Alice. Okay?' Benjamín urges quietly. I nod my head at him. The sun is low on the horizon, but the heat is still overpowering. The four walls of the desert close in on us like a clay oven. My throat feels like someone has reached in and ripped a Band-aid off it. Every breath drawn is like swallowing dust, then the dust grows to sand, after that to the size of pebbles. I experiment with shallower and shallower breathing until I find a small space to suck the oxygen through where it hurts the least. There's a funny sour taste in my mouth when I do this. I think I identify it as hope dying.

The next time I look at the sun it's as though someone has placed a sheet of tracing paper over it. The sky is drained of colour as day diffuses into night. I close my eyes. I long for blackness. I long for oblivion. I long for everything. I want to go home. Not Temerosa home, not London even, but the nostalgia and safety of childhood, before the mistakes are made and the dreams are shattered.

'Benjamín?' I hear myself croak, and my voice is a tiny person's voice.

'*Sí, querida,*' he answers, and his use of the endearment makes me want to cry again.

'What are your children called?'

'Clarita,' he says. 'Clarita, Jaime and Rosalita.'

The next time I open my eyes I'm leaning against Benjamín, sort of propped up against his good shoulder. The time after that my head is resting on his legs and his hand is heavy on my hair.

'M-E and Jack,' I murmur. Will they ever forgive me? And my cowboy builder? Would he ever know what had happened? Would he understand?

'That's what you came here for, isn't it?' he said. 'The blind step in the dark and the freedom to take it.'

I close my eyes and see his face illuminated in the glow of the fire. He lies on his back and watches silently as I undress for him.

Later I stir to find him still watching me.

'Why aren't you sleeping?'

'I was thinking there was a cactus I never showed you,' he says. 'And I wanted to show you because it's absolutely my number one cactus of them all. It's the Night Flowering Cirrus, or the Midnight Cactus as some people call it, and most of the time it's just an ordinary unremarkable little plant, but one night a year it blooms and nobody knows why and nobody knows when, but when it does it's the most heart-stoppingly beautiful thing you ever saw.'

'What happens to it after that?'

'It dies.'

'Bummer.' I kiss him. 'So which one of us here is the ordinary unremarkable little plant?'

'Ah well, maybe both of us.' He draws his arms around me. 'Maybe one night like tonight, one extraordinary midnight moment, is the best you can ever hope for.'

'What if I want more?'

'Then you have to pay the price.' He sees my expression and laughs. 'Hey, didn't you know,' he says softly, 'the only kind of love you can have as a fugitive is a stolen one.'

'Alice.' He's calling my name from very far away. 'Alice,' he whispers, closer now.

Water stings my lips and trickles into my mouth. I choke. A hand tightens underneath my shoulders. I struggle against the lead weights of my eyelids and open them to a sky no longer white, but navy and strewn with sapphires. Duval kneels beside me, holding the bottle of water. Behind him Benjamín hovers.

'Santo Toribio,' I whisper. I try to smile and my lip splits in two. 'You heard us.'

'Don't talk.'

'You heard us.'

'Yes.' He takes the weight of my head against his shoulder. 'I heard you.'

'On the radio?'

'Shh.'

'What happened to Hogan?'

'Alice . . .'

'You found us. I can't believe you found us.'

'Hush now,' he says, but I hear the catch in his voice.

The horses stand a little way off, snickering at a half moon. Duval has lit a fire. He cleans and bandages Benjamín's shoulder. The sight of the gash, blackened and crusted takes my breath away. Afterwards he washes the cut on my head.

'I'm so sorry,' I say.

'For what?'

'Winfred . . . I—'

'It's not your fault.'

'I should never have trusted Chavez.'

'How could you have known? No one knew.'

'If I'd gone with the children, none of this would have happened.'

'But you stayed.' He strokes my hair. 'With all the reasons in the world to run, you stayed.'

31

Benjamín dozes fitfully. The fire burns and I feel safe in Duval's arms. He holds me and tells me to sleep but I'm afraid to. There aren't many hours left for us. He touches his finger to the cut on my forehead.

'How bad did he hurt you?'

I hear the edge in his voice. I'm not sure which question he's asking. I'm not even sure Benjamín has told him but it doesn't make any difference, the answer is the same.

'Not in any way that mattered.'

'I thought I'd lost you,' he says flatly. 'When I found the truck I thought you were dead. Then I found the body. I saw his face. I've never known Benjamín raise his voice, let alone his hand . . . I guessed then who it must be but I couldn't be sure. All these years I never knew what he looked like. Turrón was just another ghost I was chasing.' He stops abruptly, turns his head away. 'Can you ever forgive me?'

'There's nothing to forgive. You changed everything for me. You gave me my escape.'

'But not your reality.'

I press my face into his neck, wondering how I can ever give up this man.

'I watched you that first day you came, Alice Coleman, looking out over the mountains, shading your eyes from the sun and you stood so still and you stared so intently – as though you wanted to take something from this place back home with you, only you couldn't work out what, and I think you must have cast some kind of spell on me, because all those months I kept thinking about you until one day there you were, standing at the foot of my ladder, so angry, so haughty.'

'I was not.'

'Then sitting at the kitchen table, your plans spread everywhere, all those terrible building manuals you were trying to keep one step ahead with.'

'You were outrageously patronizing.'

He kisses my hair. 'That day Winfred carried you unconscious into the schoolroom, your leg spouting blood like a Texas oil strike – and he put you in my arms and I said your name and you opened your eyes and replied "bastard" before promptly passing out again.'

'Certainly did not.'

He chuckles. 'Yes you did and I knew then you were mine.'

'I nearly turned you in.'

'Well thanks to you and Benjamín, it seems I'm out of a day job anyway.'

I fall silent. 'What will happen to Dolores?'

'They'll put her on a bus. Send her back home. I can try to help her there.'

'And then? What will you do?'

'Ah you know,' he says lightly, 'retire. Open a little espresso bar in Ague, or perhaps an arts and crafts shop.'

'Never.'

'No never, of course never.' He kisses me. 'Maybe I'll go home . . .'

'You have a home? I thought you were a hobo.'

'A ranch in New Mexico. My father left it to me when he died. It's near the Rio Grande. In the fall, Arctic geese and Sandhill cranes come to roost in the marshes and stay through the winter. I think you'd like it.'

I touch my fingers to the creases in his jaw. How would it feel, I wonder – to be able to have something you've wanted so badly and for so long, to answer a desire that you've hidden away in the deepest part of yourself . . . 'I have to go home, Duval.'

'I know,' he says simply, 'I've always known.'

I turn away. I don't want him to see me cry.

'There's a window at the top of the house faces north', he says, eventually. You can see for miles. When I was a boy I used to watch for my father out of that window.' He turns my face back to him and smooths the hair out of my eyes. 'Now, perhaps, I will watch for you.'

I have the distinct sensation of the ground shifting beneath me. 'The only kind of love you can have as a fugitive is a stolen one.' Duval had said. In the sky a pale blue light tints the horizon. It begins to blur in front of my eyes.

'Yes,' I say. 'Watch for me.'

I dream I am high up, alone in an eagle's nest, and the straw lining it scratches my face. When the eagle returns, graceful, munificent, it allows me to cling to its back while it swoops low into the deep canyons and through the dry washes. Above us the sky is white, all colour bleached out by the sun. We fly high over El Turrón's body, his face bloody no longer, but a blank mask of dust, and I pluck a feather from the eagle's tail and watch it spiral slowly down towards him.

The shouting breaks into my dream from somewhere far away. '¡*Tenemos alimento!* ¡*Tenemos agua!*' We have food! We have water! '¡*Tenemos alimento!* ¡*Tenemos agua!*' Louder now and constantly repeated, like a church bell tolling for late worshippers. Then an exclamation from somewhere close by. Hikers! Can you credit it!' Next thing I know, there's a smell of piss and tobacco breath, and I'm being gathered up in a pair of enormous fleshy arms as though I'm no heavier than a pile of dirty washing.

'This one looks pretty cooked!'

I'm being leant upright against something hard but I'm still paralysed with sleep, every bone in my body aching and resistant.

Duval's voice now. 'What the . . .'

More shouting. 'Over here, 'nother one! A Mexcin!'

A hand grips my wrist. 'This one's got a pulse!'

Finally, I get my eyes open and, thoroughly disorientated, blink into the sweating, puce-red face of Nora.

'What the hell are you doing?' Duval has his gun out.

'Checking for dehydration.' She steps back from me, stethoscope swinging round her neck, and places a meaty hand in the centre of his chest.

'Now lay still, you're confused.'

'Good God, Nora! Get your hands off me.'

'Nora?' she echoes. 'And just who the hell are you?' Her eyes narrow then widen again with recognition. 'Duval? What in God and sinners' names . . .?' She turns from him back to me. 'Oh, sweet Jesus!' she exclaims, her suspicion turning to something approaching glee. 'Oh no, don't tell me.' A gargle of laughter bubbles up in her throat as her companion looks on in confusion.

He is in his early fifties, with an unnaturally small face. His eyes dart fretfully between us as he helps Benjamín to his feet. 'Temperature yesterday was up in three figures.' He twists the flesh on his chin like a worry bead. 'We saw the water tank all shot up and we figured . . . well, we figured we'd have a lot to do this morning.'

'We caught you with the binoculars.' Nora wipes her running nose on her sleeve. 'Spotted the horses too. I told Milt I ain't never seen no migrant on horseback, but we reckoned we'd better check it out anyways, and here y'all were, looking 'bout as dead as dead can be.'

'A few degrees hotter and you would have bin.' Milt twists his chin a little more painfully. 'But folks, I'm sorry if, well . . .' Embarrassed, he looks up at Duval.

'Sorry!' Nora snorts. 'Who's sorry! We wasn't to know Romeo and Juliet here decided to camp out and get sweet under the damn stars.'

'And what with your friend bleeding and torn up . . .' Milt turns to Benjamín, his face serious. 'Say, do you mind telling us what's been going on here?'

*

Nora moves between fridge and stove, stripping piece after piece of rough-cut bacon from its greaseproof paper and laying them on the smoking griddle. Through the window of the bar, I watch Duval tying up the horses.

'Wife's on the way.' Milt lays a hand on Benjamín's arm. 'She works part-time up at the rabbit clinic in Patagonia, she'll have you stitched up in no time.'

'And this one?' Nora stands at the small table beside us, pointing a pair of blackened tongs in my direction. 'Gonna stitch up that head as well?'

I demur politely, quite happy not to be sewn together by a part-time bunny veterinarian, however well meaning.

'Suit yourself, but we need to do something with you.' She plucks at my arm. 'How 'bout a shower then?'

'Sounds good,' Duval says, walking in.

Nora tosses him a scathing look. 'Don't get excited. I ain't wasting precious hot water on no man.'

'Always the good Samaritan, Nora.' He puts his hand on the back of my head and rubs it gently.

'Hey, leave her be, can't you see it's a woman's touch she needs now?' Nora thrusts the tongs at him. 'Make yourself useful, cowboy, and cook the damn breakfast.'

Reluctantly, I follow Nora up the narrow stairs, trying to navigate between the blisters on my feet. I hadn't wanted to move from the table. I just wanted to stay close to Duval and Benjamín and feel safe. Nora disappears into the shower and bangs around a bit before reversing out, wiping her hands on her thighs. 'Takes a while to crank up, it'll be hot in about ten.' She tosses me a towel. 'Meantime, better fix you up with some clean duds.'

I look down at my torn clothes, feeling curiously attached to them.

'Oh, don't worry, these are fine.'

Nora looks at me shrewdly.

'Worried about wearing a fat woman's clothes, huh?' She seizes me by the shoulders and turns me to the wall mirror.

'It ain't like you can look a whole lot worse than you do now, girl.'

In the mirror, a stranger looks back at me. My face is burnt and scratched. My lips dark. I put my hand up and touch the gash in my head. Around it, my hair is a witch's wig of dust and dried blood.

'Still ain't willing to say who did it to ya?' Through the glass of the mirror, Nora's eyes shine fierce.

Duval had told Milt and Nora very little. I figured he was right. Too many questions, too many implications. I shake my head, feeling suddenly very weak. It can wait, it can all wait. Wordlessly, I begin smoothing out the sepia news cuttings stuck into the frieze of the mirror. They're all disaster headlines. Bhopal, Chernobyl, a mass grave in Serbia. 'Shitty little world, ain't it?' Nora says, looking over my shoulder.

I muster a response, wanting to be left alone, but unwilling to hurt her feelings. There's a squeak of springs as she slumps down on the bed behind me. 'Top shelf of the closet, there's a tote. You'll have to reach it down yourself, I ain't a giraffe like you, but don't worry, the clothes'll fit. They're from a long time back.'

I have to stand on tiptoes to reach the container. I try to lever it out but inevitably the box tips and falls, spilling its contents onto the cupboard floor. I gather everything up and carry it to the bed. It's the usual jumble, items kept for no good reason other than nostalgia, and all representing some regret or washed-out memory: T-shirts, bits of broken jewellery, jeans, snapshots, a checked summer dress. There's even some kids' stuff. A toy bear, limp and chewed, a heavily stained baby-gro.

'Here, give me that.' Nora rakes the kids' stuff across the bedspread and balls the clothing up into the tote again. I pick up one of the photographs from the folds of the sheets and glance at it. A thinner, less time-ravaged Nora with a man, fine-featured and dark. I look closer then closer still. 'Nora, is this . . . Chavez?'

Nora dips her head coyly. 'Good-looking devil, weren't he?'

I stare at the snapshot. 'Were you two . . . ?'

'Listen, girl,' Nora gives a pneumatic wheeze, ''bout that time at the rodeo. I'm sorry I pushed ya but I thought . . .' The bed springs creak. 'Well who cares what I thought . . . sometimes a person just acts stupid, you know.'

'So you and he . . .' I can't quite get the words out. 'You two were . . . ?'

'Gettin' it on?' She does a little jiggle with her hips. 'Hey, spit it out if that's what you're trying to say . . .' Then, seeing I'm incapable of saying anything at all, she sobers up. 'Yeah, for a time but . . . well, hell, in the end it wasn't to be.'

'Unrequited love put paid to Nora,' Duval had said, But Nora and Chavez? It just didn't seem possible.

'I shouldn't have kept all this stuff, I know I shouldn't.' She knots the bag and slips in a small silver cross. 'It wasn't rightly mine, but they was just babies and this crap meant more to me than it ever could to them so . . .'

The significance of what she's saying begins to penetrate my sore head. 'These belonged to *your* children?'

'Broke my heart when they got taken away.' She stares at the wall. 'But I looked after them best I could, I swear.'

'How many children did you have?' I try to exorcize the note of incredulity from my voice.

'Three girls and two boys, and so help me God, I loved each and every one of them.'

I feel overcome with pity. Poor thin Nora, abandoned mercilessly by Chavez, her children taken by welfare.

'Didn't Chavez support you, give you any money?'

'Sure he did,' she answers defensively. 'Paid up fair and square. What do you think I bought this place with?'

'But he didn't mind, he didn't . . . you know . . . want to keep them?'

'He knew they were going to a better life, and damn him he was right. I couldn't give 'em the life they deserved. Wouldn't have been fair. Still, I'd have given anything not to let 'em go.'

'Nora.' I struggle to say the right thing. 'It's not your fault you couldn't afford to keep them.'

'Keep them!' she guffaws. 'That wasn't the problem, girl, I couldn't afford to buy 'em!'

I turn very slowly and look at her. 'Nora, what are you talking about?'

'What are *you* talking about, girl? I think that knock on the head's making you speak crazy.'

'Are you saying these weren't your children? I mean you didn't . . .'

There's another bark of laughter. 'Hell, I didn't birth 'em, if that's what you're stuttering over. I was just looking after them for him until the adoptions got sorted.' She takes in my utterly blank look of shock. 'They was border babies. Orphaned on crossings. Chavez had a soft spot for 'em. Wanted them to go to a decent home. Always did what he could for them and usually on his own dollar, too.'

I find I am not breathing. Chavez tidying up his brother's messes. Keeping his own house in order. I clear my throat. 'Nora, what happened to them, do you have any idea?'

'How would I know? It was a long time ago.' She shrugs. 'Some would have left home by now, some might still be at college, I s'pose, but I lost touch with 'em in the end. For all I know I could be a grandma by now.' She chuckles. 'Me, Nora, a grandmother!'

'Border politics comes in murky shades of grey,' Duval had said. 'The good, the bad and the ugly can all end up on the same side at different times.' Reality continues sliding away from me and for a moment I feel light and papery enough to drift away.

'But you were in touch with them?'

'I wrote them.' Her mouth turns down. 'I wrote all of them, but I never got no replies.'

My heart is pounding so loudly it feels like someone must have plucked it from my chest and held it to my ear. I'm almost too afraid to ask. 'So you have addresses. You know where they are?'

Nora makes a noise like a horse whinny. 'Of course I know where they are. I have their files! What do you think? That poor Emilio could keep that kind of shit in his office? You got any idea the kind of trouble he'd have gotten himself in if people knew what he was doing? By rights those kids should have been in Mexican orphanages or living on the streets, and for what? For what? So they could grow up and cross the damn desert and die with cactus spikes poking out of their mouths.' She heaves herself off the bed and angrily shoves the tote back in the cupboard. 'Now don't you go blabbing to anyone about this, girl, don't you dare go getting him into trouble. He's a good man and it's all in the past now. He wanted nothing but the best for them. You do understand what I'm saying, don't ya? This way they got to be American citizens!' She plants her hands on her hips. 'American citizens, girl,' she says fiercely, 'and believe me, there ain't no easy road to that.'

Duval stands at Nora's grill, his brow furrowed in concentration. He plunges a fork into a piece of steak and turns it. Fat spits and he rubs his eye. I sit on the wooden boards halfway down the stairs and watch him. It's early still and the sun is on the move. It steals through the bar's window spilling hard and white onto the floor and lighting up a path almost to my feet. I hug the files in my lap. He does not know yet. It's a curious feeling. It's a wonderful feeling – to have something so big to give him, and it makes it all okay. Duval looks up to find me watching. His mouth breaks into a smile and I think that if I can just hold on to this moment, if I can find a place to keep it deep inside me where nobody can ever touch it, then I can be the great Night Flowering Cirrus, the Midnight Cactus that will bloom forever. I smile back at him. Somewhere across the great swelling rolls of an ocean, Jack and Emmy wait for me . . .

Author's Note

I'd like to believe that I can track the inspiration for this book all the way back to the beaches of North Uist, a windy, barren island off the north-west coast of Scotland where my family spent their holidays and where, as a moody fifteen-year-old, I was first given a copy of *Frenchman's Creek*.

Almost from the moment of opening it, I became – as I imagine so many fifteen-year-old girls had before me – Daphne du Maurier's heroine, the wilful Dona St Columb, in love with her pirate, dressed as a cabin boy and outwitting boorish aristocrats. I spent that summer feverishly reading in the shelter of the sand dunes, dreaming of all manner of escapes and searching the sea in vain for the white sails of *La Mouette* on its stormy breakers.

Dreams of escape tend only to flourish under the weight of real life and a few years ago, using the excuse of writing *Midnight Cactus*, I took my children to live in the mountains of Colorado – where, some time later, in the thrift shop of our local town, amongst the old glass bottles and broken watches, I came across a battered copy of *Frenchman's Creek*.

Turning the pages that night several things struck me. First, that here, in the wilds of America's south-west, I was once again in Dona St Columb's shoes, though this time for real, with the dark and furtive world of the Mexican border my own secret creek. Secondly, that the driving themes behind *Midnight Cactus* – the possibility and impossibility of escape, the tug of war between freedom and duty – had been as resonant back in the seventeenth century as they still were today. There's a truth which underpins both these books – one that presumably Daphne du Maurier had known all along and one that I had taken a lot longer to discover for myself – that, at one point or another, life can make fugitives of us all.

So I'd like to dedicate the book to the Dona St Columbs of both the past and the future, and indeed to every fifteen-year-old girl who dreams of becoming one.

Acknowledgements

I am indebted to my friends and co-border-jumpers, John and Emily Sutcliffe, for so many things that I hardly know where to begin – so in no particular order: thank you for braving the snitches, the pimps, the drug dealers and that coyote with the bad skin. For not getting us shot in Du Quesne or having our truck, money and passports stolen in Nogales. For not being washed away in the slot canyons or arrested scrambling under the wire. For springing me from the Customs Building and for all those glorious dinners in La Roca – especially the one where the enormous Mexican with the gold bling put his hand round my ankle. Thank you for every charming Super 8 Motel and Best Western (free ironing board included), not to mention the scary lesbian B&B lady and the indecisive Mormon receptionist. Thanks for the old men singing in bars in Guadelajara, and for our enforced dormitory in Juanajuato. For Operacion Michoacan. For agent 66 and those nine-hour drives to the border I wished would never end. For sleeping in the back of the pickup and the story about the gluey mouse sandwich. For getting the giggles in the lay-by and informative tips on how to kill a man with a fire extinguisher and/or remove his kidneys when drunk. My thanks for all the margaritas that made us sick and the ones that didn't and here's to all the tequila we will drink together in the future. Above all my thanks for the humour, friendship, the shared experiences and observations, all of which I've ruthlessly plundered in my quest to get to 'The End'. This book could not have been written without you.

I am equally indebted to Carole Van Wieck, for her lifelong friendship and unflagging moral support, her constant flow of brilliant ideas, and the sheer generosity which allowed her to spend a substantial amount of her day coming up with them in order to work through my many plot holes and twists. This book would have been equally impossible without you.

My thanks also to the following:

The Castillo family: Sonja, Marlene, Jésus, Nayzeth – and particularly Pancho, whose grit, determination and goodness have given his family the right to stand up and be counted.

Jack Richmond for the hardback photographs.

Billy-Joe Moffat for the paperback photographs.

My children Mabel and Finn for posing for them in the scorching heat.

Dr Nora Price of the Samaritan Patrol.

Russell Ahr, Mario Villareal, Mike Bermudaz and Amy Thornton of the Border Patrol.

'Uncle Fester' representing the California Minutemen.

Barbara Walker and Stewart Steves.

Stacey Workman for Tijuana.

midnight cactus

Katrin and Cristoph for their ghost town.

Fernanda Goncalves, Donalda Dewar and Sarah Richardson for their loyalty and kindness.

Jack and Emmy Harries for the use of their names.

Last but so far from least – a thank you to my wonderful editor, Maria Rejt, and my equally lovely agent, Sarah Lutyens, surely two of the most patient people in the world. That either of them still take my calls is a testament to the resilience of the human spirit.